BLK

W9-BAC-809

Praise for Emma Miller and her novels

"This is truly an enjoyable tale overall."
—*RT Book Reviews* on *A Love for Leah*

"The concept of having two suitors...provides a fresh twist. It is fun trying to figure out who [the heroine] will choose."
—*RT Book Reviews* on *The Amish Bride*

"A captivating story."
—*RT Book Reviews* on *Miriam's Heart*

Praise for Alison Stone and her novels

"Stone's latest is so fast-paced and action-packed that it is hard to put down. Numerous red herrings and palpable suspense combine in this thoroughly engaging nail-biter."
—*RT Book Reviews* on *Plain Sanctuary*

"This tale quickly engages the reader with its attention-grabbing details and original twists."
—*RT Book Reviews* on *Plain Cover-Up*

"[A] well-researched tale with an engaging pace... it contains sweet romance, palpable suspense."
—*RT Book Reviews* on *Plain Peril*

Emma Miller lives quietly in her old farmhouse in rural Delaware. Fortunate enough to be born into a family of strong faith, she grew up on a dairy farm surrounded by loving parents, siblings, grandparents, aunts, uncles and cousins. Emma was educated in local schools and once taught in an Amish schoolhouse. When she's not caring for her large family, reading and writing are her favorite pastimes.

Alison Stone lives with her husband of more than twenty years and their four children in Western New York. Besides writing, Alison keeps busy volunteering at her children's schools, driving her girls to dance and watching her boys race motocross. Alison loves to hear from her readers at Alison@AlisonStone.com. For more information please visit her website, alisonstone.com. She's also chatty on Twitter, @Alison_Stone. Find her on Facebook at Facebook.com/alisonstoneauthor.

EMMA MILLER

A Love for Leah

&

ALISON STONE

Plain Sanctuary

HARLEQUIN® LOVE INSPIRED®

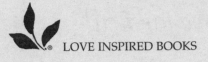

LOVE INSPIRED BOOKS

Recycling programs for this product may not exist in your area.

ISBN-13: 978-1-335-14690-8

A Love for Leah and Plain Sanctuary

Copyright © 2018 by Harlequin Books S.A.

The publisher acknowledges the copyright holders of the individual works as follows:

A Love for Leah
Copyright © 2017 by Emma Miller

Plain Sanctuary
Copyright © 2017 by Alison Stone

www.Harlequin.com

Printed in U.S.A.

CONTENTS

A LOVE FOR LEAH

Emma Miller

Delight yourself also in the Lord and
He shall give you the desires of your heart.
—*Psalms* 37:4

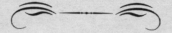

Chapter One

Kent County, Delaware
Spring

"What do you mean you won't marry me?" Thomas's eyes widened in disbelief as he stared at the young woman beside him. "Don't we go together like ham and cabbage? Bacon and eggs? Hasn't everyone been waiting for us to announce the wedding date?"

Ellie grimaced. "I'm sorry, Thomas. Truly I am." She sounded contrite.

He set her books onto the trunk of a fallen apple tree and they tumbled onto the grass. "You should be sorry," he said. "It's not easy for a fellow to propose to a girl. And when I do, you turn me down? It's humiliating."

It was late afternoon and the dirt path that ran from the Seven Poplars schoolhouse where Ellie taught, to Sara Yoder's place, where she lived, was deserted except for the two of them. The path crossed several Amish farms and this section wound through an apple orchard. The trees were bursting with new leaves and just beginning to bud from the branches on either side of the rutted lane. The only sounds, other than the thud of Thomas's accelerated heartbeat, were the buzzing of bees and the scolding song of a wren.

He scowled down at Ellie. "Why don't you want to marry me?"

"I should have never let it get this far." She looked up at him, her hands clasped together. "I knew we weren't meant to wed. But I like you and you're so much fun."

"I think you are, too. Isn't that enough? That we genuinely like each other and always have a good laugh?"

She shook her head sadly. "*Ne*, Thomas, it isn't enough for me."

In frustration, he yanked off his broad-brimmed hat and threw it on top of the scattered books. "I don't understand. I thought you wanted to be my wife."

"I never said that, Thomas."

He scowled.

She picked up his hat, brushed the leaves off it and handed it back to him. "I care for you, Thomas, but I don't want to have your babies, and I can't see us growing old together. We talked about this months ago. Remember?" Her blue eyes clouded with emotion.

"*Ya*, but I thought…" What *did* he think? She'd told him last fall that he needed to start walking out with other girls, but he hadn't, and the next thing he knew he and Ellie were running around together again.

"We're not a good match, Thomas. And if you're honest with yourself, you'll agree. I think what we have is…" Her brow furrowed as she seemed to search for the right word. "A convenient friendship."

"*Convenient?*" Needing to look her in the eye, he caught her around the waist and lifted her so that her small feet, clad in black leather lace-up sneakers, balanced on the fallen tree trunk. Ellie was a little person, and when she stood beside him, the top of her snowy-white prayer *kapp* barely reached the middle of his chest. After their first meeting he'd never thought of her as small, or different than any of the other girls he had walked out with. Ellie cast a big shadow.

Ellie's eyes registered a sharp warning. Putting his hands on her in such a familiar way was inappropriate, and they both knew it. At the moment, he was too upset to care.

A knot tightened in his throat. "Ellie, I don't understand," he said. "A convenient relationship? What's that supposed to mean?"

His face must have shown how hurt he was because her features softened. "Maybe I shouldn't have said *convenient*," she answered. "But you know exactly what I'm talking about. You and I run around together because it's easy. It's comfortable. But we're not in love with each other and you know it." With a sigh, she fixed him with a penetrating look. "Now stop feeling sorry for yourself and hear what I'm saying. It's for the best for both of us." She waited a moment, then added, "You know I'm right."

He glanced away, not ready to concede, no matter how right she was. He looked back at her and she offered a faint smile.

"Who told you to propose to me?" she asked him.

Flushing, Thomas felt a rush of guilt. She knew him so well. "My mother."

"Exactly." Ellie's eyes narrowed, making him feel as if he was one of her students who'd been caught staring out the schoolroom window instead of attending to his math.

"And what did your *mam* say?" Ellie demanded as she folded her arms. "Exactly."

He exhaled. "That it was time I had a family of my own." He ground the toe of his work boot into the soft grass. "That you were a sensible young woman who would keep me in line, and I was foolish if I didn't pop the question before someone else did."

"Do those seem like good reasons?"

He gripped his hat so hard that the brim crushed between his fingers. He was devastated…sort of. "But we get along so well," he hedged. "And everyone says—"

"That because we have fun together, we should spend the rest of our lives as husband and wife?" She shook her head. "Not good enough. Not for me. Not for you." She was quiet for a moment and then went on. "And the truth is, Thomas, you're relieved. I can see it in your face. You weren't all that eager to tie the knot with me, no matter what your mother or anyone else said. Were you?" she pressed.

He wanted to protest, but Ellie was right. He was more surprised and embarrassed than brokenhearted. And he did feel a sense of faint but unmistakable relief. "No chance you'll reconsider?" he asked lamely.

She shook her head, took hold of his hand and jumped down onto the lane. "I'm not the special one for you, Thomas. If I was, you'd know it."

"You think?" He sank down on the log. "I'm not so sure. I've dated practically every unmarried Amish girl in the county and a lot of girls from other places. My buddies all found someone they wanted to spend the rest of their lives with, but not me…" He looked at her. "Maybe there's something wrong with me. Maybe I'm not meant to be married and have a family."

"Nonsense." Ellie picked up her books and brushed off the bits of grass that clung to the covers. "Your mother's right about one thing. It *is* time you married. Past time. I think your problem is that you don't know how to find the right woman. You're looking for the wrong things. You're looking *at* the wrong things, mostly pretty faces. Married life isn't just about fun and sweet smiles, Thomas."

"Now you *definitely* sound like my mother." He dropped his hat onto his lap, leaned forward and buried his fingers in his hair. The way Ellie put it, it made him sound shallow. And maybe there was some truth to the accusation. He'd been attracted to Ellie because of her cute figure, her pretty face and her sparkling personality. He liked pretty girls. And he liked to have fun. Was that so wrong?

"I sound like your mother because she's right. I'm right," Ellie insisted. "You want a wife and a family, don't you? You want to father children and live our faith?"

"Of course. I just don't—" He sighed. "I guess I don't know how to find that."

"Exactly. So what I'm thinking is that you need some help." She poked him with her finger. "You need someone to make a good match for you. You can't just look for a pretty face. You have to look deeper than that and find what's important in a partner. You need the matchmaker's help. You need Sara Yoder."

"You think I need a matchmaker?" he scoffed, meeting her gaze.

"Why not?" Ellie shrugged. "She's very good at it and it's not as though you're a hopeless case. You have a lot to offer a woman. You have a trade—two trades, if you count blacksmithing."

He frowned. "I'm a terrible blacksmith."

"Okay, but you're a decent rough carpenter. And you know something about farming. You have that promise of land from your grandfather, and you own a horse and buggy." She studied him carefully. "And you have a good heart and a strong back," she allowed. "You've never been afraid of hard work."

He flashed her a grin, recovering some of his equilibrium. "Not to mention that girls think I'm handsome."

"Humph." She puckered her lips. "Prideful, the bishop would say. And a show-off."

"I am not," he protested, rising to his feet.

"Red and blue blinking lights on your buggy?" She shook her head and sighed. "Thomas, I'm serious. You need to talk to Sara."

He thought for a minute. It had never occurred to him to hire the services of the local matchmaker. He'd always thought matchmakers were for people who couldn't get a date. That certainly didn't apply to him. He'd walked out with more girls in the last ten years than he could count. But Ellie was a sensible woman. Probably the most sensible he'd ever known. He knew he'd do well to take her advice. "Do you really think Sara could help me find a wife?"

"Absolutely. But pray on it. With your history, even Sara Yoder will need all the help she can get."

"Why do I think the two of you invited me here for something other than my rhubarb pie recipe?" Sara Yoder asked as she took a chair at Hannah's kitchen table. Hannah, her dearest friend as well as a cousin, had sent one of her grandsons with a note to ask if she could come over at four.

Since the weather was pleasant and the two houses were less than a mile apart, Sara had walked. She liked being active. She was usually up by six and going until long after the sun had set. Not that it had done much for her figure. Despite her busy lifestyle, she remained hearty. She supposed it was partly that she loved to eat and partly because her mother had been substantial in size.

At the back door, Hannah's widowed daughter, Leah, recently returned from a long stay in South America, had taken Sara's denim coat and black outer bonnet and given her a big hug. Sara hadn't gotten a chance to get to know Leah yet, and she was pleased that she was there this afternoon.

"I'm so glad you could come," Hannah exclaimed as she dropped into a seat across from Sara. "We've been making vegetable soup and canning it. Cleaning out the cellar. Soon enough we'll have fresh vegetables again and I never like to save canned goods from one year to the next. I have a couple of quarts of soup for you. Too many to carry, but Leah can drive you home."

Leah wasn't Amish anymore, although in her plain blue dress and navy wool scarf she appeared so. When she'd married Daniel Brown several years earlier, she'd joined the Mennonite church. The Mennonites, close in belief to the Amish, were not as strict in daily lifestyle and permitted motor vehicles. Sara assumed that the small black automobile in the yard was Leah's.

Smiling, Leah brought a pitcher of cream and an old pewter bowl filled with raw sugar to the table. "Tea is such a treat," she said, joining them and pouring the first cup of tea for Sara. "I can't get enough of it. They have wonderful coffee in Brazil, but it was impossible to find decent tea."

All of Hannah's daughters were known for their liveliness and independence, but Leah was the one who residents of Seven Poplars saw as the most independent. After her marriage, Leah had left Delaware to follow her new husband to do missionary work among the indigenous people of the Amazon. There, in an isolated outpost, the young couple had operated a school, a store and a basic medical clinic. Then tragedy had struck. Leah had lost both her husband and her child to a deadly fever. Unwilling to leave her adopted community in need, Leah had remained more than a year until another team could be sent as replacements. Now, she'd returned to her childhood home to pick up the pieces of her life.

Leah might have been the rebel of the Yoder girls but, of all of Hannah's daughters, she was certainly the prettiest, Sara decided, looking across the table at her. Her red hair, blue eyes and flawless complexion made her a real beauty, more attractive even than Violet Hershberger, who was considered the cutest and most eligible girl in the county. But Leah's almond-shaped eyes held a depth of sorrow that gave her a fragility of spirit not evident in Violet or any of the other young women in the county. Leah seemed cheerful and strong enough physically. She laughed as readily as her sisters, but Sara could sense a vulnerability in Leah that tugged at her heart. It was obvious that she was still in pain from her loss, but Sara could see that she was making an effort to be a part of the world again. And she seemed to be succeeding.

Sara considered herself a sensible woman, one not easily swayed from the right path by emotion or hasty decisions. But she couldn't deny that she felt drawn to this girl and felt an instant desire to do whatever she could to help her. "It was nice of you to invite me for tea, but did you ask me here for the reason I suspect?" Sara asked.

Leah smiled and her cheeks blushed. "I think it's time I wed again and my family's in agreement."

"I'm glad you called on me, then. I've brokered a few Mennonite marriages, though you may have to be patient with me while I talk with some friends at the local church."

"Actually," Hannah said. "Leah has decided—" She broke off abruptly as her youngest daughter, Susanna, came into the kitchen with a basket of clothing she must have just taken in off the clothesline. Susanna had been born with Down syndrome and she and her husband David, also mentally challenged, made their home with Hannah and her husband Albert.

"The wind is picking up, isn't it?" Sara said to Susanna. She could smell the wholesome scents of sunshine and spring breezes on the clothes the young woman carried in the basket.

Susanna, red cheeked and beaming, nodded. "*Ya.* Almost blew me over."

"*Ach*, Susanna. You're about to lose your scarf." Hannah rose and went to her daughter, untied the navy cotton scarf and retied it in place over her daughter's braided and pinned up auburn hair.

"*Danki, Mam.*" Susanna giggled, her round face creasing into folds of pleasure. "As soon as I…" Susanna's forehead crinkled as she struggled to find the right words and pronounce them correctly. "Fold the sheets," she managed. "David's gonna show me new kittens in the loft. He said 'Susanna, you help name them.'" She nodded excitedly. "They need names!"

"That sounds wonderful," Sara exclaimed, and then waited for Susanna to take her leave. Sara didn't need to be reminded not to speak of matchmaking business in front of Hannah's youngest. As delightful as Susanna was, whatever she heard, she repeated. It was impossible for Susanna to keep a secret. Arranged marriages were confidential between the candidates and the matchmaker, not food for neighborhood gossip.

Hannah took the laundry basket from her daughter. "Would you like me to help you fold? We'll take these sheets upstairs and put them away and then you can go and see the kittens."

"*Ya, Mam.*" Susanna giggled again. "I'm gonna see the new kittens. We're gonna name them, me and David. I love David."

Hannah smiled lovingly. "I know you do. Now come along."

Leah waited until her mother and sister were out of the room before adding more tea to Hannah's cup and her own. Then she took her cup in both hands, gazed down into the swirling liquid and said, "I want to marry again, Cousin Sara." She sighed. "It's been more than a year since I lost my Daniel and our little one and… I'm the kind of person who needs to be married. It's what God has always wanted for me." Her eyes teared up. "I want a husband and children." She looked up, unashamed of her tears. "Can you help me find a husband?"

Sara leaned forward. "Of course. As I started to say, my contacts among the Mennonite faith are not as extensive as—"

"Oh, I'm sorry," Leah interrupted. "I didn't make myself clear. I mean to return to the Amish church. I became Mennonite for Daniel, as was right. I believe it was God's plan for me at the time. And now, I think He means for me to accept the Amish way of life again."

Sara reached for a sugar cookie on a blue-and-white plate. "I assume you've considered this carefully? You've lived with many conveniences since your marriage. Are you sure that you can live Plain, as you did as a child?"

Leah didn't answer at once, and Sara liked that. This was no flighty young woman who chose first one path and then another on a whim. Sara nibbled at the cookie and sipped her tea.

"I've thought of little else since I left Brazil," Leah said finally. She offered a half smile. "I loved my husband. I've mourned him with all my heart. I think I will grieve for him until my last breath, even though I know he's in heaven. Grieve for myself, I suppose. But ours was a good marriage, a strong one, and I want that again. I'm young enough to bear more children, as many as God will send me, and to marry again just seems…right."

"Children are our greatest blessing," Sara said. She had never been fortunate enough to have a child, but she had loved many children and hoped to love more. Why God chose to not give some women children— or to take them away—she would never understand. "The ways of the Lord are often a mystery to us, aren't they?" she murmured.

"Ya," Leah agreed. "I thought I would lose my mind in those first months after I lost them. I know I shed enough tears to raise the level of the Amazon River,

but, fortunately, I had our work. We had a small school and Daniel's clinic. He had been a nurse and I learned so much from him working at his side. After he was gone, there was no one else to help and I had to make do." She looked up and Sara gazed into the depths of those cornflower-blue eyes. "I delivered babies, sewed up knife wounds and set broken arms and legs. I was too busy to think much about what I wanted for myself when I could come home."

"But you knew that you wanted to come home to Seven Poplars?" Sara asked.

Leah nibbled absently at a knuckle. Her hands were slender, her nails clean and filed. They were strong hands to go with her strong spirit, Sara thought.

"There was no question of my staying in Brazil as a woman alone. I wouldn't even have remained there as long as I did, but there was unrest. Trouble between the lumber contractors and the native people. And there were floods. They were so bad that our clinic was cut off from the nearest town for quite some time. It wasn't safe for a new team to come in. It was a blessing, really. I had a chance to say my goodbyes and see the school and clinic put in good hands before I left." Leah shook her head. "But I won't bore you with my memories. If you think you can help me, then I want to tell you what I require in a husband."

"I could never be bored with tales of your experiences in Brazil," Sara assured her. "But it would be helpful if you tell me what your expectations are in a husband."

Leah steepled her hands and leaned forward on the kitchen table. "First, he must be Amish, of strong faith and respected in the community. I would prefer a mature man, a middle-aged widower, someone who may already have children. How old doesn't matter, so long as he isn't too old to father children."

Sara pressed her lips together to keep from smiling inappropriately. This adventurous child of her cousin was certainly outspoken. Whether it was her nature or a trait she'd picked up in her travels, Sara wasn't certain. It was all she could do to not show her amusement. "You're still a young woman," she said. "Not yet thirty. Are you certain you wouldn't prefer a younger bachelor?"

"*Ne*. I'm sure of it," Leah said firmly. "I've been the wife of a young man. I married for love. I'll never have that again, and I know that. I'm a realistic woman, Cousin Sara. I know that affection and respect may lead to a different type of love someday." She met Sara's gaze. "I want someone different for a second husband, someone I'll not ever compare to my Daniel."

Sara nodded thoughtfully, and while she didn't know that she was in agreement, she certainly understood what Leah was saying. "Do you have a choice of occupations?" she asked. "Farmer? Carpenter?"

"It matters not. I'm used to making do with few material goods. I ask only for a husband who isn't lazy and will be a good example for our children. He must know how much I want more children." Leah's voice took on a breathy tone. "I could not bear it if I never rocked another baby in my arms or woke to see my precious child's shining face beaming in wonder at the new day." She inhaled deeply. "So you see, it might be best if my husband-to-be already has children. I can adapt to any personality, but he must be someone who will welcome children and not treat them harshly."

"Or treat you harshly," Sara suggested.

Leah shrugged. "I can accept whatever the Lord sends me. I'll be a good and dutiful wife, so long as he knows that my children must come first. My Daniel was an indulgent father. He adored our..." Tears glistened in her eyes again. She looked down, took a moment, then looked up at Sara again. "I want to be sure I'm being clear, Cousin Sara. What I want is a marriage of convenience, a union entered into for the purpose of forming a solid family. I'm not afraid of hard work, and I'll be the best wife and helpmate I can. But I need a sensible man, a practical man who doesn't expect more than I can give." She hesitated. "Because part of me died in Brazil, Sara. All I can do is go on with what I have left."

"You don't believe in the possibility of a second love?" Sara asked gently. "Not when you see how happy your mother is with Albert, after the death of your father?"

"I'm not my mother," Leah replied, sitting back in her chair. "I honor her, and I love her, but we are not the same. She and my father had many years together and time to form many memories. Daniel and I... It went by so quickly. Too quickly."

Sara considered the young widow's words. "Wouldn't your Daniel want you to be happy?"

"Of course." Leah smiled through the tears. "But I know myself. I know what I want. Offer me no light-hearted, carefree noodle-heads. I'm seeking a sober and steady husband, one with gray in his hair, who knows what it is to suffer loss. Can you find me such a man?"

Sara reached across the table and took Leah's hands in hers. "I will do my best to find what you need in a husband. But you must remember, I can't promise you children or happiness. We are all in God's grace and we cannot see the path He plans for us."

"I understand," Leah agreed. She squeezed Sara's hands and then pulled free. "And I was hoping that you would have room for me at your house. Where I could stay."

"Certainly," Sara agreed, genuinely surprised by the request. "But what about your mother? Surely, Hannah must want you here with her."

"I don't think that would be best," Leah said firmly. "You know my mother. She'd want to put her spoon in my soup pot. I love this house and I love my family. But I'm not ready to fall into the habit of being a dutiful child again. You know exactly what I mean. I'm sure you've seen it before. A young widow returns home to her parents' house and the next thing you know, twenty-five years have passed and her mother is still cooking her supper and hanging out her laundry. No. I'll come to your home and put myself in your capable hands."

She rose and picked up her teacup to carry to the sink. "Find me a husband, Cousin Sara."

Chapter Two

Leah drove her little car slowly down her mother's driveway, savoring the familiar sights of green fields, grazing cows and her brother-in-law plowing with a four-horse team. Beside her sat Sara, several quarts of vegetable soup in a basket at her feet.

"It's so strange to be back in Seven Poplars," Leah said as she came to a stop at the edge of the blacktop and looked both ways for traffic. A buggy passed the mailbox, and several automobiles approached from the opposite direction, so she waited until it was safe to pull out. "One minute I feel like an outsider, and a few minutes later, it's as if I never left home."

"For me, it's much like that, too," Sara agreed. "I haven't been in Delaware that long, but most of the time, I feel like I was born and raised here. Your mother and I have been close since we were children, but I didn't know anyone else until I got here. It was a pleasant surprise to find all of Seven Poplars so welcoming."

"I'm so glad." Leah smiled at her. Plump Sara's hair was dark and curly, her eyes the shade of ripe blackberries and her complexion a warm mocha. Although a generation older, Sara was a widow like Leah. And Sara had also made major changes in her life after she was left alone.

When it was safe, Leah turned onto the blacktop in her little black Honda and smiled to herself, suddenly glad she'd decided to put her future in Sara's hands. She instinctively felt she could trust Sara, maybe even more than she could trust herself right now, which was why she'd decided to hire a matchmaker to find her a husband.

"Do you have a preference on where you live?" Sara asked, breaking into Leah's thoughts. "Does it have to be in Seven Poplars, or just in Delaware?"

Leah nodded. "I'd love to stay in Seven Poplars, but I know that's not likely. Though maybe you'd find a man looking to relocate here. Anywhere in Delaware would be fine. I just don't want to live so far from my family and friends that I can't visit again. I missed them so when I lived in Brazil."

"I can understand why you'd want to stay here. This is a special community. Still, many young women might wish that they had had your opportunity—to travel so far to another country," Sara observed. "To see so many different kinds of people and to live in a jungle."

"It was an amazing experience. I feel blessed to have served God as a missionary. I already miss the friends I made there." Leah's throat clenched as she remembered the Brazilians standing on the muddy riverbank to wave goodbye. Small Pio clinging to his grandfather's leg, gentle Caridade nursing her new baby girl, and the collection of village elders, all in their finest basketball shorts, rubber-tire flip-flops and feathered headdresses. And around them their most precious possessions—the beautiful children, shrieking with laughter, heedless of the ever-present dangers of poisonous snakes, caimans and piranhas in the swirling, dark water.

"Their lives are so different from ours, harsher, and less certain," Leah murmured. "I went to teach, but ended up receiving far more than I gave."

"And do you have a timeline in mind? How soon would you like to marry?" Sara asked pointedly.

"As soon as possible." Leah gripped the wheel, confident in her response. "It's time I was married, and God willing, I want another child as soon as possible." It felt good that she could finally keep her voice from breaking when she spoke of being a mother again. God truly was good, and time, if it didn't heal wounds, made them easier to bear. "Is that a problem?" she asked Sara.

"Not at all," Sara answered warmly. "You're past the mourning stage of widowhood. At your age, most would agree, the sooner the better."

Leah nodded as they approached a tall Amish man striding along on the shoulder of the road. Recognizing him, she slowed and waved. It was her brother-in-law Charley's friend Thomas Stutzman.

Sara waved and then glanced back at Thomas as they passed him. "Wait! Stop the car."

Startled, Leah braked, looking anxiously to see if she'd barely missed some hazard. "Something wrong?"

"Ne." Sara shook her head and motioned toward the side of the road. "Pull over onto the shoulder, can you? We should… I want to give Thomas some soup for his grandparents."

"Of course." Leah pulled over and put on her flashers.

Sara got out of the car and motioned to the man.

"Thomas! Hop in. We have some soup here for your grandparents."

Leah watched in the rearview mirror as Thomas approached the car. He and Sara exchanged words, but Leah couldn't make out any of what they were saying. Then Sara turned back toward the car. "No more than you could have expected. Ellie's quite set in her ways," Sara said as she walked back to the car and opened the rear door. "Get in. Leah won't mind driving you home. You can hardly walk and carry quarts of soup down the road. But you're headed in the opposite direction. You weren't headed home, were you?" She gave a wave, indicating again that he should get in. "No matter."

Thomas, seeming to realize there was no sense arguing with Sara, folded his long frame and climbed into the back. His head nearly brushed the roof so he removed his hat and dropped it into his lap. "Leah," he said in greeting.

"Thomas." Her backseat was small, and Thomas had broad shoulders. He took up most of it, even before he removed his hat.

Leah had seen him at church services the previous week. He was Charley's age, older than she was, but he'd always seemed younger. Her sister Rebecca had told her that Thomas was still unmarried, but walking out with the little schoolteacher. Leah wished her well. Thomas was a good guy, though not the sort of man she'd be interested in. Thomas was far too immature and happy-go-lucky to suit her. And too self-centered.

"Your mother lets you keep a car at her house?" Thomas asked, glancing around the vehicle as he put on his seat belt. "I know you Mennonites drive, but…" He didn't finish whatever it was he was going to say.

"We do drive." Leah put the car into gear and eased back onto the road. "This car belonged to my late husband's cousin. Ben moved to Mexico to serve as a missionary and he gave it to me."

"Hannah doesn't object to Leah driving." Her arms crossed, Sara looked over her shoulder at Thomas. "Leah's Mennonite sister Grace drives every day, doesn't she? And Leah's stepfather has his pickup for veterinary emergencies. Bishop Atlee approved." She chuckled. "Leah isn't a child anymore. She respects her mother, but she doesn't ask for permission on how to conduct herself."

"That's what I tell my mother," Thomas said. "About me."

Sara made a small sound of disbelief. "And how does that work?"

"Not very well."

"Didn't think so," Sara replied.

"Doesn't work so well with my *mam*, either," Leah said with a grin. "It's why I'm going to stay at Sara's." She kept her eyes on the road. "I'd be happy to drop the soup off at your grandparents'," she assured him, "if you're headed somewhere else?"

"I'm going to Sara's actually," Thomas admitted sheepishly. "I left my horse and buggy there. Ellie— she's my girl—*was* my girl—Ellie likes to walk home after school on nice days like this. I thought it would be a surprise if I walked over and carried her books home."

"Ach," Sara said. "And it was you who got the surprise, wasn't it?"

"Ya," he admitted. He exhaled and went on. "I asked her to marry me and she turned me down."

"I'm sorry to hear that." Leah glanced at Thomas in the rearview mirror again. He didn't seem all that upset for a man who'd just proposed to a girl and been turned down. Seemed more put out than anything.

"Tough to be told no, but tougher to marry the wrong girl," Sara observed. "No need for you to take it personal, though, Thomas. Ellie's been saying for months how happy she is teaching at the school. You just weren't listening. You know the board wouldn't keep her on if she married. She likes her independence, our Ellie."

"I knew that she said that," Thomas said. "But how was I to know that she meant it?"

Leah turned into Sara's driveway.

"By tonight, everyone in Seven Poplars will know Ellie refused me," Thomas went on. "I'm going to look pretty foolish."

"Ne." Sara shook her head. "Not true. You're not the first one to be turned down in Seven Poplars and you won't be the last. But maybe this will teach you to listen to what a woman says. She told you she wasn't going to marry you. I heard it myself."

"Guess I should have listened," Thomas admitted.

"I do know a thing or two about compatible couples," Sara said. "Which reminds me. I'm giving a get-together on Friday night in my barn. You should come, Thomas. There will be eligible young women there. I want to have games, as well as food and singing."

He shrugged. "I'm not sure I'd be good company."

"Nonsense," Sara replied. "I could use your help setting up. And if you don't come, you'll just sit home feeling sorry for yourself."

"I suppose I could make the effort. If you need me, I could come for a while, just to help out."

"It will do you good. Take your mind off losing Ellie." Sara clasped her hands together and turned to

Leah. "And you should come, too. It should be a lively evening—you'll enjoy yourself. And you and Thomas can catch up."

Leah eased the car to a stop near Sara's back door and Sara handed Thomas two quarts of the soup from the basket on the floor beside her feet.

"Thanks for the ride," Thomas said, getting out on the driver's side, a jar in each hand. "And for the soup. I know my grandparents will appreciate it."

"No trouble." Leah smiled at him, leaning through the window. "It's not as though I took you far."

He started toward his buggy, parked on the far side of the barnyard, then turned back to her. "It's good to have you home again, Leah." Then he grimaced. "That didn't come out right. I mean, I know that you'd rather not have… that…" He looked down and then up at her, meeting her gaze. "I'm really sorry about Daniel and your little one."

Leah was touched by the emotion she heard in his voice. "Please don't feel that you have to tiptoe around me. This is a new start for me. What better place than home, where I have so much support?"

"Ya," Thomas agreed. He stood there for a second, then offered her the handsome grin that Amish girls all over the county talked about. "Well, see you."

Leah turned in the seat to face Sara as soon as Thomas was out of earshot. "I hope you weren't thinking of Thomas for me."

"Nothing wrong with Thomas that a little attitude adjusting can't fix," Sara said, getting out of the car.

Leah shook her head. "I wasn't criticizing him. It's just that he's too young, too…" She shrugged. "I don't know. Not a man I could call *husband.*"

"Don't worry," Sara assured her, picking up the basket with the soup. "I think I know exactly what you need." She closed the door and leaned down to speak through the open window. "Which is why you should come to the frolic."

Leah groaned and rested her hands on the steering wheel. "It's been a long time since I was single. I'm afraid I'll feel out of place with the younger girls and fellows."

"You won't. I've invited people of all ages. And it will give you a chance to reacquaint yourself with the singles in our community. There's a vanload coming from Virginia, as well, so there will be plenty of new faces." She held up one hand. "I know, no Virginian, unless he's willing to relocate. I just mean there will be interesting people to talk with—men and women."

"*Mam* tells me that you've made a lot of good matches. Still, I have to admit that I'm nervous."

"You won't be alone in that, but we'll muddle through." Sara chuckled. "We should have a nice-sized crowd Friday night. And Hannah told me that you have a lovely singing voice. We can always use another strong voice. Would you like to come in and see the room I have for you? You can move in as soon as you'd like."

"I don't need to see the room. I'm sure it will be fine." Leah glanced in Thomas's direction as he untied his horse's tie rope and slipped on the bridle. "I think I'd like to come tomorrow, if that suits you."

"It suits me fine." Sara watched as Thomas climbed up into his buggy. "He's a good man, Leah. Don't sell him short."

Leah pursed her lips thoughtfully. "He doesn't seem all that broken up over losing Ellie."

"Because she wasn't the right one for him." Sara

smiled and held up the basket. "I do appreciate not having to cook supper tonight. Your mother makes good soup."

"I know," Leah said. "It was one of the things I kept dreaming about when I was in Brazil—my mother's cooking." She paused. "You don't think I'm rushing it, do you? You don't think it's too soon to look for a husband?"

Sara smiled kindly. "*Ne*, I don't think you are. It's only right that we grieve for those we've loved and lost. But it would deny God's gifts if you couldn't continue on with life. A new marriage will give you a new beginning. I promise you, Leah. I'll find someone who will lift the sadness from your heart."

"It's what I want, too," Leah agreed, starting the engine of the little black car. "God willing, we can do this together."

Thomas stepped into the kitchen of Sara's hospitality barn. Bright lights illuminated the immaculate food-preparation area. The kitchen wasn't large, as Amish kitchens went, but it had a propane-powered refrigerator, double sinks, a freezer, a commercial stove and new butcher-block counters. Leah was the only one there, and she was busy making sandwiches.

"Hey," Thomas said. He leaned jauntily against the double-door refrigerator. "Could you use some help?"

"Thanks, but I'm almost done." Leah deftly spread some of her sister Ruth's famous horseradish mustard on a slice of homemade rye bread and stacked on ham, cheese and pickles. "I thought Sara had too much food, but apparently not." She chuckled. "A hungry bunch, those Virginians."

"Probably the long ride. They're staying over until

Monday. Fred Petersheim told me that there's talk they'll come quarterly. He's the short, gray-bearded farmer you were talking to."

"Ya." Leah nodded. "He talks a lot."

Thomas grinned. "About his Holsteins." Thomas had noticed that the older man had cornered Leah earlier in the evening. "He told me he lost his wife last winter. Does he have children?"

"Six, but two are grown and out of the house," Leah responded. "The rest are girls."

"He seems like a respectable man. I doubt Sara would invite him if he wasn't." Seeing that there were dirty dishes and silverware in the sink, he rolled up his sleeves, washed his hands and began to run warm water over the dishes. "I may as well wash these up," he said. A dishwasher was the one appliance Sara didn't have. With so much available help, she'd never seen the need.

"Are they still playing Dutch Blitz?" Leah placed the sandwich halves on a tray one by one. "I saw you won the first round."

"Lost the second," he said. *"Ya,* they're playing. Couples now." He reached under the sink for the dishwashing soap. "So, you've decided to let Sara make a match for you?"

Leah glanced over at him. "God willing. Sara seems pretty optimistic." She gave him a quizzical look. "Is she trying to find a wife for you?"

"I'm thinking about it. Ellie suggested it." He made a face. "I haven't had any success on my own."

Leah tried to open a quart jar of spiced peaches, but the lid was stuck. "Do you think you could open this?" Her vivid blue eyes regarded him hopefully. "Sometimes these lids are on so tight that it's impossible to get them off."

"Sure." Thomas dried his hands on a towel and took the peaches. The ring gave easily under his strength. Without asking, he opened the other jar that she'd put on the counter beside the sandwiches. "Here you go."

"Danki."

Leah smiled her thanks and he was struck again by just how attractive she was. She didn't look like a woman who'd been married and had a child. She hardly looked more than nineteen. Before she'd wed Daniel Brown and gone to Brazil with him, most people said she was the prettiest girl in Kent County, Amish or Englisher. He and Leah had never dated because she was a lot younger than he was and didn't run with the same crowd. It was a shame she'd suffered such loss. But it did his heart good to see her here, still able to smile after all she'd been through.

Leah dumped the peaches into a blue-flowered bowl. "I'm surprised that you and Ellie are still speaking, let alone her giving you advice on finding a wife."

He grimaced. "I'll admit that I'm still smarting from the blow of her refusing me, but we're too good of friends to let that come between us."

"Sensible."

"She's special, Ellie. She'll make some man a good wife. I'm just sorry it won't be me."

"It says something about you, Thomas," Leah said, "that her being a little person didn't matter to you. If you had married, your children may have been short statured, like her."

"Ya, I did think about that. But it would have been in

God's hands. And who's to say that being six feet tall is any better than being four feet tall?"

"Your parents didn't mind?"

Thomas returned to washing the utensils in the sink. "My father huffed and puffed, but my grandfather reminded him that he had an uncle who had only one arm. He said that Uncle Otto could outwork any man he knew. And once *Mam* and *Dat* got to know Ellie, it wasn't a problem anymore."

"Your grandfather sounds like a wise man."

"And a good one. He's been good to me. My brother will inherit my father's farm, but my grandfather has promised his to me. I was supposed to take up his trade, his and my *dat's*, of smithing, but I'm not sure it's what I want to do." He lifted a dripping colander from the soapy water and rinsed it under the tap.

"Were you trained as a blacksmith?"

He nodded. "*Ya.* I was, but I think everyone is beginning to realize I may not be cut out for it. *Grossdaddi* has arranged for a new apprentice, Jakob Schwartz from Indiana. He's arriving tomorrow." Taking a clean towel, Thomas carefully dried the colander and put it in the cabinet under the sink. "Jakob's little, like Ellie, but *Grossdaddi* says he has the makings of a fine smith." He glanced at her. "You need the strength in the arms. Height doesn't matter."

Leah removed her oversize work apron. She was wearing a dark plum dress with a starched white Mennonite prayer *kapp*. "I suppose I should get these sandwiches out there."

"The platter is heavy. Let me," he offered.

"I can do it. I'm used to lifting heavy objects. Once, one of our parishioners brought home a quarter of a cow." Leah rolled her eyes. "I didn't ask where he'd gotten the beef. There was always a running feud between the farmers and the indigenous people." She picked up the tray.

"What was it like, living among them?"

"Wonderful. Awful. I never knew what kind of day we were going to have, one where nothing happened or one where the world turned upside down." She chuckled. "A fine missionary I turned out to be. I could never even pronounce or spell the name our people called themselves. They are listed in our rolls as the St. Joseph tribe or the St. Joes."

"I'd like to hear more about them," Thomas admitted. "I'm curious as to what they're like."

She gave him a surprised look and set the tray down. "Really? You're one of the few to ask. Since I've come home, I mean."

He nodded. "*Ya*, I'm sure. But I've always been interested in the English world." He grimaced. "That didn't sound right, did it?"

She chuckled. "*Ne*, Thomas, it didn't. I wouldn't expect you to know, but I can't imagine a life more un-English than our village. But to them, it is all the world. Like us, most of the St. Joes want to remain apart, with their customs and their jungle."

He felt a flush of tingling warmth at the way she said his name, slow and sweet. He shifted his feet, suddenly feeling the conversation was getting too serious. "But what about that mysteriously acquired beef? Did you eat it?"

She laughed. "We all did. It was the season when protein is scarce. There were hungry people to be fed, so I asked the women to light the cook fires and we had a feast. Our refrigeration unit was very small, just used for medicine. Daniel was concerned that it would set a bad precedent, but I said, 'Eat the cow or let her go to waste, and that doesn't sound very sensible.'"

"And did Daniel eat the meat?"

Leah shook her head. "It didn't keep me from enjoying every bite."

Thomas laughed, then grew more serious. "This has got to be hard…coming home. Starting again."

"Ya," Leah agreed.

Thomas's throat tightened. Leah had suffered a great loss. He had to admire her courage. "So I guess this—" he motioned toward the gathering beyond the door "—is as awkward for you as it is for me?"

"It is," she said. "I didn't want to come." She shrugged. "But Sara is very persuasive."

"Truer words," Thomas agreed as he picked up the platter of sandwiches. "So…back we go to meet Sara's likely candidates and hope for the best."

"Ya." Leah's smile was mischievous. "And be prepared to hear a lot more about Holsteins."

Chapter Three

Thomas pushed open the sliding wooden doors to his grandfather's forge to catch some of the midmorning breeze. It was stifling inside, and he'd started to beat the last of the wrought-iron hinges into shape. Returning to his task, he used long-handled tongs to lift a smoking hinge into the sunlight to get a good look at it before plunging it back into the glowing coals.

His grandfather watched, faded blue eyes narrowed with concentration. *"Goot,"* he said. "A little more. Feel the shape in your mind, Thomas. Strike hard and true."

Thomas swung the hammer again and again. The shock resonated through his body, but he paid it no mind. He was used to it. He didn't mind hard work. It was *this* work he disliked.

Patience, he told himself.

Again and again he struck hammer to iron. Slowly the iron yielded to the shape he wanted. He knew it was good and he should have been pleased, but he took little pleasure in the forge. He much preferred digging in the soil or building with wood and brick. He'd been born to a family with a tradition of blacksmithing going back to the old country, but he had no heart for it. Never had.

"Ya." Obadiah nodded. *"Ya.* That is the way. Was that so hard?"

Thomas placed the finished piece beside the others to cool and turned toward his grandfather. The gray-haired man held out a small bucket. Thomas took it, drank and then dumped the remainder of the cool well water over his head. It ran down his neck and shirt to wet his leather apron and forge trousers, but he didn't care. The pants and shirt would dry soon enough and both trousers and apron were scorched and riddled with holes.

His grandfather chuckled. "Always with you the heat, Thomas. The heat never bothers me."

And it never did. For sixty-five years Obadiah Stutzman had labored in a forge, and the flames and red-hot metal had only made him tougher. Past eighty now, his shoulders were still formidable and the muscles in his arms were knotted sinews. Thomas loved him as he loved his mother and father. He couldn't imagine what life would be like without *Grossdaddi* watching over his shoulder, hearing the raspy voice hissing in *Deitsch,* "Strike harder, boy. Feel the iron." Thomas had always wanted to please him, but spending his life within the walls of this forge, he didn't know that he could do it.

Thomas walked to the open doorway and squatted on the hard-packed earth, letting the warm sunshine fall full on his face. He ran a hand through his damp hair and let his muscles rest from the strain of swinging the hammer.

In the distance, a calf bawled, its call quickly answered by the mother's deeper mooing. The farmyard stretched out in front of Thomas, familiar and comforting as always. Chickens squawked and scratched, earnestly searching for worms or insects. One hen was trailed by six fluffy chicks and a single yellow-and-brown duckling. Thomas smiled at the sight, knowing that when they came to the first puddle the foundling would terrify its adopted mother by plunging in and swimming. *Maybe I'm that duckling,* he thought, *always ready for fun, never quite fitting in or doing what I'm expected to do by my family.*

His grandfather came to stand beside him. "A sight you look," Obadiah said. "*Goot* thing your mother is to the house. Doesn't see you without a hat to cover your head in God's presence."

Thomas glanced guiltily at the wall where his straw hat hung on a peg. He never wore it in the forge for fear of it catching fire. *Grossdaddi* wore an old felt dress hat with the brim cut off over his thinning gray hair, but Thomas wasn't ready to be seen in such a thing, so he worked bareheaded.

"When do you expect Jakob to get here?" he asked. His father had told him at morning milking that the new apprentice was arriving today. He'd be staying with them in the big house.

"Anytime now. Hired a driver to bring him from the train station in Wilmington."

"I liked Jakob when I met him. I hope he works out," Thomas said. "Hope he likes Seven Poplars."

"Be a change from Indiana," his grandfather answered. "You know those folks don't even have tops on their buggies? Winter and summer, no tops. Their bishops won't allow it."

"I'd heard that," Thomas said.

"How was your social last night? Too bad Jakob couldn't have been here in time to go along," Obadiah said.

"It was fine. Good food."

"Any new girls catch your eye? Your mother said she spoke to Sara yesterday about possibly making you a match."

"*Ne*. No one in particular; I spent most of the evening talking to Leah Yoder." Thomas shook his head. "Honestly, I'm having second thoughts about this matchmaker thing. Don't see why we need to lay out the money. I've never had trouble finding dates."

Obadiah turned a half-bushel basket upside down, sat on it and took out a penknife. Absently, he began to whittle at a small piece of wood he carried in his pocket. They sat in silence for a few minutes and then his grandfather said, "People say Sara knows her trade. They say give her a chance, she'll find you a proper wife."

"Seems foolish, though, docsn't it? Having her find me a wife? When I could do it myself?"

"But you haven't." His grandfather sighed. "Thomas, what can I say? Time you grew up. Started working in the family business. Trouble is, you think you can stay free and single year after year. You like the pretty girls. I can see it. But when talk turns serious, you're off after the next one."

Thomas felt heat flush his face. "It's not like that. I thought that Ellie and me would…" He trailed off, not wanting to talk about Ellie. That was still a sore subject. "I'm not certain Sara can find me a match I'd be happy with. She wanted me to meet this woman last night— Hazel something or other. One of the ones who came up from Virginia in the van. Sour as an October persimmon. Little beady eyes and a mouth screwed up so tight I thought she didn't have front teeth until I saw her eating. I couldn't imagine looking at that face across a breakfast table every morning."

Obadiah chuckled. "So, not pretty enough for you?"

Thomas shook his head. "That wasn't it. Hazel would have been attractive if she hadn't been so ill-tempered. Not a good word to say about anyone or anything. One complaint after another. She even complained about the potato salad. Said she preferred German potato salad to Sara's and left it on her plate."

"One wasteful woman doesn't ruin the batch. You're being stubborn. Time you started walking out with a respectable girl."

"I thought I was when I was with Ellie. And you all liked her."

His grandfather ignored that and went on. "Bishop Atlee asked me last week if you were planning on going to baptism classes. Way past time, Thomas. I'm going to retire in a few years. Don't know how much longer I have on this earth. I know I've always told you that I wanted to leave this farm to you, but you worry me. I'm starting to have second thoughts. Maybe you mean to drift away from the faith. Maybe you're too flighty to entrust our family farm to."

Thomas winced as if his grandfather had struck him. This was the first he'd heard of his grandfather's hesitation about leaving him the farm. Since he was a boy, he'd expected it would be his someday. His throat clenched. "That's up to you, *Grossdaddi*."

"You should be married. You should have married five years ago. I could have great-grandsons and granddaughters to spoil. I've stood up for you to your mother and father, took your side when maybe I should not have." He exhaled. "You don't give Sara a chance to find you a wife, I have to take it into consideration that maybe you've lost track of what's important in life."

Thomas opened his mouth to respond, but his grandfather's shepherd raised his head and let out a single yip, then leaped up and ran toward the house. Thomas heard the beep of a car horn and the dog began to bark in earnest. "That must be Jakob coming now," he said, rising to his feet.

"Must be," his grandfather agreed. "But you think on what I said. I'm worried about you, boy." He met Thomas's gaze. "Prove to us all that you are ready to take over this farm. Find a wife, get to churching and be quick about it."

Sara smiled at Thomas as they shook hands across her desk. "So we're in agreement. I'll make you a match. Keep an open mind, and I'm sure I can find someone who will suit you and your family."

It had been more than a week since Sara's barn social. Thomas had spent days wrestling with the idea of asking for help in finding a wife. He'd prayed on it, and he'd considered asking the bishop to add his name to the upcoming classes in preparation for baptism in the fall. But he hadn't been ready to take that step yet. One obstacle at a time. Maybe finding the right girl would erase the last doubts he had about a Plain life. As much as his parents wanted him to join the faith, they wanted it for the right reasons. It had to wholeheartedly be his choice, not someone else's. The Old Order Amish lifestyle was a lifetime commitment, one you were supposed to enter with joy.

Tonight, he'd come after supper, as Sara had asked.

He hoped that he wouldn't run into Ellie or Leah. It wasn't that he was embarrassed about using a matchmaker. It was more that a man's personal business ought to be private. And what could be more personal than choosing a wife?

Thomas hadn't mentioned to Sara that his grandfather was threatening to leave the farm to someone else. The possibility of losing the farm hurt, but if Thomas hadn't thought that maybe his grandfather was right, he would never have agreed to make an official agreement with the matchmaker.

He started to rise from his chair, but Sara waved him back into his seat. They were in her office in her home, a spacious room with comfortable furniture, deep window seats and a colorful braid rug.

"Don't go yet," she said. "I have a fresh pot of coffee and a blueberry pie that's just begging to be sliced." She made a few more notations on the yellow legal-sized notepad and tucked the sheet into a manila folder.

"How long do you think it will take?" Thomas asked. He rested his straw hat on one knee and looked at her.

"Slicing the pie or finding you a wife?"

He grimaced, still not entirely convinced this whole matchmaker thing was a good idea. "Finding somebody for me."

"Actually, I already have someone in mind."

"Not that Hazel girl you introduced me to the other night," he protested. "I didn't care for her at all."

She chuckled. "Not Hazel. Funny you should mention her, though. She and Fred Petersheim hit it off. It seems he didn't care for my potato salad either."

Thomas laughed. "I thought it was great."

"I'm pleased. Now," she said, rising, "you make

yourself at ease. I won't be a moment. How is it you like your coffee?"

"Sugar and milk. Two sugars."

"You like it sweet."

"*Ya*, I do. I could come out in the kitchen with you," he suggested. "No need for you to—"

"No. Stay where you are, Thomas." She walked from the room, closing the door behind her.

Thomas tapped the heel of one boot nervously. He glanced around the room. The pale blue walls were hung with cross-stitch family trees and several large calendars. One showed a farmer plowing with a six-horse team against a rural background. Another showed a mare and newborn foal, the little filly tentatively trying out her new legs in tall clover.

In one corner of the room stood a battered green filing cabinet. He wondered if there was a manila folder in one of the drawers that would hold his future. It was exciting and a little frightening to put his life in Sara's hands. He was tempted to wander over and take a peek. He wasn't normally a snoop, but if he just—

The door opened and Thomas turned his head to see not Sara but Leah. She was carrying a tray with slices of pie and three cups of coffee. "Oh!" he said. "You startled me." He rose and hurried to take the tray, realizing that although he'd hoped they wouldn't run into each other this evening, he was pleased to see her.

"Sara asked me to bring this in," Leah explained with a smile. "She said she'll just be a minute." He put the tray on the desk, and she took a seat opposite him and motioned to the coffee. "Please, go ahead. It's nice and hot."

He noticed that she was wearing glasses. He didn't

think that she had worn them at the barn frolic. But they did nothing to hide the intelligent sparkle of her bright blue eyes. Leah should have been as plain as a barnyard dove in her worn gray dress, apron and headscarf, but red-gold tendrils of hair framed her heart-shaped face, and merry dimples gave her a mischievous appearance.

He wondered if Sara could find him someone like Leah. But maybe not so pretty, he thought. Ellie had warned him that he needed to look beyond an attractive face and neat figure.

A minute or two passed. Leah cupped her coffee mug in her hands and inhaled the steam. She didn't speak, and Thomas realized that the silence between them wasn't awkward. Rather, he found it peaceful. Most girls he knew liked to fill every second with chatter.

He tasted his own coffee. It was good. He would have to ask Sara what brand it was. His mother was an excellent cook, but her coffee left something to be desired. It was either too weak or something. It never tasted as good as Sara's. This was hearty, with a brisk, bright flavor.

"I guess it was quiet in the jungle," he remarked. "No traffic, not many people."

Leah smiled and shook her head. "Not noisy like here in the States, but certainly not quiet. There were so many insects, buzzing, flapping, whirring. For the first month I was there, I found it hard to sleep. And the monkeys? Some kinds scream, others howl. They all chatter nonstop. And sometimes you'd hear a deep rumble, like a cough in the night. Iago said that when I heard that noise, I should stay inside the house or clinic hut because it was a leopard and I would make a fine meal for a big cat."

Thomas gave her a sharp look. "A leopard? Did you ever see one?"

"No, but Iago said that they came to our side of the river in the rainy season. One had killed a child from the nearest village two years earlier. He wasn't given to tall tales, so I believed him." She rested her mug on the wooden arm of her chair. "You would think him odd if you saw him. He wasn't as tall as me; he had a potbelly, and his hair was cut like a cap just below his ears. Even though he was a great-grandfather, his hair was still as black as soot and coarse as a horse's mane. Iago's tattooed face was wizened like a winter apple and his legs were bowed, but he was stronger than you can imagine. He was my dearest friend other than my Daniel, and I shall never forget him. Iago taught me so much about life. It was his wisdom and patience that made it possible for us to live and work among the St. Joes."

"I would like to have met your Iago," Thomas said.

"You would have liked him. He told such stories that I could listen all day."

"He spoke English?"

Leah chuckled and shook her head. "Only a little. His granddaughter translated for me, and Iago was a fine actor. He used such expressions and hand movements that it was easy to follow."

"Who was easy to follow?" Sara asked as she entered the room.

Thomas stood. "Leah was telling me about some of her adventures in Brazil. It seems she was nearly eaten by a leopard."

"I didn't say that." Leah laughed.

Sara took her place behind her desk and helped herself to a slice of pie. "Mmm. Coffee's still hot. Good."

She motioned to the other plates of pie. "Well, what are you waiting for? It's for eating, not looking."

Thomas took a plate and handed it to Leah.

"I should leave you two alone," Leah said, rising, her plate in her hand. "If you and Thomas have business."

"We do." Sara wiped a drop of coffee from her lip. "And so do you and I." She glanced from one of them to the other. "What? You really haven't guessed, have you?"

"Guessed what?" Thomas asked. He looked at Leah, who had sat down again, then back at Sara. "Wait. You don't mean—"

"Ne," Leah pronounced firmly, looking at him and then at Sara, too. "Not Thomas. Not for me." Her cheeks took on a rosy glow. "It's nothing against you, Thomas," she hastened to explain, glancing back at him again. "But you're not what I—" She turned her attention to Sara again. "I was very clear what I'm looking for. An older man. Settled. With children."

Thomas shook his head, wondering what Sara could be thinking. "We've known each other our whole lives. You don't think—"

"Stuff and nonsense!" Sara interrupted him, seeming perturbed. "Listen to the two of you. Who is the expert here? I've made more matches than you can imagine, and I think I know my business. You're perfect for each other." She pointed at him with her fork. "You're badly in need of a wife, Thomas. And Leah doesn't want to leave Seven Poplars and her family. What could be a better solution?"

"But Thomas isn't…" Leah murmured.

"She…she doesn't—" Thomas struggled to find the

right words. If she wasn't interested in him, he certainly wasn't going to be interested in her.

"Look. Either you have faith in me or you don't," Sara said crisply. "Leah, you wanted an arranged marriage, someone of the faith that your family would approve of. And Thomas, you've been hopeless at finding someone on your own." She fixed him with a determined gaze. "So here's what I propose. Six weeks of dating. That should give you each time to consider the pros and cons of the other."

"But I don't want to date Thomas," Leah insisted. "He's the last sort of man I'd want to marry."

Her words hurt him a little, and he felt his own ire rise. "She's not what I'm looking for," he blurted. "I won't consider—"

"Oh, but you will," Sara said rather firmly. "You will both agree to give this match a fair chance. Because if you don't, if you won't even open your minds to the possibility, then I'm not the matchmaker for you." She sat back in her chair, crossing her arms over her chest. "And I'll wash my hands of both of you."

Chapter Four

Leah didn't know what to say. She didn't know if she was more disappointed in Sara or upset with her that she would suggest such a thing. Hadn't she just told Sara the other day that Thomas was all wrong for her? A terrible match. Of course, he was a good person. This was awkward, so much so that she almost wished the floor would open and let her drop through to the cellar. Anything to get out of this chair and away from Thomas.

"Well?" Sara said. "Are we in agreement, Leah? Six weeks?"

"I... I'm just afraid it would be...a waste of everyone's time," Leah hedged. "Not helpful for..." Her fork fell off the plate. She grabbed for it and missed. The fork clattered to the floor leaving a trail of blueberry-pie filling across the hardwood. Her face felt warm; she knew she was blushing. She reached to pick it up but Thomas was quicker. He grabbed the wayward utensil and dropped it onto his empty saucer.

Leah seized a napkin off Sara's desk and wiped at the mess. It smeared and she got down on her knees to get the last of the blueberry smear.

Sara cleared her throat.

Leah got up hastily, crumpling the dirty napkin and shoving it into a spacious apron pocket. She glanced toward the door, wondering if she should make a run for it.

Sara folded her arms again and looked at Thomas. "What about you? Are you willing? Would you date Leah for six weeks?"

He started to rise and then settled back into his chair. "*Ya*, I suppose I could. I mean…" His tanned complexion flushed. "It's just that I wasn't expecting…"

"You can see that it wouldn't work," Leah blurted, finding her voice. "He doesn't want—"

"Nonsense," Sara interrupted. "What Thomas wants or doesn't want clearly hasn't been working, has it? That's why he came to me." She turned and their gazes locked. "And you came to me. You asked for my help. My opinion. And I'm giving it to you. My opinion is that you and Thomas may be a good match. An excellent match." Sara steepled her hands and leaned forward, elbows braced against the desk. "And if nothing else, six weeks will give you time to settle in to Seven Poplars again. What is it the sailors say? Get your sea legs?"

Leah was in no mood for humor, but what could she say? She had hired Sara and she had put her trust in her abilities. And it wasn't as if she could go door-to-door knocking at farmhouses, asking if there was an eligible bachelor available. She'd wanted a matchmaker so that she wouldn't have to make a decision, so that the weight would be taken off her shoulders. Her plan was that whoever God sent, she would accept.

"I… I just…" Leah didn't know what to say.

"Come now, it's not as though I'm asking you to cry

the banns next Sunday," Sara said. "And Thomas is an acceptable escort. You might have fun. And if the two of you go to frolics, singings, socials, who knows—you might meet someone you really like." She hesitated. "Humor me, Leah."

Leah looked at Thomas. "What do you think?"

"I see no harm in it." Thomas shrugged. "And it could be fun."

"Ya," Leah replied. "You *would* say that."

He chuckled. "Sorry. I do like having a good time."

"Well?" Sara asked.

Leah looked from the older woman to Thomas and back to Sara. "At the end of six weeks, if we both feel the same way, will you find me the older widower I asked for?"

"Of course," Sara agreed. "And if I've made a mistake and wasted your time, I'll consider a substantial reduction in my fee for your new matches."

"Could we talk?" Thomas suggested. "Just Leah and me?" He glanced at her. "If you're agreeable, Leah?"

"Ya," she said.

"Fine." Sara got up from her chair. "Take all the time you want. But I'll leave the door open, for propriety's sake." She paused on her way out. "You two need to trust me. I know what I'm doing."

"I wish I was certain of that," Leah admitted, once she and Thomas were alone.

"Want to sit down?" Thomas motioned toward the chair she'd vacated. "Talk about this?"

Leah nodded, taking Sara's seat, putting the desk between them. "I'm sorry about you being put on the spot this way. I had no idea that she was going to suggest—" she began.

"Me neither," he said, cutting her off. "Sorry, I didn't mean to interrupt. I just don't want you to think I was in on this."

"I know you weren't. It's fine. This is just so—"

"Awkward," he finished for her.

"*Ya,*" she agreed, and found they were both chuckling as though they shared a joke. And perhaps they did. Sara's ruse. "I suppose we're stuck with this," Leah ventured.

"*Ne.* Not if it doesn't suit you. If you find me that…" Thomas seemed to search for a word. "Distasteful."

Leah shook her head. "It's not that. I like you, Thomas. You're a good man. Just not…"

"What you were looking for," he supplied. "I understand."

"I'm glad someone does." She nibbled at her bottom lip. "I thought it would be easier than this."

His dark eyes lit with humor. "It would have been if I'd taken a fancy to Hazel."

"And if I liked Holsteins more." She returned Thomas's smile with one of her own. She felt her annoyance slipping away. He was sweet. What harm could it do to humor Sara? It would only be for six weeks, and then she would get on with the process of making a serious arrangement. "I think we should just give in gracefully," she admitted. "I think Sara has us in a corner."

"Actually," he said. "You might be doing me a favor. It will give me some time to get my family off my back." He arched a brow questioningly. "Are you in?"

Leah nodded and offered him her hand. "I think we have a deal. Six weeks and no hard feelings when we break it off."

His stood again and strong fingers closed around

hers as he reached across the desk to shake on it. "Six weeks," he echoed quietly. "We walk out together, have some fun, and everyone is satisfied."

"And then we get on with our lives," she finished.

"*Goot* enough." He squeezed her hand and then released it. "So, will you let me walk you home after church services tomorrow?"

"Tomorrow?" Her eyes widened in surprise. "Are you sure? So soon?"

"*Ya*, tomorrow," he answered steadily. "Why not tomorrow? We've made a bargain, haven't we? When I agree to something, I keep my word."

"All right," she said, smiling at him again. "Me, too."

"A good sermon," Leah said. "Not too long."

Thomas nodded. "Your sister's husband is a good preacher. When Caleb first came to Seven Poplars, we thought he might not be a good fit, but we were wrong. We like him." He grinned at her. "Partly because he doesn't speak to hear the sound of his own voice."

"But what he said was powerful," Leah replied. "A good preacher doesn't need to shout to deliver God's message."

"*Ya*, I agree." Thomas bent to pick up a stick lying on the edge of the blacktop and tossed it into the woods. "When a sermon is too long, a man's thoughts drift. I like the short ones best."

It was late afternoon and they were on their way back to Sara's house after worship. Ahead of them, a few hundred yards, walked a young family: a mother, father and three children. Some distance behind them, another couple strolled. Buggies passed at regular intervals, followed by an occasional automobile or pickup truck, but this was a narrow country road with little traffic other than locals, a safe road for walking.

The Kings' farm, where services had been held today, was two miles from Sara's, but the weather was mild and the spring sun warm on his face—so warm that Thomas looked overdressed in his coat and vest. She suspected that he would rather remove the coat and walk home in shirtsleeves, but it wouldn't be proper on the Sabbath. Thomas seemed *fast*, almost reckless at times, but he wasn't outright rebellious.

Leah was comfortable enough in her gray cotton dress and black leather oxfords. She considered herself a good walker, and although Thomas's legs were a lot longer than hers, she had no trouble keeping up.

Thomas groaned and patted his stomach. "I think I might have had one too many helpings of Anna's shoofly pie."

"Greedy. You should have stopped at one slice."

He chuckled. "I thought it was delicious, but I couldn't be sure until I ate a second piece."

"Three," she reminded him. "You had three slices."

"Small slices," he admitted, and laughed with her. "This isn't so bad, is it? Walking out with me? Unless you'd rather be driving."

She shook her head, thinking of her little black car parked behind Sara's chicken house. "I don't mind walking," she answered. "It's good exercise. We walked all the time in Brazil. There are no roads where we were. It was travel by boat down a river, fly or walk. Mostly, we walked. It could take hours or days to get to a sick patient or a village where Daniel was preaching."

"You walked for days through the jungle? Weren't you afraid?"

"Sometimes. Not often. Most of the tribespeople are quite shy of strangers. We always traveled with a guide, someone who could speak their language. Usually, we were welcomed into their villages and treated as honored guests. If I was afraid of anything, it was the snakes." She shuddered, just thinking of them. "There are several that are extremely poisonous. Deadly, even with modern treatment. I never learned to lose my fear of snakes."

"You said there were lots of insects. Mosquitoes?"

"Far too many. And some carry diseases such as malaria and dengue fever."

"And here I thought Delaware mosquitoes were bad."

"They can be." She rubbed her arms. "Don't remind me. They aren't out yet, and it's much too pleasant to think about them."

"August was bad last year. We had a lot of rain and they hatched by the millions. Huge and hungry."

"Lovely," she said. "I can't wait."

Thomas chuckled. "Well, I guess we raised a few eyebrows when we left the Kings' together."

"I'm sure we set them all atwitter," she agreed. She was surprised at how much she was enjoying the day. She'd expected having Thomas walk her home from church would be awkward, but she found him comfortable to talk to. He had an easy laugh, and it was nice having him beside her.

"My grandfather saw us and nodded his approval." He made a reluctant sound. "I feel a little bad about deceiving him, letting him think that we're walking out together."

"But, we are, aren't we? We did promise Sara a six-week trial."

"I suppose you're right," Thomas said. "It isn't really a ruse. Not if we do date like we promised. Even if we both know that this isn't going to work out."

"Exactly," she agreed. "You know, honestly, I can't see why you haven't found someone. There's nothing wrong with you that I can see."

"I'm glad to hear that."

His tone seemed a little stilted. "Don't take it personally, Thomas. And who knows? Maybe Sara will prove us wrong. Maybe we'll fall madly in love."

He chuckled with her. "Right."

Leah stopped walking and looked up into his face. "But I warn you, you'll have to be careful what you say. My sisters are relentless. They'll try to drum every bit of information out of you. They'll interrogate you just like one of those detectives on the television shows."

"Have you watched a lot of television?"

"*Ne.* Not much, but you can't help but see it now and then when you travel a lot."

"I suppose you miss it now that you're living with Sara."

"*Ne.*" She shook her head. "I don't. Mostly television is reporters shouting about fires or shootings or some movie star's latest scandal or people running around and blowing up things. Life is better without it."

"I suppose." He took her arm, guided her off into the grass as a truck passed and then released her.

Leah felt a warm rush of pleasure. How long had it been since she'd felt a man's touch? It felt good, and the realization made her wonder how she could so quickly forget that she had once been a married woman. And now was Daniel's widow.

Subdued, she turned the conversation to Thomas

after they had walked a short way. "Your family must be eager for you to settle down and start a family. As much as my family wants me to marry again."

"You could say that."

When she didn't comment, he found himself telling her about the conversation he'd had with his grandfather about the farm. "I wasn't expecting that," he concluded. "I never thought that he'd threaten me about the land."

"What will you do?" she asked.

"I'm not sure. I wanted to shout back at him. To tell him that he couldn't pressure me into marrying just anyone. But I bit my tongue. I just…"

She nodded. "I understand. It isn't easy with those we love. They want to help, but they cause more problems. It's one reason I decided to stay at Sara's. *Mam* pities me because of what happened to Daniel and our baby. She wants to protect me and to tell me what to do with my life at the same time." Leah flashed a brilliant smile. "But I'm not letting her get away with it."

"Still," he said, "you must have…" He wanted to say *suffered* but, instead, just trailed off. "It was a great loss," he finished.

Leah swallowed back the surge of hurt that threatened her peaceful day. "I have to believe that they're in a better place. It helps that I know the two of them are together in the Lord's care. And that if I live a good life I'll see them again." She forced a smile. "I know that. Just as I know that my Daniel would have wanted me to live on, for all of us."

"*Ya,*" Thomas said. "I see the wisdom in that." He touched her arm lightly. "I think you are a brave woman."

She shook her head and chuckled wryly. "Not brave.

Just trusting that God has a path for me and that all I have to do is to try and find it."

They walked a little farther in silence, and then he said, "You make me realize that my problems are small."

"Finding a wife?"

"That is an obstacle. But it's more than that. My grandfather, my father, my whole family expect me to follow tradition and become a blacksmith. But it's not what I want. It's not how I see my life. Does that make me selfish?"

She stopped and looked up at him. "You shouldn't feel guilty because you don't want to be told what to do for a living. My family certainly didn't want me to marry a Mennonite and go to Brazil as a missionary. But it was my choice. Surely, each person has the right to choose what's best for them."

"*Ya*. It's what I think, too. But it's hard to disappoint my grandfather and my father. It means so much to them."

"But you are your own man, Thomas. You should be. Otherwise, you're just a shadow of them."

He smiled. "It doesn't sound so bad when you say it that way."

"So what would you do with your life, if you could choose? Sara told me that you work construction sometimes and that you help on your grandfather's farm. Do you prefer one or the other? Who knows? Maybe you haven't found your place yet. Maybe that's why you haven't settled down."

"I do like farming, but not the way my grandfather wants me to farm. Corn. Soybeans. Hay. The same old crops, fields of them. Commercial fertilizer. I don't think that's the way to go. If I could do anything, I'd like to start small, raise organic vegetables. I read the farm magazines and there's a growing need for heritage crops produced locally without insect sprays. Of course, if you did that, you'd need bees. They're everything when it comes to pollination."

"Daniel subscribed to *Modern Organic Farming.* We practiced it as much as possible. Easy there in Brazil, where chemicals and commercial fertilizers are too expensive to use. But jungle soil is thin. If you want to raise vegetables, either you move your gardens regularly, as the indigenous people do, or you find a way to enrich the earth. We buried fish guts and compost in our kitchen garden."

Her mood lightened as she remembered the joy of working with her plants in the early morning, loosening the soil around them and pulling the weeds. The village children had helped, making a game of plucking insects from her tomatoes, squash and peppers. Although she'd never been certain why they'd dropped each beetle, grub or ant into a tiny bark container and carried the insects away. Suspecting that the protein may have strengthened the family stew pot, she'd never had the nerve to ask.

"So you understand the idea," Thomas said eagerly. "Raising food without poisons. It's becoming popular with the Englishers, but you know our people. They like the high yields commercial fertilizer delivers. Once they get used to doing something in a particular way, they don't accept change easily."

"*Ya,* exactly," Leah agreed. "It was the same with the village elders. They were used to sending the young men out with nets to catch fish, but sometimes the river was so fast that it tore the nets, and sometimes there were few fish. Daniel and I built a fish pond behind the clinic. We used the natural fertilizer that the fish provided to feed our garden and then drained the excess water back into the pond. We could catch fish for dinner whenever we pleased. At least when the predators or our neighbors didn't get them first." She laughed. "A fat fish in the missionary's pool is a temptation that's hard to resist."

"But you had a steady supply of food."

She nodded. "We were always trying to come up with small projects to improve the villagers' lives. We never did get them to stop drinking river water, but we managed to convince the elders to divert a stream upriver, filter it through charcoal and sand, and pipe it into the village. That way people weren't filling their cooking pots where the children bathed. They thought we were peculiar, but they humored us when they saw that fewer babies took sick and died in infancy."

"So you don't think my ideas are foolish?" Thomas asked.

"Ne," she protested, warming to the idea of a new project to put her mind to. "Not at all. Who would you sell to? I don't know how well organic produce would sell at Spence's market."

"I was thinking that maybe I could sell to restaurants. Maybe specialty markets."

"That's a brilliant idea!" She smiled up at him. "I would imagine there's real money to be made if you could connect to the restaurants or the specialty markets in the cities. Daniel has a cousin—second cousin, really. Richard… Richard something. Hunziger, that's it. He lives near Lancaster. He and Daniel used to email back and forth. Richard grows organic fruits and vegetables and delivers them to restaurants in Philadelphia. He also makes a good profit on his laying hens. Even English people don't like store eggs once they've eaten ones from free-range chickens."

"Really? I'd love to have a chance to talk to him. But…" Thomas shrugged.

Leah thought for a moment. "Why don't you let me contact him for you? I don't have his address, but I'm certain that Daniel's aunt would. I'll ask Richard if he'd be willing to have you come out to Pennsylvania and see his operation. If you're interested?"

Thomas's features brightened. "Of course I'm interested. I could hire a driver and—"

"Why would you need a driver when I have a car and a license?" she asked. "It's not that far. We could easily go up and spend the afternoon. Actually seeing what he's doing would give you a better idea of what's involved. I know that growing organic vegetables and fruits is more expensive than regular, but Daniel said the profits were better, too. At least you'd be in a better place to make a decision, wouldn't you?"

"I would," Thomas said. A smile spread across his face and lit his intelligent, dark eyes. "You know, Leah, there's a lot more to you than people realize. You're not only pretty, but you're smart, and you're a good listener."

"Danki," she replied, thinking that perhaps there was more to Thomas than she'd thought, too. "But it's not such a big thing," she went on. "A trip to Lancaster would be fun, I think. And I would like to meet Richard's wife and family."

"So when can we go?" he asked eagerly.

"As soon as I can arrange it," she promised.

"And you have to let me pay for the gasoline and buy you lunch."

"I would like that," she assured him. "I'll warn you that I'm fond of hamburgers and fries. In Brazil I used to dream about crispy French fries from American fast-food restaurants."

"It's a date," he said as they turned into Sara's driveway. "And one that I can honestly say I'm looking forward to."

"Me, too," she agreed. And she had to admit that she was. Thomas might not be the man for her, but he was always fun to be with, and who wouldn't enjoy an unexpected holiday?

Chapter Five

Thomas lowered his window and gazed out at the rolling Pennsylvania farmland. The growing season was several weeks behind Seven Poplars, but it was full spring here all the same. The trees were bursting with new green leaves of every hue, and tractors and teams of workhorses plowed the wide fields. "A little rocky," Thomas pronounced, "but this looks like rich soil."

"Some of the best in the country, Daniel said," Leah replied. "The topsoil is deeper than a man's arm is long and the Pennsylvania Dutch are good stewards of the land."

"I think that some of my grandmother's people came from north of here. Some valley." He shifted in his seat to find more room for his legs. Leah's compact car was a tight fit for him. His head nearly brushed the roof, and even with the seat pushed back as far as it would go, he was cramped. Not that he cared about a little discomfort. He was enjoying the day, the new sights, and a break from the routine of everyday work. And they hadn't even reached Richard Hunziger's organic farm yet.

Leah signaled, slowed and turned off the wide road

onto a narrower, hilly one. The houses on either side of the blacktop were a mixture of older stone residences and newer clapboard or brick. Young Amish children played in the yards, and women hung clothes on lines, swept porch steps and planted seedlings in large gardens. In one yard, a boy, no more than four years old, tugged at the halter of a fat brown-and-white pony. Pulling out of a driveway was an Amish man in an odd type of gray buggy, enclosed in the front as a normal buggy would be, but open in the back for carrying larger items.

"Amish pickup," Thomas said. "Pretty handy to have. I could use one of those for transporting lumber and building material."

Leah chuckled.

"What's so funny?"

"Not what you said. I'm sure a buggy like that would be useful. I was thinking about how far away this is from the Amazon. When the St. Joes didn't walk, they traveled by river in dugout canoes that barely rose above the waterline. Sometimes they'd load them down with entire families—fathers, the mothers, infants, kids and elders. I wondered why they didn't sink, but they never did."

"Mothers?"

Leah shrugged and grimaced. "Customs change slowly in the Amazonian jungle. It used to be common for the best hunters and the leaders of the St. Joes to have more than one wife at a time. Daniel and I did our best to discourage the practice, but…"

Thomas shook his head, amazed at what this young woman had seen and half wishing that it had been him traveling to faraway places and witnessing unfamiliar and outlandish customs. "Aren't there crocodiles in those rivers?"

"Some, but what we saw were a kind of alligator called a black caiman. Vicious beasts that grow to over sixteen feet long. The river also was home to poisonous snakes and flesh-eating piranha. Delicious, but very dangerous."

"You ate piranha?"

She laughed. "I'm sure we did. It wasn't considered polite to ask what your hostess put in her cook pot. Food, especially meat, is difficult to come by in the jungle. When the locals offer you food, you accept with thanks, ask a silent blessing that you won't die from it, and you eat it."

"So I wouldn't think you did much swimming in the river?"

She laughed again. "Hardly. The St. Joes swim naked."

Thomas felt his throat and face flush. Nudity was hardly a proper topic of conversation between a man and a woman, especially those who were dating. Not that this was a date. He'd come with her to learn more about organic-farming practices. As much as he enjoyed being with Leah—and she was always fun—she had a way of making him uneasy. She was so outspoken... so experienced. Not like other Amish girls he knew. He wondered if she'd ever be able to return to the quiet life in Seven Poplars or any other Old Order community after her life in the English world. Pity the man who did marry her. It wasn't natural, a woman knowing more than her husband.

"I don't think it's far now to Richard's farm," Leah said.

They passed an open courting buggy with a couple in it and several more gray family buggies before turning into a lane marked with a cheerful green-and-white sign that read Eden Hill Organic Fruits and Vegetables. A stone wall enclosed a pasture on one side with a flock of black-faced sheep. On the far side of the driveway were tidy rows of young apple trees.

A dog barked as the car pulled into the farmyard. The back door of a tidy white cottage opened and a middle-aged African American woman wearing a calf-length denim dress, a flowered apron and a head-scarf cap much like Leah's came out onto the steps. "You made it!" she called. "Richard! They're here!"

A husky redheaded man with a neatly trimmed beard followed her out onto the stoop. He came out to the car, followed by his wife, and shook hands with Thomas. "Did you have any trouble finding us?" Richard asked.

Leah shook her head. "*Ne.* Your directions were excellent."

"This is my wife Grace," Richard introduced. "The boys are in school, but you'll get to meet them later. They have a short day today for some reason."

"Teachers' conferences," Grace supplied.

Leah greeted Grace with a warm embrace.

"It's so good to see you. We've been worried about you," Grace told Leah. "We were so shocked by your loss. But you've been in our prayers every day."

Leah nodded. "I appreciate that. It means a lot."

"And I appreciate you taking the time to show me around your farm," Thomas told Richard.

Richard rolled up his shirtsleeves. "Glad to do it."

Grace chuckled. "Believe it. There is nothing Richard likes better than someone new to share his ideas with," she said.

"This is just a small place," Richard explained, leading the way across the yard. "Seventeen acres. And a lot of it is too steep to till for regular crops. But we're blessed with two springs that never go dry and some

really fertile fields. By concentrating on growing only
the best vegetables, I've been able to build up a steady
demand for our crops, at top prices."

"And you think the market is there to make the extra
expense of growing organic profitable?" Thomas asked.
Leah and Grace fell in behind them.

"I do. It's hard work—I won't tell you otherwise—
but I find it extremely rewarding, not just in financial
reward but in knowing that I'm growing the healthi-
est food possible, food I want to feed my family. And I
know I'm not polluting the ground or the water."

"That's one of the things that drew me to the idea
of growing organic produce," Thomas said. "In many
ways, it's the traditional way of farming, as our great-
grandparents did."

Richard nodded enthusiastically. "You can start
small, but land is the most expensive outlay. And you
need something that hasn't been worked commercially.
Otherwise, it will take a lot longer to meet the qualifi-
cations for organic crops."

"The acreage I have in mind has been in pasture for
decades," Thomas explained. "It has good drainage and
the soil's not too sandy."

"That sounds perfect. But finding your buyers is cru-
cial. That's Grace's department around here. She carried free strawberries to a dozen of the best restaurants
in Philadelphia and convinced the head chefs of two of
them to give us a try. Since then, our farm has been in
the black, and we've doubled and tripled our fancy-fruit
sales. Farming has always been a hard way to make a living, but this has the greatest potential that I've seen, especially if you can find help to do the picking and packing."

"Which I think I can," Thomas said, thinking of the

young Amish men and women in Seven Poplars who'd recently left school.

Richard led the way to the first of three greenhouses and pushed open the nearest door. "This is where I grow our salad greens and start seedlings," he explained. "With a combination of solar power and propane, I can keep the temperature high enough to grow tomatoes, lettuces and peppers, even in bitter weather."

Thomas stood back to let Richard's wife and Leah enter first. He noticed that Leah was carrying a clipboard and pen.

"To take notes," she said when she saw him looking at her. "You might like to know what varieties of cucumbers and squash grow best in a greenhouse, and what varieties Richard may have had problems with."

"I should have thought of that," he answered. Thomas was pleased that Leah showed so much interest in Richard's farming practices. For more than an hour they followed Richard up one aisle and down another, listening to him as they inspected the greenhouses and then went to see the field greens and strawberry patches.

"Blackberries and raspberries provide an excellent return," Richard said. "But they're labor intensive. They have to be picked, packed and delivered at the peak of ripeness. My customers love them, but the season is relatively short."

Duplicating what Richard Hunziger had done here would take years of work, Thomas mused, but the possibilities seemed endless. Finding markets for his products near Kent County, if he managed to grow them successfully, would be a problem. There were restaurants in Dover, but it was a much smaller city than Philadelphia, and Philadelphia was too far from Kent

County to easily deliver fresh produce. But those were problems that could be worked out. What was important was that Richard was doing exactly what he'd dreamed of, and was doing it in a manner that supported his family.

Thomas and Leah had planned to be home early, but there was so much to learn from Richard and Grace and they were having such a good time that it had been impossible to refuse Grace's invitation to share a late lunch. And, after that, seeing that Richard had transplanting to do, it seemed only fair that he and Leah pitch in to help. They didn't leave the farm until almost supper time.

On the ride home, Thomas and Leah couldn't stop talking about all they'd seen. And he hadn't realized that he was hungry again until Leah pulled the little black car into a fast-food place. They purchased hamburgers, fries and lemonade from the drive-through window and ate it parked in the back row of the lot behind the restaurant. His double cheeseburger was so juicy that grease ran down his chin, and Leah had to mop it up with a napkin. They laughed over that and a dozen other silly incidents that had happened that day as they finished the last of the salty French fries and drained the last drops of lemonade.

"Not as good as Sara's," Leah pronounced.

"No, but it's cold and wet," Thomas replied. And then, chuckling and exchanging guilty looks like naughty children, they drove around to the drive-in window again and bought ice cream with chocolate and whipped cream on the top.

"Is it as good as you thought it would be when you were in the jungle?" he asked, indicating the ice cream.

She licked her spoon and grinned. "Absolutely."

All the way home they discussed all the possibilities of his starting his own organic-farm project that spring. Leah had good suggestions, and he was surprised by how much she had absorbed of what Richard had told them. "It's finding the markets that worries me most," he confided. "It won't be any good to grow organic vegetables if I can't find a place to sell them profitably."

"What if you tried the beach?" she asked as they drove back onto the highway and turned south toward home. "Rehoboth and Lewes? I think there are lots of high-quality restaurants there, and I know they must have the customers who would want organic produce."

"But how do I deliver the fruits and vegetables?"

She thought on it for a moment. "Horse and buggy wouldn't work, would it?" she said.

"Hardly. It must be forty, fifty miles from my place to Rehoboth Beach."

She braked at a traffic light. "So maybe you need to go to Rehoboth and talk to some people at some restaurants. See if anyone's interested."

"I don't know who I would talk to. I can't just walk in the door. I'd probably have to have an appointment."

She glanced at him. "Actually, just walking in probably *would* be better. If you asked for an appointment, they could say they were busy. But if you walk in the door, a manager or a chef or maybe even an owner would probably talk to you just because you're Amish."

He frowned. "What do you mean *because I'm Amish*?"

"All day long they serve Englishers. Tourists in tiny bathing suits and short shorts and fancy clothes. How many Amish men come in? They'll be curious. You can take advantage of that curiosity. It's how Daniel and I met the more isolated tribes. We were a curiosity to them." She chuckled. "All we need is a few minutes of the restaurant manager's time. And if you could bring fresh organic vegetables to their back door, it would be a big help to their business, wouldn't it?"

He ran a hand through his hair. "What we haven't figured out is how I'd get those vegetables to them."

"One problem at a time," Leah said. "First we find you customers, then we'll worry about how to get the vegetables delivered."

Traffic began to back up. They came to a stop again, this time a long way from the light. Sirens wailed and an ambulance and several police cars passed. "I think there must be an accident ahead," Leah said. "I hope no one is hurt."

Thomas rolled down the window and strained his neck to see, but whatever had caused the trouble was too far ahead to make out.

On the left, a big sign flashed, advertising a bowling alley. "Oh," Leah said. "Bowling. I haven't been bowling in years. When I was little my *dat* used to take us. Do you bowl?"

"I've never been," he admitted. "Well, not since I was a teenager. And then, I was terrible."

"Me, too," she admitted.

They waited. More police cars passed. Not a vehicle in the lanes moved. There were cars in front of and behind them and a bumper-to-bumper line on the left. People began to get out of their automobiles.

"I think we may be here for a while," Leah said.

"It looks like it." He glanced at the flashing bowling ball and then back to Leah. "Maybe we should go bowling. It would be better than sitting here."

"Are you serious?" she asked.

He shrugged.

"Why not?" Leah exclaimed.

"And did you go bowling?" Leah's sister Rebecca asked as she reached for another of her mother's raisin sticky buns. They were seated at Sara's kitchen table with Ellie, enjoying a leisurely Saturday-morning visit. Rebecca's toddler, Jesse, was sprawled on the floor playing with a bag of wood alphabet blocks that Ellie had found in Sara's toy chest.

"Did they ever!" Ellie laughed. "Leah beat him at bowling. Slaughtered him."

Rebecca chuckled. "I don't know if Sara would approve. It doesn't sound like very good behavior for a first date."

"It *wasn't* a date," Leah protested. She glanced from one to the other. "It wasn't! We went up to visit Richard and Grace so that Thomas could see Richard's farm and hear about his organic-vegetable business. It's something that Thomas is interested in. He doesn't want to be a blacksmith."

"Wait. Wait, let me get this straight," Rebecca teased. She was red-haired like Leah, like most of her sisters, and prone to sunburn. Since she'd been busy in her garden that week, she was sporting a crop of new golden freckles, sprinkled like cookie crumbs across her sweet face. "It wasn't a date. Yet the two of you, you and Thomas—the same Thomas who Sara wants to match you with—traveled out of state together, shared dinner with the Hunzigers, went to a restaurant, went bowling and didn't get home until after midnight? And you want us to believe that it wasn't a date?"

"It sounds like a date to me," Ellie agreed. "And a pretty racy date at that. Even for a Mennonite."

"It wasn't like that!" Leah declared. She knew that their kidding was good-natured, but it didn't stop her from flushing with embarrassment. "We went to get information about organic farming. We had to eat something on the way home."

Jesse's block tower tumbled and he began to fuss. Ellie got down on her knees to help soothe his distress. "Like this, Jesse," she said, and then handed another block to the chubby, ginger-haired boy. He was still young enough to wear a baby gown, the garment that all Amish children in the community wore until they were out of diapers. He had a full head of hair that Rebecca kept cut straight across his forehead that fell around his ears in auburn ringlets, and he had the cutest button of a nose.

Leah looked at her nephew with a lump in her throat. Strangely, it was becoming more and more difficult for her to remember her lost baby's features. She closed her eyes for just a few seconds and gathered her resolve. Her baby wasn't gone forever. They were just separated for a little while. She was here and, Lord willing, she would have other children to love. And they would all be together in heaven someday.

Rebecca nibbled on a piece of sticky bun. "If you want my advice, sister, I think you should give Thomas a chance. I think that's only fair to him. You *did* tell Sara you'd agree to get to know him."

Leah wiped the crumbs off her mouth with a worn linen napkin. "She didn't really give me—give *either* of us—a choice. This isn't all on me. Thomas wasn't thrilled with the idea, either."

Rebecca and Ellie exchanged looks.

"He *wasn't*," Leah protested. "Thomas only agreed because his family is putting pressure on him to find a wife."

"Because I turned him down," Ellie put in.

"It's more complicated than that," Leah told Ellie. Then she turned to her sister. "You weren't there in Sara's office, Rebecca. You know how it all came about. Sara asked me to get to know Thomas and if it didn't work out, after six weeks, she agreed she'd find the kind of match I'm looking for. An older widower, someone settled in his life who needs a wife for his family."

Rebecca raised her Yoder blue eyes to meet Leah's gaze. "What you're talking about is a marriage of convenience," she said.

Leah got up and went to the stove on the pretense of warming her coffee with more from the pot. Of all her sisters, Rebecca had always understood her the best. Rebecca gave the impression of being easygoing, but she could go directly to the heart of a matter with unerring accuracy. "Is that so wrong?"

"Not wrong. We all know good marriages that have been arranged by family or friends, or even…a matchmaker," Rebecca said. "But your marriage to Daniel was very different. You fell in love. You went against your family and your church to marry him because you knew he was the one for you. You let your heart decide, not logic."

"I'm just…at another point in my life." Leah took care to choose the right words. She wasn't comfortable talking about this. About her feelings. Not with her sister. Not with anyone. She was still too raw from Daniel's and her baby's deaths. Too raw deep inside. "I don't want the same things that I did when I left Seven Poplars with Daniel." She threw her sister a pleading glance. "I wouldn't change my decision for the world, but I'm not certain that I would make the same one again." She inhaled, then sighed. "Let's say that I've come to value the quiet joys of life. I don't need excitement or romance. What I'm looking for in a husband is settled companionship, a partnership where each of us knows our place. No more jumping the traces for me. All I want is the peace of our community and our faith."

"I think it's early days yet," Ellie advised. "Don't be so sure that God wants you to be the wife of a man old enough to be your father. There's much to be said for a young man with spring in his step. What if that young man God means for you is Thomas? There's more than a few men and women in Seven Poplars who say Sara plays a part in God's intentions when it comes to marriage. That she's His instrument."

Leah placed her cup on the edge of the counter, not sure how to respond. She had heard enough from her mother to know Sara's matchmaking skills were the best. That was why she'd come to Sara in the first place. But she saw nothing wrong with telling Sara what she wanted. Didn't everyone, man and woman, who came to her do that?

There was a sound of the back door opening and Leah let out a sigh of relief. "Need any help, Sara?" she called.

"Not a bit. Clothes are on the line." Sara entered the kitchen from the utility room, her cheeks rosy. "We have a visitor. Someone who's come to see you this morning, Leah."

"Who is it?" Leah asked.

"Your brother-in-law. Anna's Samuel. I asked him to come in, but he said maybe you'd rather just come out to the buggy."

"Ach," Rebecca said. "I wonder what Samuel wants with you? I should be going, anyway. I've got a dozen things waiting for me at home, and Caleb and I want to ride over to look at a new driving horse this afternoon. It's a bit of a drive, so we told Amelia we'd pack a lunch and make a picnic of it."

"You sure you have to go so soon?" Leah frowned. It felt so good to be with her sisters again. She hadn't realized just how much she'd missed them until she returned to Seven Poplars. "I feel like you just got here. But you're not far away now."

"And we'll see plenty of each other," Rebecca assured her, retrieving her son.

Leah went to her sister and hugged her, then bent to give small Jesse a squeeze. He giggled and claimed whatever bit of her heart he hadn't earlier. "Come again soon," she urged Rebecca.

"And you come over to see me. The road runs both ways, you know." She kissed Leah's cheek. "And stop and talk with Caleb sometime. He's wiser than his years, sister. He may be able to give you spiritual comfort. You remember, he suffered a terrible loss, too."

"Maybe I will," Leah replied, thinking she would do no such thing. Her grief for Daniel was private. She couldn't imagine what her sister's husband could tell her that she hadn't already heard from a dozen other well-meaning people.

Curious as to what Samuel wanted, Leah left Rebecca to say goodbye to Ellie and Sara and went out into the yard. He was standing by his horse's head feed-

ing the animal bits of carrot and stroking the bay's neck
and nose. The horse saw her coming and raised its head,
nickering softly.

Samuel turned to her, his expression solemn. He
was a kindly man, one that Leah knew made her sister happy. Samuel was a good father and a pillar of the
church community, but being almost a generation older,
she'd never known him well and had always held him
in a kind of awe.

"Samuel. Good to see you," she called.

"I'm afraid I'm here as a deacon of the church
rather than your brother-in-law," Samuel said. He was
a big man, tall and wide of shoulder, with a full beard,
streaked with gray.

Nervously, Leah thrust her hands into her apron
pockets and waited.

Samuel took a deep breath. "I don't like doing this,
and I hope you won't allow it to…" He broke off and
started again. "You know as deacon, it is my duty to
point out errors in the behavior of—"

"Behavior?" she asked. Now she was really curious.
She'd barely been in Seven Poplars three weeks. "What
have I done wrong?"

He grimaced. "Not wrong. Just unseemly. Bishop
Atlee called on me early this morning and said that he'd
had a disturbing report from someone in our community. You were seen returning at a late hour last night,
in the company of a man."

Leah's eyes narrowed. "Aunt Martha reported
Thomas and me to the bishop, didn't she?" She should
have known that her interfering aunt would make a
fuss. "There was no misbehavior, Samuel," she said.
"Thomas and I went to Lancaster to visit cousins of my

late husband and discuss organic gardening. Then we had something to eat, went bowling and drove home from Pennsylvania. Unfortunately, my car had a flat tire in front of Uncle Reuben and Aunt Martha's place. Uncle Reuben was in the barn delivering a calf, saw our flashlight and came down to the road to see what happened. He watched Thomas change the tire, and then I drove Thomas home and came back to Sara's."

"But you and Thomas *are* dating. And you were out all day and part of the night without a chaperone." He tugged on the brim of his straw hat. "I know you, Leah. I've known you since you were a child. You're a good girl. You wouldn't behave in a way that would shame your family. But Thomas has the reputation of being a bachelor who cuts a wide swath. It doesn't look good, Leah. Your aunt doesn't approve, Bishop Atlee doesn't approve and Anna and I are concerned for your reputation."

A knot twisted in the pit of Leah's stomach and she tamped down her rising ire. "I'm not baptized in the faith. I'm a grown woman, a widow. Surely, I can stay out after dark without my mother's approval."

Samuel shook his head. "That's part of the issue. You've been in the outside world for years. Now you've asked our bishop to return to the fold. It's important that you demonstrate that you can live by our rules. And you can't be accused of setting a bad example for younger women who look up to you."

She drew in a deep breath, resting her hands on her hips. She wasn't annoyed with Samuel; she understood that this was his responsibility. She just didn't like people telling her what to do. Not anyone. "So what does Bishop Atlee want me to do? I'm supposed to be getting to know Thomas. That's what everyone wants. How am I supposed to get to know him if we don't spend time together?"

"It's not about you spending time with Thomas," Samuel responded patiently. "It's about the circumstances. You were unchaperoned."

"The bishop wants me to take my mother and stepfather with me next time Thomas and I go to Byler's for ice cream?"

Samuel frowned. "Anna said you wouldn't take this well. We mean only the best for you, Leah. We love you, and we want you to be accepted fully into the community. Bishop Atlee understands how difficult your position is. He asks that if you are out after dark, or if you and Thomas leave Seven Poplars in each other's company, you have a chaperone with you to prevent any uncharitable gossip. And it doesn't have to be your mother. Anyone will do." His expression hardened. "There is more at stake than your own situation. English people are quick to notice what we do. I know that you wouldn't want to cause our community to be a topic of criticism."

"Ne," she agreed reluctantly, crossing her arms over her chest. She was still annoyed, but she knew he had a point. "I wouldn't."

"Goot." Samuel's features softened. "Then I'll tell the bishop that you understand and you've agreed to use a chaperone when necessary. *Ya?"*

Leah cut her eyes at him. Then she sighed and dropped her arms to her sides. *"Ya*, fine, I'll agree to it. I just won't agree to like it."

Chapter Six

Midweek, Leah drove to the Stutzman farm in search of Thomas. While picking up groceries for Sara, she had run into a young Amish couple in Byler's Store who were friends of her sister Ruth. They had recently bought a small farm in Maryland, not far from Seven Poplars, and were raising organic asparagus and selling it commercially. They'd invited her and Thomas to visit, and she'd been impressed enough by what they had to say that she felt she needed to tell him about them.

The Stutzman place, consisting of two attractive houses, several barns and a handful of outbuildings, as well as the blacksmith shop, was set back off the road on two hundred and ten acres of high ground. Thomas's father kept a herd of dairy cows, which, along with the successful smithy, provided a comfortable living for the extended family.

Leah followed the gravel driveway from the road to the farmyard and parked her car near the blacksmith shop. A buggy stood near the open front doors. There was no horse between the shafts, but Leah could hear the ring of a hammer on steel and guessed that one of her neighbors was having an animal shod this morning. She was about to go in to search for Thomas when his grandmother came out of the house. "Morning," Leah called in *Deitsch*.

The older woman smiled as she recognized her. "Leah Yoder. I expect you're looking for our Thomas." Alma pointed. In the second field over, Leah saw a man turning up pastureland with a one-horse plow. "If you've a mind to save these old legs of mine, you can carry this iced tea out to him." She indicated a quart mason jar on a sideboard on the porch where she stood. "Plowing is warm work, and he's been at it all morning."

"I'd be glad to," Leah replied.

Two men came out of the smithy. One, Leah's sister's husband Roland, was leading a gray driving mare. The horse picked up her feet gingerly, obviously testing a new shoe. Roland nodded and smiled. "Morning."

She returned the greeting. She liked Roland. With him was Jakob, the new blacksmith come to work for Thomas's grandfather. She'd met Jakob before so she wasn't surprised by his appearance. Jakob was a little person, like Ellie. And, like Ellie, despite his short height, he was an attractive and cheerful person. Leah was sure he'd be an asset to the community and she couldn't understand why Ellie seemed to have no interest in socializing with him. The man was a ginger, with thick, dark auburn hair. He had broad shoulders to balance his stocky build and his high forehead and large, cinnamon-brown eyes gave him an intelligent and pleasant appearance.

"Good day to you, Jakob," she called.

He smiled and raised a hand in a friendly way.

"A nice young man," Alma said, coming down the

porch steps with the iced tea. "A help he'll be to my husband and son, I know. He comes as an apprentice, but there is little he needs to be taught. A good man with iron and gentle with the horses."

"I'm glad," Leah said. She put out her hands to take the jar of tea. "I'd best get this to Thomas before the ice melts."

"*Ya*, but best you take off your shoes before you walk out to them fields," Alma advised. "We had some rain last night and you'll get them good sneakers soaked through."

Nodding agreement, Leah removed her new navy blue cross-trainers and left them by the car before setting out to deliver Thomas's cold drink. As she walked into the first newly plowed field, she found herself chuckling aloud. The warm earth felt good on her bare feet, and the scent of fresh-turned soil made her almost heady with childhood memories. She'd gone barefoot in Seven Poplars much of the time, a pleasure that she couldn't allow herself in Brazil because of the poisonous snakes and fire ants.

She stopped and shaded her eyes with a hand, watching as Thomas reached the end of the field and turned back. What a beautiful picture he and the big bay Belgian made, almost like a painting on a calendar. They made a good team, the horse and the man, striding forward, muscles surging in unison as though they were one.

She'd always loved horses, especially the huge draft animals used for pulling wagons and doing the heavy fieldwork. She and her sisters had often taken turns riding on the horses when her father plowed or cultivated the crops. Sometimes, they'd run behind to pick up earthworms that were turned over by the plow. Later, after supper, her *dat* would take them all fishing. How she'd missed all this in the years she'd been away from Seven Poplars. And how she ached to have more children of her own that could grow up here and experience the wonderful life that she'd had.

"Please, God," she whispered. "Find someone for me who will make that possible." The glass canning jar felt icy cold between her fingers as she started slowly toward Thomas and the long dark cuts the plow had sliced through the thick sod of the pasture.

As she drew closer to the field that Thomas was working, she found that she couldn't take her gaze off him. Somehow, just watching Thomas and the sturdy draft horse made her smile. This was the life that she knew, simple and honest, and Thomas was the kind of man she understood best. If only he was older, more established, more mature. If only… But he wasn't, and that was that.

She had to be patient. Sara would find her a settled and respectable widower who needed a wife.

So why did watching Thomas Stutzman send a skittering sensation down her spine? And why was she walking faster, eager to reach him and tell him about her new friends? And why had she lain awake the night they'd gone to Lancaster thinking of what a good time she'd had? She pushed those thoughts away. Thomas was her friend. He was fun to be with, and that was all.

"Leah!" Thomas reined in the horse, and the plow jerked sideways and came to a halt. Thomas looped the lines around the handles of the plow, lowered it onto its side and came to meet her. "What's that? For me?" He grinned as he reached for the tea, removed the screw top and took a long drink. "Ah, good." He drank again, and she watched as beads of condensation dripped from the glass jar to run down his sweat-streaked neck.

He was dressed in everyday work clothing: denim trousers, lace-up leather work shoes and a short-sleeved blue shirt. The knees of his pants were patched, and his shirt was faded from long hours in the sun, but he didn't appear poor or shabby. With his tall, lean frame, narrow waist and broad shoulders, Thomas cut as sharp a figure as ever, she thought, and then chastised herself for doing so. *This is only a favor for Sara*, she reminded herself sternly. *Six weeks of being together, and she'll find a suitable match for me.*

Thomas drained half the jar of tea, wiped his mouth with the back of his hand and sighed. "You have no idea how thirsty I was." He placed the jar in the grass and removed his straw hat. His dark hair was as unruly as ever, thick and shaggy.

"You need a haircut," she said. "I could…" She broke off. She'd always cut Daniel's hair, and she'd almost offered to do the same for Thomas. She averted her gaze as she felt a warm flush creep up her throat and cheeks. Such familiarity wasn't accepted between unmarried couples. Had he been her brother or other close relative, or if he'd been a child, it would have been fine. "Could…mention it to your grandmother," she finished hastily in an attempt to cover her mistake.

"Ne." Thomas laughed. "I wouldn't let her near me with a pair of scissors. *Grossmama* never wears her glasses. The last time she cut my father's hair, he looked like a sheep that had just been clipped. On one side, she cut a good two inches shorter than the other."

Leah chuckled, grateful that he'd not pressed her on

her near offer. But then he tilted his head and eyed her mischievously. "Unless, you'd like to—"

"Not me," she protested, putting her hands up, palms out. "I'd do a far worse job of it."

He didn't reply. Instead, he retrieved the mason jar and finished the rest of the tea. "Thank you," he said when he had drained the last drop. "You saved my life."

"I doubt that."

"Absolutely." He grinned at her and she couldn't resist a smile. Thomas was being charming and he was hard to resist.

"What do you think of this as a spot to plant my garden?" he asked, encompassing the newly plowed field with a sweep of his hand. "The soil is rich, and since *Dat* put in the pond, the land is draining good."

"It's decent-looking soil, for certain."

He nodded. "I thought I'd start with tomatoes, peppers and greens."

"Where will you get your plants? It's a little late to start tomato seedlings, isn't it?"

"I found someone who will sell me organic seedlings that are a little more mature. I'm going to put in all heritage varieties: Brandywine, Old German, Nebraska Wedding, Cherokee Purple and Mortgage Lifter. I haven't found a source for organic plum tomatoes, but I will." He pushed back his hair and put his hat back on, pulling it down tight on his forehead. "You did me a tremendous favor when you took me up to Lancaster to meet Richard and his wife. I appreciate it."

She shrugged. "It's nothing. We had a good time."

"The best," he said. "Although it *did* get us in trouble with the bishop." Together they chuckled, and then he glanced back to where the horse stood patiently. "Actually, I was about to quit for dinner. *Mam* doesn't like us to keep her meal waiting. Would you like to eat with us?"

"*Ne*, I didn't want to interrupt your workday. It's just that I met someone at Byler's and…" She hurried to explain to him about the asparagus and the ready market for the crop. "I thought maybe you'd like to go and take a look," she suggested. "Of course, it takes years for asparagus roots to take hold, but once they do, it's easy to care for them and harvest."

"I'd like that," he said. "When can we go?"

"Anytime, I suppose. I've finished up my chores at Sara's." She hesitated. "Honestly, I'm going a little stir-crazy. I'm used to being busy from sunup until evening. It's strange not having my own home, my own work to be done."

He met her gaze and something in his told her he understood. "How about this afternoon?"

"Aren't you going to finish plowing the field?"

Thomas shook his head. "*Dat* needs the horse to bring in a load of logs from the woods. If you'll stay for *Mam's* fried chicken and dumplings, we can go right after dinner."

Then she remembered her conversation with Samuel. The same conversation, she learned, he'd had with Thomas first. "Are we supposed to have a chaperone?"

"Are we leaving Seven Poplars?" he teased.

She frowned. "But we'll be back early. It won't be dark." She pursed her lips. "Honestly, Thomas. I think the whole chaperone thing is a little over-the-top. Why should two grown adults need chaperones?"

"We follow church rules, Leah. I should have thought of it before Samuel had to speak to us. I blame myself.

You've been away from it all, but I don't have that excuse. It's a small thing, a chaperone. And if you want to live Amish, you might as well get used to it."

"*Ya,* so I tell myself."

He smiled at her, his dark eyes warm and sparkling. "If you'll wait while I unhitch Dickie, we can walk back to the house together. I know my mother would be pleased to have you take bread with us. She and my grandmother always cook enough for twenty and then fuss about all the leftovers."

Leah wasn't entirely sure she should be sitting down to dinner with Thomas's family. If they were truly dating, with the intention of soon becoming engaged, that would be one thing, but this—what they were doing—she just didn't know if she felt comfortable joining the family. But she really did want to stay.

"Come on," Thomas urged. "You know you like chicken and dumplings. And there will be rhubarb pie. I cut the rhubarb yesterday."

"Fine." Leah chuckled. "You've convinced me." She followed him back to where he unhooked the singletree from the plow and carefully knotted the long reins and hung them over the Belgian's collar. Once Thomas had the horse under control, she approached and stroked his neck. "He's beautiful," she said. "I've missed horses. We didn't have any in Brazil. They don't thrive in the jungle."

Thomas spoke soothingly to the big horse and began to lead him back across the field toward the house. Leah hurried to keep up. "I remember you riding your father's horses when you were a kid," he said. "You Yoder girls were something else."

"I loved to ride the draft horses," she admitted.

"Their backs were so wide I wasn't afraid I'd fall off. Miriam showed me how to braid the horse's mane and pretend that it was the reins."

He stopped and looked at her. That mischievous smile slid over his face. "Would you like to ride now?"

"Now?" She knew her eyes got big. "But—"

Thomas cut off her protest by stepping close to Dick and cupping his hands for her to use to step up. "Dare you," he teased.

She glanced around. Who was there to see? Laughing, she caught a handful of Dick's thick mane, thrust her bare foot into Thomas's make-do stirrup and scrambled up onto the horse's back. Once she was up, she turned sideways and sat on him with both feet dangling and her skirt back over her knees, where it belonged.

He nodded approval, took hold of the gelding's halter and began to lead him once more.

"If we get in trouble for this, it's your fault," she declared, but she didn't care if it wasn't considered seemly for a woman to be riding a horse. Being up on Dick's back, feeling the familiar rhythm of the horse's gait beneath her, was exhilarating. "So if we need a chaperone this afternoon, where are we going to find one on such short notice?" she asked.

"Oh, don't worry, we'll find someone," Thomas promised. "My mother, my grandfather, maybe even both my grandparents. We'll have such a strict chaperone that even your aunt Martha won't have a word to say in criticism."

Leah chuckled as she remembered her aunt's disapproving face when she and Uncle Reuben had found them changing the tire in the dark. "Maybe we'd best play it safe and ask Aunt Martha herself," she joked.

"Ne," Thomas protested. "Not her. I'd rather Bishop Atlee and both preachers, all crammed into the back of your car and fighting for a window seat."

The image of that in her mind made her laugh so hard that she had to tightly grip the horse's mane to keep from slipping off.

Several hours later, Thomas held open the car door so that his grandmother could get out. "Are you sure that double-dip cone didn't spoil your appetite for supper?" he teased. *Grossmama* had agreed to go with them to the asparagus farm, but Thomas had had to promise they would stop for ice cream on the way back. His grandmother loved ice cream. Strawberry. Always strawberry. Luckily, Byler's Store usually carried strawberry, and it was one of the places where you could still buy an old-fashioned ice-cream cone. Leah had chosen butter pecan, his personal favorite, a single dip, and he'd had two dips of rocky road.

Somehow, in the time that he'd gone into Byler's to purchase the ice cream, his grandmother had convinced Leah to return to the house to share supper with them. Thomas almost wished she'd refused. While his family had embraced her at the noon meal, he'd felt a little awkward. No one in his family knew that this wasn't a prelude to a real courtship. Leah had made that clear. He hadn't thought it was fair to get his family's hopes up, when in all likelihood, the dating would go nowhere.

The evening meal was a much simpler one: vegetable soup, buttermilk, crusty loaves of yeast bread and another helping of the delicious rhubarb pie. Jakob joined them as he did most evenings, and everyone had lots of questions about the visit to the Masts' asparagus fields.

Thomas always enjoyed this time of evening with his family. Supper was a time for leisurely eating and talking. Sometimes they would sit at the table for more than an hour, and afterward his grandfather would read a short passage from the Bible before everyone scattered.

"I should be going once we clear up the kitchen," Leah said to his mother. "I'm afraid that I've imposed on your hospitality today."

"Ne," his mother answered, smiling. "We were glad to have you. Thomas never brings young women home with him."

"And if you hadn't come, Leah, I wouldn't have gotten ice cream," *Grossmama* reminded her. "You come every day, if you've a mind to it. I'm always free to go here or there."

Even Jakob seemed taken with her. "I like hearing about far-off places," he said as he settled down for a game of chess with *Grossdaddi*.

Leah offered to wash dishes, but his mother shooed her out of the kitchen. *"Ne, ne.* We can handle this. You and Thomas go sit on the porch and digest your meal."

"I really should be getting back," Leah protested. "Sara will wonder what happened to me."

His grandfather had shaken his head and rubbed his generous belly. "No need to rush away. It will give you a bad stomach. Go and sit on the front porch with Thomas for a little while. And see if you can convince him to let his mother get that splinter out of his thumb."

"He has a splinter?" Leah asked.

"Ya, and first thing you know, it will turn bad, and he'll be swollen up to his elbow." Thomas's grandfather waggled his finger at him. "A fellow I knew one

time, got a little splinter of wood in his foot and ended up with a wooden leg."

Thomas curled his fist, hiding the offending thumb with its dime-sized, puffy red infection. "It's nothing. The splinter will work its way out. They always do."

"Would you let me have a look at it?" Leah asked. "I won't touch it unless you want me to. But I've had a lot of experience removing thorns and splinters at our clinic. Once, I removed a rusty fishing hook that had gone through a child's hand. Your grandfather's right, you know. Splinters can cause a great deal of trouble if they aren't removed and the wound properly cared for."

Feeling trapped, Thomas looked from one to the other. "All right," he agreed reluctantly. "I'll let you look at it."

"Goot," his grandmother said as she wiped her hands on her flour-streaked apron. "I'll get the tweezers."

"And a needle," his mother added. "Just in case."

"Where do you want him?" *Grossmama* asked. "There may be more light by the window."

"I think we can go out on the porch," Leah suggested.

"Just Leah and me," Thomas said. His mother was handing Leah a spool of thread with a needle thrust through it.

"Tweezers might be better," his father suggested.

Thomas held open the back door for Leah. "We could sit on the step," he said. "Or the swing." This was ridiculous. He didn't need anyone to dig the splinter out of his thumb. He could do it himself. A little infection made it easier to slide out. He felt foolish and a little ashamed that such a small thing could make him uncomfortable. But he hated needles. He always had. Still, he couldn't look like a child in front of Leah. What would she think of him?

His mother tried to follow them through onto the porch, but he stood his ground and narrowed his eyes. "*Mam*," he said softly. "I think Leah and I can manage one small splinter."

She rolled her eyes and laughed. "*Ya*, you young ones want to be alone. I should know that."

His father called, "Wife."

His mother handed him the tweezers. "Tell her that the needle is clean."

His *grossmama* came to the screen door with alcohol and Dr Ivan's All-Cure Liniment. It was the same liniment that they used on the livestock, more smell than antiseptic as far as Thomas was concerned, but it was easier to take it than argue. He pulled the wooden door firmly closed behind him and heard his mother and grandmother whispering. His father laughed, and Thomas joined Leah on the porch swing.

"Let me see," she ordered him.

Nervously, he extended his left hand. She took it between her smaller ones and turned it to examine the infected splinter. "It's nothing," he insisted.

"Let me be the judge of that," she said. "I'm the nurse." She glanced up and chuckled. "Well, not really a nurse, but close. And don't worry. I'm not going to poke you with a sewing needle."

Her fingers were warm. Gentle. He felt himself relax. They were probably right. He should have done something about the splinter before this. He couldn't afford to lose days due to an injury that didn't heal properly. Seeing the asparagus fields had made him even more eager to see what he could do with organic vegetables.

And Leah's enthusiasm and suggestions added to his certainty that this was something possible.

"It must be sore," she said.

"Not bad." It was, but he wouldn't admit it. He glanced down. The red circle was growing, but the splinter was in deep. Getting it out wouldn't be pleasant. "What do you think?" he asked.

"Either we get it out or you go to the emergency room," she said. "This kind of infection can spread quickly. You can't afford to let it go any longer."

He nodded. "You're probably right. Do your worst."

"First, we soak it in warm water with salt in it. And then I'll see what's in the first-aid kit in my car. If your mother has ice, we can numb your thumb before we attempt to remove it. Sound like a plan?" She smiled at him.

An hour later they were still sitting side by side on the porch swing, and Leah was once again holding his hand. Between the soaking in warm water, the ice, Leah's soothing touch and her first-aid kit, they'd gotten the splinter out and cleaned up the inflammation. Except for a tiny pinch when the wood came out, it hadn't hurt. And the small discomfort was more than made up for by the gentleness with which she applied antibacterial ointment and carefully bandaged his thumb.

They'd talked easily about the day, about the rhubarb pie and about the possibility of asparagus and beets and cucumbers, and they'd laughed about his mother and grandmother's fussing over him. It had been a long time since he'd had such a good time with a young woman, and he'd never spent time with one that he'd been willing to be so open with. He didn't want the evening to end.

Shadows began to fall across the porch and still they

laughed and talked as if they did this every day. Thomas found himself studying her: her eyes, her freckled nose and her lips. What would Leah do, he wondered, if he tried to kiss her? He'd kissed Violet and Mary and Jane, to name a few girls. It had been fun and he'd liked it very much. But, suddenly, he wanted to take Leah into his arms and not just kiss her, but hold her. And he got the feeling she felt the same way.

He leaned closer. For an instant their gazes locked. He looked deep into her clear blue eyes and she began to lean toward him.

And then the moment was gone.

She pulled back and got up. "It's getting late. It's been a wonderful day, but it's time I went back to Sara's."

He jumped up. Had he misread her? He was usually good at knowing when a girl wanted to be kissed. And he was pretty sure he hadn't been mistaken. Not the way she'd looked at him. "Leah."

"Thank your mother for dinner and for supper," she said. "And your grandmother for going with us today, to act as chaperone." She moved away from the swing.

"Leah," he repeated. "I..."

"Good night, Thomas." She hurried down the steps and across the yard to her car.

He stood there watching her go, wishing she wouldn't, wondering if what he thought was happening between them really was.

Chapter Seven

Leah shifted her weight on the wooden stepladder and rubbed hard at the schoolhouse windowpane with her cleaning cloth. On the other side of the glass, Ellie wiped away ammonia spray as she continued her amusing story. One of her first-graders had found a frog on his way to school that morning, had put it in his lunchbox and forgotten about it until he opened the box. The frog had leaped out onto the head of one of the Miller girls and continued on hopping from desk to desk, causing an uproar among the students.

Leah laughed along with Ellie. How she wished she'd been here to see the turmoil caused by one small frog. It was four thirty in the afternoon on Friday. The children had gone home for the day, and Leah had come to help Ellie wash the schoolhouse windows. It was odd being back at the school where she'd spent so many happy years as a child. Ellie's stories reminded her so much of similar events when she was a girl, but she couldn't believe how much smaller the building seemed now. For years her mother had been the teacher at the Seven Poplars school, and her sisters and many of her cousins had been here with her. Good days, she mused, carefree days.

Other than the addition of the back porch and a closed-in area for coats, boots and lunch boxes, not much had changed since she'd been a student here. The scarred hardwood floors, the plain white vertical wainscoting and the smell of chalk and Old English furniture polish hadn't changed. The school consisted of a single room with an old-fashioned blackboard, rows of tall windows, and a potbellied stove that stood in the center and provided heat and a place to warm hot chocolate or soup on cold winter days.

"It was sweet of you to volunteer to help," Ellie said from the other side of the glass. Her friend's high voice pulled Leah out of the past and back to the present. "The school year ends next week and I want the building to look its best for parents' night," Ellie said.

"Glad to help." Leah finished the last pane and descended the ladder. The adjoining window was the last on this side of the schoolhouse, and she wanted to complete this section before Thomas arrived to pick her up. "More hands make every task easier."

Ellie pushed open the window and reached out to take hold of the top of the stepladder to steady it as Leah moved it into place. Practical Ellie had her sleeves rolled up and wore an oversize apron over her bright blue dress. She'd removed her *kapp* and tied a navy scarf over her neatly braided and pinned blond hair. As usual, Ellie was a delight to spend time with. Leah liked the woman more every day because when you were with her it was impossible to be gloomy. No wonder the students adored her. Ellie's love of life was infectious.

"Where is Thomas taking you today?" Ellie asked.

"Nowhere in particular. Just for a drive." Leah continued washing the windowpanes, taking care not to miss any spots. "I mentioned how much I missed traveling at the speed of a horse and buggy the last few years. And he offered to quit work early today and take me for a drive. He borrowed an open courting buggy so we wouldn't need a chaperone."

Ellie's heart-shaped face lit up with mischief as she pushed up the window. "I guess that depends on where your ride takes you."

Leah gave her a questioning look.

"If he goes by Tyler's Woods Road, he might just stop to water his horse at the pond. You remember how young people like to go there. It's off the road. Pretty with all the trees coming out in bud this time of year. But I warn you, if you agree to go there with him, don't be surprised if Thomas tries to steal a few kisses."

"Why would you say that?"

Ellie laughed. "Because he tried it with me." She shrugged. "It didn't work, but he made the attempt."

Leah shook her head. "It's not like that with us."

Ellie stifled another sound of amusement. "*Ne*, of course not."

"Really," Leah protested. "He's fun to be with, but—"

Ellie leaned on the windowsill and gave her a disbelieving look through the open window. "You like Thomas and you know you do. Admit it."

Leah resisted the urge to toss her dirty sponge at her friend. "I do like him, but not in that way. Thomas and I are friends. I'm helping him find out more about organic farming. He thinks that's what he wants to do, and I think it's an excellent idea."

"So is Thomas thinking about how he'll provide for a wife and children?"

"Eventually." Leah chuckled. "But even if he is, it doesn't mean…" She didn't finish the sentence. The other night on the porch at his house, Thomas had come very close to kissing her. She hadn't let him, of course. She'd ended the evening before she had to tell him she didn't want him to kiss her. Or maybe she'd ended the evening so quickly because she was afraid she might have let him kiss her.

Ellie giggled. "*Ne*, of course he's not thinking of you. Just because you're courting."

"We're not—" Leah cut herself off. She wasn't going to have this conversation with Ellie again. Instead, she said, "I'm sure Thomas will make a fine husband for someone. He's just not what I'm looking for."

"Or me." Ellie dropped her cleaning rag into a bucket. "But he isn't hard on the eyes, you'll have to admit that."

"Looks aren't everything," Leah said. "I want an older husband, someone settled. I've had excitement in my life." She unconsciously lowered her voice. "Now, I just want a peaceful life, a new baby to hold in my arms, someone to walk to worship with, a husband who will take care of us and make the decisions."

Ellie's blue eyes clouded with concern. "Are you certain that's what you want, Leah? I haven't known you all that long, but I know Hannah and your sisters. You don't seem like the kind of woman who wants her husband to think for her."

Leah didn't answer. Instead, she climbed down the ladder, emptied her bucket of dirty water and joined Ellie inside the schoolhouse.

Ellie came to meet her and took Leah's hands in her small ones. "I'm sorry," she said. "I need to learn to hold my tongue. I shouldn't have pressed you about your private business. You know better than me what will make you happy."

"*Ne*, it's all right," Leah insisted. She could feel the emotion gathering in her chest. In another moment, she'd be bawling like a baby. "I do think that's what I need, but..." She shrugged and forced a smile. "The truth is, sometimes I don't know what I want. Thomas is wonderful but he's so...so...lighthearted."

"He just plays the part of the cutup because that's the sort of person everyone expects him to be. He's really quite sweet."

"But he wasn't right for you."

"No, he wasn't," Ellie agreed. She released Leah's hands and perched on one of the first-grader's desks, her sneakered feet dangling over the edge. "I want to marry someday. I want a family. Children. But I've never met a man that suited me. And..." She gestured around the schoolroom. "I really love teaching the children. I can't imagine giving this up."

"Because you haven't met the right man." Leah felt relief that the conversation had moved on from her personal life to Ellie's. "You know, I had supper with Thomas and his family the other night, and Jakob asked about you. He seems intrigued."

"Don't tell me that."

"Why not?" Leah asked. "Jakob's single. And he is a very attractive man."

"For a little person, you mean?"

"Don't put words in my mouth. That wasn't what I was thinking." Leah folded her arms. "What I was thinking was that Jakob Schwartz may be short, but he's still a hottie."

"Leah!" Ellie's eyes widened in surprise and then together the two of them burst into giggles.

"Well, he is," Leah said when she could talk again. "And he's nice. I like him. You should give him a chance."

"Absolutely not," Ellie said with a shake of her head.

"What? You don't like him because he's little?"

"I don't want anything to do with him because everyone—including your mother—is trying to shove us together. Just because we're both little people. From the first time he came to Seven Poplars for a visit, Jakob this and Jakob that is all I've heard. And now that he's living here, it will only be worse. I'm not picking a husband because of his height." Ellie slid down off the desk, pulled her cleaning rag from a bucket and began washing the blackboard. "No more talk of Jakob. Agreed?"

"Agreed," Leah said. "But only for now, because—"

"Look!" Ellie pointed out the window. "Here comes your Thomas. And he's driving that fancy sorrel horse of his."

Leah glanced out the window and she couldn't help the quiver of anticipation that ran through her. "It's a beautiful horse, isn't it?"

"Beautiful and fast…like his master," Ellie teased.

Leah reached up to make certain that her *kapp* was in place and then untied the big work apron and hung it on one of the iron hooks along the back wall.

"Take a sweater," Ellie advised. "Unless you are depending on Thomas to keep you warm."

"Stop," Leah protested. "I am *not* sweet on Thomas. There will be no hugging and certainly no kissing."

"*Ne*, of course not," Ellie replied. "Because you're

not sweet on him." Her laughter echoed in Leah's ears
as she hurried out of the schoolhouse and walked across
the grass toward Thomas.

"Can't you get Irwin to weed this for you?" Leah asked
her mother. Irwin was a boy her mother had taken in years
ago, and was a member of the family now. She'd stopped
by for morning coffee and found Hannah in the garden
cleaning up her strawberry patch. The berries weren't
fully in bloom yet, but they soon would be. Here and there
a white blossom peeked through the lush green leaves.

"Irwin has a part-time job with the Kings helping build
lawn furniture. He's there today. Besides, I like getting
out in my own garden," Hannah replied as she stooped to
yank out an offending sprig of dandelions from under the
edge of a strawberry plant. "These are Pocahontas," she
explained. "They ripen later than the Surecrop, but they're
sweeter. They make the best strawberry shortcake."

Leah dropped to her knees on the opposite side of the
row from her mother. In Brazil, she'd sometimes worn
a light blouse and a split skirt, with knee-length trousers under it, for working in her garden. Since they had
visitors only rarely and the St. Joes wore next to nothing in the hottest season, she hadn't felt that she was too
immodest. But she'd given away the skirt and the pants
when she'd said goodbye to her jungle home. The Old
Amish residents of Seven Poplars would never understand or accept such laxity in dress in one of their members. Fortunately, she'd worn her oldest dress today, and
either the garden dirt would wash out or it wouldn't.

Her mother raised her head and smiled at her. "It's
good to have you home, Leah. You'll never know how
much we missed you."

"I missed you all, too," she replied as she dug out the root of a stubborn chickweed. "Every day." She'd left Seven Poplars for a different life, and she'd done her best to serve God and to be the wife that Daniel deserved. If he hadn't died, she would be there now, working beside him. But coming home, being with her family, walking the fields and woods that she had while growing up had gone a long way to healing the unbearable pain of losing Daniel and her child.

"I prayed for you to come back to us." Her mother's gaze was full of compassion. "I just didn't expect it to be this way."

"Me, neither," Leah replied. She and Hannah had so much in common—both had been widowed far too young. What she didn't know was if she possessed the strength her mother had. "I just hope I'm making the right decision in asking Sara to find me a husband."

Hannah looked up. "Have you prayed on it?"

"*Ya.* And I feel in my heart that this is what I should do. That it was right to become Mennonite, and now it's right for me to join all of you and become Amish again."

"And you have no doubts about taking on the responsibility of our faith?" her mother pressed.

Leah smiled. "None at all. I'm looking forward to it. I know it's where I belong."

"It eases my mind to hear you say it." Hannah went back to weeding. "Now you need to stop worrying and let Sara do her job. It will all come out right. You'll see."

"I hope so."

From the side yard, Leah heard her sister Susanna's laughter as she and her husband David tossed a ball back and forth. It was a large plastic ball, nearly the size of a basketball and bright orange, but neither of them could manage to catch it on the first try. Instead, they giggled and squealed and chased the rolling ball across the grass. Susanna's *kapp* hung askew, her face was smudged with dirt and her hands and dress were grubby, but she was clearly having a wonderful time. Susanna, like Ellie, had the gift of enjoying every moment of life.

When Ruth had written that their mother had given her permission for Susanna to marry David King, Leah had been surprised. Growing up, Leah had always thought Susanna the light of their home, one of God's special people. But she'd never expected Susanna to wed. She was childlike in so many ways. Now, seeing how happy Susanna was, and getting to know David, who'd also been born with Down syndrome, Leah was beginning to understand her mother's decision.

"Thomas is working this morning," Leah explained to Hannah, "but he'll be off by one. We were thinking of going to Rehoboth this afternoon to talk to some of the managers of local restaurants about possible markets for Thomas's organic vegetables."

Hannah dropped a handful of weeds into a pile and looked up with a serious expression. "Would you like me to come along as your chaperone?"

"*Ne, Mam.* I would not," Leah replied firmly. "I thought that—"

Hannah laughed, and Leah broke off in midstatement. Realizing that she'd been had, she began to chuckle as well.

"How about Irwin?" her mother teased.

Leah shook her head. "Absolutely not."

"You have to have someone. You can't go to Rehoboth for the day without a chaperone."

"Actually, I thought maybe that Susanna would like

to ride down with us," Leah said. "I could take her to see the ocean and buy her cotton candy. You know how she loves to ride in the car."

"I do. Maybe more than is good for her. But you're right—she would enjoy it." Hannah got up and dusted the dirt off her skirt. "I'll tell her to wash up and change into her church dress and bonnet."

"I can do it." Leah glanced down at her own dress, streaked now with garden soil and grass stains. "I need to freshen up myself. I have another dress in the car. I'll go and change before Thomas gets here."

"You watch your sister close," her mother warned. "You know how she is. And I wouldn't want her to come to harm out among the English."

"I'll take good care of her," Leah promised. "And I'll have Thomas to help me."

"And that's supposed to make me feel easier, with his reputation for mischief?"

"I think that was when he was younger," Leah said. "He's been very responsible around me."

Hannah looked skeptical. "I hope he appreciates your help. And you. He couldn't find a finer wife anywhere."

Leah rolled her eyes. "*Mam*, I told you before. I don't see this working out. I'm just giving it the six weeks because that's what Sara and Thomas and I agreed to."

Her mother studied the strawberry bed with its spreading rows and straw-laden aisles. "Better," she pronounced. "Much better. Martha always thinks her strawberry bed is the best one in the county. Wait until she tastes my Pocahantases and Raritans."

"If I didn't know you better, I'd think you were a little prideful," Leah teased.

"Maybe a little," her mother admitted. "It's a fault I

own to. And the good Lord knows I have more than a few to repent of."

"You're not alone." Leah smiled and hugged her. "I've missed you more than I can ever say."

Hannah's lips were warm on her cheek. "Go and have fun. Just don't let Susanna out of your sight."

As she'd suspected, Susanna was delighted by the prospect of a holiday. Her round face glowed with excitement as she bounced from one foot to the other. "Cottoned candy! I like cottoned candy. Blue."

"We'll see if they have blue," Leah agreed as she urged her into the house. "But we have to hurry. Thomas will be here soon, and we have to be dressed and ready."

"Ready!" Susanna agreed. "Ready for cottoned candy."

Twenty minutes later, Thomas came striding up her mother's lane. Leah and Susanna were on the porch waiting. "We're all set," Leah said, getting eagerly to her feet. She was almost as excited as Susanna was—she was just better at hiding it. "Susanna's coming with us. She was thrilled when I asked her to be our chaperone."

"Goot, goot," Thomas replied with an easy grin. "I'll talk with a few of the restaurant managers and then we can take a stroll on the boardwalk. I'll buy my girl some Thrasher's French fries. Best anywhere."

"Thomas's girl." Susanna clapped both hands over her mouth and giggled.

Leah let his comment pass without correcting him. The three of them were nearly to the car when her mother came across the yard. "Wait," she said. Smiling, she took Susanna's hands and looked into her face. "You do what Leah says, and stay with her. Do you understand?" Squeezing Susanna's hands tenderly, she kissed her on the cheek.

Susanna nodded vigorously. "Leah said…said blue candy. Cottoned candy."

"Try not to get it in your hair," Hannah advised. She straightened Susanna's bonnet and tied her *kapp* strings under her chin.

"She'll be fine, *Mam*," Leah assured her.

Her mother's gaze turned to her, running up from her black leather shoes to her black tights and calf-length Lincoln-green skirt, topped by a white blouse and black cardigan. Leah's cheeks grew warm as her mother inspected the lacy white scarf that she'd tied over her hair in place of her usual conservative Mennonite prayer *kapp*. "If you're to be one of us, you'll have to give up fancy clothing," she advised gently.

"I will, *Mam*. But I don't have to just yet."

Hannah sniffed, reached behind Leah's head, untied the scarf and retied it beneath her chin as she had Susanna's. "So the ocean wind won't blow it off," she said.

Leah looked from her mother to Thomas. He grinned and shrugged.

"I might know you'd take her side," Leah said. She brushed her mother's cheek with a kiss and took Susanna's hand. "Time to go."

Thomas climbed into the front seat. Leah fastened Susanna's seat belt in the back and then slid into the driver's seat. She was just about to start the car when David trotted toward the vehicle, waving his arms.

"Me!" he cried. "Me, too. Going!"

"Wait for King David!" Susanna cried. "Come on, King David."

Leah tried not to smile. David was dressed in his Sunday black coat and trousers, and wore a fast-food paper crown on his head. Leah looked at Thomas. "We can't say no." The backseat was small, barely large enough for two small passengers. And David was definitely not a small person, but there was no way she could leave him behind.

Thomas said, "Get in, David. We'll make room for you. And be sure to fasten your seat belt."

Susanna squealed with pleasure and clapped.

"Ya," David agreed as he squeezed into the back. "Make room."

Leah looked out the window to where her mother was standing by the gate.

"Naturally, your sister is bringing her husband along. They're inseparable." Hannah waved. "You young people have fun!"

Leah glanced over at Thomas. He shrugged, and they laughed together. "We will," Leah called to her mother as they drove out of the lane.

But when she reached the end of the drive, she stopped the car long enough to untie her scarf and retie it as it had been when she'd come out of the house. She waited for Thomas to comment, but when he wisely held his peace, she said, "Now you know why I'm staying with Sara."

Thomas laughed, and Susanna and David giggled. As they drove south toward the ocean resorts, Thomas turned on the radio and found a Christian station. When a familiar hymn that was popular at the social gatherings began, he started to sing along with it. Susanna and David, both loud and off-key, joined in enthusiastically.

We're going to have fun today, Leah thought. She knew that she should admonish Thomas for the forbidden radio, but she didn't have the heart. And by the time they reached Dover and turned onto Route 1, she'd shed her doubts and was singing along with the rest of them.

Chapter Eight

"What did he say?" Leah asked as Thomas came out of Breeze, a popular new eatery on Rehoboth Avenue. It was the last restaurant on his list for the day and she was eager to hear how it had gone.

Thomas smiled and nodded. "I think it went all right." He glanced to the wooden bench on the sidewalk where David and Susanna were enjoying their cotton candy. "Those two good?"

Leah looked over her shoulder. Her sister and brother-in-law were safely where she'd left them, heads together, talking, so she turned back to Thomas. "They're great. Enjoying their cotton candy. Don't keep me in suspense. What did they say? Were they interested in buying your produce?"

He took her hand, guiding her away from the door. "A definite maybe," he said in *Deitsch*. He switched to English. "The manager listened to what I had to say."

"So a firm maybe?" she asked. They'd had two definite nos, restaurants that had other sources they were happy with, one yes and another maybe.

Leah had enjoyed seeing how much Thomas's confidence had increased with each restaurant he walked into. Dealing with Englishers wasn't always easy for the Amish and she understood his nervousness. But today everyone Thomas had approached had been kind, and they hadn't treated him as if he were some quaint oddity or a nuisance.

He nodded. "A definite maybe. They'd like me to stop back when I have salad greens and berries to show them. Breeze is known for healthy food, but I wouldn't have to have the certified organic vegetables. They wanted to know how many days a week I could deliver produce." His expression was serious, but Leah could read the excitement in his eyes.

She smiled up at him, making no effort to free her hand. Vaguely, she was aware of passersby studying them with interest, but she ignored them. It was natural that they look. How often did you see such a good-looking Amish man in his best black coat, hat and trousers in the midst of a sea of tourists in flowered shorts, bright-colored T-shirts and oversize sunglasses? "What did you say?"

"I told him I could deliver every two or three days, depending on what was in season and how much they were willing to take. And I made it clear there would be no Sunday deliveries." Thomas grimaced. "The big question is *how* I'm going to deliver."

"You're resourceful," she answered. "I'm sure that if you can find reliable customers, you can find a way to get your produce here. Maybe you can hire a driver with a van or something."

He smiled down at her. "*I'm* resourceful? If it wasn't for you, I wouldn't have gone to see Richard's farm or the asparagus fields. And I know I never would have thought to come directly to restaurants to find a market.

You're an amazing woman, Leah." He grinned. "Not just a pretty one."

She felt herself flush with pleasure. Thomas was a flirt, and he probably said things like that to girls all the time, but she was glad she'd taken the trouble to wear something nice today. She shouldn't have cared so much what he thought, but for some reason, she did.

Confused and conscious of her quickening heartbeat, she pulled her hand from his and stepped away, putting distance between them. Thomas knew that it was unacceptable for the Amish to display affection in public. Even married couples were expected to refrain from holding hands or hugging, let alone kissing, as she'd seen an English girl and boy doing on the street just a few minutes ago. She put a hand to the back of her head, checking her scarf. "We need to get back to Susanna and David," she said, to cover her loss of composure.

"They're fine." Thomas gazed intently at her, as if he was seeing her for the first time.

Leah's heart fluttered again. It had been so long since she'd felt this way about someone. Too long.

When she realized the direction her thoughts were going, she reined them in. *Thomas,* she told herself, *this is just Thomas. We're friends, nothing more. He isn't the man I'd want to spend the rest of my life with.* But she found herself unable to break eye contact with his warm brown eyes. She couldn't tear her gaze away. He took a step closer and, against her will, she felt giddy. The honk of cars, the voices, the clatter and hum of the busy street faded, as if in the midst of all this activity, they were the only ones on the busy sidewalk.

"Leah?" Thomas took her hand again.

She felt a tingling sensation that started at her hand

A Love for Leah

where he touched her and drifted upward. She tried to say something, but her mind went blank. Her lips formed his name, but no sound came out.

"Leah, I…" He leaned toward her and she had the strongest suspicion he was going to try to kiss her.

And if she didn't break this intimacy immediately, she was afraid she would let him this time.

"Leah—"

"We…we should go. You—you don't know Susanna," she blurted as she hastily backed away. "When she wants to, she can move as quick as a cat's paw. You can't imagine what mischief she can find to get in to." The outer wall of the restaurant loomed behind her, keeping her from retreating any farther. "One time she snuck out in the middle of the night, hitched up the pony and cart and drove off to be with David." Leah knew she was babbling foolishly, but it didn't matter. *She had wanted him to kiss her.* She still wanted him to. She had to get control of her emotions before it was too late.

"They look innocent enough to me." He took another step toward her.

Leah glanced at her sister. Susanna was still sitting on the bench, black stockinged legs crossed at the ankle and bonnet seated snuggly on her head. Apparently, she and David had finished every bite of their blue cotton candy and were well into their tub of Fisher's caramel popcorn.

"I'm not sure what's happening here between us, Leah," Thomas murmured, searching her gaze. "But I think we should…talk about it."

She shook her head, unable to break eye contact with him.

When he spoke again, it was a whisper. A whisper meant only for her. "What is it you want, Leah?"

"French fries!" The words just came out of her mouth. She blinked. "*Ya*, Thrasher's French fries. You promised you'd buy us fries." She could feel her cheeks flaming.

Thomas broke into a grin and took a step back. But Leah felt like she hadn't fooled him. He knew what she'd been thinking. He knew she wanted to be kissed as much as he wanted to kiss her.

"I did, didn't I?" He gestured toward the ocean, a few blocks away. "Let's go. I'll get you fries. And pizza, if you want it. Whatever you want, I'm your man."

Once they'd purchased boardwalk fries, Thomas looked around for a bench where they could sit and enjoy them in the warm afternoon sun. There were a lot of people on the boardwalk: couples and families strolled down the noisy walkway amid the blaring music from the children's rides and the calls of hawkers urging passersby to play their games, as well as the bustle of the many fast-food stalls. Seagulls added to the clamor with their squawks and diving forays to snatch fallen bits of pizza, popcorn and corn dogs.

David and Susanna walked just ahead of him and Leah, hand in hand. The boardwalk was too crowded for them to walk four abreast, and guiding David and Susanna was a little like herding cats. Distracted by the colorful sights and smells, both of them were apt to dart away in opposite directions without warning. Ten paces down the boardwalk, Thomas realized why Leah wanted to find a place to sit as quickly as possible.

Thomas spied a bench just being vacated by a family and was about to direct them that way when Susanna stopped short in her tracks.

"Ooh!" she cried. "King David! Look!" She pointed

toward a booth boasting a wall of plush stuffed skunks with huge silky tails and enormous bows around their necks.

David slowly began to smile. He turned and walked toward the stall, followed by Susanna. Leah tried to hold her back, but there was no stopping her once she got something in her head.

"Susanna!" Leah hurried to catch up with her.

David came to a halt in front of the counter. He pushed his black-framed glasses up on his nose and studied the game. Thomas came up behind David and scanned the interior of the stall. Oversize white soda bottles formed a square, and stacks of colored hoops waited on pegs just out of reach. Strings of colored lights blinked on and off to the blare of music. The purpose of the game was to successfully toss the hoops over the necks of the bottles. It appeared simple, but Thomas knew better.

"Step right up! Try your luck! Win a prize for the little lady!" the attendant called.

"No," Thomas said. "He doesn't want—"

But David had already pulled a ten-dollar bill out of his pocket and handed it to the fortysomething sunburned man wearing a Dolle's Taffy T-shirt and a straw cowboy hat. The man slid David's money into the pocket of his canvas apron, but Thomas gave him a stern look. "Five dollars only," he said. "Give him change from his ten."

The man frowned. "It's three throws for a fiver."

Thomas stepped closer to the booth. "Change," he said firmly.

With a shrug, the man did as he asked.

Susanna giggled and hopped from one foot to the other excitedly. "I want that one," she said, pointing at the nearest stuffed skunk. "Please." Susanna's speech was difficult to understand, but it was clear to Thomas what she wanted.

"Ya," David said, stroking his neatly clipped beard. "For Susanna."

Thomas looked helplessly at Leah. She shrugged. Games of chance on the boardwalk probably weren't what Hannah had in mind when she'd allowed Susanna and David to come with them to Rehoboth, but David clearly knew his own mind. His Down syndrome condition might be clear to anyone who looked at him, but after spending time with him, Thomas understood that, although speech was difficult for him, David was less challenged than Susanna in many ways. And the money was David's. He had a right to try to win a skunk for his wife if he wanted to. Interfering might be worse than letting him lose his five dollars. Thomas glanced back at the attendant and nodded. Leah took David's frozen lemonade.

"Win a prize with every hoop!" the man called out.

Several teenagers had stopped to watch. "You can do it!" one of them called.

"Yeah, go for it," another chimed in.

David's grin faded as he took the first hoop from the man. Susanna patted his arm and stood on tiptoe to whisper something to him. He pulled back his arm and threw the rope ring. It bounced off the lip of one bottle, seemed ready to settle onto another and then slid between them. David groaned.

Susanna put out her hands for the stuffed animal.

"Ne," Leah explained. "David has to get the ring on the bottle."

"'Nother one," David said in *Deitsch*.

A Love for Leah

More fun seekers had stopped to watch. David suddenly had a cheering section of sunburned Englishers. Thomas was so glad that Leah had been able to convince David to leave his paper crown on the backseat of the car and wear his straw hat.

"Throw it easy," urged one of the kids.

There was a general moan as David's second attempt missed the bottles altogether. Susanna clapped. David looked at her and a smile spread over his round face. The man handed David his final ring. The onlookers grew quiet. Thomas wondered if God would forgive him if he prayed that David would make this one. David tossed the ring. Again, it struck the lip of a bottle, bounced and spun. But this time, the hoop flipped and settled solidly over the neck of the end bottle in the row.

"Winner!" the man cried. "We have a winner here!"

One of the teenagers slapped David on the back. "Way to go, bro!"

The crowd clapped as the attendant unhooked the stuffed animal skunk Susanna was pointing at and handed it to her. She clutched it and stared at David with shining eyes.

Thomas made eye contact with Leah. She was wiping away tears and smiling, too. "Thank you," she murmured.

"Don't thank me," he said. "David made the winning throw. He won the prize."

David beamed and threw back his shoulders.

"Try for a second one?" the huckster asked.

"Ne," Thomas said as he ushered his charges away. "One skunk is plenty."

David took Susanna's hand in his and they walked together down the boardwalk until Leah spied two empty benches. She settled Susanna, David and the stuffed skunk onto the first one facing the boardwalk and then glanced at Thomas expectantly.

Thomas flipped the back of the other bench so that they could sit the opposite way, with a view of the ocean. Leah slid onto the bench and looked out at the waves. Thomas sat next to her. Neither of them spoke, but after a while he took her hand in his. He knew he was taking a chance, but he couldn't help himself.

He saw her cheeks color, but she didn't try to free her hand.

He sighed, content. The breeze off the ocean, the sun on his face and the smell of caramel popcorn and salt water... It was a glorious day. He couldn't remember ever having such a good time.

"No kissing!" Susanna hollered suddenly in English. "No kissing, sister!" This time, to Thomas's dismay, her words came out so clearly that a woman pushing a baby carriage heard her and laughed.

"Shh." Leah raised a finger to her lips. "Church voice, Susanna."

"No kissing!" her sister repeated just as loudly, falling into *Deitsch*. "King David and me can kiss. *Mam* says 'married kissing.' 'Door-closed kissing.' But you can't kiss Thomas. You have to marry Thomas. Then kissing."

"Thomas and I aren't kissing," Leah answered quietly, in *Deitsch*.

"Holding hands. I see you." Susanna waved a chubby finger. "You like Thomas. But no kissing."

"All right, no kissing," Leah agreed. Chuckling, she looked at Thomas. "You heard our chaperone."

Thomas gave her hand a squeeze. He was so happy

he felt as if he'd burst with joy. *I really am falling in love*, he thought. *Even Susanna can see it. I'm falling in love with Leah Yoder.*

Carrying a willow egg basket, Leah climbed barefoot over the stile that led from Sara's pasture to her aunt and uncle's farm. It was a gorgeous May morning, and the fields and woods were tinted a dozen shades of green. It had rained the previous night, and the grass glinted with water droplets like so many diamonds. Her mother's strawberries were ripe and promised a bumper crop. Hannah had invited her to come and pick some, and the back lane that ran through her mother's orchard was the quickest way to get there. Leah wanted to pick several quarts and would surprise Sara with a strawberry shortcake.

As she crossed the lot where Sara's mules were corralled and then the meadow, Leah let her thoughts stray. She'd dreamed of Daniel last night. Not a bad dream or a sad one, but she'd awakened feeling that there were things that had to be said between them.

After their baby had died of the fever, Daniel had lingered, his temperature soaring to dangerous highs and then receding, giving them hope that he would survive it. They'd had time to talk, time to say their farewells and time for Daniel to tell her that she must be strong.

She paused on the far side of the stile, her feet cushioned on the thick moss, a chorus of birdsong around her, and let Sara's basket slip to the ground. She remembered every word that Daniel had said to her that last night. He hadn't been afraid of death. He'd been secure in his faith. Daniel had been the strong one, and she'd clung to him, begging him not to leave her alone.

"But God is with you," he'd whispered, his voice low and urgent. "Never forget that, Leah. God has a plan for you. All you have to do is let Him take control. Follow where He leads you." She'd wept, telling him that she didn't want to live without him, that life held nothing without him and their baby. But he'd refused to accept that. "I know you," he'd rasped. "You Yoder girls are as solid as granite. You won't crumple when storms batter you. Find a good man and marry again. Have more children. You have to promise me that you will."

"I can't," she'd answered, but Daniel had insisted. How could she refuse him anything at that moment? And so she had agreed.

And now, finally, after more than a year, she could see that he'd been right and she'd been wrong. She only wished she could tell him.

Leah looked around. On a branch overhead, a wren scolded her, and, higher up, she caught sight of a squirrel. But there were no humans around, not a single person to hear her and think she'd taken leave of her mind.

She closed her eyes. She didn't know if Daniel could hear her up in heaven, but she liked the idea that maybe he could. She certainly felt as if he'd been watching over her since he'd been gone.

"Daniel?"

She concentrated, trying to picture Daniel in her mind. She could summon a fuzzy memory, but nothing sharp or definite. "Daniel, if you can hear me, I want you to know that I'm all right. I'm doing what you said. I didn't think I would ever laugh again or take pleasure in a hot cup of tea or the soft feel of a new-hatched chick. But I do. It hasn't been easy. You know me. I hate to give up control. But I'm trying to just let go, to be a leaf in the wind, to see where God takes me. And it's good, Daniel, really good."

She opened her eyes. The love she felt for Daniel and her baby was still there. It would always be there. But so was God's love. His mercy had set her free to live again…to seek a second chance at being a wife and a mother. She wondered if she should tell Daniel that.

But then she guessed he already knew.

A smile spread over Leah's face as she picked up the basket, her heart feeling lighter. She had gone a hundred yards when she was startled by the crash of underbrush and a frantic bellowing. She looked up to see a brown-and-white cow come charging out of the woods straight at her.

"Stop her!" shrieked a woman. "Don't let her get away!"

Leah jumped aside and the cow thundered past, a rope trailing behind her. The animal skidded on the path, pitched forward, scrambled up and continued on at an awkward lope into a huge open field.

Out of the trees came a disheveled and red-faced woman brandishing a broom. "You let her escape!" she shouted at Leah. "She ran right by you."

"Nearly ran me down," Leah agreed, trying not to smile.

Aunt Martha's once-white apron was muddy, and her faded lavender dress had a three-cornered tear in the skirt. One sleeve had come unstitched at the shoulder seam and hung down, exposing six inches of her upper arm. A blue scarf and tangled lengths of gray-streaked hair dangled down her back, and a twig with three leaves sprouted from the crown of her head. She wore men's rubber muck boots that came to her knees, probably not her own as they were several sizes too large. Worse, the boots were caked with something that smelled suspiciously of barnyard fertilizer, some of which had stained the hem of her dress.

"What are you staring at?" Breathing hard from the chase, Aunt Martha dropped the broom, scrunched her hair into a messy bun and tied the scarf firmly over it. "Why didn't you catch her?" The twig with the three leaves still protruded from under the scarf.

"Sorry," Leah mumbled, trying hard not to laugh.

"Worthless heifer." Her aunt wiped her muddy hands on her skirt. "I told your uncle that she was nothing but trouble. She'd be more use if we sent her to Gideon's butcher shop for hamburger." She stopped her tirade, caught her breath and advanced on Leah. "Where are you off to? Your mother's, I suppose. I'm sure you weren't planning on stopping to spend time with me."

"*Mam's* expecting me," Leah explained, still trying to control her impulse to giggle. She'd noticed a chicken feather clinging to her aunt's scarf. A tall, thin scarecrow of a figure with sharp features and a narrow, pinched mouth, Aunt Martha could never be truthfully called more than a plain woman. This morning, however, she looked as though someone had put her in a burlap bag full of garden dirt and shaken her.

"Has ideas on her mind, that one," Aunt Martha said.

"Excuse me?" Her aunt couldn't be talking about Hannah, could she?

"The heifer." Aunt Martha's lips firmed into a thin line and her voice dropped to a whisper. "Those beef cattle of Samuel's. He has a new bull. And that one…" She gestured in the direction the cow had gone. "Sweet sassafras, Leah, you were a married woman. I shouldn't have to spell it out for you."

"Oh," Leah replied. "Your heifer is running after Samuel's—"

"What did I just say? Some things shouldn't have to be said straight out, should they? But then your mother always did let you girls run wild. When you married that Mennonite boy and went off to God knows where, I said to her, 'Hannah, now you see what comes of it.' Thank the Lord you've seen the error of your ways and come home to the faith. But had she listened to me, you'd have married your own kind to begin with."

Leah didn't know where to begin answering that and so she didn't say anything.

Aunt Martha didn't seem to notice. "And speaking of marriage, you need to remember what's expected of one of our girls. I saw you and that Thomas walking home just about dusk the other night. Right down this path. I wouldn't have noticed if you didn't cut through my farm. I mind my own business, you know. Anyone can tell you that." Her aunt gave her a probing look. "Seeing a lot of him, aren't you?"

"I am, but…" Leah drew in a breath and prepared to defend herself. "But we were chaperoned. Anna's son Peter was with us."

"Saw the two of you. Didn't see him."

"But he was with us. Bishop Atlee said we needed a chaperone after dark or to travel out of Seven Poplars, and we've done as he asked."

Martha nodded. "So you should. A widow or not, a young woman has to guard her reputation, and that Thomas, he's always been a wild one."

"Sara arranged the match," Leah said. "She thinks—"

"Oh, I know what she thinks. And this time, I have to agree with her. You know Thomas's name was mentioned for my Dorcas. Everyone said, 'Thomas is going to come into a bit of land and he has a trade.' But my Reuben and I, we thought she could do better. We told her to wait. The right man would come along." She picked up her broom. "That heifer will be long gone by now. Reuben will have to send the hired boy to fetch her home."

"Well, it was good to talk with you, Aunt Martha." Leah shuffled her feet. "Sorry about your cow."

"You go on, pick your strawberries. Ours haven't come on yet. I expected your mother to invite me to come over and pick, but she hasn't. Too many of her own to feed, I suppose, to think of a sister-in-law." She sniffed. "But you mind what I said, Leah. Listen to the bishop and don't do anything that could cause rumors of misbehavior between you and Thomas." She smiled. "Come to think of it, I may have been the one to put a bee in Sara's bonnet about the two of you. 'That Thomas might be perfect for Hannah's Leah,' I told her. 'Both of them being a little odd.' And Sara took my advice and matched you up. I told Reuben that you were walking out together as soon as I heard. And he said, 'You're right, Martha.'" Martha walked away, talking to herself now. "I'm right so often about who should be courting whom, maybe *I* should become a matchmaker."

Chapter Nine

When Leah arrived back at Sara's after driving her sister and nephews to the dentist, she didn't expect to find Thomas there and busy at work. He was digging a hole in the side yard using a Bobcat, a small specialized tractor with a backhoe on the rear. Thomas saw her and waved before shutting off the engine. "You're out early," he called to her.

"Dental checkups for Johanna's older boys. No cavities."

She got out of the car and crossed the lawn to the edge of the excavation.

"They keep you busy, driving to doctors and such," he said. "Your sisters."

"Not just my sisters. Friends, family, half the people in Seven Poplars, I think," Leah replied, tickled to see Thomas, even though she wasn't expecting him. "I won't be allowed to keep the car once I join the church, but until then, I'm glad to help out the community. Saves them paying a driver. *Grossmama* needs to go to the lab for some blood work soon. I promised Anna I'd take her."

She was also driving Ruth to the midwife for a

checkup, but that wasn't information she intended to share with Thomas. Her sister was in the family way, something women liked to keep private until their condition became obvious. "What are you doing? Don't tell me Sara is putting in a swimming pool?"

Thomas chuckled. "Close enough. She wants a fishpond with a fountain. It's going to be solar powered."

"I didn't know you could drive one of those things." She pointed at the Bobcat. How handsome he looked, she thought. Just the sight of him on this bright June morning made her want to clap for joy.

"There's a lot about me you don't know," he replied with a grin.

Typical Thomas, always ready with a smart answer. She looked at the hole in the lawn and then back at the machine. "I meant, I didn't know that the elders approved of tractors. Shouldn't you be digging this with a shovel?"

He shook his head. "It would take a *lot* of shoveling. The community voted to allow heavy machinery on a limited basis." He chuckled. "So I'm fine as long as I don't use it as transportation. I just can't drive it home."

She laughed. "How did you get it here?"

"The equipment-rental place delivers." He climbed down off the tractor seat and pointed to the excavation. "Sara asked me if I wanted to put in a bid for the pond, a screened-in gazebo and an arbor. She wants a welcoming place where her couples can sit and talk privately while remaining in full view."

"It will be lovely, but she didn't say a word about it," Leah said.

"That's Sara. She likes to have all her ducks in a row before she talks about her plans. This shouldn't take too long, and it will give me extra money to put into my garden. Speaking of which…" He pointed at her. "Would you like to come over after work and see my peppers and tomato plants?"

"I would." The two of them spent three or four evenings a week together and she never grew bored with being with him. Sometimes they just went for a walk or fishing in the pond, but often they made themselves busy planting seedlings or even weeding his small but growing garden. "Any idea when the first tomatoes will be ripe enough to sell?"

He considered. "Let's see. This is the first of June. So far, we've had excellent weather for growing. If we get enough rain, I should be picking cherry tomatoes by early July. Four or five weeks. God willing."

"*Ya*, God willing," she repeated. They had much to be thankful for. So far, Thomas's plans for raising and selling his organic vegetables had gone smoothly. He was excited about it, and she was as well. It was good to have a new project to help bring to fruition. "Is it too late to put in more spinach? *Mam* has had luck with a heritage variety that stands the heat better. And those baby eggplants. Maybe there'd be a market for those."

"Leah, are you keeping Thomas from getting my fishpond dug?" Sara came from the house carrying glasses of iced tea.

"We were talking about Thomas's garden," Leah explained. "His heritage tomatoes are growing well."

Sara chuckled. "You were talking, all right. I shouted out the window to see if you'd like something cold to drink, and you were so intent on your conversation that you never heard me."

"Sorry," Leah said. She smiled, feeling a little bit as

if she'd been caught doing something naughty. But it was Sara's idea that they see each other, so she refused to feel guilty about it.

"I'm just teasing you." Sara handed each of them a glass of tea. "I've been wanting to catch the two of you together. Do you realize that your six weeks is up?"

"What?" Thomas nearly choked on his tea. He started to cough, and when he'd cleared his throat he shook his head. "It can't be. Six weeks?"

Leah thought for a minute. Could six weeks really have gone by so quickly? But when she did the math, she realized Sara was right. It *had* been six weeks since she and Thomas had agreed to see each other. Almost seven weeks. She gave a little laugh. "She's right. The time has flown, hasn't it?"

Sara planted her hands on her ample hips. "So?" The question was directed at Leah.

"So…what?" Leah repeated.

"So, what do you think?" Sara pointed at Thomas. Then she gave a wave in his direction. "No need to ask you. I already know you've fallen head over teacup for our Leah." She returned her attention to Leah.

Leah took a breath. She hadn't contemplated what she would say because she hadn't thought she'd ever be in this position. But facts were facts and she wasn't afraid to admit she'd been wrong. "You were right, Sara. Thomas and I are a good match." She went on, matter-of-fact. "I didn't think so when you first brought up the idea. In fact, I was *sure* that he wasn't what I wanted." She gave him a warm look. "Nothing against you, Thomas. I just thought… Well, never mind what I thought. What matters is that I was wrong. We're compatible." She shrugged. "So I guess we should move forward."

Sara narrowed her gaze. "So, you two have talked about this?"

"Not…exactly," Leah went on. "But, you're fine with this, right, Thomas?" She glanced his way.

He nodded rapidly, looking a little surprised.

It was just like a man to be surprised by something so apparent as this. She and Thomas were compatible— they had the same values, the same desire to live in a way that was pleasing to God. And they both needed spouses. It was really that simple. Leah looked at Sara again. "Thomas and I are both seeing Bishop Atlee for baptismal classes. We're happy with each other, so I don't see any reason why we shouldn't begin official courting. We could probably be married in autumn, once both of us have been baptized."

"You seem to have your mind made up," Sara said, looking directly at Leah. But then her gaze drifted to Thomas. "I see no reason you can't court, but I'm not sure you're ready to set a wedding date."

Leah looked down at the watch locket that she wore on a chain around her neck. "Oh, look at the time! I've got to pick up Anna and *Grossmama*. I hate to run, but I promised I'd be at Anna's early. It's not so easy getting *Grossmama* dressed and into the car. Her health really seems to be failing in the last few months."

"Will you be home for supper?" Sara asked.

"*Ne*, don't wait on me." She turned to go, then back to wave. "See you later at your place, Thomas. Have fun with the Bobcat."

Thomas drank the last of his iced tea and watched Leah drive out of the yard in her car. Vaguely, he was aware that the tea was icy cold, just the way he liked it.

The tea quenched his thirst and the June sun was warm on his face. Still, he felt a little odd, even out of sorts. Had he just heard what he thought he'd heard? That Leah didn't just want to marry him? That she wanted to set a date for their wedding? It was what he'd wanted, what he'd prayed for. So why, now that it was going to happen, was he not bursting with excitement?

"You look confused," Sara said.

"Shocked, I think," he admitted. "Leah and I have been really enjoying each other's company and getting to know each other. I'd hoped she'd want to move forward. I *think* she has feelings for me and I definitely..." He felt his cheeks grow warm. He'd never been shy about talking about a girl before but maybe because he'd never felt this way before. "It's just... I..." He stopped and started again. "I guess I didn't realize that we...that Leah was ready to take the next step."

"But you are, too, aren't you?" Sara's gaze was direct and a little uncomfortable. "You're ready to move toward marriage?"

He nodded. Honestly, he was a little bewildered by Leah's casual declaration. He had just assumed that at some point he and Leah would talk about the original arrangement they'd made with each other and how it had changed. When they'd agreed to see each other seven weeks ago in Sara's office, he'd thought he'd been buying himself some time with his grandfather. And Leah had agreed to date him to please Sara with the understanding that if it didn't work, the matchmaker would find her an older widower. Neither had thought they'd end up discussing marriage. What had he missed?

Of course, he'd never seriously dated anyone like this before. Maybe it wasn't something you were supposed to talk about to each other. "I'm in love with Leah," Thomas said quietly. "So that means that we should be courting. And marrying in the church."

"Is she in love with you?"

He dropped his gaze to his boots.

Sara made a sound in her throat. "You've not discussed your feelings for each other or the idea of marriage." It was a statement, not a question. "You would feel easier if the two of you had talked it out before Leah said something to me?"

He squinted, thinking. "Should we have? I mean, is that what couples do?" He shrugged. "This is all new to me. I've never seen my mother and father talk about personal stuff."

"But you wouldn't hear private conversations between your parents, would you?" Sara said. "Matters that are private between a couple are not for others to hear, not even a dear son."

Thomas scratched his head. "So…are you saying Leah and I *should* have talked about this? Alone?"

Sara pursed her lips. "It seems to me that if you and Leah intend to marry and spend the rest of your lives together, that decision should be made together."

"So…we should talk about it?" he said. "We need to?"

"I think you two need to get in the habit of talking things through. Not just thinking the other knows what's going on in your head."

He nodded, thinking, staring at the toe of his boot. "Leah's not a big one for talking about how she feels. She's more one for just doing. But I have my own faults. And I want Leah for my wife." He looked up at Sara. "I want her any way I can get her. And that's the truth."

Sara smiled. "You must be cautious, Thomas. Marriage is for the rest of your lives. Once joined, you are together until death. You might feel differently in ten years, even twenty. And it isn't fair to change the rules then. You need to establish things now, before you make that commitment."

He continued to look at her, not certain where this conversation was leading. "Establish them how?"

"There is nothing wrong with telling Leah that you want to talk things out before she makes decisions for both of you. Even when you agree with what she thinks, it's important that you both have your say."

He nodded. "I'll think about it, Sara. I will."

"Be certain you do. These things need to be worked out between you before you exchange vows. There's nothing that says you have to marry this fall. Not if you're not ready. Marry in haste. Repent in leisure."

"But…" He handed her his iced-tea glass. "I don't understand, Sara. You're the one who said we were right for each other. This match is your idea. Now are you saying it's not?"

"That's not what I'm saying, Thomas. But I've been doing this for a long time. Every couple has issues to work out. And they are best worked out *before* marriage. That way there are no unpleasant surprises for either of you later."

"I don't see any problems between us."

"I'm glad of that. But you need to take this one step at a time. You're not a raw boy. You're used to doing things a certain way, which is natural. And Leah has been through a lot. You're not marrying a twenty-year-old girl."

"I know that." He hesitated. "About your fee. Do I pay it after the wedding or—"

"No need to worry about it. Hannah and Albert are taking care of Leah's portion, and your grandfather has already come to an agreement with me."

"So you think that fall would be too soon for us to marry?"

Sara shook her head. "No, I didn't say that, either. Plenty of time to set a date for a November wedding. What's important is that you each marry with a free heart, that you find what you want in the union."

"I want to make a home with Leah, to have children if God sends them, to serve Him and our community."

Sara smiled. "I can't think of better reasons to marry." She patted his arm. "You're a good man, Thomas, and Leah is fortunate to find someone like you."

"And me, her." He grinned at Sara. "But I'd better get back to work on this pond. They charge rent by the hour, and we're talking on your pocketbook, when I should be digging."

"I'll leave you to it, then." Sara took the glasses and went back to the house.

Thomas let out a sigh of relief. He couldn't wait to get home this afternoon and tell his family that he and Leah intended to set a date for their wedding. That should please them—especially his grandfather. It pleased him well enough.

He climbed back into the seat of the Bobcat and started the engine. Maybe there was something to what Sara had said about telling Leah they needed to talk things out between them. But, right now, he was happy that she'd agreed to be his wife.

* * *

Two days later, Leah, Thomas and Ellie were driving back from Rehoboth on Route 1 in Leah's car. Thomas had delivered assorted orders of lettuce, spinach and strawberries to three restaurants, and Ellie had come with them as chaperone. They'd all enjoyed a walk on the beach after the vegetables had been delivered, and both Ellie and Leah had gotten slightly sunburned.

"Next time, we'll remember to put on sunscreen," Leah said as she glanced into the mirror to see her sunburned nose. Her sister Miriam tanned, but she never did.

"I offered to lend you my hat," Thomas teased. He tapped the edge of the wide straw brim. He had the hat in his lap because he was tall and the car had a low roof. Ellie, in the backseat, had plenty of room.

"Wouldn't that be a sight for the Englishers?" Ellie said chuckling. "But it wouldn't be right for you to go without your head covered, Thomas. You would have to wear one of our *kapps*."

Leah and Thomas both laughed at the thought. Traffic was light, and Leah was enjoying the drive. The whole day had been fun. She always enjoyed being with Ellie, and having her along was easy, without any awkwardness. Nothing fazed Ellie, not the noise and clamor of the boardwalk or the open stares of the tourists and their children.

"Does it ever bother you, Ellie?" Leah asked. "Having people point at you in public?"

"Because I'm short or because I'm Amish?"

Leah laughed. Her friend had a good point. And she liked the fact that they didn't have to avoid the subject of her stature. "Because you're short."

"When I was little, it frightened me that people were always staring," Ellie admitted, "but then I decided it was because I was pretty, not because I was little."

Leah grinned, glancing at her in the rearview mirror. "Only you would say such a thing."

"*Ya*, but it's true, isn't it? I'm short, but I'm cute. And God gave me a brain. I have my health and my eyes and two hands and two legs. Why should I feel sorry for myself because I'm not taller? If I—"

"Did you see who that was?" Thomas said, interrupting Ellie. "Walking along the highway?"

"*Ne,*" Leah answered. "I was concentrating on that pickup. He's switched lanes multiple times and I was just trying to stay out of his way."

"Where's the next turnoff?" Thomas asked, looking over his shoulder. "We have to go back."

"Go back? Why?" Ellie asked. "Who was walking along the road?"

Thomas pointed to a traffic light ahead. "There," he said. "Make a U-turn. I think that was Jakob."

"Jakob? You mean Jakob Schwartz?" Leah asked. She put on her signal, moved over and guided the car into the turn lane. "What do you suppose he was doing walking?"

"He was going fishing today on a boat out of Bowers Beach. A driver picked him up before daylight this morning. I'm sure it was Jakob," Thomas insisted.

Ellie groaned. "It's not like little people are as common as cows around here."

Leah looked in the mirror as she made her turn and saw the sour expression on Ellie's face. "You wouldn't want us to leave him by the side of the road, would you?" she asked.

"*Ya*, I would. Unless you plan on putting him in the trunk. If anyone in Seven Poplars sees me in the backseat of this car with him, my life is over."

Leah accelerated in the southbound lane. "Why will your life be over, Ellie? I've met Jakob. He's a very pleasant person. Smart. And funny. You two should—"

"*Ne*, we shouldn't. Your grandmother asked me after church when we were crying the banns, me and the little man. And your aunt Martha said out loud during one of the hymns that us both being little didn't mean our children would be short. We could have normal children."

"But that isn't Jakob's fault," Thomas defended.

Ellie sniffed. "If you'd heard as many hints and suggestions and offers to have us both to dinner as I've heard since that man first came visiting to our community, you'd understand. When I marry, *if* I marry, it won't be because my husband has to be a little person. And as for our children being normal, I think I *am* normal," she fumed. "It's the rest of you who are too tall."

Leah spotted Jakob, made the next U-turn and pulled to the shoulder of the road behind Jakob, who continued walking. She put on her flashers. Pulling off like this made her nervous. Seeing Jakob walking the busy highway made her even more nervous.

Thomas got out and shouted. "Jakob! It's Thomas!"

The little man turned, grinned and waved, and trudged back to the car. In one hand, he carried a saltwater fishing pole and reel, in the other, a tackle box. "Glad to see you, I am, Thomas."

"Get in," Thomas told him.

Jakob leaned in the open passenger window. "I didn't think to be picked up by a friend. Leah." He nodded a greeting, then glanced into the backseat, saw Ellie and did a double take. "Ellie Fisher." His smile spread until his whole face crinkled with good humor. "God is truly good to me."

"The tackle box will go in the trunk," Thomas said, taking it from him. "Fishing pole, too, if I break it down." He made his way to the back of the car as Leah released the trunk latch. "You can jump in the back."

"Or ride in the trunk with the tackle box," Ellie muttered.

Leah stifled a chuckle. "Be nice," she warned, turning to look into the backseat.

Ellie grimaced. "Maybe Thomas would like to ride back here with him."

"Thomas barely fits back there." Leah made a face. "He's too tall."

"We could fold *him* in half," Ellie suggested.

"Fold who in half?" Thomas asked, closing the trunk. "Hop in, Jakob."

Ellie slid over and Jakob got into the backseat with her.

"Sorry if I smell like a fishing boat," he said. "I'm afraid I will stink up your car."

Ellie drew herself up stiffly and moved over closer to the door, leaving a space between them. *"Ya,"* she agreed. "You do smell like a fishing boat."

"What happened?" Thomas asked, getting back into the front seat. "Why are you walking? What about the driver who picked you up?"

"The bay was rough. The driver got seasick," Jakob explained. "So seasick somebody else had to drive him home. They offered to take me, but he lives way south of Dover, so I decided the best thing to do was start walking."

"It's a long way from here to Seven Poplars." Leah checked her rearview mirror and eased back onto the road. "At least twenty miles, maybe more. You should have called the chair shop or another driver."

"Don't know any others," he said. "It never occurred to me that the Englisher who drove me to the dock wouldn't take me home. And I don't have the number of the chair shop." He shrugged. "I don't have a cell phone. And I've walked farther than this before. I might not have got back to the farm until after dark, but I would have gotten there."

"I'm glad we came along when we did," Thomas said. "Did no one else offer you a ride?"

"Two Englishers," Jakob said, "but they'd carried a cooler of beer onto the boat. I don't hold with alcohol, and I'll not ride with anyone who's been drinking."

"Did you catch any fish?" Thomas asked.

Jakob shook his head sadly. "Nothing I could bring home. And I had my heart set on fried fish."

"I like fish, too," Leah said, changing lanes to get around a tractor trailer hauling chickens. "Saltwater fish are my favorite. Especially flounder or trout."

"How about you, Ellie?" Jakob asked. "Do you like fish?"

"Can't abide them. Not the smell, not the taste."

"I'm sorry for that," Jakob replied. "You don't know what you're missing."

"I think I do," Ellie said.

Leah glanced at Ellie in the rearview mirror. She was staring straight ahead, her hands fisted at her sides. Her cheeks were pink and her mouth set in a thin line. Leah was surprised. She'd never seen Ellie so out of sorts, and it was unfair to blame Jakob, who'd done nothing but have a bad day. Leah hoped he wouldn't notice her friend's rudeness.

"Tell you what," Thomas said. "Let's stop in Wyoming. There's a family restaurant there that serves good food at fair prices. I'll treat you all to supper. And Jakob, they always have fish on the menu. You can enjoy your fish supper after all."

"That's a great idea," Leah said. "Ellie?"

"Lovely," Ellie said in a tone that clearly said she felt otherwise.

"Goot," Jakob exclaimed. "But the treat will be mine. Nothing I like better than to share a meal with friends." He smiled at Ellie. "Especially such pretty friends."

Chapter Ten

"Hey, Leah!" Thomas waved from his perch on one of the rafters of Charley's partially constructed house. "Up here!" Leah and several of her sisters were walking across the yard below. "Leah!"

She looked up, saw him and waved back. Her sisters laughed and waved, as well. "Hold on!" Leah shouted back. "We don't want to have to rush you to the emergency room with a broken leg!"

"I'll try to remember that!" Chuckling, Thomas returned to his task of hammering in a wooden peg, securing one rafter securely to the ridgepole of the house. Heights had never frightened him and he was having the time of his life. From here, it seemed he could see half of Seven Poplars: the chair shop on the other side of the road, Samuel Mast's barn and the brick chimneys of his house, Hannah's house and barns, even Johanna and Roland's farmstead. Working on either side of him were Leah's brothers-in-law Charley and Eli, and two stories below, directing the project, was James Hostetler, a local contractor and carpenter with a lifetime of experience in building houses.

Charley couldn't have picked a better day for the house raising if he'd tried. June was a busy month for farmers, and most of the men who worked in trades outside of Seven Poplars still had work to do on their own farms and homes on weekends. But the entire community and many from other church districts in the county had come to lend a hand on the house. The weather was perfect, temperature in the seventies with clear blue skies. Thomas counted more than twenty men directly involved in the construction, while more carried lumber, sawed wood and assisted the women in setting up the long tables for the midday meal under the trees. He wouldn't even attempt to count the children. The smaller ones were running back and forth and playing, while the older kids were either helping with the coming picnic dinner or running errands for the workmen.

Until now, Charley and his wife had shared a house with one of her sisters, but rumors were that after a long wait, the couple was expecting a second child. Charley's horse breeding and training was a successful sideline to his farming skills, and it was time that his family had room to grow. And, according to tradition, the Amish community and some of the local Englishers had turned out en masse to help. Helping one another was expected. Charley and his wife had done their best to support and aid fellow church members, and now their hard work and dedication would be repaid by their neighbors and friends.

Thomas gave the peg a final blow with his hammer and grinned as it drove without splitting to the depth of the predrilled hole. From below, on the first floor, Albert Hartman, the local veterinarian and Hannah's husband, began the first chorus of an old hymn, and all over the house and yard, men joined in, blending their voices together amid the rhythms and din of hammer and saw. Thomas sang with them, his chest swelling with the warm feelings of unity and faith that united him to these people.

On the far side of the roof, at the top of a ladder, clung Jakob, a huge leather work belt slung over one shoulder and a hammer in his hand. Thomas would have expected Jakob to choose tasks that kept him closer to the ground due to his size, but the little man could climb better than Thomas could. His strong arms and powerful shoulders made up for his lack of size. Jakob's addition to the family blacksmith shop had, so far, been a resounding success. Thomas knew that his grandfather was pleased with Jakob's work, and the customers all seemed to like him, as well. Jakob started work before breakfast and would continue at the forge until long past the ringing of the supper bell if someone didn't urge him to bank the fire and come to the table.

Thomas moved to another rafter. He glanced up at the sun. Nearly noon. His belly had been grumbling for an hour. House building was hard work. He liked hard work, but he'd been thinking about the feast the women were preparing. He could smell fried chicken, roast beef, *schnitz und knepp*, and baking bread. A pit and turnspit had been prepared and teenage boys had meticulously turned a whole pig for twelve hours over a bed of coals. Thomas could almost taste the juicy slices of pork with its crisp skin and delicious interior. There would be salads, green beans, scalloped potatoes, *kartoffle bolla*, mashed potatoes, buttered beets, stewed tomatoes, English peas with dumplings, cakes, pies and enough gravy to swim in. Every woman would have brought her finest dish, not out of pride but wanting to share her best with her neighbors and family.

"Running short of nails yet?" Jakob called.

Thomas shook his head. "I've got plenty."

"I'm out." Jakob motioned to the area where he was working. "You want to give me a hand with this?"

"No problem." Thomas moved cautiously along the rafter and then walked toward his new friend. "Going good. We should be laying—" His foot slipped and he lost his balance and fell but caught himself with his arms. His heart pounded as he sucked in lungfuls of air, his feet dangling.

"Hang on!" James shouted from below. "Someone will—"

"Got him!" Jakob yelled. He grabbed Thomas by the shirt collar, then the arm, and helped him scramble back up to sit on the narrow beam. "Take your time," Jakob said to Thomas.

"I'm all right." Thomas's heartbeat slowed to somewhere near normal as he glanced down at the distance between where he had just hung and the solid ground far below. He quickly looked back at Jakob. "Whew," he said.

"God is with you," Jakob said. He offered a broad hand, and Thomas took it and slowly rose to his feet. Jakob grinned. "What's important is that you caught yourself. Back home, I saw a man fall off the roof of a barn and break his back. He lived, but he never walked again, and he had a wife and five children to care for."

"*Ya*, I guess I got a little overconfident." Thomas returned the smile. He couldn't help scanning the dinner area to see if Leah had witnessed his near miss, but she'd been wearing a green dress and he didn't see any.

All the women seemed to be clad in various shades of blue, brown and lavender. Several had their heads together and were pointing at the roof, but none of them were his Leah. *Just as well*, he thought.

"Slow and steady works best when you're up this high," Jakob said. "But anybody can slip. Shake it off."

Thomas removed his hat and wiped the sweat off his forehead. His shoulder ached from swinging the hammer, but it was a satisfying twinge. The beam felt solid beneath his feet and he released his death grip on the nearest post and stopped breathing in quick, hard gasps. *God is good*, he thought. And merciful. He swallowed, and attempted to ease his dry throat. "That was a little too close," he said to Jakob.

"But you survived it, and all the girls will be finding an excuse to talk to you during dinner." Jakob grinned again, his high forehead wrinkling with good humor. "And they will be telling you how brave you are. It's almost worth it."

Thomas chuckled. "Only one girl I care to impress. And I don't think she saw me doing my trick."

"A pity," Jakob offered, and they both laughed. And then Jakob said, "How are the baptism classes going?"

"Good. I think." Thomas replaced his hat, tugging it firmly into place. "You already baptized?"

"When I turned eighteen. Back home in Indiana. It was either accept the life or leave home without a penny in my pocket. My father was pretty firm on the subject. But it didn't take much persuasion. I would have come to it in a year or two anyway, once I'd had my fun. This is my faith, and I wouldn't know any other way to live."

"Still, it's a serious decision," Thomas admitted. "Not as easy as I always thought it would be."

Jakob threw him a sympathetic look. "Probably easier when you're younger. You don't consider the magnitude of the decision." He waited and then went on. "But if you have questions or doubts, you don't have to wrestle with them alone. I'd be happy to talk with you, and so would any of the others." He indicated the men working below them.

Thomas nodded. "I appreciate that."

A dinner bell rang loud and clear.

"Guess that's the signal we were waiting for." Jakob started down the ladder. "I don't know about you, but I'm starving."

"I'm not sure I could eat a horse and plow," Thomas replied, following him, "but I could give it a good try." When he reached the bottom floor, Jakob was standing there waiting for him. Other men were descending the ladders, taking off their tool belts, laying down tools, but none were close enough to hear.

"What you said before," Jakob said quietly. "About your concerns. You know we have more than one leader. Preacher Caleb seems sensible. And he's a lot closer to our age than the bishop. You might want to talk to him if you're having any reservations. Now's the time to do it, not after you've joined the church. That's where some make a big mistake."

"It's the practical side that keeps nagging at me," Thomas said as he hung his own tool belt over a nail. "Leah having access to that car, being able to deliver my crop directly to the good markets, that means a lot."

"She's Mennonite, isn't she?"

"Was. Raised Amish but joined the Mennonites when she married. Now she's planning on returning to the faith. She's taking classes, too, the young women's class, of course."

"Are you thinking about becoming Mennonite, instead? Then the two of you could keep the car." Jakob shrugged. "It might be the answer to your dilemma."

"I don't know. That would be a bigger step than going through with the baptism."

Jakob nodded. "*Ya*, but not wrong if your heart leads you in that direction. We choose to live apart from the world, but it's not for everyone. How does Leah feel about it?"

Thomas shrugged. "I don't know. We haven't talked about it."

Jakob paused in the doorway and glanced back at him. "Then you shouldn't be talking to me—you should be discussing it with the woman you intend to marry. It's a decision that you and Leah need to make together."

"You're probably right, but I haven't gotten it straight in my own head. I'm not sure how I feel or what I want. I wasn't sure I should trouble her with the idea until I knew what I wanted." He took off his straw hat again, rolled the brim and slicked back his forelock before replacing the hat.

"There's something in what you're saying," Jakob agreed, "about thinking this through before approaching Leah with it, but—" He broke off and motioned toward the windmill in the yard. "There's your girl, now."

Thomas looked up. It was Leah in her green dress and dainty white lace *kapp*. She was carrying a tray piled high with biscuits, and walking beside her was Ellie, her hands balancing a four-layer chocolate cake.

"A pretty sight," Jakob observed, "those two."

"Leah's taken," Thomas teased. "But Ellie's single

and she's not interested in anybody special, not since we broke up."

"That's right. She broke up with you, didn't she?" Jakob asked.

"Turned me down flat when I asked her to marry me."

Jakob laughed. "Shows what good sense she has. I have a feeling she was waiting for me to show up in town."

Leah saw them approaching and smiled. Ellie frowned, turned on her heels and marched back in the direction from which she had come.

"I don't know about that. She doesn't seem all that infatuated with you," Thomas teased.

"Don't believe it. She adores me. Who wouldn't?" Jakob threw out his arms in a dramatic gesture. "I'm handsome. Hardworking. And very modest."

Thomas chuckled at his antics. "Ellie can be tough, but she's going to make someone a fine wife. Don't give up on her if you're interested."

"I'm not giving up on the pretty little schoolteacher," Jakob replied, still watching Ellie retreat. "She had me from the first time I laid eyes on her. She's going to be my wife. She just doesn't know it yet."

"Ellie? Where are you going?" Leah called.

Rebecca came up behind Leah. "Let me take those biscuits. *Mam* wants you to fill the water glasses. There's a pitcher on the side table over there."

"Like old times, isn't it?" Leah smiled at her sister as she handed her the tray. "When we were all living at home. *Mam* always took charge, even when it wasn't her dinner."

Rebecca laughed. "*Mam* hasn't changed, Leah, and neither have you. The trouble is, the two of you are too much alike. I think you both like to give orders." Her dimples flashed as she smiled. "It's so good to have you back with us again."

"Good to be back." Leah brushed her sister's cheek with a kiss. "I have to admit, I did miss your pointing out my failings."

"See?" Rebecca laughed again. "I am good for something."

When they were small, they'd always joined together as a team making a united front against Miriam, Johanna, Anna and Ruth, who'd seemed so grown-up and in charge. Leah had never doubted that all of her sisters loved her and would come to her aid if she needed them, but she had to admit, for all her ideas, Rebecca was her favorite. "You really think I'm like our mother?"

"Absolutely," Rebecca pronounced. "*Mam* even says so herself. And you know she's rarely wrong."

"We need biscuits at this end of table!" their sister Ruth called.

Rebecca rolled her eyes. "A woman's work is never done."

"It's hardly work, though," Leah answered. "More of a holiday with everyone here."

Rebecca nudged her with an elbow. "There's your Thomas over there with the new blacksmith. They're watching you, or at least Thomas is."

"*Ne*, he's not," Leah replied, although she knew he was. "He's just hungry for his dinner. Thomas is always ready to eat." Just saying his name made her want to laugh. She saw him almost every day, but still, seeing him here today was exciting. It made her feel like a giddy teenager again.

"You're blushing," Rebecca teased.

"*Ne*, I'm not."

"There's nothing to be ashamed of. Thomas and you will make a wonderful couple, and you'll be a beautiful bride. Don't you remember how it was when you met Daniel? You were so happy. I'm glad to see you happy again."

Leah pressed her lips together, suddenly feeling a twinge of guilt. It wasn't the same as Daniel. It couldn't be. No one could take Daniel's place in her heart. It wasn't possible. "It's not like that with me and Thomas," she protested. "Not the same at all. I told you this weeks ago. Thomas and I are marrying because it makes sense. He needs a wife. I need a husband and this is the solution."

Rebecca set the tray of biscuits on the long table, grabbed Leah's arm and tugged her aside. "Come with me," she said, walking away from the bustling women and children. "Did I hear you say what I thought I did?" She didn't stop until they were partially hidden by a large lilac bush. "Are you telling me you don't love Thomas?"

Leah shook off her sister's hand on her arm. "Sara arranged this match. It's not... It was never supposed to be romantic. I told you that."

"I know what you told me when you started seeing each other, but I assumed things had changed between you and Thomas." Rebecca held Leah's gaze. "You've certainly been acting like things have changed." She lowered her voice. "I thought you were in love with him."

Leah squared her shoulders. "I like Thomas. I respect him. But our relationship is about companionship...friendship. Not everyone who marries is madly, romantically in love with each other."

Rebecca frowned, crossing her arms over her chest. "Maybe it's too soon for you to be thinking of marriage. Maybe you need longer to mourn what you've lost. Give yourself more time. You loved Daniel so much. I wouldn't rush into marriage again if you're not ready, because that would be a mistake. And unfair to Thomas."

"I'm not making a mistake. Thomas understands. I told him from the first my reasons for wanting to marry again."

"All right, if you're sure." Rebecca sighed, looking unconvinced. "You know I just want what's best for you. Remember what happened with Johanna. She thought she was in love with Wilmer and look how that turned out."

Leah sighed and stared at her bare feet. "Thomas is not Wilmer. They are nothing alike, and I'm not Johanna. I know what I'm doing. Don't worry about me."

"It's just that I care about you, and I want you to be happy."

"I am happy," Leah insisted.

Rebecca looked at her.

"I *am*," Leah repeated, opening her arms wide.

Seeming to sense she'd pushed hard enough, Rebecca changed the subject. "How are the baptismal classes going?"

"Good."

"And Thomas's?" Rebecca asked.

"Okay, I suppose." She grimaced, knowing that she

could never deceive Rebecca. "The truth is, I think he's struggling a little."

"Second thoughts?"

"Nothing like that. I think it's just that he's been a bachelor for so long, having fun, avoiding responsibility, that taking classes with the bishop means that this is for real."

"It's not cold feet? Because I'd hate for you to be the one dumped after everyone has planted fields of celery for your wedding."

Leah rolled her eyes. "Thomas is not dumping me." She shook her head. "It's not about me. I think he's just a little nervous, is all. About the responsibilities of a man in our community."

"And you've talked about it?"

"We talk all the time," Leah assured her.

"Leah! Rebecca!" Miriam appeared around the corner of the house. "What are the two of you doing over here? *Mam's* been looking for you. The food is ready for the first sitting. And Thomas is looking for you, too, Leah." She glanced over her shoulder. "Over here, Thomas." Miriam looked back at Leah. "Did you see him almost take that dive off the roof?"

"What?" Leah asked.

"Scared me half to death." She brought her hand to her heart. "He fell off one of the roof rafters."

"Nothing for you to get upset about," Thomas assured her as he joined them. "It was a stupid mistake on my part. I caught myself." He waved one hand. "No harm done."

Stunned, Leah stared at him. He'd almost fallen off the roof? She struggled to draw a breath. "But...but you're all right?" she asked, feeling a little light-headed. "You caught yourself? You didn't fall?"

He grinned boyishly. "*Ne*. I didn't fall far. Didn't even get a scratch."

She had an impulse to run to him and hug him, but she couldn't. Not with her sisters both standing there.

But she wanted to hug him. She wanted to hold him tight. Which she found a bit bewildering. She'd just told her sister she didn't have romantic feelings for Thomas, and here she was, wanting to throw herself into his arms. Everything she had said to Rebecca made perfect sense. It was this feeling in her stomach, in her heart, that was confusing.

Leah forced a smile. "You must be hungry," she said to Thomas. "For…dinner. Dinner's ready."

The last bell for the first seating rang.

"You'd best get to the table," she said hastily. "Before grace." She looked at her sisters. "And we…we need to get back to work." Without waiting for Thomas to respond, she rushed off toward the kitchen. She needed to think this out, and she couldn't think when Thomas was around. Later, she promised herself. Later, she'd figure all this out.

Chapter Eleven

By nine thirty Saturday morning the pancake breakfast at the Mennonite church was in full swing. Leah
stood at the six-burner stove in the big kitchen flip-
ping pancakes, while Daniel's aunt Joyce stirred up another batch of batter. The cheerful room, with its large
windows overlooking picnic tables and a children's
playground, was buzzing with activity. Caroline, Aunt
Joyce's daughter, was loading the commercial dishwasher while her sister Leslie poured orange juice and
another woman, Gwen, wiped down the counters. Eight-
year-old Yasmin, another of Daniel's cousins, darted in
and out of the kitchen carrying napkins and fresh jugs
of maple syrup.

Daniel and his aunt had been close, and Joyce had
always been kind and welcoming to Leah. So when
Aunt Joyce asked her to help with the fundraiser for the
Mennonite school, Leah was only too happy to pitch
in. When Thomas heard she was going, he offered to
go, too, saying he liked the idea of seeing what her life
had been like as a Mennonite woman. Everyone at the
church had been pleased to have an extra set of hands

and Thomas had immediately been put to work serving the breakfasts with the other men. Always the good sport, he hadn't even complained when Aunt Joyce had tied an oversize white apron around him.

"We're just waiting for the final approval from the court," Aunt Joyce said, continuing with her update on the impending adoption of her foster child, Yasmin. "We applied over a year ago, after she came to live with us, but there's a great-grandmother objecting to the placement. Yasmin lived with her when she was an infant, but the grandmother is elderly and in poor health. Social Services thinks our adoption application will still be approved, but the process is slow."

"The entire church is praying for your family," Gwen said as she sprayed the counter with cleaner. "You can see how happy the child is. When she first came she was so shy and withdrawn she hardly said a word to anyone. Look at her now."

"I'll keep you in my prayers," Leah assured Joyce.

"As you remain in ours." Joyce turned on the mixer. When the contents of the bowl were sufficiently blended, she carried the pancake batter to the stove. "We expect another run soon," she said. "The Janzen family hasn't arrived yet, and they said they were bringing their neighbors."

Leah nodded. "I'll get started on another batch, but we can pop them in the warm oven when they're done. We don't want to serve anyone a cold breakfast." She smiled. "And who knows, the Janzens all might want bacon and eggs instead of pancakes." She used a spatula to remove the pancakes that were done and slid them onto serving-sized plates as Thomas came in through the swinging doors, carrying an empty tray.

"Three more for pancakes," he said.

Leah turned to look at him. His straw hat was pushed up on his forehead, and his name tag hung precariously from one strap of the apron. "Were any of the guests surprised to find their waiter was Amish?" she teased as she dried her hands on her apron and approached him to straighten his name tag.

Thomas shrugged. "If they were, they had the good manners to not say so. Except for one little boy, who asked me if my mama hadn't taught me to take my hat off in the house."

She adjusted his name tag, smiling up at him. "What did you say?"

"What could I say?" Thomas grinned. "I told him that I was carrying food and had to keep my hat on or wear a hairnet."

"Good answer. You can take those." She stepped back, indicating the pancakes she'd just taken off the griddle.

Thomas scooped up the big oval plate that had both blueberry and plain pancakes on it and deposited it on the tray, then reached for a serving plate of bacon. He grinned and winked at her as he hurried back out of the kitchen with the tray. Leah couldn't help chuckling. Some Amish men were uncomfortable with women's work, but not Thomas. She liked that about him; he reminded her of her father, who had not been above grabbing a dishcloth and helping wash dishes after supper.

Leah walked back to the stove and used a ladle to pour more batter onto the hot griddle. As she replaced the bowl on the counter she made eye contact with Aunt Joyce. To her puzzlement, her usually good-natured aunt was frowning. "What's wrong?" Leah asked.

Aunt Joyce shook her head. "Later."

Leah glanced around the kitchen. Everyone was still working steadily. Had she missed something? "Aunt Joyce—"

"Later, dear," Aunt Joyce repeated, and turned her attention to putting away a stack of clean dishes.

The older woman's odd behavior nagged at Leah, though, and when Joyce headed outside to carry scraps of food to the compost bin, Leah followed her. "Aunt Joyce," she said, quickening her step to keep up with the older woman. "Have I said something to upset you?"

Joyce stopped, considered Leah and took a deep breath. "It's simply that… I have to tell you that it pains me to see your behavior with that young man. It's…not appropriate, Leah."

"What behavior's not 'appropriate'?" she asked, trying not to get her feathers ruffled. "What did I do?"

"Making eyes at him, of course. And…touching him. All the flirting. I'm not a prude, Leah. I was young once. But you aren't a girl. You're a widow. In my mind, you shouldn't be putting your hands on a man not your husband. It's not a good example for the younger ones in our congregation. Or in our family. It's clear to me that you're besotted with the boy. The two of you are as giggly with each other as a pair of teenagers."

"I'm sorry," Leah said, crushed at the criticism. "I didn't even realize I'd—" Then she remembered she *had* adjusted Thomas's name tag a few minutes earlier in the kitchen. And when he'd untied her apron strings in fun, their fingers might have caught for just a moment. But nothing had been *inappropriate*. And she'd certainly not been *making eyes* at him. "Aunt Joyce, I'm sorry. I thought you knew that Thomas and I are courting." Courting couples were generally given more lee-way in their behavior because a couple who announces a courtship is announcing their intentions to marry if all goes well.

"Courting, are you?" Joyce sniffed.

Leah softened her tone, wondering if she hadn't been as considerate of Aunt Joyce's feelings as she should have. Maybe it had been a mistake to bring Thomas. "It's been over a year since Daniel died. My family and I agree it's time I marry again. It's what Daniel wanted." She hesitated. "Do you think it's too soon?"

Joyce's brow wrinkled. "Of course not," she answered tersely. "No one expects a widow of your age to remain alone. It wouldn't be natural. But…" She stiffened and walked on purposefully. The church was deeply con-cerned with earth-friendly practices and had installed a series of covered bins along the wall of a storage shed. Food scraps went into a compost bin that was turned regularly to produce clean garden soil. Joyce lifted the lid and deposited the contents of her bucket. "I'm just going to come out and say this, dear. It's fine that you remarry. It's your duty. But it isn't…it just isn't respect-ful to Daniel to take up with someone like Thomas."

"'Someone like Thomas'?" Leah repeated, having no idea what she meant.

"I have nothing against Thomas," Joyce said with a sharp nod of her chin. "He's quite likable, in fact. Witty. A handsome face. So full of life." She leaned closer. "Which makes him totally unsuitable," she said, low-ering her voice, "for a second marriage."

"What do you mean?"

"I mean there's nothing wrong with following one's heart's desires, a *body's inclinations*, the first time around. But out of respect for your deceased husband and for his family," she said pointedly, "you need someone more appropriate. A woman in your position doesn't marry for love."

"I'm not in love with Thomas," Leah argued. "This is an arrangement made by a matchmaker."

"You should come to supper tomorrow night," Joyce went on, not seeming to have heard her. "There's someone I want you to meet, a member of our church. Eldon Goosen. He's older, a widower with children who need a mother, and he's asked about you. He thinks you seem like a good worker. Eldon's going to Poland to take up a mission in July or August. Plenty of time for the two of you to become acquainted. And an excellent second marriage for both of you."

Leah took a step back, feeling a little numb. What would make Aunt Joyce think she was in love with Thomas? "A Mennonite man won't do. I've decided to become Amish again. It's important to my family and to me. I've already started my classes. I'll be baptized in late summer."

Aunt Joyce frowned. "Fine. Then surely there's an appropriate Amish widower looking for someone to cook and clean for him. Someone with a readymade family. It's best you leave young men like Thomas to women who've not yet had a husband."

Leah glanced down at the grass, not sure how to respond to that. "I... I'd better get back to making pancakes." She turned away. "We wouldn't want anyone waiting too long."

"Just think on what I've said, Leah," Joyce called after her.

All Leah could do was nod and hurry away.

* * *

A few nights later, Thomas stopped by Sara's after dinner. Leah and Sara were sitting on the porch with Hiram, Sara's hired man, Ellie and Florence, a young woman from New York State who'd come to Delaware to be married.

Leah got to her feet as Thomas came up the steps. Ever since her conversation with Daniel's aunt, she'd been feeling out of sorts. Not with Thomas, but with herself, though why, she wasn't quite sure. "Ellie just made lemonade," she said. "Would you like some? Or a slice of chocolate pie?"

"The pie sounds good." Thomas nodded a greeting to Sara and the others. "But it's such a nice evening. I was hoping you might like to take a walk with me." He glanced at Sara. "Maybe I could have that slice of pie when we get back."

"If Hiram doesn't get to it first." Sara stroked the gray cat curled in her lap.

Hiram's face reddened and he ducked his head. "A man can't help it if you make a good pie. A man can't help it if he likes good pie."

"Would you listen to that?" Sara teased. "Hiram just said more than ten words in one stretch. Better keep an eye on the weather, Thomas. It might just snow."

"Needn't take on so," Hiram muttered. "I'm a man of few words, unlike some around here." He threw a look Thomas's way.

Thomas chuckled. "True enough, Hiram." He glanced at Leah. "What do you say? Do you feel like a walk?"

"Sure," Leah agreed.

Thomas looked back at Sara. "You're welcome to come along," he offered. "If you'd like to chaperone."

Sara shook her head. "I've been on these feet too long today." She wiggled her bare toes. "I'm content to sit right here, enjoy this lemonade and tease Hiram. You two go on and enjoy yourselves. But behave. I've got my eye on you, Thomas. You know I do."

Leah followed Thomas off the porch and into the yard. "Where did you want to walk?"

What Daniel's aunt had said at the pancake breakfast had troubled her, but she hadn't mentioned the conversation to Thomas. It seemed disloyal to tell him that Joyce was trying to match her with a Mennonite widower. She wouldn't want Thomas to think that she'd consider it. But Joyce's words lingered in the back of her mind and nagged at her until seeds of doubt sprouted. Joyce's suggestion that Leah was marrying Thomas because she had fallen in love with him was ridiculous. As ridiculous as her insinuation that Leah was stealing a young, good-looking man from younger girls better deserving.

Leah matched her pace with Thomas's and they walked without speaking through the late shadows of the day out of the farmyard and down the back lane. The weather was perfect with just a slight breeze that kept the mosquitoes away. They passed through a gate and strolled across the back pasture where the mules grazed in the light of the setting sun, and on to the edge of the wood line, where Thomas stopped her with a quick gesture. Leah stood absolutely still and watched in delight as a wild turkey hen strolled out of the trees, followed by a line of babies. The turkey poults were about the size of doves, miniatures of their mother and so cute. They trailed the mother in perfect formation, one after another, staring around with bright eyes and imitating her as she pecked at the ground.

After a few minutes of watching the birds, Thomas abruptly clapped his hands together. At the sound, the turkeys flew up, exploding up in a flurry of feathers and long necks, and then flapped and darted into the woods.

"*Ach*! Why did you frighten them away?" Leah asked.

"I didn't want the little ones to become too accustomed to us. If they're not afraid of people, they'll end up on someone's table." He shrugged. "I warn you, I'm not much of a hunter."

She smiled at him. "I'm glad. I always felt sorry for the animals that the St. Joes hunted in the jungle. Monkeys, sloths, turtles. I didn't blame them because I knew they needed meat to feed their families, but it made me sad to see them come home with dead creatures hanging from poles."

"You have a gentle heart, Leah."

"Or a foolish one. I grew up on a farm. I know where hamburger and fried chicken comes from. But I still hate to see wild things killed." She peered into the woods, half-expecting to see the bright flash of parrot feathers or hear the haunting cry of a jaguar. But the jungle was faraway. And so were the graves she'd left there. She turned back into the light. "I'm glad we saw the turkeys," she said. "I think they're beautiful."

"*Ya*, I think so, too." He smiled, turning to face her. "You don't see them often." He gazed into her eyes. "But that's not all that's pretty out here."

She looked away, her cheeks warm, but she didn't protest when Thomas took her hand and kissed the back of it. "I'll take care of you, you know," he said quietly. He raised her hand to his face and pressed it against his chin.

Leah shivered as she felt the prickle of a new growth of beard. Thomas had shaved that morning. She knew because he shaved every morning, but his dark hair and beard grew quickly. Once they were married, it would be easy for him to grow a full beard. She thought it would make him even more handsome.

"I want you to know that," he continued. "You'll never go hungry or lack a roof over your head. I'll work hard, you can count on it." He unfolded her hand and ran fingertips over her palm. "I love your hands," he confided. "Such small hands, but so strong and graceful."

Leah felt herself blush. She pulled her hand free, conscious of the nails broken by gardening and the one thumbnail she'd bitten to the quick. "You're sweet to say so," she managed, "but my hands are a mess." English girls, she knew, often had their nails polished, but she was content when hers were clean and sensibly shaped. She rubbed lotion into her hands every night after her bath, but canning, housework and outside chores often left them callused and reddened.

"I think your hands are beautiful," Thomas insisted. "And not just your hands. All of you. I always thought you were the prettiest girl I'd ever known."

"Stop." She looked at the grass at their feet. "You're embarrassing me. You shouldn't say such things. You'll make me vain."

"*Ne*, Leah. Not you. I wanted you to know…that I think so. That you're beautiful. And good. And I want you to know how much I care for you, because…" He lowered his gaze. "Because we haven't talked about our feelings…for each other."

She didn't know what to say. She didn't want to talk about her feelings for Thomas because she was so confused. Her plan had been a good one: a matchmaker, a marriage of convenience. What she hadn't planned on was this man she'd known her whole life who'd brought laughter into her heart again.

He leaned down and picked a tiny bouquet of wild violets from the moss at the edge of the trees and pressed it into her hand. "I'll plant flowers in my garden just for you. Would you like that?"

"I would," she admitted. "I love flowers." She raised the violets to her nose and sniffed the sweetness, thinking they should start back.

"You know," Thomas ventured, looking down at her. "I almost think I should do what Sara told me not to."

"What's that?" She looked up at him and, before she realized what he was about to do, before she could react, he leaned close.

His lips brushed hers, resting there for just a few seconds, caressing and tender. For an instant, it felt strange. No man had ever kissed her before, except for Daniel. She wanted to pull away, to tell him no, but the warmth and the sweet touch of his mouth was more than she could resist.

It was Thomas who released her and stepped back. Which was a good thing because she didn't know if she'd have had the strength to do it. She felt breathless, and her knees were unsteady.

"That was nice."

She touched her lips with a fingertip and smiled at him. "Too nice," she murmured, taking a step back and then another. She had known the kissing would come. Certainly in their marriage bed, but it hadn't occurred to her that she would like it so much. Suddenly the world felt off-kilter and she could barely find her voice. "I think we better go back."

Thomas chuckled. "*Ya*, we better." He took her hand and she let him, and they started back the way they'd come. "But I've been wanting to talk to you about something."

"Okay," Leah heard herself say.

"It's about my baptism classes. My joining the church."

She looked up at him, trying to move past the kiss. Talking was better. "You said they were going well."

"They are. I just… I've been wondering about something, Leah."

She stopped to give him her full attention. "What's that?"

"Well, I wondered if maybe we're going about this all wrong. Maybe this isn't what we were meant to do."

"I don't understand."

"I'm talking about both of us being baptized in the Amish church. Maybe…" He seemed to be struggling to find the right words. "Leah, do you think you should consider staying Mennonite and I should join the Mennonite church?"

She stared at him, thinking she must have misheard. "You want to become Mennonite?"

"I don't know. That's what I'm saying. Do we need to rethink this? If I became Mennonite, we could keep the car or even buy a truck for the deliveries. I assumed you would become Amish to marry me, but what's to say I shouldn't join your faith instead of you having to change yours for me?" He gazed earnestly into her eyes. "What do you think, Leah?"

Chapter Twelve

Leah stepped back and stared at him with a horrified expression. "You want to abandon your faith?"

"I didn't say that," Thomas protested. "I've just been thinking and I wondered if it was fair to you to—"

"You *knew* that I wanted to become Amish again," Leah interrupted, the anger in her tone startling him. "It's why I came to Sara for a husband." She threw up her arms. "I don't believe this. Why do you think I'm going to baptismal classes?"

Thomas stood there for a moment, stunned. Had he known she was going to react this strongly, he'd have never brought it up. It was just that everyone was encouraging him to talk with Leah about things. "I'm not saying it's what we *have* to do," he defended. "I just... I thought we should talk about it. Sara said it's important for couples to—it was just something I thought about and wanted to—" And again, before he could finish what he was trying to say, she lashed back at him.

"*Ne.* I don't want to hear any more." She held up her hand. "It's not what I want. It's not what I agreed to. I won't agree to it. I won't marry you." She folded her arms and stared at him with brimming eyes.

Remorse swept over him, making his gut clench. "Don't say that, Leah. I love you. I want you to be my wife. I'll do whatever you—"

"*Ne*. No more." She whirled around and walked away from him, then stopped and glanced back. "You would give up our whole way of life for the sake of a car?" Her lips puckered as if she'd tasted something bitter. "Being able to drive means more to you than sitting in worship with our families? Than raising children in our fathers' faith?"

He could feel his own temper rising. She was being unfair. That wasn't what he'd said. It certainly wasn't what he'd meant. He was thinking of her more than anything. And he hadn't said he wanted to become Mennonite—he'd only said the idea had crossed his mind. Why was she acting like this? He had just wanted to talk this thing out with her. "There's no need to over-react. I was just asking."

"Don't tell me how I should feel, Thomas!" She shook her head adamantly.

"I think we both need to cool down and discuss this calmly," he said, walking toward her.

"What is there to talk about? I know what I want. And clearly, you don't. So this is not going to work. I won't marry you, Thomas. I thought we…" She shook her head again. "It doesn't matter. We obviously don't want the same things in life."

"You're behaving irrationally, Leah. You don't walk away from what we've found together because we've had a disagreement." He gestured with one hand. "This isn't even a disagreement. I just wanted to talk it over with you."

She continued to shake her head. "I'm sorry, but it's over between us. Find someone else, a girl who wants motor cars and electricity. I'm not that woman."

Leah raised her foot from the pedal of her mother's old Singer sewing machine and glanced up from the seam she was finishing. "This is good material," she said to her mother. "It's been so long since I've worked with anything this nice. At the mission, I had to put in a request for cloth and hope that I got something close to what I needed." She'd left her own sewing machine behind when she'd returned to the United States. The family that replaced her would have a greater need than she would.

"I'm glad you like the ticking," her mother said. "It's so nice to have all of you girls here and working together on the pillows. Just like old times."

"It is, isn't it?" Leah agreed. When Rebecca had stopped by Sara's that morning to ask her to come, Leah had been thankful for the invitation. She'd always liked making pillows. Hannah was one of the few women who still made them the old-fashioned way. All year, she and Johanna saved down from their geese for stuffing. It took a lot of work, but the resulting pillows would last for years. Best of all, it was a great excuse to get together with her sisters and mother, to laugh and share the latest family news.

It was just what she needed after the awful breakup with Thomas earlier in the week...the breakup she still hadn't told anyone about.

She just hadn't been ready to answer the questions

she would be asked. She had no right to repeat Thomas's doubts about remaining in the faith. That was private and personal, not something to be discussed by the community until he made a final decision. But she was glad he'd come to her when he did because there was no need to drag out their courtship if it wasn't going anywhere.

Maybe her dreams of remarrying were just that. Dreams. Maybe she wasn't meant to find happiness in another marriage, or to be a mother again. She had other options. She knew that she could find a home with *Mam* or any of her sisters. Someone would have to care for Susanna and David when her mother and Albert grew older. Could it be that God meant for her to spend her life caring for her little sister and helping her family? She could still return to the church, still be with those she loved.

She sighed and returned to the seam she'd been reinforcing on the pillow casing. The dull ache that had haunted her since her confrontation with Thomas threatened to ruin the day. Just as it had ruined the previous day.

And the one before.

She steeled herself to not allow her regrets to drag her down. She could withstand this disappointment. Prayer and faith would carry her until the pain of losing Thomas faded.

A flash of blue and flying pigtails caught her attention, yanking her from her thoughts. Anna's small daughter Rose darted across the sewing room and thrust chubby hands into the basket containing the goose down.

Giggling, she seized handfuls of down feathers and

tossed them into the air. "Snow!" she shrieked in *Deitsch*. "Snow!"

"*Leibchen*, how did you get in here?" Anna laughed as she laid down the embroidered pillowcase she was hemming and scooped up her little daughter. "Ruth, can you come get this escapee?"

Leah's throat constricted at the sight of her sister and child. So beautiful, she thought. Did Anna have any notion of how fortunate she was? Goose down settled on the child's butter-yellow hair and clung to her blue dress, a perfect copy of the one Anna wore, complete with white apron. Anna had braided Rose's hair into two tiny plaits secured by ties of white ribbon, plaits that stuck out on either side of her perfectly shaped head.

Hannah laughed. "She loves to be in the center of the action, don't you, pumpkin? Give her to me, Anna. *Grossmama* will tend to her."

Anna passed her daughter over and Hannah took a clump of down out of the child's hair and tickled her nose with it. Rose giggled and patted Hannah's cheeks.

"Thirsty," Rose said. "Want milk."

"Do you?" Hannah asked. "How about if you come down to the kitchen with me and we'll fix a snack for you and your cousins?"

Rose's head bobbed in agreement. *"Ya."*

"Goot," Anna said. "You go and help *Grossmama*. And stay downstairs. I don't know how you got away from your aunt Ruth."

Susanna and Ruth had taken the children into the front room, where they were playing with an assortment of wooden blocks and farm animals that Albert had carved for them. Usually Rose was quite happy bossing Ruth's twin boys around and feeding cookies to Miriam's little son or rocking one of the babies, but she had an independent streak and was as mischievous as Rebecca had been as a child. No stranger, looking at those innocent blue eyes, red cheeks and sweet lips, would suspect Rose of being the ringleader of her nephews' troublemaking.

"You think I'm joking," Anna said to Leah when their mother had led Rose out of the sewing room. "She's a handful. Mashed potatoes in her father's work boots, kittens in the bread box and coloring all over her father's latest copy of *The Budget*. And that's just since the Sabbath."

"But she has a good heart," Rebecca defended. "No one could be more gentle with the babies. And she can't stand to see the boys squabbling. She never cries if she falls and skins her knee, but she wept a bucket of tears over one of the chicks that died hatching out of its egg."

"Samuel would spoil her rotten, if I let him. And the older children give in to her. It was one thing when she was a baby," Anna said, taking up her needle again and searching for a spool of thread, "but I'll do her no favors if I let her do as she pleases."

Leah smoothed out the pillow casing and examined the double line of stitching. "I still can't get used to hearing *Mam* refer to herself as *Grossmama*. I keep thinking that she's talking about *Dat's* mother."

Anna nodded. "I would have liked to bring her with me today. I think she would have enjoyed being with us. But she's failing. The doctor says her heart is weak. She sleeps a lot."

"I'll come to see her tomorrow," Leah promised. She felt guilty. She hadn't spent much time with *Grossmama* since she'd come home. "*Mam* said that she'd gotten very quiet, but I didn't realize that she had serious health problems."

"Other than her wandering mind, you mean?" Rebecca put in. "I don't think she knows who Anna is anymore. She's always calling her Hannah."

Leah grimaced. "Is she cross with you?" she asked Anna. She and their *mam* never got along very well.

Anna shook her head. "*Ne.* I think she lives in her own world most of the time. She likes to sit and rock in that big chair by the window. Sometimes she hums hymns, but mostly she sleeps. I don't think we'll have her with us long."

"She hasn't gone to the Senior Center in months," Rebecca said. "She used to teach other women how to make rugs, but she's not able to do that anymore. She wants her sewing bag beside her chair, but she doesn't open it. It makes me sad. I think I'd rather have her fussing at us."

"The Lord will take her in His own time," Anna said. "Samuel has talked about bringing one of his cousin's daughters here to help me if *Grossmama* can't get to the bathroom on her own. He's so good with her." Anna smiled. "She thinks he is our father, and Samuel doesn't tell her different. He can coax her to eat when none of us can. I was truly blessed to find such a husband."

"*Ya,*" Rebecca agreed. "Samuel is the best of men." She stuffed another handful of down into a bulging pillow casing. "Best of all, he cherishes you, Anna."

Anna's full cheeks flushed a deeper red. "Such things you say."

"It's true, everyone knows it," Rebecca insisted. "And it's no more than you deserve."

Leah took another length of material and began on

a new pillowcase. From downstairs came the sounds of children's high-pitched voices and her mother's laughter. She was so glad that she'd come today. Being in her mother's house, in the place where she'd grown up, in the bosom of her family, was just what she needed.

"Can I ask you something?" she said, looking at Anna.

Her older sister smiled. "You know you can ask me anything."

"When you and Samuel married, were you sure he was the one God intended for you?" Leah folded the casing and averted her gaze.

Anna gave a hearty laugh. "Absolutely. I couldn't believe that a man like Samuel would care for me."

"But why not?" Leah asked. True, Anna was a big woman, round and healthy and plain as rye bread. But her heart was the most generous of any of her sisters, and she was as good a cook, mother and homemaker as their mother. "Why wouldn't Samuel love you?"

Anna's cheeks reddened and her round face creased into a bashful grin. "Oh, my little sister, that you should ask. I was a fat girl with a face like a pudding. *Ne*, don't try to argue. No one ever called me pretty, and with good reason. But God was good and he sent me a wonderful husband and children to love. And I know that He will do the same for you. I know that you and Thomas will—"

"I don't want to talk about Thomas," Leah said, looking down.

"But we have to," Rebecca said. "At least we have to talk about your wedding. Have you picked a date?"

Leah shook her head, afraid to look up at her sisters

for fear she would start to cry. "I've need to tell you… Thomas and I have—"

A giggle came from the doorway. "Leah loves Thomas." Susanna walked into the room with a plate of whoopie pies. "Chocolate." Obviously, Susanna had already tasted the oversize cookies because she had crumbs on the front of her dress and at the corners of her mouth. She giggled again. "Leah and Thomas getting married. Like me and King David."

Leah's throat tightened and her eyes welled with tears. "*Ne.* We're not."

"Not what?" Rebecca asked.

"Not…getting…married," Leah managed to say between sobs. She jumped up, letting the ticking material fall to the floor unheeded. Clapping her hands over her face, she ran from the room and down the hall to her old bedroom. She dashed inside, slamming the door behind her and threw herself on the double bed. She pulled a pillow over her head to muffle her weeping, but it did no good.

All three of her sisters followed her into the bedroom. Susanna, who could never stand to see anyone cry, began to wail herself. Rebecca tried to comfort Susanna while Anna sat on the bed beside Leah and pulled her into her arms.

"Leah, Leah, what is it?" Anna asked. "What's wrong?"

"Nothing," Leah sobbed.

"Something certainly is wrong," Anna said.

Susanna dissolved into tears again. "Don't…don't cry, Leah."

Leah sat up and wiped her eyes. "I'm sorry." Anna's arms were strong and warm, and she leaned against her sister. "Thomas and… I…we…"

"You argued. It happens." Rebecca sat on the other side of the bed. "What did you quarrel about?"

"It doesn't matter," Leah said. "I can't marry him. We broke up."

"Have you told *Mam*?" Anna asked her. "You have to tell *Mam*."

"*Ne*. I can't." Leah sniffed. "I don't want to."

Rebecca stroked her arm. "All couples have spats," she said. "You can talk it out. In a day or two, this will be behind you."

"It won't," Leah said, fresh tears welling in her eyes. "It's over. I can't explain. But neither can I be his wife. Not now, not ever."

"Whoa, whoa." Thomas took a firm grip on the halter and soothed the nervous bay horse. "Easy, boy. This won't hurt." The gelding rolled his eyes. He laid his ears back and shifted his weight from one leg to another. "Careful," Thomas warned Jakob. "He might kick."

"Not if I can get this leg up, he won't," the little man answered.

Smoke rose from the forge, curling up to lie thick beneath the roof of the smithy. It was raining out and they'd had to bring the horse inside to shoe him. The confines of the building made it all the more important that they keep the animal under control. Had it been up to Thomas, they would have taken him across the yard to the barn and done the work in a stall, but Jakob assured him that they could manage here.

"The horse will be fine," Jakob said. "He just likes to act up a little to show us who's boss. Once we convince him otherwise, he'll calm down."

"I could blindfold him," Thomas offered. It was an

old trick of his grandfather's for dealing with skittish animals.

"*Ne*, no need." Jakob stroked the horse's rump and spoke to the animal in a soft, singsong voice. He ran his hands down the gelding's hip and leg, then pressed his weight against the horse as he lifted the back hoof. The horse gave a nervous snort, caught its balance on three legs and stood still. "See, what did I tell you?" Jakob said. He pried away the old shoe and cast it aside. With a curved knife, he trimmed the hoof, traded that tool for a pick and cleaned the hoof.

Thomas scratched under the horse's chin. "Good boy," he repeated. The animal's nostrils flared and he trembled, but he didn't make any attempt to break free.

"I took the wagon down to the chair shop to pick up a chest of drawers for your grandmother," Jakob said. "And who do you suppose was there to use the telephone?"

Thomas sighed. "I can guess."

"That pretty little schoolteacher, that's who." Jakob fitted the new shoe against the hoof. "She pretended not to see me, but I know better. I offered to give her a ride home in the wagon."

"And what did she say to that?"

Jakob laughed. "She likes me. I can tell. But she's a lot like this horse. Trying to bluff me. You were right. She's tough. But she'll come around."

"You think so, do you?" Thomas chuckled.

"Why wouldn't she? Now that you're getting hitched, how many handsome, charming single men are there left in Seven Poplars?"

"Including yourself in that group, are you?"

"Truth's truth, Thomas. I'm a catch, if I do say so

myself. I'll make a fine husband. And I've decided that Ellie's the one."

"Not doing too good so far, are you?"

"No need to be negative," Jakob said, driving the first nail into the horse's hoof. "The Lord helps those who help themselves. I've got plans."

"I can't wait to hear them."

"You and Leah are getting married. Between you, you're related to most of the people in the county. It will be a big wedding and you'll need lots of attendants. I'd like to offer my services to be one. Since Leah and Ellie are friends, Leah is bound to ask her. I'll arrange to have us paired off together for the work and later, sitting together at the wedding dinner." Jakob grinned. "Nothing like a wedding to make a young woman inclined to think of love."

"Just one problem with your plan," Thomas said, rubbing the gelding's nose. His voice sounded strange in his own ears. "Leah and I aren't getting married."

"What happened? Don't tell me you're getting cold feet? You can't stay a bachelor forever, you know. Leah's perfect for you."

"*Ne*, apparently not. She was the one who broke it off with me."

Jakob's voice tightened. "You didn't get fresh with her, did you?"

"Of course not," Thomas said. "Who do you think I am?"

"A fool if you don't marry her."

"I'm telling you. She won't have me."

"Why not? What happened?"

Thomas shook his head. "I don't really know. I... I was trying to talk to her about something. You know...

kind of wanting to think something through out loud and she just…she got really angry with me. Flew right off the handle, which isn't like her." He glanced at Jakob. "Not like her at all," he repeated, as much to himself as to Jakob.

"You can't let your courtship end like that," Jakob said. "You've got to talk it out. Be sure the argument is about what you thought it was about."

"What?" Thomas said, pushing his hat back off his head.

"Be sure she's mad about what you think she's mad about. Women can be funny like that sometimes. They're complicated. You think she's upset about one thing when she's upset about another. You said yourself that her reaction didn't make sense. Talk to her."

"I don't know," Thomas hemmed. "I'm not sure she will even talk to me."

"Don't give up, I'm telling you. Don't take no for an answer," Jakob insisted. "You have to patch this up and go on with the wedding. You'll never be happy if you lose her, and I'd have to come up with a whole new plan to charm that little schoolteacher."

Chapter Thirteen

Leah, Sara and Ellie were clearing away the noon meal when Thomas drove his horse and open buggy into the yard. Hiram's dog barked, and Leah turned away from the window, her heart suddenly thudding in her chest. "It's Thomas," she said. "I don't want to see him."

"Don't want to see him?" Ellie repeated. "Have you two had a fight? I knew something was wrong." She cast a knowing look at Sara. "Didn't I tell you? Leah's been moping around for days."

Hiram jumped up from the table where he'd been finishing a second cup of coffee. "I got chores to do." Grabbing his hat from a hook on the wall, he hurried outside.

Leah put the dishes she'd carried from the table into the sink and untied her apron before turning to Sara. "I was waiting for a chance to tell you." She didn't make eye contact. "We've broken off the courtship. I can't marry Thomas."

Sara uttered a sound of exasperation. "If this is serious, you should have come to me. Why didn't you?"

"You aren't my mother," Leah said.

"No." Sara's mouth pursed in barely concealed pique.

"I'm your matchmaker. You hired me to find the right husband for you. And if there is a problem—"

"I'm an adult. I don't have to explain to someone else why—" Leah broke off, suddenly mortified by the realization of how rude she sounded. "I'm sorry, Sara," she said, suddenly close to tears. "It's just that the reason we can't… It's personal. I didn't feel free to discuss it with anyone." She glanced out the window again. "He's coming. I can't talk to him." Running away might make her appear to be a foolish child, but she couldn't face him. "Please, Sara, I just can't—"

"Stuff and nonsense. Of course you'll speak to him. Whatever went wrong, we'll get to the bottom of it. Unless—" Sara's dark eyes narrowed. "Thomas didn't behave in—"

"*Ne*, nothing like that." Leah felt her cheeks grow hot with embarrassment. "Thomas would never attempt anything that would damage my honor—or his. He's a good man, the best, but—" She made a sound of distress. She didn't want to talk about this. She didn't want to think about it. "It's not Thomas that's the problem, Sara—it's me."

The screen door squeaked and Leah heard Thomas's footsteps on the porch.

"I've got mending to do," Ellie proclaimed before darting out of the kitchen.

Sara looked at Leah directly. "Sit down. Running away isn't the answer."

Leah felt light-headed. "I don't want to talk to him. There's nothing to say."

"Courtship is serious. You have every right to break it off. And so does Thomas," Sara said. "But there's a proper way to do it."

Leah slid into a kitchen chair. She had considered fleeing anyway, but she wasn't certain her legs would carry her. She wanted to cry. She felt so bad. Breaking up with Thomas had been the right thing to do. He deserved better. She just wasn't sure she could face him without bursting into tears again. This never would have happened if Sara had matched her with a settled older widower like she'd asked.

Leah heard footsteps and then Thomas's tall frame filled the doorway. He snatched off his hat, gripping it so hard between his fingers that it crumpled. "Leah. We have to talk." His dark eyes were bloodshot, as if he hadn't slept. She could well understand that. She couldn't sleep, either. She felt sick.

"Sit down, Thomas." Sara rescued his hat and pushed a cup of coffee into his hands.

"Give me another chance," he said, staring at Leah. "I love you, Leah. I'll do whatever you want."

"Sit!" Sara pointed to a chair across from her. "Look at the two of you. Miserable as hens in a puddle. Long faces. And all because of a silly quarrel."

Thomas sat down hard. Leah felt his gaze on her, and she looked away and then down at her hands in her lap. Looking at him made it even harder to explain how she felt. She sat, hands laced together, knees trembling.

"I want to talk," he said. "That's all I was trying to do, to talk something out, but Leah thought I meant I'd made a decision and—"

"I overreacted," Leah blurted. "I did. But that's because…" She exhaled. "I can't marry Thomas. I just can't. I'm sorry I let it get this far. It was a mistake. I know that now."

"Leah, please," Thomas said. "You can't just walk

away from me. What we have…what we've done together means something. Whatever is wrong, we can fix it. I don't understand—"

"Exactly," she burst out. "You couldn't." She glanced at Sara, saw the disappointment and impatience in her eyes and found the strength to rise to her feet. "I respect you, Sara. You've been good to me, and I know you mean well, but I'm not right for Thomas and there's no sense in us talking about this. Find someone else for him. He deserves a good wife. It just can't be me."

With that, she walked away from him, out of the kitchen, and ran up the stairs to her bedroom. She closed the door behind her and went to the window, fighting tears. She leaned her face against the windowpane as waves of emotion surged through her. The sense of loss she'd felt when Daniel had died returned in full. "Help me," she prayed. "Please show me the way I should go."

Downstairs, Thomas looked at Sara. "What do I do now?" he asked. He got to his feet. "How do I fix this between us if I don't know what's wrong? If she won't even talk to me?" He shook his head. "The whole conversation was about whether or not we should consider being Mennonite instead of Amish. I never said that was what I wanted. I just wanted to talk to her about it. I wouldn't have brought it up if I'd known this would happen."

"I see." Sara nodded. "All right. So, in your heart of hearts, what would you rather do with your life? Would you rather remain in the Amish church or become Mennonite?"

"Amish. If it were my choice alone, there would be no question. I was only thinking of Leah and what she would have to give up." He gripped the back of a chair with one hand. "She's right. I don't understand." He scowled. "Was it so wrong of me to bring the question up to her?"

Sara scoffed. "Of course not. It's what couples do, certainly what married people should do. But I don't know that this is about religion. I think it could be about something more."

"That's what Jakob said." Thomas hung his head. "He said sometimes you think a woman is upset about one thing, when really it's about something else."

"Sounds likes Jakob knows something about women. At least relationships." She considered and then went on. "Go home and come back tomorrow. Leah may be willing to talk to you when she's calmed down."

"And if she doesn't?" he asked.

"I can't make her marry you, Thomas. If you love her, if you truly believe that she is the one the Lord wants for you, then you have to have patience. You know that our Leah is headstrong. She likes to do things her way." A hint of a smile played over her lips. "Not unlike you, Thomas. But I think we can bring her around and get her past whatever made her react so badly to your attempt to talk to her about the Mennonite church." Her smile became a full one. "It wouldn't hurt to pray, not for what you want, but for what He thinks is best."

Thomas nodded and turned away. "I'm not going to give up on her," he said, feeling a little better with Sara's encouragement. Because he really did believe God meant Leah to be his wife. "Whatever I've done wrong, however I've hurt her, I'll make it right."

He carried that hope home with him and all the following day until he finished his work in the garden and returned to Sara's house. But there, standing on the front porch, once again, he was disappointed. "Leah still won't see me?" he asked Ellie.

"She isn't here. She went out after breakfast, and we haven't seen her all day."

Thomas stood there, feeling awkward, unsure what to do next. He wondered if he should try to find Leah, go from one sister's house to another asking for her. Anything was better than doing nothing.

"Thomas. I've been waiting for you." Sara came out of the house, dressed in her best church bonnet and black dress and cape. "Good, you came with your horse and buggy?"

"Ya."

Ellie stepped into the house.

"I have an idea, but I can't do this on my own. I want you to drive me to Bishop Atlee's house. But first we have to stop and pick up Hannah."

"Why are we going to see the bishop? Is Leah at Hannah's?"

"Grace picked her up this morning on her way to the veterinarian clinic. But I doubt she took Leah to work with her. She's probably at Anna's or maybe Rebecca's. But before we can approach Leah, we have to get the bishop's approval. And her mother's." She took a deep breath. "Well, Thomas, what are you waiting for? Bring the horse around. We want to catch Bishop Atlee before he retires for his evening prayers."

Thomas held the door open for her. "I'll take you wherever you want to go, but why won't you tell me what you're planning to do? Surely, you aren't going to ask Bishop Atlee to try and convince her to marry me?"

"No sense in explaining my plan over and over,"

Sara said. "You'll find out soon enough." She folded her arms and regarded him sternly. "Now, are you in or not? Because if you've changed your mind about wanting to make Leah your wife, then this is a waste of time."

"Ne," he stammered. *"Ne.* You know I do."

Ellie came out of the house wearing her own black bonnet and dress cape. "Wait for me," she called.

"You're coming, too?" Thomas asked.

"Wouldn't miss it," Ellie said as she scrambled up into Thomas's buggy. "When Sara gets an idea, it will be too good to hear about secondhand." She looked at the dashboard. "I just hope you don't intend to turn on all these flashing blue lights tonight. It may not put the bishop in the best frame of mind to listen to what Sara has to say."

"Bishop Atlee has company," his wife said when Thomas knocked at his screen door. "But I'm sure he won't mind if all of you come in." She pushed open the door and welcomed them into her cheery kitchen.

Thomas waited for Sara, Hannah and Ellie to go first, then he entered, followed by gangly Irwin and his dog Jeremiah. Hannah had been just as puzzled and intrigued by Sara's invitation as Thomas had been. He hadn't expected Hannah's teenage foster son Irwin to climb into the buggy, as well.

"Ne." The bishop's wife pointed to the dog and shook her head. "Dogs stay outside."

Irwin, who'd been in the process of removing his straw hat, stopped short. "Jeremiah can't come in?"

"Your dog can stay on the porch," the woman said. "I'll even give him a nice bone I have left from our roast. But in my house, *ne*. Let me see how long he'll be." She held up one finger and disappeared down the hall. A moment later she was back. "Go on through. You know the way. My Atlee will be pleased to see you."

"If he has someone here, we can wait," Hannah offered.

"Atlee says you're to join him in the parlor," the bishop's wife insisted, stepping back to let them pass.

Irwin's plain face fell. "Guess I'll stay out here on the porch with Jeremiah," he said.

"Maybe I can find you an apple dumpling and a glass of milk," their hostess offered. "Growing boys are always hungry."

"Ya." Irwin nodded. *"Goot.* I like apple dumplings."

Thomas followed the women into the front room and was surprised to see Leah there ahead of him. "Leah?"

She rose from the bench where she'd been sitting across from the bishop. "Thomas?" Her cheeks reddened and she averted her eyes. "I didn't expect…" She glanced back at the church leader. "How did he know I was here?"

"We didn't," Sara said. "But it's best that you are. This will make my task easier." She nodded to the bishop. "Bishop Atlee." The others exchanged greetings.

"What a nice surprise." Atlee Borntrager chuckled and extended his arms. "Sit, sit, all of you. I'm very glad to have you in my home." He slid his thumbs under his suspenders. "First comes our Leah and now her young man, Thomas, with mother, friend and matchmaker. Mother!" he called to his wife. "Bring something cold to drink for our guests."

"I'll help her with the glasses," Ellie offered, slipping back out of the room.

Hannah and Sara settled themselves on a sofa that

had seen better days. Thomas took a straight-backed wooden chair. He kept glancing at Leah, hoping she would favor him with a smile, but she didn't. She remained cool and formal.

"I'll get right to it, Bishop," Sara said. "As you know, these two, Leah and Thomas, have been walking out together."

He nodded and tugged unconsciously at his gray beard. "It's no news to me, Sara Yoder." He chuckled. "They're both taking my baptismal classes. Have you come to discuss the wedding plans?" he asked Thomas.

"Ne," Leah said. "There isn't going to be a wedding. Not between me and Thomas."

The older man looked at Leah thoughtfully. "Which is why you came to me, I suppose?"

She nodded.

"I think they've had a serious disagreement," Hannah explained. "We'd like to take every opportunity to help them work it out."

"Mam." Leah's eyes widened. "This is my affair. You shouldn't be involved."

"Why shouldn't I?" Hannah asked. "Who cares for you more than I do? I want you to be happy, with or without Thomas."

"Without," Leah said. "Definitely without."

"Is this a spiritual matter?" the bishop asked. "Something that I can be of help with?"

"What the two of them have is a lack of communication," Sara said. "And *ya*, you can be of help. I've thought of a way that would improve their communication, but it will require your approval."

"I'm all ears," Bishop Atlee replied. He snapped one suspender against his dark blue shirt and crossed his ankles. Thomas noticed that he was in stockinged feet. One white sock had a neatly stitched patch on the heel.

The bishop's wife returned with tall glasses of home-made root beer. Ellie came after her carrying a plate of oatmeal cookies.

"What none of you seem to understand is that I can't marry Thomas," Leah said. "He's a good man. He'll make some woman a fine husband, but it can't be me. So there's no need for us to have better communication. Any communication."

"Did I tell you?" Hannah fussed. "Stubborn like her father. Always wanting to prove that she's right and everyone else is wrong."

Leah looked at Thomas. "I can't believe that you'd go along with this. You should know that what's between us is personal."

Bishop Atlee took a deep drink of his root beer and then set the mug down on the table beside his chair. "I, for one, would like to hear what Sara has to say. She's had a lot of experience in arranging marriages. And since we're all already here, I think we ought to listen to her."

"So do I," his wife agreed. "I think young couples are wise to listen to older heads. Marriage is a serious decision, not to be taken lightly." She squeezed in on the sofa beside Hannah. Ellie perched on a stool.

"Leah, Thomas, will you listen to my suggestion?" Sara asked.

Thomas nodded. "I brought you here, didn't I? I'm willing to try anything that will make things the way they were between me and Leah."

Leah twisted her hands in her lap.

She looked small and vulnerable to him. He wanted

to take her in his arms and hold her against him. He wanted to smell the clean fragrance of her hair and feel her warm skin pressed to his. But she no longer wanted him, and he had to sit there, unable to comfort her.

Vaguely, he was aware of Sara saying something, but he was concentrating so hard on Leah that he didn't pay attention until he heard the bishop's wife give a gasp of astonishment.

"…bundling was sometimes used in my community in Wisconsin. The couple—"

"Bundling?" Leah squeaked. "You want me and Thomas to sleep in the same bed?"

That got Thomas's attention.

Sara spread her fingers in a calming motion. "Listen to me before you make up your mind. Bundling has always been a respected tradition among our people. True, you don't hear so much of it today, but it was done for many years in previous generations. Successfully."

"You're suggesting that Leah and Thomas do this?" Hannah asked.

Leah crossed her arms over her chest. "Absolutely not."

Bishop Atlee leaned forward in his chair. "Let's hear her out, Leah. I've heard that this is done in parts of Kentucky in some conservative communities. The bundling is well chaperoned, isn't it?"

"Usually by the girl's mother," Sara replied. "The couple is wrapped tightly and then sewn into separate blankets with a board between them so that they may not touch. A bed is set up in a common area, usually a parlor, and the prospective bride and groom spend the night together. A single candle lights the room, but the chaperone or chaperones remain awake. They keep a constant vigil to prevent any hint of impropriety."

"You're suggesting that you do this bundling at your home?" the bishop asked.

Sara shook her head. "I think her mother's home would be more appropriate. That is, if Hannah agrees."

Thomas swallowed. Spend the night in the same bed as Leah? Lie beside her in the darkness? He would agree to anything that would bring them together again, but there was no chance that Leah would do it.

"What would be the purpose?" Bishop Atlee asked. "In this instance? Wasn't it done with arranged marriages when couples didn't know each other?"

Sara nodded. "Sometimes. But the purpose is to provide a way for couples to get to know each other. It gives the man and woman privacy and the opportunity to talk in an intimate situation without the loss of reputation or morals." She looked from Thomas to Leah and back to the bishop. "I honestly believe that these two are perfect for each other. But they've hit an impasse. I think that confining the two of them to a bundling bed will ease the tension and let them discover how to communicate. Only by communicating can they get to the bottom of their disagreement."

The bishop looked at Hannah. "What would your husband think of such a proposal?"

"Albert?" Hannah considered. "He's a sensible man. Usually, he agrees with me in matters of my children. But I'd have to ask him."

Bishop Atlee nodded. "Do you approve of this scheme?" he asked Hannah.

"It doesn't matter whether she approves or not," Leah protested. She got to her feet. "I'm having no part of this. I can't believe that you'd ask me to do such a thing. And I know Thomas wouldn't—"

"Thomas wouldn't what?" He rose and extended a hand to her. "I would, Leah. I'd do anything to have you consent to be my wife. But…if I can't have you…then I think I deserve to know what I did wrong."

Leah wiped at her eyes. When she spoke, her voice was choked. "You didn't," she answered. "It's me. This is all my fault."

"You're scared," Ellie said.

"Scared?" Leah repeated. "That's not it at all."

"It is," Ellie insisted. "And Thomas is right. He deserves to know what went wrong between you."

"Spending the night sewn up in a blanket couldn't possibly change anything," Leah began.

"Maybe not," Thomas said. "But maybe it would. I think we should do it."

"Ne," she protested. "It's a waste of time. Nothing will be resolved."

Sara set her hands on her hips and met Leah's gaze. "Then what have you got to lose?"

Chapter Fourteen

"I can't believe that I've agreed to do this," Leah exclaimed. Three of her sisters were making up the bundling bed in her mother's front parlor and setting the room to rights for that evening. "This won't change anything," she insisted. "It will just make me feel stupid and give Thomas reason to hope that our relationship isn't over."

"I think it's old-fashioned," Miriam said as she tucked a corner of the sheet neatly under. "And a little odd. But if Sara, *Mam* and the bishop all think there's a reason for trying it, then I think you should go through with it. I trust them, and I know they only want what's best for you."

"I agree," Anna said. "Sara has had a lot of experience in matching couples. Why would she suggest this if she didn't think it was right? Besides, what's the worst that could happen? You could be right and all of us could be wrong. You love being right, Leah."

Leah glanced around at her sisters. It was impossible that they had all been won over by this absurd idea of Sara's. Why couldn't they see how much this was upsetting her? How could she bear to spend an entire night lying next to Thomas? It was wrong. It had to be. If it wasn't, why would she feel like this? "I think I'm sick," she said to Miriam. "I can't do it."

Miriam grimaced and threw her arms around her. "You'll be fine, baby sister. You're the tough one, remember? The one who went to the jungle and fought twenty-foot snakes and ate cannibal fish for Sunday breakfast."

"Be fine," Susanna echoed. She dropped the pillow she'd been stuffing into a pillowcase onto the mattress and came across the room to join in the hug.

"It wasn't twenty feet long," Leah protested. "It was seventeen. And I had to chase it away because it was trying to get through the window near the baby's bassinet."

"Exactly." Miriam chuckled.

Just the thought of her baby made her throat tighten. That loss ran so deep that she tried not to think about it. No mother should have to bury her child. And she shouldn't have to lay her precious baby in the ground when her husband lay close to death racked by the same tropical fever.

That day had been a nightmare. It was the rainy season in the Amazon. Water had poured from the skies, drenching her hair and clothing, filling the tiny grave with water. She'd wanted to go into the ground with her precious little one, but she couldn't allow herself to give up. God's strength had kept her upright and moving when she'd wanted to surrender. But she'd still had her husband to fight for, the man who had been the love of her life, the man she'd given up home and family to go with into the wilds of an unknown world to follow his dream.

Leah had shared that dream. She'd given herself wholeheartedly to ministering to the St. Joes and teaching in the one-room school. But hard work and good intentions hadn't been enough to protect them from the sorrows of the world. Sickness had come with the rains, devastating the villagers. When Daniel became ill, she'd prayed that he would survive the fever, but it ravaged his mind and body as swiftly as it had taken their beloved baby.

Two days, two long nights, and both were gone, lost to her on this earth. She would see them someday in heaven. She believed that with all her heart and soul, but *someday* stretched before her.

Close to tears, Leah went to the window and threw up the sash. She stared out at the green lawn and flowering shrubs that filled the air with a sweet and familiar scent, feeling lost even in her mother's home. She'd carried a seed of hope that here among her people she could find happiness and a new family, not to replace the dear ones that she had lost, but to help fill the emptiness inside her. Now she wondered if that had all been wistful thinking.

"Leah." Susanna stood beside her, tugging on her dress sleeve.

Normally, Leah would have gone out of her way to do anything for her sister, and she'd never ignore her. But Leah was so full of sorrow and grieving that she knew if she turned away from the window, she'd fall into a desolation of weeping. Crying always upset Susanna. And crying wasn't something that had been encouraged growing up in her mother's house.

"Save tears for the suffering of the long-ago martyrs," Hannah would say. She was always quick to kiss a scrape and hug a wailing child, but it was plain what was expected. "Stand tall, take your bumps and laugh at small injuries." No sissies under the Yoder roof. They came from a long line of strong women who'd faced death and torture to stand by their faith.

"Leah…" It was Susanna still.

"Leave her, sweetie," Anna said warmly. "Come on, Susanna, Miriam. We'll see what *Mam's* up to in the kitchen. Sister needs some private time." Chattering, her sisters had all left her alone in the parlor.

Gratefully, Leah let her thoughts drift back to that small clearing in the jungle and the home she and Daniel had made out of a rough storage building with holes in the roof and vines climbing the inner walls. They'd learned to sleep in hammocks to avoid the ants and other biting insects that didn't fly, and she had done daily battle with biting flies, giant cockroaches, horned beetles and hungry mosquitoes.

They'd gone to serve a society of indigenous people where they were unwanted, and they had created a family of friends and faith. She'd been happy there at the mission with Daniel, so joyful in doing God's work, in bringing basic medical care and education to their community, that the hardships didn't matter. She'd been rich in everything that mattered, and she'd lost it in the space of hours.

Should she have come home at once? Would that have changed anything? Would she have gotten her grieving over quicker if she'd returned to Seven Poplars immediately after Daniel's death? But there had been no one to take her place. Villagers who she'd come to

love and respect were ill and threatened by encroaching
cattle ranchers and farmers who wanted to cut down
the trees and build roads through the jungle, destroying
the wildlife ecology and putting an end to the ancient
way of life of the St. Joes. She'd been so busy, trying
to do her job and fill Daniel's shoes that she hadn't had
time to mourn or think of her loss. She'd risen before
dawn and fallen into her hammock at night, exhausted.
And, gradually, she'd found herself able to smile at a
baby's laughter and found peace in the light of a glorious sunrise.

In time, perhaps, she would have found the satisfaction of her work that she'd known when Daniel was
alive. Would she have remained there if the Mennonite
committee had allowed it? She didn't know. She had put
her trust in God that He knew what was best. And when
the orders came for her to return to the States, she'd returned eager to wrap herself in the familiar scents and
smells of home.

A mockingbird lit on a branch of the lilac bush near
the window. Its song was so sweet that Leah couldn't
help but smile. Strange that the jungle, with its beauti-
fully plumed birds didn't have one that Leah thought
could compete in voice with the quiet tones of the mockingbird.

Her mother's voice cut through her reverie.

"Leah, look who's here."

She turned back to see her mother and Aunt Martha
entering the parlor. Leah steeled herself to keep from
showing her dismay at the visitor. Her aunt had always
been a plain woman and the years since Leah had been
away had taken their toll. Tall and thin as a garden
rake with a tight mouth and small, deep-set eyes, Aunt

Martha always gave the appearance of a woman who smelled something distasteful on someone's shoe and was searching for the source.

"Leah, dear," her aunt said. "I'm shocked that you would consider such a thing. I told your uncle, I'll just march over there and have a word with Hannah. To think that she'd condone bundling under her own roof. No one does it anymore. At least not here. Maybe in one of those backward communities in the Western states. But it just isn't done among the pious. I wanted you to know that you're putting your reputation in jeopardy by spending the night with this runabout ruffian."

"Thomas is hardly a ruffian," Leah defended.

"Bishop Atlee has allowed it," her mother said. Leah could tell that her mother was fighting her amusement. Often, it was either laugh at Aunt Martha or be vexed by her interfering behavior. Usually, Hannah chose laughter.

"Humph." Aunt Martha sniffed. "Very odd. But Hannah's daughters have always had her stubborn nature. If you're determined to go through with this, it's my duty to make sure that no high jinks take place. I told your mother that I'd sit up with her tonight, just to make sure."

Leah gritted her teeth. "That's kind of you, Aunt Martha, but there's no need. *Mam* will have Sara with her. And, of course, Albert."

"Your stepfather. Practically a stranger to you." She picked up the corner of the beautiful quilt that Ruth had made and examined the stitching before wrinkling her nose in disdain. "And him fast asleep upstairs in his bed, no doubt. I know men and the good they would be in such a situation." She dropped the quilt, sighed as if to dismiss the needlework and smoothed it out. "No, indeed. Sara or no Sara, I'm staying. I want no one pointing fingers at you and whispering behind your back. A young widow must guard her reputation. What if you spend the night with Thomas and he still refuses to marry you? What then?"

"I'm not marrying Thomas," Leah said.

Aunt Martha gasped. "Then why are you sleeping with him?"

"To prove a point," Leah answered. "And to satisfy Sara and my family."

"And you won't be deterred from this nonsense?" Aunt Martha huffed.

"*Ne*, Aunt. I won't."

Standing slightly behind Aunt Martha and out of her line of sight, Hannah shrugged and gave a helpless expression. "I suppose, if you insist on staying, Martha, I won't turn you out of my house."

"I should think not. This is my late brother's house. And I remember him if others don't." Her aunt lifted the top quilt and inspected the wooden barrier that ran from the headboard to the footboard and divided the two sides of the bed. "And where did you find this?" she asked, rapping on the wood with her fist. "I wouldn't imagine that you had a bundling board tucked up in the attic."

"Sara asked James to make it for her," her mother explained. "She gave him the specifications. Who knows, if this works, it may catch on in Seven Poplars."

"Adequate, I suppose." Aunt Martha sighed heavily, ignoring Hannah's jest. "But I still believe you're wrong to agree to it. You'll regret it or she will. Mark my words."

For once she's right, Leah thought. *I regret it already.*

* * *

Leah closed her eyes and counted to three hundred. Thomas didn't say a word but she could hear him breathing, slow even breaths. It was unnerving. The sheets that were sewn tightly, making a cocoon around her body, the wooden board that ran the length of the bed, and the light of the single candle did little to allay her nervousness.

Thomas was lying inches from her in the semidarkness. They were supposed to be talking. Communicating. But he hadn't said anything. Goose bumps rose on her arms and the back of her neck. She was alternately too hot and then chilled. This was unnatural. There was a man in her bed and he wasn't her husband, and there were four people on the other side of the closed door. Custom aside, the bishop's permission aside, it was unnerving. It didn't matter that they were both fully dressed from head to toe; this felt more intimate than the days and evenings they'd spent driving in her car or walking on the boardwalk in Rehoboth.

She lay perfectly still, afraid to move, not knowing what he'd do or say if she did move. Her own breathing seemed too fast, too erratic. Her heart raced. She wanted to call out to her mother or to Sara and tell them that this was a huge mistake. She wanted out. She wanted to be away from Thomas and this farce of a courtship. But Aunt Martha was here in the house. If she weakened, her aunt would seize on it. She would know that she'd been talked into something that she couldn't fulfill. She would appear weak and vulnerable.

Weakness was ammunition you never wanted to give Aunt Martha. Like a bullying hen who rules the chicken run with pointy beak and sharp claws, her aunt would seize any weakness and take advantage of it. Worse, she would spread the news far and wide that Hannah's Mennonite daughter wasn't as much as she thought she was.

Not that she cared so much what Aunt Martha thought of her. Aunt Martha had never been fond of Hannah or of her and her sisters. But weakness would also make Hannah look bad. It would give Aunt Martha pleasure in some twisted kind of way that wasn't Amish at all. And she didn't want to do anything that would make her mother look bad. She couldn't. She owed her that much. So Leah would stick this out. She'd be here in the morning, just as determined not to wed Thomas as she was at this moment. She'd do it if it killed her.

So why wasn't he saying anything? Had he realized how useless this whole fiasco was and simply gone to sleep? Could he sleep wrapped up as tight as a cured ham? And if he could, what did that say about all his protests that he loved her? It was demeaning, really. According to Sara, she and Thomas were supposed to communicate. They were supposed to exchange thoughts and hopes. At least, that's what Sara had said.

But Sara was wrong. As were her mother and the bishop and most of her sisters. Susanna didn't really understand what was happening. She'd thought it was funny when Sara had stitched her up in the sheet, and she'd giggled loudly when Mam did the same for Thomas. Her husband David, who'd followed her into the parlor, had chuckled, too.

"Time you two were abed, as well," her mother had said to Susanna. "Tomorrow is library day, and you and David will have to be up early to watch for book borrowers."

"Ya," Susanna agreed. Her eyes sparkled with excite-

ment. "Librar-ry day." And then, as she'd been leaving, she'd giggled and wagged a chubby finger at Leah and Thomas. "No kissing!" she admonished. "Only married kissing."

Kissing. Leah grimaced. That was the last thing on her mind. "Thomas," Leah whispered. "Are you awake?"

No answer.

"Thomas?" He had to be asleep. How insulting. What suitor would agree to bundling with his intended and then go to sleep? She wriggled, trying to get more comfortable. She wasn't used to lying down with her prayer covering on and she knew it had fallen down out of place, but she couldn't get her hands loose to adjust it. "Thomas?" she repeated.

"Tell me about Daniel." His voice seem to float in the air.

"What did you say?" she asked.

"He must have been a special person. Tell me about him and your life together at the mission."

"He was special. He was everything to me. Daniel…" She trailed off as tears flooded her eyes. "I don't want to talk about Daniel."

"Why not?" Thomas's voice was low, but she could hear every word he uttered. "When you talk about Daniel, you honor him."

"I don't feel like I'm honoring him." She swallowed. Tears ran down her cheeks. She struggled to get an arm free and heard the tiny rip as threads pulled loose. Immediately, she lay perfectly still. Had Thomas heard the threads tearing? Sara had sewn these seams. She was an excellent needlewoman. Her stitching shouldn't have come undone.

"Why would you say such a thing, Leah?" His voice was warm and gentle. "What do you think you've done wrong? If you had died instead of Daniel, would you have expected him to live alone for the rest of his life? Is that what he wanted for you?"

If Thomas had raised his voice or if he'd insisted that she answer him, she could have stood firm. But the tender cadence of his question touched something deep within her. *"Ne,"* she whispered. "The last thing he said to me was to remarry and have more children."

"He must have loved you very much."

Grief so powerful that she was helpless against it swept over her. She cried softly, as she remembered Daniel's insistence that she live for both of them. Thomas said nothing, but she could feel his nearness. And then, as her sobs subsided, she began to relate incidents of her life with Daniel, some funny, others solemn or poignant. And once she'd begun to talk, the words spilled out of her.

She talked for what seemed like hours and in that span of time, she gradually loosened the stitches in her sheet so that her left arm and hand were free so that she could wipe her eyes or scratch her nose when it itched. A nagging guilt told her that getting partially out of the sheet might be against the rules, but it wasn't as if she meant to do anything wrong. Was it her fault if Sara had used old thread?

Thomas rarely interrupted as she spoke. Sometimes, if the tale she was telling was amusing, he would chuckle, or sometimes he would comment briefly, but mostly, he listened.

Now and then, the parlor door would open and the beam of a flashlight would pass over them. Leah would hear her mother's murmur or her aunt's brusque tone or Sara's matter-of-fact statement, "All is as it should be." And then the door would squeak closed, and she and Thomas would be left alone again.

Sometime after the midnight chime from the grandfather clock, the breeze through the open window caught the flame of the candle. The candle sputtered and then went out, leaving them in total darkness except for the moonlight that spilled into the room.

She had just finished telling Thomas about the time she and Daniel and two of the St. Joes had gone on a fishing trip on the river and gotten caught in a thunderstorm, when Thomas abruptly spoke up.

"I'm sorry I upset you so much by bringing up the subject of me becoming Mennonite instead of you joining the Amish church."

"I thought you knew how much I wanted to be Amish again."

"I thought that you had made the decision so that you could be one with your family again," Thomas said. "I didn't realize how important it was to you."

"I see that now," she said, "but I would never have believed that you would waver in your faith."

"It was for you," he said. "I didn't want you to sacrifice your religion for me. Besides, your faith didn't waiver when you became Mennonite for Daniel." He exhaled. "I just wanted to talk about it."

"And I wouldn't listen," she whispered. "That was wrong of me. You had the right...*have* the right to decide for yourself. Not everyone is called to our faith."

"For myself, I'd never walk away. I was born Amish and I'd die Amish. But I'd do anything for you, Leah."

"So you don't want to be Mennonite?"

"Nope."

"Not even for the convenience of the car?"

He chuckled. "Nope."

She lay there in the darkness, wondering how she could have hurt him so thoughtlessly. Why had they never talked like this before? Things could have been so different.

"I wondered," Thomas mused. "Is it the same? When you're sitting in a Mennonite church service, do the hymns lift your heart in the same way?"

"They do." She found herself smiling in the darkness. "When Daniel asked me to marry him and I decided to become Mennonite for him, it seemed an easy decision. With him and in our home, it was easy. But outside, among other members of the church, it always felt like a new pair of shoes—useful, handsome, but not quite as comfortable as my old, worn pair." She exhaled softly. "I never told Daniel that."

"*Ne*, you didn't want to burden him with the thought that he had led you away from something you loved."

"If he'd lived, I never would have thought of returning to the Amish faith. But after he died, I prayed about it every night. I asked God to show me His plan for me. I put my life in His hands, and He led me back home. It's why I can't bear the thought of changing again. In my heart, I'm already Amish," she admitted.

"You won't miss driving the car or the freedom you've had?"

"I don't think I will. It's not giving up the world—it's embracing something more real. I want to marry, to have more children, and to raise them in the faith I grew up in. I want that peace for them."

"You could have just said that," Thomas said. "You

didn't have to become so emotional, to start an argument with me. You didn't have to break off our courtship because I asked a question about our future."

"Ne," she admitted. "I didn't." And then, suddenly, the truth was as clear as day to her. About what had happened that night on the walk. After the kiss they had shared. The kiss she had enjoyed very much. "I don't think it was so much what you said, Thomas. I think... I think I was looking for a reason to break it off with you."

"Because you don't love me?"

"Because I do, Thomas. Don't you see?" Sobs shook her body, making it hard to speak. "Daniel was the love of my life. So how can I love you? How can my heart skip a beat when I see you walking toward me across the field? How can I feel such longing to have you kiss me?"

"But you meant to marry. You asked Sara to find you a husband."

"A husband," she repeated. "Someone I could respect, a companion, a father for my children. I never thought she'd find me a man I could love. Because loving you feels like betraying Daniel."

"Did your mother love your father?" Thomas asked.

"Of course she did," Leah answered.

"And does she love Albert?"

"Ya, of course. But not like she loved *Dat*."

"How do you know what's in her heart? And if she does love Albert every bit as much, do you blame her?"

"Ne," Leah insisted.

"So if Hannah's loving Albert isn't wrong, then you loving me can't be, either. You aren't betraying Daniel," Thomas said. "You're fulfilling your promise. Living for him, living for both of you. And if you believe God led you home to Seven Poplars, can't you believe He led you to me, as well?"

"Oh, Thomas." She sat upright, tearing out the stitching that confined her left side. She reached over the bundling board to touch his face, just as his arms came around her. "Thomas?"

He sat up and pulled her against him.

"How did you?" she began. "My mother's stitching shouldn't have torn out."

"Not unless she intended it to," he answered, smoothing her hair. "I suspect neither Hannah nor Sara intended us to remain apart all night."

Leah shivered as his warm lips fit perfectly to hers and they kissed, a kiss so sweet and tender that she didn't want it to end. "I love you," she murmured. "Love you, love you." She gazed into his eyes, their noses touching.

"Enough to become my wife?" he asked breathlessly.

"Can we be married as soon as we're baptized?"

"As soon as Bishop Atlee gives his blessing."

"Then, yes, Thomas, I will marry you."

He kissed her again, and she wasn't sure if she would have had a third kiss if the door hadn't opened and her aunt Martha hadn't shrieked, "Sara! Hannah! Come quick! The fox is in the henhouse!"

Epilogue

One year later...

Leah parked next to a Do Not Litter sign and turned off the ignition. It was early morning, and the sky was just beginning to fade from dark to light. They were close enough to the shoreline that she could hear the ocean waves through the open windows of the vintage black truck. Around them, in the scrubby salt pines, birds were coming awake, and rabbits and mice were beginning to stir.

Thomas walked around the truck and opened the driver's door. Leah turned toward him and he caught her by the waist to lift her down to the ground. "Wait," she said. "Let me take off my shoes."

"Let me, *leibschdi*."

Sweetheart. Her throat clenched at the endearment.

Tenderly, Thomas untied her sneakers and removed them one at a time. After each shoe slid off into his hand, he set it back inside the truck and tenderly massaged each of her feet, taking care to concentrate on her sensitive arches and toes.

"That tickles," she teased, but she liked it. She loved the feel of Thomas's hands, so strong and yet so gentle. When he stepped back, she slid down off the seat. The surface of the parking lot was pleasantly cool on her feet. "Better take off your shoes, as well. Sand in them won't be fun."

"*Ne*, I suppose it wouldn't." He tugged off his boots and socks and tossed them into the back of the truck.

They had been up for hours, loading the truck and driving south from Seven Poplars. After some persuasion on Leah's part, Bishop Atlee had decided to allow her to own a motor vehicle. The rules were that she could drive to deliver Thomas's organic fruits and vegetables to the restaurants and to take community members to doctor and dentist visits. It was a trial period, which the elders could extend, so long as Leah and Thomas used the horse and buggy at home and didn't use the vehicle for personal use.

She had traded the little black car for an old black truck with a reliable motor. Their first delivery today was in Ocean City, across the state line into Maryland, but it was early yet, and Thomas had wanted to take the time to stop and see the sunrise over the ocean.

"I hope we won't be late," she said. "New customers and—"

"We won't be late," he answered. And taking her hand, he led her away from the truck and down the wooded path to the beach. The boardwalk gave way to hard-packed sand, and the smell of the sea blended with the spicy scent of pine needles. Here, it was still night, and the trees loomed black against charcoal foliage. But the sound of the surf was louder now, and Leah's heartbeat quickened in anticipation.

They traversed another bend in the trail and Thomas held a pine branch up so that she could duck under it. Suddenly, they were out of the dunes and onto the beach. It stretched out on either side of them, with the ocean directly ahead and filling the horizon.

Shorebirds were there ahead of them at the water's edge. Long-legged shadows darted back and forth on the sand, bobbing rhythmically as they searched the wet sand for the ocean's bounty. Noisy gulls flapped and dove overhead. From behind them, Leah heard the hoarse cry and the muffled flapping of a blue egret's wings.

The ocean was a dark mass, lit now by rays of iridescent light. Clouds piled one upon another, pink and peach and lavender, and shining through, seemingly borne of the surface of the waves, came the glory of the sun. Leah stopped short, made speechless by the beauty of the sunrise. Thomas let go of her hand and slipped an arm around her shoulder. For minutes, they stood there, watching, mesmerized as dawn banished the darkness. Leah swallowed against the constriction in her throat and blinked back tears. "Wonderful," she whispered.

"It is, isn't it?" Thomas answered. "Whenever I see a sunrise, over the water here or the fields at home, it makes me think of God's love for us."

"Ya," she agreed. "Me, too."

"I think the beauty of a sunrise is here to tell us that love is like the light," Thomas said. "You can't measure it out in cups or bushels. It just is, and it is eternal."

"Sometimes, I think you would make a good preacher."

"Me?" Thomas snorted. "Hardly."

"You have a deep core of wisdom," she confided.

"You understood what I didn't." She leaned against him, pressing her face against his chest. "Thank you for bringing me here to see it."

"You're part of it," he said. "Part of the beauty."

She chuckled. "Hush, you shouldn't say that. You'll make me guilty of *hockmut.*"

"Leah, you are a woman with more reason than most to feel pride in her appearance, and yet you show it least." He smiled down at her. "I doubt very much that the bishop will be admonishing you for showing pride."

She slipped her arms around his neck and stood on tiptoe. He bent and their lips met. His mouth was sweet and she thrilled to the sensation. "You will lead me into wicked thoughts," she teased.

"I might. I never made any bones about the fact that I liked to have fun. And two people who love each other are sometimes tempted to play."

"But temptation doesn't always have to win out." Laughing, she whirled away from him and ran through the sand to the water's edge. Waves were breaking close to shore and salt water foamed and washed around her ankles.

"Watch out. You'll get caught in one and end up wet to the neck," Thomas warned.

In answer, she caught up her skirts and waded deeper into the water. It was cool and invigorating. She felt like a child again, playing tag with the waves. Venturing out, only to run for the beach when a larger wave threatened.

"Be careful," Thomas said.

Another waved crashed around her, splashing salt water to her knees. "Come try it!" she dared.

Thomas looked up and down the beach. Leah did the same. The only living thing she could see was a sand flea digging out of the hard-packed sand, a line of fiddler crabs and the birds.

"Chicken!" she cried.

"Really? We'll see who's chicken." Thomas pushed down his suspenders and stepped out of his trousers, leaving him clad only in his shirt and one-piece white cotton undergarment. It was sewn of heavy white cotton and consisted of a short-sleeved undershirt and drawers that came down halfway to his knees. English men wore much less when they went into the water. All the same, it was hardly an exhibition that the elders would approve of by a baptized member of the church, even on a swimming beach.

"You wouldn't," she said, suddenly not so certain what he would or wouldn't do. She was so busy watching Thomas that she forgot to watch the ocean. A big wave rolled in, drenching her halfway to the waist and nearly knocking her off her feet.

Thomas doubled up with laughter.

"Not funny!" she shouted back, although it was funny.

But what was he up to now? Leah gaped in surprise as Thomas removed his shirt, folded it and laid it on the sand and put his hat carefully on top of it. "Thomas…"

Wearing only his undergarment, he dashed down the beach, splashed past her and dove into the water. He swam out to where the waves were breaking. A wave crashed over Thomas, and Leah lost sight of him. Fearful for his safety, she pulled up her skirt and waded deeper. Water wet her up to her thighs.

"Thomas!" She was about to go in after him when he bobbed up, laughing, a few yards away. Thomas had never told her that he could swim like a fish.

"Come in." He gestured to her.

Leah backed toward the shore. "I don't think so."

"Maybe I'll catch you and throw you in." He got to his feet and moved toward her, but she fled to the beach. He followed and caught up with her on the sand.

He wrapped his dripping arms around her and kissed her. "I love you," he said.

"And I love you," she replied. He was wetter than she was, but she didn't care. The warmth of the rising sun enveloped them both, and she clung to him as he kissed her again.

"Are you happy?" he asked her. "Have I made you happy?"

She looked up into his dark eyes. "And why wouldn't I be happy?" she murmured. "You've given me everything that I could want—a home, work that I love, a future."

He nuzzled the crown of her head. "I think I could have coaxed the skirt off you," he teased. "You'd make a beautiful mermaid."

"My skirt, maybe," she replied. "But not my shift or my scarf."

He chuckled, but then she felt his muscles tense and his tone grew serious. "You're not sorry you married me, are you, Leah?"

"This would be a fine time to decide that," she answered. "And me, a respectable Amish wife, alone with a half-dressed man on a deserted beach."

"Your half-dressed *husband*," he corrected.

She laughed and stepped away, smoothing down her wet skirt and shaking out some of the sand. He reached out and cupped her rounded tummy in his big hand. Shyly, she covered his hand with her own. "Soon, I'll be so fat that you could roll me down to the beach," she whispered.

"I don't care how fat you get," he said, leaning down to speak to the little one growing under her heart. "I love this little one more than fried chicken and dumplings. And you will, too."

"We'll have no chicken or dumplings if we don't get those vegetables delivered," Leah reminded him. Her hand rested protectively on her belly. "You said we were coming to look at the ocean sunrise."

"And we did, didn't we?" Thomas grinned at her as he went to retrieve his clothing. "Life isn't all work. Sometimes you need to stop a moment and just enjoy it."

"I do," she said. "Every day, living with you, being your wife." How could she explain the joy he'd brought her? It was a new beginning. Life with Thomas was different than life with Daniel, but it was no less fulfilling.

Together, they were building a new house, building the farm and planning for the child that would be born to them in the late fall. "Have you thought what you'll name the baby, if it's a girl?" she asked as he dressed. He'd let her pick a boy's name, and she'd chosen Jonas, after her father.

He pushed back his damp hair and settled his straw hat on his head. "I'm thinking either Hannah or Martha," he teased.

"Martha?" she cried. "You wouldn't do that to our innocent baby, would you?"

"Well," he explained as he led the way back to the truck, "that might get us back in your aunt Martha's good favor."

"Good try," she answered. "But nothing would keep

us there long. You have to remember that I'm one of Hannah's girls."

"Fair enough," Thomas said with a grin. "Then Hannah it will have to be."

Laughing, they climbed back into the truck and Leah backed out of the parking space and pulled carefully back onto Coastal Highway. "Hannah Stutzman," she murmured. "It has a nice ring to it, doesn't it?"

"It does," Thomas agreed. "But not nearly as *goot* as Leah Stutzman."

"Oh, Thomas, what a thing to say. What will our baby think if she hears you?"

"She'll think that her *dat* is head over heels for her *mam*. And what's wrong with that? Besides, it's going to be a boy. Jonas. A good name for a farmer."

"Or a blacksmith," she teased.

"Or a blacksmith. Whatever he wants to do for a living will be fine with me, so long as he remembers that all blessings come from a merciful God."

Leah could add nothing to that. And when Thomas began to hum and then to sing a joyful hymn as they rolled along, she joined in with him. Together they sang the old beloved verses of a song they had learned as children as they drove into the bright, sunny morning, full of hope for whatever lay ahead.

* * * * *

PLAIN SANCTUARY

Alison Stone

To Scott, with love, forever and always.

Give all your worries and cares to God,
for He cares about you.
—*1 Peter* 5:7

Chapter One

"Walker." Deputy U.S. Marshal Zachary Walker answered his cell phone and held it in front of him set on speakerphone. He dropped his duffel bag on the floor of his rarely used hunting cabin. He hadn't had a chance to open the windows to air out the place before the call came in. It was probably just as well considering the rain pelting the sides of his family's cabin.

"Hi, Zach." It was his boss, Dave Kenner, at the U.S. Marshals Service at the Western District of New York headquarters in Buffalo. And if his boss was calling him late on a Friday night at the start of what was to be Zach's vacation—a vacation his boss had to force him to take—he knew it wasn't to make small talk. "Are you in Quail Hollow yet?" Zach pulled out a chair at the kitchen table and waited for his boss to get to the point.

"Yeah, just got here." He cleared his throat. "Remember that vacation you told me I had to take?"

"You never thought you'd have a nine-to-five job as a U.S. Marshal, did you?" Dave exhaled sharply over the line. Something was seriously wrong. "You see the news?"

"No." Zach had left the office at six, stopped to visit a college friend and his family for a few hours, then listened to an audiobook on the hour drive to Quail Hollow. It was his attempt to decompress. Transition. Leave the stress of the job behind. So, no, he hadn't listened to the news.

"Let me bring you up to speed."

"Am I no longer on vacation?"

"That remains to be seen."

"Hold on." Zach stood, set his phone on the counter, grabbed the remote and aimed it at the nine-inch TV sitting on the kitchen counter. The laugh track of some sitcom filled the quiet room. He immediately hit the down arrow on the volume and then played with the bunny ears mounted on the TV. He refused to pay for cable at his getaway cabin.

"Let me fill you in."

"I had no doubt you would." Zach didn't try to hide his frustration. He had worked for Dave long enough to know when he was avoiding getting to the point. That could mean only one thing: the news had to strike a personal chord.

Zach flipped the channels blindly, sensing his blood pressure spiking.

"It's Brian Fox."

And there it was.

A headache exploded behind his eyes. He dragged a hand over his mouth. Just then he clicked on a channel and a live news broadcast appeared on the screen. Searchlights lit the stone walls of Peters Correctional Facility like a scene out of some prison break movie. A woman with a blond bob and a red coat stood with a mike in one hand, pressing the other to her ear, waiting for directions from her producer or whoever called the shots at the studio in a situation like this. The words on the bottom of the screen scrolled past. Zach had to squint to read them as the reception cut in and out to the old-school TV: "Convicted murderer Brian Fox escaped Peters Correctional Facility at 8:15 p.m."

He swallowed hard as disbelief made the words flicker even more.

Over two hours ago.

Zach muttered under his breath. "You gotta be kidding me. He escaped? How in the…?" He rubbed his temples with his fingers. The image of his little sister, bloodied and sprawled on his back steps with a trail of blood leaking from her head, flashed in his mind. Bile rose in his throat. People had told him he'd have closure when Fox was convicted. Put behind bars. The people who'd claimed that had never experienced the brutal death of a loved one. Peace. Closure. They were elusive.

"How did this happen, Dave?"

"Initial speculation is that he had help from the inside."

"Help?" Zach paced the small space. "Who helps a convicted killer escape?" He closed his eyes against the flickering image on the TV, feeling a migraine coming on.

"A female employee may have provided him tools. She's missing now, too. He's resourceful. Fox dug a hole through the cement wall in his cell. Got into the bowels of the prison, then, it appears, he got out through the sewer system."

Zach fisted his hand. "You're kidding me. He was able to do this without anyone noticing?"

"Apparently he knows how to turn on the charm.

Had this woman wrapped around his finger..." His boss's words trailed off when he realized he had opened mouth, inserted foot. Fox had turned on the charm with Zach's sister. Married her. Then showed his true self when it was too late. "I'm sorry. I know this is personal for you."

Zach ignored the last comment. That was the only way he got through each day. The only way he was able to do his job. Each day he did his best to catch the bad guys, something he did in memory of his little sister. But he had yet to find a way to do his job and not be haunted by the horrific scene in which she died.

He was successful in shutting down the dark thoughts maybe 20 percent of the time, at most. Despite helping other people, he'd never get past failing the one person who had spent her entire life looking up to him.

I'm sorry, Jill.

"Brian Fox's on the run." His boss got back to the facts.

"Any idea where he's headed?"

"His first wife moved to Quail Hollow about nine months ago. She's renovating an old house. Word is she's opening a bed-and-breakfast."

"She's here in Quail Hollow?" Dread pooled in the pit of his stomach. This wasn't the first time Zach had wondered how a guy like Fox landed not one, but two wives. "Does Fox know where she is?"

"Not sure. But his cellmate said he's fixated on her. Blamed her for putting him in prison."

"Great. The jerk kills my sister and he blames his first wife for his imprisonment. What a delusional idiot."

"About that vacation…" his boss said, a hint of hesitancy in his voice.

"I'm officially off vacation."

"I need you to track down his ex-wife. Put her in protective custody until we have Fox back behind bars."

"Give me her info."

Dave rattled off an address for the woman. "Listen, we couldn't find a phone number, but we found her current address from a public real estate transaction. Fox could do the same thing."

"Well—" Zach sighed "—Heather Miller hid for ten years from this guy. She only came out of hiding to testify against him in my sister's murder case. I owe her."

"Keep your head on straight. If it gets too personal, I'll send someone else in."

Zach gritted his teeth. "I'm already here."

"I know. That's why I called. Besides, they have every law enforcement agency in Western New York tracking Fox. I can't spare another person. Stay cool. And I'll let you know as soon as we have him in custody. It shouldn't be long. And let me know when you make contact with Miss Miller."

"Will do." He ended the call and grabbed the car keys from the table. So much for rest and relaxation.

A crack of lightning illuminated the night sky in the distance. The stillness felt electric. A sense of expectation hung in the air. Swallowing around a knot of emotion, Heather Miller adjusted the plain roller shade on the bedroom window. A light breeze blew in from the cracked window and with it a mist of rain and the scent of country air.

Her *mammy* had lived out her life in this home, look-

ing out this same window at the barn and the seasons
that cycled through tall rows of corn and barren land.
How had her *mammy* been able to look at that barn
every morning and night? The dilapidated structure
hunkered in the shadows, a silent reminder of a tragic
event that had changed the course of all their lives. Back
then, could her *mammy*, Mariam Lapp, ever have predicted that her descendants would be living as outsiders, defying their Amish roots?

Heather had been six years old when her father
slipped out of town with his three young daughters in
their long dresses and bonnets. That was the last time
she had seen this house, her *mammy* and her Amish
wardrobe. Their father had stopped at a superstore outside of town and purchased his daughters cheap sneakers and *Englisch* clothes and they'd never looked back.

The memories of that day were both disjointed and
etched in her memory. The bright white sneakers. Her
first pair of jeans. The colorful unicorn on her T-shirt.

Her heartbroken father had taken what was left of his
family and carved a life for them in the outside world.
Leaving the Amish was one of a handful of events that
had shaped Heather into the woman she was today.

Today was yet another milestone. A happy one.

Heather was back in Quail Hollow, an *Englischer*,
planning to run a bed-and-breakfast for all the tourists interested in seeing the Amish countryside. The
inheritance had come as a surprise and Heather hoped
her grandmother wouldn't mind that her eldest granddaughter had opened her home to the outside world in
this way.

Heather was excited by the possibilities. She had
come a long way since she had fallen for a charmer

when she was only nineteen. Now she was making a second—no, a third—go at life in a place that held her roots, yet she'd never felt more free.

She would learn to live in the moment and let go of the past.

Moving away from the window, Heather flipped back the covers and climbed into bed. She pulled up the hand-stitched quilt passed down to her through generations. She was exhausted but feared she wouldn't sleep. Without a TV or Wi-Fi, her options for wasting time were limited to reading and her eyes were too tired for that. Besides, she needed to try to rest. She had another long day ahead of her. The house still needed work before opening weekend in a couple weeks. Just in time for the peak autumn colors. She had hoped to remain in her nearby apartment until renovations were completed, but time and money had run out.

Just as she settled her head on the pillow, a thunderclap made her jump and the resulting rumble vibrated through the walls of her new home. A whoosh of wind rustled the oak tree on her front lawn. A vague memory whispered across her brain. Had her father brought her back here to play on a tire swing hanging from its limbs? Or was that a memory from before their family moved out of the home they shared with their *mammy*? Her mother had been an only child, a rarity in the Amish community, and she and her husband had moved into the home with Mariam to start their family. When Heather's mother died and her father left Quail Hollow, her *mammy* had been left alone in this big house.

Heather closed her eyes and imagined the wind blowing through her long flowing hair—free from the constraints of a tight Amish bun—as she pumped her legs on the swing. Despite the vivid memory, or maybe it was a dream, her father claimed he had never gone back to Quail Hollow. He couldn't face the tragic past. Heather forgave her father that. His wife—Heather's *mem*—had been murdered by a stranger passing through town, or so they suspected. No one was ever arrested. Every corner, every face, every waking moment in Quail Hollow had reminded him of all he had lost.

All *they* had lost.

Heather threw back the quilt, climbed out of the bed and was drawn again to the window. Thick drops of rain pelted the glass and screen. She pushed down on the frame and it slid with a loud screech, making the hairs on her arms stand on edge. A shadow in the distance, near the rows of corn, caught her attention. She blinked rapidly. It was gone.

Am I imagining things?

Heart racing in her chest, she flattened herself against the wall, careful to stay out of view.

An old, familiar fear coiled around her lungs, making it difficult to breathe.

Heather focused on each intake and release of breath as the walls seemed to close in around her.

In through the nose, count to three, out through the mouth…

In through the nose, count to three, out through the mouth…

She was safe. The man who had tormented her was in prison. A hint of guilt twined with her fear and pressed heavily on her lungs. Somehow in her warped perspective, she felt guilty that after she escaped her violent marriage, he had sought out another victim.

His new wife hadn't been able to get away.

Brian Fox killed his second wife, landing him in prison. Finally granting Heather her freedom.

She closed her eyes and said a quick prayer for Jill's soul, the only remedy that gave her some modicum of peace.

Heather opened her eyes and focused on her reality. She was standing against the wall, still afraid of the bogeyman from her past. Perhaps she wouldn't have been so jumpy if the Amish workmen had completed the installation of the new window in the breakfast area. Large plastic tarps stapled over the huge opening may keep the rain out, but not a determined intruder.

She rolled back her shoulders, trying to dismiss her racing thoughts. She blamed Brian Fox for the lingering fear, the paranoia that always hovered just below the surface. A person didn't live in constant fear for ten years and not escape unscarred.

The wind picked up and the tree branches scraped the side of her home. She climbed back into bed and shuddered against the chill despite having closed the window. She'd have to hire someone to trim the branches. The dragging sound was unsettling.

Heather finally drifted to sleep when a loud crash downstairs startled her awake. She bolted upright in bed, her heart jackhammering in her chest.

"It's just the storm," she muttered to herself. "It's just the storm."

A creaking sounded in the hallway. On instinct, she slipped out from under the warm quilt and grabbed her cell phone from the nightstand. She moved to the bedroom door, considered locking herself in, or perhaps dragging the tall chest of drawers in front of it. Indecision kept her rooted in place. Why had she thought it was a good idea to move way out into the country all by herself?

In spite of her past fears, Heather decided she'd live life as a strong, independent woman, not letting her ex take that away from her, too. However, in reality, she was defenseless out here. Even if the spotty cell phone reception allowed her to call 9-1-1, how long would it take for help to arrive? Could law enforcement reach her before a potential intruder did?

Grabbing the golf club she always kept in the bedroom closet—this new home was no exception—she tucked her cell phone under her arm and opened the bedroom door. The loud creak of the hinges set her nerves on edge.

Since her grandmother had been Amish and she meant to recreate an Amish-like experience for the tourists, there was no light switch close by. Instead she'd have to take the time to turn the knob on the kerosene lamps mounted on the walls in the hallway.

An unease threaded its way up her spine as she tiptoed down the hallway toward the stairs. She grabbed her cell phone out from under her arm and used the back of her hand to feel along the wall in the dark. The other hand was wrapped firmly around the handle of her driver.

Dear Lord, please keep me safe.

Heather navigated the stairs, each one creaking under her weight. Breathing heavily, she made her way to the new addition off the kitchen, where she hoped to serve meals to large groups of tourists staying in her home.

The plastic sheets the Amish workmen had hung over the opening for the window flapped in the wind. The snapping sound—along with the rumble of thunder in the distance—was disconcerting in the dark of night.

For a long moment, Heather stared at the rippling plastic, trying to decide if she should barricade herself in the bathroom and call 9-1-1 because someone had slipped in through the opening or if perhaps the wind had somehow torn the plastic sheeting from its staples.

With her back flat against the wall, she didn't let go of the golf club. Her eyes adjusted to the shadows. A crack of lightning illuminated the new breakfast nook. A metal mop and broom had been upended and had come to rest in the corner.

A shaky groan of relief ripped from her throat as the need to both laugh and cry at the same time overwhelmed her. The metal bucket must have made the crashing sound. Not an intruder. She set the golf club against the wall, then examined the plastic sheet more closely. She couldn't leave it like that or the rain would warp the plywood that formed the base of the new hardwood floors that were scheduled to go in soon.

She glanced at the time on her cell phone. The workmen wouldn't be there till morning. And she couldn't very well call her Amish handyman this late at night. Even though he was allowed to have a cell phone for work purposes, she doubted he kept it on his bedside table as she had. The rules provided limits.

Come on, you can do it, a little voice inside her head nudged her. *You want to own a business? You gotta get your hands dirty. Put on your big girl britches.*

Rolling her shoulders, she tried to ease out the kinks. She might as well replace the torn plastic and seal the window opening because the adrenaline surging through her veins wasn't going to allow her to catch a wink of sleep anyway.

She turned on a kerosene lamp in the sitting room, then jogged up the stairs to throw on some clothes. On the way back down the stairs, she could hear the rain pelting the roof.

"Being a business owner is highly overrated," she muttered.

She grabbed an umbrella from the front hall, then put it back. She'd need two hands to carry the supplies from the shed in the back corner of the yard. She had noticed her Amish handyman, Sloppy Sam, putting them away this afternoon. The Amish people's tendency to use nicknames to distinguish between the same names was both creative and charming. She doubted she would have had a nickname because her name wasn't all that common among the Amish. Her mother's love for flowers influenced the names of her daughters: Heather, Lily and Rose. But the girls never had to worry about their unique names while living in Quail Hollow because they were ripped away from their extended family as little girls.

Focusing on the task at hand, Heather plucked her rain slicker from a hook by the door and stuffed her arms into the cold sleeves. She psyched herself up to run across the wet yard, get the stuff she needed from the shed and then return to the house. It would take no time. No time at all.

She laughed at herself.

She really was a chicken.

But she figured she came about it honestly, after being terrorized by her husband for years.

Brian Fox was in jail, she reminded herself.

And she was safe in Quail Hollow.

She unlocked the back door, a useless lock considering there was a large hole in the back wall of the house.

She darted back into the kitchen and grabbed a flashlight from the junk drawer and felt the weight of it in her hand.

What could happen to her in her own backyard?

Zach drove past the house with the address his supervisor had given him for Heather Miller, made a U-turn about a mile up, then returned, pulling in alongside an Amish buggy that had been abandoned across the street and partially obscured his truck. Based on his limited interaction with Heather Miller during Fox's trial, he'd learned that she had gone off the grid for ten years, fearful for her life. But a year ago she resurfaced after Fox's arrest for murdering Zach's sister. Heather's testimony had been instrumental in putting him away for a long time.

For that, Zach was grateful.

Then, nine months ago, according to his boss, this real estate transaction in Quail Hollow popped up with her name on it. Poor woman probably let her guard down after Fox was arrested, figuring she'd be safe.

She should have been safe.

Drawing in a deep breath, he knew he had a job to do. He had to push aside his personal demons. His personal need for revenge. His job was to get Miss Miller into protective custody until Fox was back rotting in jail.

Zach killed the headlights on his truck, then studied the property, wondering why Fox's first wife had moved to a farm in Quail Hollow. From what he knew about her, she had grown up in Buffalo, New York. Not exactly the country. Maybe this was her way of starting over after Fox's imprisonment.

The reason why Heather Miller was out here in the middle of nowhere wasn't important right now. Securing her was.

Fox wasn't likely to announce himself, and the darkness didn't help. Zach thought he knew dark. But the blackness in the country during a rainstorm was unlike anything he had experienced. The wipers smearing the rain didn't help the cause.

He grabbed his cell phone from the middle console of his truck and called his boss. The call took a few extra minutes to connect. "I'm sitting outside Heather Miller's house. I'm going to check out the property before I try to make contact."

"Okay. Once you have her secure, report back in. And, Zach…be careful. Local law enforcement reported that Fox may have stolen guns from a home near the correctional facility. There was a break-in shortly after his escape."

Zach ended the call, then tucked the phone into the interior pocket of his jacket. He climbed out of the truck and closed the door with a quiet snick. The sound of thunder rumbled in the distance and the rain was still coming down steadily. The temperature had plummeted with the storm, not unusual in September in Western New York.

Maybe that meant Fox was hunkered down somewhere and not stalking his ex-wife.

As long as Fox wasn't hunkered down here.

Zach crossed the street, giving the house a wide

berth, as if it might hold secrets. He noticed a light on in the kitchen that hadn't been on when he pulled up.

He scanned the landscape. There were a lot of out-buildings for a person to hide in. He was making his way around the back of the house when he heard a rustling at the back door. Sliding his gun from its holster, he rushed toward the door, focusing intently on the sound.

A person—a woman, based on her petite stature— stood on the porch with a flashlight. *What's she doing?* Before he had a chance to announce himself, she let out a scream that sent all his senses on high alert. The flashlight fell from her hands and landed with a thud on the porch. The light went dark. She spun around, pushed through the open door, then slammed it shut.

Zach froze in his tracks. He holstered his gun and lifted his hands in a nonthreatening gesture. He didn't want to frighten her any more than he already had.

"I'm calling the police," she yelled from inside the door. "Leave now!"

Zach reached into his coat pocket and pulled out his credentials. "I'm Deputy U.S. Marshal Zachary Walker. We met last year at Brian Fox's trial. I don't think my ID will fit under the door. Go to a window. I'll show you."

"Go away."

"Not gonna happen."

"Come back during the day. That's what a normal person would do."

"Ma'am, I wouldn't bother you so late at night if it wasn't important."

Silence stretched between them. He didn't hear any movements on the other side of the door, so he assumed she was still standing there debating what to do. After a moment, he heard rustling behind the door that sounded much like a dead bolt sliding out of place. The door opened a crack. A brass chain glinted when he lifted the flashlight she had dropped. A swift kick would have snapped the chain on the door, but he needed her cooperation, not her fear.

Heather squinted and lifted her hand to block the beam of light.

"Sorry," he muttered.

"Slip your ID between the crack. Hurry up." She spoke with an authority he hadn't anticipated.

Zach passed his ID through the narrow opening between the door and frame. She slammed the door shut. The dead bolt snapped back into place. After a long minute, he heard the slide of the chain and she opened the door.

Heather Miller planted a fist on her hip and a dark shadow crossed her face. "Marshal Walker. This can't be good."

"No. I'm sorry to have to tell you this. Brian Fox escaped and we fear he's coming for you."

Chapter Two

Heather glared at the U.S. Marshal standing on her back porch in the middle of the night, his familiar face reminding her of how far she had come. His mere presence making her feel like everything she had worked so hard to build these past nine months was about to slip away.

No, no, Brian Fox was locked up in Peters Correctional Facility.

"May I come inside?" The deputy U.S. Marshal had a valid request. The small porch provided little protection from the weather. And the wind and rain pelting against the metal roof of the overhang was scraping across her every last nerve.

"Yes, of course." She would not allow herself to melt into a puddle of panic. She was not the woman she used to be. Despite her best efforts, her gaze drifted to the darkened yard beyond her porch and a chill crept up her spine. "Come in, Deputy U.S. Marshal." She opened the door wider for him.

"Thanks, and please call me Zach." He slipped in past her, the rain from his coat dripping on the floor.

He turned slowly to face her. In the yellow glow of the kitchen, she noticed the handsome angles of his face. The same intensity in his eyes from when she'd first met him at Brian's trial was still evident. Her ex-husband had murdered his little sister.

"How did Brian get out? I don't understand. He's in a maximum-security prison. You must be mistaken." Her mouth suddenly went dry and her knees threatened to give out from under her. She sensed she was standing on the edge, feeling like the unstable cliff she had built her new life upon was about to crumble beneath her.

"I understand he had help from the inside."

"No… How? I don't understand…" She shook her head slowly. The man who was standing in her kitchen grew blurry.

The marshal took a step toward her. "I know it's hard to comprehend, but we have reason to believe he's coming for you."

The man's words became jumbled and sounded like they were coming from the other end of a long, narrow empty tunnel. She blinked slowly, feeling as if she was floating above her body. Maybe if she pinched herself, she'd wake up from this nightmare.

Brian escaped. Brian escaped. Brian escaped.

Unable to wrap her mind around that simple concept. No, not a simple concept. A completely impossible concept. How did someone escape from a maximum-security facility? Even with help? She turned and placed the flat of her hand on the cool countertop, trying to ground herself. "Explain what's going on. *Now.*" Her fear came out as anger.

"Would you like to sit down?" He pulled out a chair at the small kitchen table, the one she'd sat at earlier planning the future of the bed-and-breakfast. Her future…

It took Heather a moment to hear his words, process their meaning. She looked up at him, trying to keep her lips from trembling. When had he moved to stand so close to her? Her anxiety spiked and she slid closer to the door. Away from him. Toward her escape.

Always have an escape.

That had been her mistake with Brian. She had been swept off her feet as a young girl. Married him. Then when things turned violent, she had no job. No place to run. No escape.

Until not escaping would have meant certain death.

It had for his second wife.

A shudder coursed through her and she wrapped her hands around the edge of the sink, ignoring the man's offer to sit down. Lifting her gaze to the window, she saw her hollow eyes reflecting back at her.

Was Brian out there watching her?

She spun around and squared off with the U.S. Marshal who had come to share this horrible news.

"What happens now? I'm renovating this bed-and-breakfast. I have plans…"

She looked up and tuned into the narrow wood shelf lining the top of her grandmother's plain pine cabinets. Her grandmother had a collection of hand-cut wood blocks that Heather recognized as buildings located in the center of Quail Hollow. She wondered if the Amish would have allowed such frivolous decorations, but Heather assumed her grandmother may have bent a few of the rules after losing so much. What punishment could the Amish elders have dished out to her *mammy* for a few wooden decorations when she had already suffered the worst fate: her daughter had been murdered and her son-in-law left Quail Hollow with her three young granddaughters never to return?

What would her *mammy* think if she knew her granddaughter had almost suffered the same fate as her daughter? However, her mother had died at the hands of a stranger. Heather had been threatened by the man she had once loved. Were some families prone to violence?

Heather shook her head at the ridiculousness of that thought. Her mind had a tendency to race when she was stressed. To think the most random thoughts.

Focus.

Heather grabbed a glass from the cabinet and filled it with tap water. Then she turned to face the man in her kitchen. "Why do you think he's coming for me?"

But she knew, didn't she?

Her hand began to shake and she set the glass down. "I haven't had contact with him since…the trial." That was when she had finally faced the man who had abused her for years. When she finally stood up to him.

An emotion she couldn't name flitted in the depths of his eyes. "We have reason to believe he's obsessed with you and may be headed your way."

Thick emotion clogged her throat. "How is that possible?" But deep down she knew. Brian Fox was an egotistical psychopath and she had escaped his clutches. He'd also vowed that he would kill her if she ever left him. Her ex-husband didn't like to fail. Now he was taking his one shot at freedom to right his one failure.

Her.

Heather's entire body shook. The yellow light in the kitchen of the old farmhouse made her pallor more pronounced. She pulled out the chair and slumped into it, placing her elbows on the table and digging her fingers into her hair.

"Do you have someplace you can go?" Zach hovered over her, then realized he might get a better response if he sat down across from her. Less threatening.

After a moment, she glanced up. A silent tear slid down her cheek. Law enforcement officers learned to separate their feelings from the job, but this case was too personal not to feel heartache for this woman.

"No, I don't have someplace to go. I spent every dime I had on renovations. I moved out of my apartment today. *Today!* It's like he knew how to mess with me." She held up her palms, disbelief threading her tone. "I'm opening a bed-and-breakfast. I've decided to name it Quail Hollow Bed & Breakfast. Simple, but appropriate. Renovations are nearing completion. I've worked so hard." Her tone had a weary quality, probably a mix of her frustration with the contractors and the new bomb he had dropped on her: her violent ex-husband was tracking his way across Western New York to continue his reign of terror.

"Could you delay the opening? Just until Fox is back in custody?"

"Maybe he won't find me. It's not like I'm on social media or anything advertising where I live." The hope in her voice was like a knife twisting in his heart. How could one man cause so much havoc?

"We were able to track you down through a real estate transaction. Easily. He could do the same." Zach resisted the urge to reach out and cover her hand. Comfort her. But it wasn't his place. He hardly knew Heather. He only knew what she had done for his family. She stepped up at his sister's murder trial when it counted. Now he had to keep her safe.

Heather straightened and pounded a fist on the table. "That jerk took my twenties from me. I refuse to let him take any more."

Anger pulsed through his veins. "Fox could take your life."

Heather jerked her head back as if she had been slapped, but instead of crumbling, she seemed to grow angrier. She pushed back her chair. It slammed into the wall behind her, then crashed to the floor. She stepped over it and paced the small space. Then she turned to face him, jabbing her index finger in his direction. "Don't you think I know that? I left him in the middle of the night with only a few dollars and the clothes on my back. I made sure I stayed off the grid. I lost touch with my family. I moved every few months when I thought he might be closing in. I don't know when he stopped looking for me, but I know when I stopped fearing him. When he went to prison for murdering—" her voice faltered "—for killing your sister." She pressed her palms together and touched her lips with the tips of her fingers. "There's not a day that goes by that I don't pray for Jill. And there's not a day that goes by that I don't thank God for sparing my life."

Heather bent over and righted the chair and tucked it under the table. Wrapping her hands around the back of the chair, she leaned toward him. "I'm not going to run. I don't want to bring danger to anyone else's doorstep. I've run too often in the past to have established any solid friendships to impose upon. And I have no money to leave on my own." She placed her hand on her midsection. "It's like I'm trapped all over again."

"There have to be options. It shouldn't be long before they track Fox down. They have NYS Troopers, FBI Agents, and every other law enforcement agency between Quail Hollow and Peters Correctional Facility looking for him. They'll find him soon. But you must lie low for a few days."

A determined look settled in her eyes. "I've worked too hard. I refuse to let him control me again. The bed-and-breakfast is booked for opening weekend in a couple weeks. I have lots to do to get ready before then. If this place isn't ready and I cancel the reservations, I won't be able to pay my bills. I fear everything will spiral downward from there." She crossed her arms again and gritted her teeth. "I'm not going to live in fear anymore."

Zach stood to meet her frantic gaze. He knew this was anger and fear speaking. Not logic. "It's only temporary," he spoke softly.

She locked gazes with him. "I'm not leaving. I bet you can call your boss and convince him to have someone stay here to protect me."

He scrubbed a hand over his face, no longer bothering to hide his frustration. "My superiors are going to insist you go to a safe house."

"It's not going to happen. I'm staying here so I can continue getting this place ready and your office is going to see that I'm kept safe."

He cocked his eyebrow. "If I can't convince you to leave, how do you suppose I'm going to be able to convince my superiors to allow me to stay?"

"Because New York State won't like the bad press if they not only allowed a killer to escape from one of their *secure* correctional facilities, but in doing so, they let him get to one of his prior victims." Her tone was oddly cool, as if living in fear had made her numb. Or maybe she had reached the end of her rope and instead of letting go, she had decided to swing out with her legs and kick with all she had.

Heather held up the plastic sheet while Zach used the staple gun to secure the edges. She was glad she had something to occupy her hands, but she wished she could say the same thing about her mind.

Brian was out of prison and headed her way.

Her ex-husband had haunted the periphery of every part of her waking life and he had visited many of her nightmares.

But ever since he had been locked up in Peters Correctional Facility, she had allowed herself to hope, to dream, to make plans for a brighter future. Push him out of the center of her mind.

Tonight, Brian had come roaring back. The worst possible scenario was laid out before her. Despite her rioting emotions, she was not going to let him ruin this dream.

Erring on the side of caution, Zach had searched her house for any intruders. Thankfully, everything other than the construction zone was secure.

"The workmen will be here in the morning, but if we'd allowed this rain to keep coming in, it would have ruined the plywood. I'd hate for the workmen to install the new hardwoods on top of warped subflooring," she said, feeling the awkwardness of the silence stretching between them.

"Yeah, no problem."

Cha-chink. Cha-chink. Cha-chink. Three more staples went through the thick plastic into the raw wood. Per Heather's instructions, Zach carefully aligned the staples so any holes they left would be hidden by the frame of the new window.

After they finished the task at hand, they sat in the rockers quietly, interrupted only by the occasional polite chitchat. Heather was unwilling to leave and Zach was unwilling to leave her alone. Heather's bones ached by the time the sun crept over the horizon. Finally she stood. "I'll make us some coffee." She started toward the kitchen when a knocking on the front door drew her attention. She glanced at the clock on the wall, surprised since it was so early.

"Hold up," Zach said, stretching out his hand to block her from going to the front door.

Heather did as he said, her heart in her throat. *Would Brian actually knock on the door?*

A soft voice floated in from the entryway. "Um, is Heather here?"

Ruthie! Heather rushed to the front door to find her Amish friend standing there with a basket full of fresh fruits and vegetables. "Hello, you're here early."

"I figured you'd be up, ready to start the day. If not, I figured I could let myself in and start without you."

Heather had forgotten she had given Ruthie a key.

"*Gut* morning." Ruthie cocked her bonneted head and gave Zach a pointed stare. "Have you hired extra help?"

"Um, no." It was too early to think on her feet.

Ruthie held up her basket of fresh foods. "I thought you might be low on groceries. Meanwhile, knowing what's in season, we can plan the menu for your first guests before the days get away from us. We have lots to do."

"Of course." Heather led the woman past Zach toward the kitchen. "It will be good to plan ahead." Get her mind off Brian.

As they passed near the new addition, Ruthie whispered, "You don't have to hide the fact that you hired workmen outside the Amish community."

Heather's lips formed into a perfect O, but she didn't know what to say. She didn't want to alarm her friend and employee. Nor did she want to offend her. Ruthie had recommended her good friend's work crew.

Guilt threaded through her. Was Heather placing others in jeopardy by not going into hiding? How long would it really take to capture a fugitive?

Heather racked her brain about how to best explain Zach's presence, when Zach approached and extended his hand, making the decision for her. "I'm Zach Walker, a friend of Heather's." Ruthie tipped her head in greeting but didn't take his hand. Zach smiled and dropped his hand. "I stopped by to see how the new construction was going." He pointed toward the window. "Good thing. The rain was pouring in the opening for the window."

"Another early riser?" Ruthie muttered, then turned her attention to the plastic covering the window. "I'm so sorry. Sloppy Sam should have had the window in already."

"I believe there was a delay by the manufacturer," Heather said, eager to ease Ruthie's concerns.

"I'm sorry for your inconvenience."

Heather waved her hand in dismissal. "It's fine. I suspect he'll have it in today. Then we'll have a beautiful new eating nook." She wandered over to the far corner of the window and inspected the staples. "I trust they'll be able to stain the woodwork the same color as the original wood throughout the house."

"My friend is *gut*. Just let him know, *yah*?" Ruthie nodded at Heather. "I'm going to take inventory of the canned goods in the pantry. I've been doing a little shopping since you hired me. We need to start planning our menu."

"Okay." Heather watched Ruthie walk away. She dragged her hand along the unfinished edge, marveling that yesterday her sole concern was getting the addition completed on time.

"Ruthie is going to help me with the day-to-day operations of the bed-and-breakfast."

Zach nodded his understanding.

Heather drew in a deep breath. She loved the smell of raw wood. She started to smooth her hand along the drywall when her eye caught something on the wall near the corner. In red permanent marker it read: Brian + Heather 4Ever.

Nausea swirled in her gut. She spun around, fear blurring her vision as she struggled to focus on Zach's face. "Brian. Brian Fox was here."

Chapter Three

"I've already searched the house. He's not inside. Not anymore." Zach touched Heather's arm in what she assumed was intended as a comforting gesture, but how could she possibly be comforted?

Her ex-husband had been in her house. *He's here in Quail Hollow.*

Stars danced in her line of vision. Less than twelve hours ago this room had held so much promise for the future. For all the potential customers to her quaint bed-and-breakfast. Now its walls and the graffiti pulsed. A hot flush of dread crashed over her. She was suffocating. Trapped. She tugged on her collar and focused on her breathing.

"Are you *sure* he isn't still in here?" Her lower lip quivered. "Hiding." She found herself whispering to protect Ruthie from her past. Her chest grew tight at a memory of a confrontation with Brian. She had been out with friends. Having fun. Something she hadn't done much since they got married. Brian hadn't let her. But she had been uncharacteristically defiant. Determined to reclaim some of her life.

A mistake.

Brian had been waiting. In the dark. Insanely jealous that she had been out with her friends. He had accused her of picking up guys. Something she would never do. She had grown to fear Brian, but she had never been unfaithful in her marriage.

That was the first time he had hit her. His fist had struck her, hard and fast, a shocking surprise in the darkness. She had been an easy target backlit by the hall light.

"Yes. I checked the house thoroughly." Zach interrupted her racing thoughts. "But we can't stay here. He's close."

"Who's close?" Ruthie asked, concern etched onto her pretty features, free of makeup, as she returned from the pantry on the other side of the kitchen. "Did someone break in?" She tugged nervously on the loose strings of her white bonnet.

Heather smiled tightly. "I'll explain in a minute."

Zach pulled back a corner of the vinyl sheeting covering the window. "What's in the building in back?"

"You saw the shed. It just has supplies for the remodel." She pointed to the stapler and vinyl. "The barn's empty. Needs some repairs." A thumping started in her head. "He's hiding in there, isn't he? He's in there." The hysteria welled in her chest, squeezing her lungs, making it difficult to breathe.

"Look at me," Zach said, a determined forcefulness in his tone. *"Look at me."*

She met his eyes and saw warmth, compassion and something she always saw in her own eyes when she looked in the mirror—anger. Anger aimed at a man who had ruined so many lives.

"I am not going to let anything happen to you. I promise."

Something about the sincerity in his voice, in his eyes, made her believe him. But hadn't she also believed her husband when he told her he'd never hit her again? That he was sorry.

She had been fooled by a charming liar.

But Zach wasn't Brian. Zach had come here to protect her. She had to trust him.

But trust didn't come easily.

He pulled back his jacket and she noticed his gun, immediately relieved that they weren't sitting ducks. He plucked his cell phone from his belt. "I'm going to call the local sheriff. Let them know Brian Fox may be close."

At the mention of his name a shudder raced through her. Apparently sensing her renewed dread, he reassured her that she'd be safe. "I need you and Ruthie to go to a room that locks. Your bedroom? A bathroom? And stay away from the windows."

Instinctively Heather reached out and grabbed his wrist. "No, wait for the sheriff before you go into the barn looking for him. Brian's evil."

Zach shook his head. "I need to go out there and check the buildings. I can't risk him getting away." He leveled his gaze at her. "You have a cell phone?"

She nodded, her palms growing slick as she grabbed her cell phone out of the rolltop desk in the sitting room. "The service is terrible out here."

His brows furrowed. "I haven't had trouble. Different carriers, I suppose." He ran a hand across his stubbled jaw. He flicked his gaze toward the back door. "Listen, time isn't on our side. Can you go upstairs and lock yourself in a room? I'll call the sheriff."

Heather swallowed hard and grabbed Ruthie's hand. "Come on. Let's go upstairs. I have a dead bolt on my bedroom door." She had installed one there for security for when she opened her house to strangers. She had never dreamed she'd have to use it to keep her ex-husband out.

"What's going on?" Ruthie asked as she begrudgingly followed her up the stairs, her boots pounding up each step.

When they reached her bedroom, Heather ushered Ruthie inside and spun around, slammed the door and turned the bolt. Why did she think a flimsy lock on a hollow wood door would keep out Brian when a maximum-security prison had failed?

Zach waited at the bottom of the stairs until he heard the bedroom door close and the bolt slide into place. He made a quick call to the sheriff's department. Pulling his gun out of its holster, he moved toward the back door and muttered, "I'm coming to get you, Fox. You're not going to get away from me now."

He exited through the kitchen door, where he had first run into Heather last night. He prayed the sheriff and his deputies didn't take their time in getting here. Zach feared if he picked the wrong outbuilding, Fox might be able to make his escape while he was otherwise occupied. Or worse—make his way into the house through the construction zone. To Heather.

After Zach cleared the shed, he heard sirens growing closer. One patrol car pulled up the driveway. Two others sped past before coming to a stop somewhere out of view on the other side of the house. A call like his had probably gotten the attention of the entire Quail Hollow Sheriff's Department.

A tall man unfolded from his patrol car, his hand hovering over the grip of his gun. Zach waved to him silently and pointed to the barn. The man in turn gestured to his officers. The four men surrounded the barn under Zach's silent directions. Two stayed outside watching for any sign of the fugitive while the tall officer and Zach checked the interior. Thanks to several missing planks and a large hole in the roof, most of the interior was well illuminated except for a few dark corners.

Zach cautiously checked the shadows behind a tractor with no rubber on its wheels, an old shell of an Amish buggy and a few hay bales that smelled ripe from dampness and age.

"Clear," he hollered after checking the last stall, where horses must have been kept at some point in the past.

The two law enforcement officers exited the barn together.

"You really think the fugitive made it all the way to Quail Hollow?" The officer looked at his watch as if that might give him the answers. "Isn't Peters Correctional Facility about a hundred miles from here? Guy had to have resources to get to Quail Hollow so quickly."

"He's determined. And he's had help," Zach said bluntly. He offered his hand, introducing himself.

The officer shook his hand. "I'm Deputy Conner Gates. Tell me. Why Quail Hollow? We're a small Amish community."

Zachary glanced up at the house and he saw Heather standing in the upstairs window. This had been her chance at a fresh start after the mayhem Fox had un-leashed on her. Yet Fox had found her again and was toying with her.

Zach wasn't going to let this jerk get to Heather. He hadn't been able to save his sister, but he was going to make sure nothing happened to Heather Miller.

"The escapee knows the owner of this property. She testified against him." Zach paused a half second. "And Heather is Brian Fox's ex-wife."

"Oh, man." Gates planted his hand on his hip.

"What makes you believe he's actually here?"

"He left some graffiti on the wall of the residence. He's close."

"Okay," the sheriff's deputy said, "I'll call it in. We have to immediately make plans. Grid the area. Fan the search out from here."

Zach held his hand up. "Don't let me hold you up. My job is to secure Heather Miller. Keep her safe."

"Heather Miller, you say?" The sheriff's deputy rubbed his jaw. "I didn't realize she had moved back. Shame what happened to her mother."

Zach plowed a hand through his hair. He hated to ask. Apparently he didn't have to, because the offi-cer continued, "My father was sheriff back when her mother was murdered. Heather and her sisters were just little girls. Her father moved away from Quail Hollow with his three daughters and never looked back."

"Can't say I blame him. It's a small town. Every-where he turned must have reminded him of his wife." Unease twisted his insides. He hadn't realized Heather had so much tragedy in her past.

"They left everything, including their Amish com-munity."

Zach did a double take. "Heather grew up Amish?"

Deputy Gates nodded. "Sure did. Her mother's murder turned this entire town upside down."

Heather stepped away from the bedroom window, her nerves humming from all the law enforcement activity on her quiet little farm.

Not so quiet anymore.

"I'm sorry you had to get caught in the middle of this," Heather said as she crossed the room to Ruthie, who was sitting quietly in the chaise lounge Heather had put in the corner of the bedroom where she'd envisioned herself escaping with a good book. Not escaping from her fugitive ex-husband.

"Can you tell me what's going on now?" Ruthie dragged her fingers down the edges of her apron over and over. "We have lots of work to do before the bed-and-breakfast opens."

"It looks like everything is safe. For now." From the upstairs window, it looked as if Zach and the sheriff's department had come up empty-handed.

"What is going on? Who is this person they're searching for?" Ruthie's eyes grew wide as she searched Heather's face for answers.

Heather lowered herself onto the edge of the chair and met Ruthie's wary gaze. How did she tell her Amish friend that her ex-husband had escaped prison and had tracked her down in Quail Hollow?

Wasn't this part of the reason the Amish lived separate from the world? There was too much evil out there. Case in point.

Living the Amish way hadn't saved her mother.

"You deserve the whole truth." Heather swallowed

hard and ran her hands up and down her thighs. "A long time ago, I was married to a man who turned out to be abusive."

"This man they're looking for?" Ruthie stopped fidgeting with her apron and stared at her. The fear and uncertainty in her eyes made Heather feel like she had somehow betrayed her friend.

Heather nodded in response to Ruthie's question. "I got away from him—" she fast-forwarded ten years, not wanting to weigh Ruthie down with her past "—but he remarried and killed his second wife."

A quiet gasp escaped Ruthie's lips as blotches of pink fired in her fair-skinned cheeks.

"The man you met downstairs isn't a friend of mine. He's actually a law enforcement officer. Deputy U.S. Marshal Zachary Walker came here to warn me that my ex-husband had escaped prison and was on his way to hurt me."

"I'm so sorry this has happened to you," Ruthie said. "How can I help?"

Heather's breath hitched before she caught herself. This wasn't the response she had expected. Shock, maybe. Questions, definitely. But sympathy and a show of support? Perhaps Ruthie had more exposure to the harsh realities of the outside world than Heather had realized.

"I'd completely understand if you decided you didn't want to work here." Heather felt it necessary to offer her young friend a way out. She couldn't put her in danger.

"I've been looking forward to working here," Ruthie said softly. "It's a pleasant change from the greenhouse."

A knock sounded on the door followed by Zach

Walker's authoritative voice. "Fox is gone. It's safe. Come on out."

Heather brushed the back of her hand across Ruthie's sleeve and smiled. She stood and crossed the room to unlock the door. Hoping she could mask her apprehension, she squared her shoulders before opening it.

"We can talk downstairs," Zach said, all business.

Heather led the way downstairs followed by Ruthie, Zach trailing behind.

"It's safe?" Heather repeated his words, although she doubted she'd ever feel safe. She should have never believed she could. As long as there was evil out there—namely Brian Fox—she'd never feel safe again.

Once they reached the new addition, Zach widened his stance and crossed his arms, looking down at her. "It won't be safe here for you until Fox is back in custody. That's nonnegotiable. You need someplace secure to go for the duration."

"For the duration?" Heather's mind spun. She hated the high-pitched quality of her voice. "I can't just leave. I'm in the middle of renovations. The workmen should be here any minute." Even as she said the words, she realized how ridiculous she sounded. Of course she couldn't stay here. Brian had already found her. Tingles of panic bit at her fingertips and threatened to spread up her arms and consume her with the all-too-familiar fight-or-flight response.

She turned her back to Zach, trying to hide the red flush heating her face. She needed time to think.

The sound of a few Amish workmen speaking in Pennsylvania Dutch floated in from the backyard through the plastic lining covering the opening for the window that was yet to be installed. "I should offer them coffee."

"I'll get the coffee." Ruthie hurried past her and into the kitchen.

"Can we sit down?" Zach asked. "Talk about this?"

Heather had long passed the point of trying to ignore this entire nightmare. She held out her hand, directing him toward the sitting room. Two rockers sat in front of a wood-burning stove, where the tourists were supposed to relax after a day of sightseeing. Not where she was supposed to discuss her ex-husband, who had escaped from prison.

This is too crazy to comprehend. Like a nightmare come true.

The U.S. Marshal leaned forward and rested his elbows on his knees. "You are one of the strongest women I know. It took a lot for you to come forward to testify against Fox in my sister's trial. I'm grateful."

Her stomach twisted at the personal nature of his comment. After she escaped, Brian had killed *Zach's sister*. Zach didn't owe her his gratitude. If she had been braver sooner…

"I didn't have a choice but to testify." She measured her words, fighting back a groundswell of emotion, guilt riding the crest. If she hadn't escaped from Brian, he might not have killed his sister.

You would have been the one he killed…

Heather dragged a hand across her hair and blinked her gritty eyes. Every fiber of her being ached with exhaustion. Frustration. Regret.

"I've put everything into this place. I have nowhere else to go." Even she could hear the fight draining from her argument.

"The sheriff's deputy told me you have two sisters."

"How did he...? Of course..." Heather slowly shook her head. Quail Hollow was a small town. Despite having kept to herself—except for getting to know Ruthie's family—since she moved into a nearby apartment to start renovations, the residents still knew her story. She didn't truly believe she could be a Miller in Quail Hollow and not have people know about her past, but she had hoped to live a quiet life. *So much for that.* "I can't move in with one of my sisters. I'm not going to put either of them in danger. I can't."

"A relative. Someone Fox doesn't know about."

"My father moved us away from our family. We've lost all ties. Last I heard, my two uncles and their families moved to another Amish community. I suppose I'm the only Miller foolish enough to live in Quail Hollow."

"Friends?"

"I never stayed anywhere long enough to establish friendships. And the friends I had before..."

Pulse thudding in her ears, she slowly turned to meet Zach's steady gaze. "I was married to the man. He knows everything about me. I'm not safe *anywhere*." Her voice cracked over the last word.

"You may feel that way, but I can take you to a safe house."

"You're asking me to run?"

"I know." The look of compassion in his eyes spoke volumes. He knew what he was asking her to do.

"What will happen to this place when I'm gone? If I run, Brian wins. Again." She bowed her head and threaded her fingers through her hair and tugged, frustrated. But even as she made the argument, her resolve was fading.

"It's only temporary." His smooth, calming voice washed over her. If only she could believe that.

"I hid for ten years from Brian." She lifted her gaze, wondering if he could read in her eyes the blame she felt for not coming forward. For not stopping Brian before he had a chance to meet, marry and then kill Zach's sister. As irrational as that thought was, it always came back around to haunt her. In the long chain that had connected Brian Fox to Zach's sister, Jill, she had been a pivotal link.

"The difference this time is that every law enforcement agency in New York State is searching for this guy. It *will* be temporary. He's not living as a free man."

"You can stay with me."

Both Zach and Heather spun around to find Ruthie walking into the sitting room holding two mugs of coffee. "You'll be safe at my home."

"I couldn't," Heather said, accepting the coffee from her Amish friend.

"Wait," Zach said, "that's not a bad idea. Fox wouldn't know to search for you there. You've only recently become friends, right? There's no way Fox would make the connection."

"*Yah*, well, my *mem* and Heather's *mem* were friends a long time ago."

"I can't imagine Fox would connect the dots," Zach said.

"I can't put Ruthie in danger."

"No one will know you're there." Ruthie's eyes shone brightly, the eagerness of only the young and the innocent. "You can even wear my Amish clothes. We're about the same size."

Heather's eyes widened at the young woman's suggestion. Heather might have thought Ruthie had watched a lot of TV to come up with such a crazy plan, but that obviously wasn't the case. She was just a clever young woman.

Zach leaned forward, resting his forearms on his thighs. His golf shirt stretched across his broad chest. "It's not a bad idea."

"You live with your parents?" Zach asked.

"My *mem*. My *dat* died last year. Now it's just the three of us. I have four older sisters, all married and living nearby. My little sister is fifteen."

"I can't imagine your mother would be happy with having an outsider in her home." Maryann had been nothing but kind and welcoming to Heather, but she wasn't so sure about this. This involved some level of deceit: pretending to be Amish. Would Ruthie's mother go for it?

Ruthie planted her hands on her hips. "She won't mind. My *mem* and your *mem* were best friends. She'd want to help you. I know it."

Surprise trapped a response in Heather's throat.

Zach pushed to his feet. "It's worth asking."

A throbbing started in Heather's temples. "What if he follows us there? I can't... I just can't."

Chapter Four

Zachary paced the small space between the rocking chairs and the wood-burning stove. "We can take extra precautions to make sure Fox doesn't follow us back to Ruthie's home."

Heather stared up at him, worry lining her pretty eyes. "I don't think this is a good idea."

"I'm not letting you stay here." Zach winced at the way he'd framed the words. He suspected Heather wouldn't take kindly to being forced to do anything. He stopped pacing and sat down on the rocker across from hers. "Don't get me wrong. I'm not going to force you into anything. However, it's against my better judgment and all my training to leave you here. Fox has been here." He pointed in the general direction of the graffiti on the wall. "Please let me—" he looked at Ruthie "—let *us* help you."

He shifted to catch Ruthie's attention. "Do you know the workmen here?"

"*Yah*, Sloppy Sam is a *gut* friend."

"Sloppy Sam?" Zachary couldn't help but smile. Then

he turned to Heather. "You hired someone named Sloppy Sam to do home renovations? Seems like a risky move."

Shrugging, Heather mirrored his smile and flicked a quick glance at Ruthie. "Sloppy Sam came highly recommended."

"A lot of Amish have nicknames because so many people have the same name. I know—" Ruthie lifted her hands and held up her fingers. "I know at least seven Samuels. And trust me, Sloppy Sam is a very fine craftsman. He got his nickname when he was a little boy. He tended to enjoy his meals so much that his father kept calling him sloppy. It stuck."

"Well, maybe Sloppy Sam can give you a ride home in his wagon. You can talk to your mother, run the plan by her, then I'll see to it that Heather makes it there, albeit in a circuitous route. Sound like a plan?"

"Yah."

"Please don't tell Sloppy Sam or any of the other Sams you know. The fewer people who know where Heather is, the better."

"I understand." Ruthie pointed toward the back window. "I'll see that the workmen install the window before I leave. Make sure no one else can get in."

Zach met Heather's gaze. She knew as well as he did that no one could stop a determined Fox from getting in.

"Thank you," Heather said. "You've been a good friend. But please, if I arrive and your mother doesn't want me in her home, please tell me. I don't want to put your family out."

"It'll be fine. You'll see." Ruthie smiled and went outside to talk to the workmen.

"Why don't you grab a few things? I'll drive you to the sheriff's department, and then we'll make alternate plans to get you to Ruthie's house. I don't want Fox to follow us from here."

Heather dragged the charm back and forth across the gold chain on her necklace. "How long do you think it will take before they capture Brian?"

Zach rubbed the back of his neck. "I understand Fox has a lot of experience surviving in the woods. He was big into camping, right?"

Heather nodded. An expression suggesting she was remembering an unhappy camping trip flitted across her features.

"He's more equipped than most to make a go of it out in the woods."

Heather's shoulders sagged, as if she had lost some of her initial bravado. "Do you think I'm foolish to stay in Quail Hollow? Maybe I should put more distance between us."

Zachary leaned forward and reached out to take her hand, but stopped short of touching her. "You can go round and round with this. I think our initial plan is a good one. We can reevaluate if either I or the sheriff's department feels your safety is compromised."

Heather raised her eyebrows. "You're not leaving Quail Hollow? I thought your job was to make sure I'm secure."

"It is. And the only way you'll be one hundred per-cent secure is if Fox is back in custody. Until then, I'm sticking close by."

Heather closed her eyes and shook her head. "I'll grab a bag. It won't take me long. I haven't even had a chance to unpack since moving in here."

The hammering of the workmen clashed with the pounding in Heather's head as she jogged up the stairs to grab a few things. Between the lack of sleep and her plans for the future crashing down around her, she wondered why she had ever allowed herself to dream. To hope for the future.

Tragedy followed her as if she had a flashing neon arrow over her head.

Rely on your faith. Her father's words drifted through her mind. Despite losing his wife and the only life he'd ever known, her father had raised his three daughters to be strong in their faith. To not let their circumstances weigh them down. That God would provide.

Yet her father had worked the last twenty years of his life in a dark factory and died of a heart attack on the way home to his two youngest daughters while riding a public bus during a snowstorm. Help hadn't arrived in time to save him.

God had not provided, but Heather refused to allow that to shatter her faith. She owed that much to her father.

Heather snatched her sweater off the back of the chaise lounge in her bedroom and crammed it into a bag.

Time to go. Hide from Brian. Again.

Her heart ached with the reality that she had come so far only to be pulled back by the man who had always been determined to keep her under his thumb.

"I'll be back," she whispered to her cozy bedroom. That was a promise. She turned and hustled down the stairs. When she reached the bottom, Zach extended a hand to take her bag. "Is this it?"

Heather tipped her head. "I don't suppose I'll be needing much, considering I'll be wearing Ruthie's wardrobe."

Lifting the strap of her bag over his shoulder, he shot her a look she couldn't quite read. "I talked to the workmen. They'll finish up here and Ruthie's going to lock up on her way out."

"And there's no way Brian will follow us to Ruthie's?" Unease twisted her stomach. "I can't—"

"You'll have to trust me on this. Come on." With a hand to the small of her back, he led her outside. His intense scrutiny of their surroundings both comforted and unnerved her. They walked down the muddy driveway, made uneven by the horses' hooves and the narrow wheels of the workmen's wagons.

Alarm coursed through her. "My sisters. They must have heard that Brian escaped. They'll be worried." She dragged her hand across her forehead. The intensity of the morning sun made her feel queasy. "You don't think he'd go after them?"

"He's here. He's coming for you."

She couldn't help but laugh, an awkward, nervous sound. "Is that supposed to make me feel better?"

Half his mouth quirked into a grin. During the trial, she had never seen him so much as crack a smile. "I didn't mean…"

Heather held up her hand. "I know what you meant. But do you think I could contact my sisters? At least let them know I'm okay and to tell them to be more cautious. To report anything suspicious."

"Of course. We can make a few phone calls from the sheriff's office before I take you to Ruthie's home." He quickened his pace, nudging her forward with a hand to her elbow. "But let's get you off this property."

Heather squinted against the sun and tented her hand

over her eyes. "Where did you park?" He was leading her across the narrow country road.

"I parked behind the buggy here. I didn't want to draw attention to my vehicle in case Fox was watching."

Still holding her elbow, he led her around the buggy and they both came up short. Her stomach bottomed out and she willed away her urgent need to throw up. The windshield of his truck had been smashed.

With two hands on her waist, Zach set her next to the buggy like she was a child who needed to be told to stay put and not move. He reached for his gun. "Stay here." He set her bag down on the gravel lot.

A flush of dread washed over her and she struggled to catch her breath. She glanced around, her vision narrowing. A crow silently flapped its wings overhead, cutting a path across the sky.

The cornfields swayed in the winds. The sweet scent of corn and dried leaves reached her nose.

A split-rail fence in need of repair.

A long-ago abandoned silo.

Yesterday, this landscape had brought her peace. Today she saw nothing but places for Brian to hide.

She flexed and relaxed her hands, trying to tamp down her panic. He was not going to destroy her life. Not again.

Leaning over, she scooped up the strap of her bag that Zach had dropped and waited. She glanced around to make sure they were alone. Zach did the same as he strode across the gravel lot.

After a closer inspection of his vehicle, he walked back toward her, all the while keeping a watchful eye on the landscape. His posture relaxed. Perhaps he was convinced the immediate threat had passed. Something made him go back to the vehicle and open his driver's door. He paused. A muscle ticked in his jaw. He stepped away from the open door with an envelope in his hand.

"What's that?" Despite her best efforts to be strong, her voice trembled.

"It's addressed to you." But he didn't hand it to her. They made eye contact briefly before he pulled out a pocket knife and slid the blade under the seal of the envelope.

Another crow cawed overhead as he pulled out a piece of paper and unfolded it. The edges flapped in the wind. She stepped closer, wanting to read the note. *Not* wanting to read the note. Blinking rapidly, her eyes watered from staring at the bright white paper in the blinding sunshine. The wavy black lines came into focus: "You can run. But you can't hide."

She let out a long breath between tight lips. She recognized Brian's handwriting. The same meticulous letters that he'd carved into notes giving her instructions on what to buy for dinner or how to wear her hair or when to be home. Or how to wash his clothes, hang his pants, fold his socks. His demanding directives had been as particular as they were plentiful.

He'd controlled her.

Heather's stomach twisted and she feared she would have thrown up if not for her empty stomach.

"I wonder why he left the note in my truck and not in your house. He had access." Zach turned the note over in his hand.

Heather turned her back to the truck, suddenly sensing they were not alone. "He wanted me to know that even you can't keep me safe."

Zach slammed his fist on the frame of the door of his truck and muttered under his breath. "We're going to have to get a sheriff to take us to their office."

"My car is parked behind the barn."

"No, it's better if we don't take your car. Too obvious." Just then, he looked up and saw Deputy Gates walking toward his patrol car. He waved to the man. Gates climbed into his vehicle and drove over, pulling up alongside his damaged truck. The officer rolled down his window. "What happened here?"

"Fox got to my truck. He might be hiding in the cornfields." Zach kept Heather close as he scanned his surroundings. He tapped the roof of the sheriff's patrol car. "Forget about my truck for now. I can get someone to tow it to a collision shop. I need to get Miss Miller out of here. All this open space is giving me the willies."

He thought he heard Heather mutter, "The willies?" under her breath.

"Can you take us to the sheriff's department?"

The deputy tipped his head toward the back of his vehicle. "Hop in."

Zach held out his hand for Heather. Hesitancy flashed in her eyes before she climbed in. He suspected not many people liked to travel in the back of a patrol car. He ran around and jumped in the front passenger seat.

Zach looked over his shoulder and smiled at Heather sitting in the backseat. "We'll get you to safety."

She stared at him with a blank expression in her eyes, seemingly unconvinced.

"Nice to meet you, Miss Miller. I'm Deputy Conner Gates. I hear you're opening a bed-and-breakfast in your grandmother's house," the deputy said casually to Heather as he pulled out onto the road.

"Yeah…" She stretched the word out, as if she were about to ask him how he knew her plans, but then realized word traveled quickly in a small town. "I hope to open in less than two weeks. I already have it booked."

"The fall foliage is beautiful. Our little hotel in town can't keep up with the tourists. You'll have a booming business, I'm sure." The deputy was good at making small talk, obviously trying to distract Heather from the events going on around her.

"That's what I was counting on," Heather said, noncommittally. Defeat slipped into her tone, as if her dreams had been forever dashed by today's events.

"The town will be happy to see the old house come to life again." The deputy flicked his gaze into the rearview mirror and Zach could imagine Heather smiling back politely.

"How far is the sheriff's office?" Zach asked, determined to get the focus off Heather.

"In the center of town. Ten-minute drive. From there, we'll get an unmarked vehicle to take Miss Miller to a safe location."

"I have something else in mind. Something Fox would never expect." Zach tapped the door handle, nervous energy from the adrenaline surging through his veins.

"Whatever you say," the deputy said.

Cornfields whizzed past in a blur. A flash of something dark emerged from the cornfields just ahead, catching Zach's eye and making his pulse spike. He held up his hand, as if that would stop the car. "Slow down."

Before the deputy slowed, the form—dressed in black—crouched low on the side of the road.

"Get down!" Zach yelled. "Get down!"

The back window shattered with an explosive sound. The patrol car skidded, weaved, then picked up speed.

The deputy scrambled for the radio controls. "Shooter on Lapp Road. In the cornfields point five miles from the Miller home. Patrol car's been hit. Send backup."

"Stay down," Zach yelled as he tried to stay hunkered down and get a location on the shooter. A ping sounded somewhere else on the vehicle. He cursed under his breath. "Stay down." He stretched his hand over the seat and touched Heather's head. She had unbuckled and taken refuge in the tight space behind the front seat.

After another half mile, Zach was confident the shooter had retreated into the cornfields. "Pull over."

The deputy did as Zach instructed. Zach climbed out and yanked open the back door, his heart racing in his chest. "Heather, Heather! Are you okay?"

Heather sat up, terror radiating in her bright brown eyes. He reached out and raked the shards of glass from her hair. "Are you hit?"

She pressed her hand to her chest. "I… No…no, I'm okay."

"Okay." Zach gritted his jaw in determination. He closed her car door, then leaned into the front passenger seat. "Take her to the sheriff's office. I'm going after him."

Without waiting for the deputy to finish his protest, Zach slammed the door and patted the roof. "Go!" Grabbing his gun from its holster, he ran back in the direction of the shooter, his senses on high alert.

Every twig snap, bird crow and rustling stalk sent his adrenaline spiking over the edge.

Fox. It had to be Fox. He couldn't let him get away.

Breathing hard, Zach reached the point where the gunman had emerged from the cornfields, and based on the footprints, the same point where he had ducked back into them. Zach had also noted the mile marker.

Pulse whooshing in his ears, he slowed, cautious not to get ambushed, fearing his need to get revenge might override his better judgment.

Examining the ground, he noticed a heavy boot print in the dirt. Sliding between the cornstalks, he followed the prints, the deeper in, the less certain the path of travel, but they seemed to be leading to woods on the other side of the fields.

Once he reached the woods, he slowed, trying to quiet his ragged breath. In the distance, he heard water, a river or creek. Pausing a moment, he let his eyes adjust to the heavily shadowed woods, except for the occasional beam of bright sunlight that penetrated the thick canopy.

Gun in hand, he made his way deeper into the woods, toward the sound of water. Once he got to the clearing, he caught sight of a man on a dock, leaning over something. A boat, maybe?

Zach raced toward the dock.

"Fox!"

The man spun around and fired without warning. Zach dived behind a tree, then shot back from the protection of his hiding place.

Another shot split the bark near his shoulder.

"You've run out of options. Drop the weapon," Zach yelled, sensing perhaps his statement contradicted his current predicament.

Another shot rang out, this one spraying the dirt at his feet.

Pressing flat against the tree, he yelled, "Fox. You've got nowhere to go. Drop your weapon. Surrender."

"Surrender? And go back to that hellhole?" Fox yelled back, his voice slightly muffled. "No way."

The sound of an engine ripped through the still air. Zach's chest tightened as he peered out from behind the safety of the tree. Fox was on a boat motoring away from the end of the dock. The water in the creek rushed from last night's rain.

Pulse pounding in his ears, Zach sprinted to the dock, the soles of his shoes sucking into the muck on the shore. The boat was about thirty feet away from the dock with the distance quickly growing.

Zach planted his feet and took aim at the man who had murdered his sister.

Chapter Five

The edge of the hard plastic chair bit into the back of Heather's thighs as she waited impatiently for U.S. Marshal Zachary Walker to return. That was how she had to think of him, as U.S. Marshal Zachary Walker, professional law enforcement officer, because if she made it personal, it made her worry too much. She couldn't imagine the bravery it took to charge after Brian Fox, her ex-husband-slash-convict.

She'd never be able to live with herself if he got hurt—*or worse*—because of her.

No, not because of you, a more rational voice whispered to her. But it was hard to separate the two. Brian Fox was in Quail Hollow because of her.

Leaning forward, she focused all her nervous energy on plucking out the shards of glass that had rained down on her as she hunkered down in the backseat of the patrol car. If Zach hadn't hollered out his warning, would her ex-husband finally have made good on his promise to kill her?

Groaning, she stood and dumped the shards she had collected in the palm of her hand into the garbage. She paced the small office area. She promised Deputy Conner Gates she wouldn't wander away because anywhere beyond the protection of law enforcement she was liable to become target practice once again for her ex-husband. Given another chance, he wouldn't miss.

The deputy had been called away ten minutes ago and she sent up a silent prayer that U.S. Marshal Zachary Walker had apprehended Brian and he was headed back to Peters Correctional Facility. But no one seemed to want to tell her what was going on.

A bustling at the door drew her attention. Deputy Gates entered followed by the U.S. Marshal.

Thank God. Zachary is safe.

She tamped down her initial reaction to gush all over him, to express her relief that he was safe.

Their relationship was strictly professional.

So why did she care so much about his safe return? Probably because she couldn't handle knowing her ex-husband had hurt another person. He had to be stopped.

Zach made his way to her. She had already given up the pretense of his official title. She lowered her gaze. Mud caked the bottom and sides of his shoes. A deep scratch lined the back of his left hand.

"You okay?" he asked, his mood somber.

"Yeah. Did you get him?" Her pulse whooshed in her ears and she feared she wouldn't hear the answer.

"No." The apology in his eyes said far more than the single word.

Her stomach plummeted. "He got away." She dragged a hand through her hair and her fingers got tangled in the snarled mess. She spun around and glanced up, refusing to cry.

"We exchanged gunfire. Then he climbed into a boat

on the creek," Zach explained. "I got off another shot before he disappeared around a bend. I'm confident I hit him, but I couldn't stop him." His monotone voice suggested even he was having trouble accepting the turn of events.

"You shot him? But he got away?" she repeated in disbelief.

"They're searching the creek. There's no way he'll get far."

She slowly lowered herself onto the familiar plastic chair. "So…what? We wait here until they bring him in?"

Zach sat down next to her and tipped his head to meet her gaze. "The deputy and I think we should move forward with our plan to take you to Ruthie's house. And with an abundance of caution, we'll take a circuitous route to make sure no one follows."

"But if he's…" She couldn't say the word *dead*. Did she really wish him dead? God forgive her. She didn't want him dead—she just wanted him safely behind bars.

Zach gently rubbed his knuckles across the back of her hand. She expected the urge to flee would overwhelm her, make her feel trapped—like it always had when someone got too close—but instead, an unexpected warmth spread up her arm. "Until we've located Fox, we can't take any chances," he said, his voice hoarse.

"You hit him?"

"Yes, I'm sure I did. But he only cranked the motor to full throttle. I was at a disadvantage on the shore."

"Your shoes."

He lifted his boot. "Good thing I had my hiking boots at my cabin."

"Your cabin?"

Zach crossed his arms and tucked his hands under his armpits and he seemed to stifle a shudder. He was probably freezing after running through the cornfields. "Yeah, I have a cabin in Quail Hollow. I had just arrived last night when my supervisor called to alert me of the situation."

Realization twisted her stomach. "If you hadn't come to my property, Brian might have gotten to me first." The image of the graffiti on the wall in her newly constructed eating area was etched in her brain. "Why didn't he attack me when he had the chance? He was in my house." Her lips grew numb with fear and she had trouble forming the words.

"I think he wanted to toy with you, but law enforcement descended too quickly."

The thought of her being terrorized—again—by her ex-husband made her realize she might never be free from this man.

Unless he's dead.

Zach reached out and gently touched her knee as if he recognized the turmoil she was in. "Will you let me take you to Ruthie's? We'll wait until dark. I promise I'll keep you safe."

Heather nodded. She didn't put much stock in promises, but with Brian most likely mortally wounded, she figured Zach's promise to keep her safe might be reasonable.

When Heather arrived at Ruthie's home under the cloak of darkness in a delivery van from the local hardware store, she suspected this was how kidnap victims felt. By the time Zach opened the back doors, her backside ached from each and every bump they'd hit between Quail Hollow's town center and Ruthie's family farm. Sitting on the hard metal surface of the back of the delivery fan wasn't exactly the lap of luxury. And the smell of fresh wood and some sort of fertilizer mingled in her nose and coated her mouth.

Zach held out his hand to her. She accepted it and climbed out, grateful to stretch her legs. She couldn't help but smile at Ruthie as she directed Zach and the driver to stack the fertilizer and wood in the barn. "You actually needed this stuff?" he asked.

"Why waste a trip? My *mem* needs supplies for the greenhouse." Maryann Hershberger and her youngest daughter, Emma, as well as her older daughter Ruthie, ran a greenhouse on the property. Heather had befriended the family after she moved to Quail Hollow, drawn to them by a letter Maryann had written to her father years ago. After getting to know them, Heather had hired Ruthie to work at the bed-and-breakfast. Heather suspected the small family needed the extra income working at the bed-and-breakfast would provide.

If they were able to get back to the required work necessary before opening day.

"How did you arrange all this?" Heather asked as she brushed the loose soil from the back of her pants.

Her question was directed to Zach, but Ruthie stepped forward, rolling up on the balls of her black boots. "The deputy reached me on the phone and he asked me if I ever take deliveries from any businesses in town."

Heather held up her hand. "Wait. You have a phone?"

Her father had grown up Amish and had taken his young family away from Quail Hollow when Heather was only six. Her sisters had been three and two. He'd told them so many stories about the Amish that'd made the young girls long for a home they were too young to remember.

Ruthie jabbed her thumb in the direction of a pole deeper in the barn. A generator hummed and a soft bulb illuminated a phone mounted on the pole. "The *Ordnung* allows us to have a phone for business purposes as long as it's not in the house. The phone serves a purpose but shouldn't interrupt our daily lives." She smiled, a hint of apology lurking in her eyes. "I have an answering machine here, too. So I can return all the calls I miss. In this case, I was happy the sheriff's department reached out. Now you'll be safe because no one knows you're here."

Zach reached into his pocket and pulled out a business card. "Tack this up near the phone in case you need to reach me."

Ruthie took the card and turned it over in her hand. "I will."

Heather cut a sideways glance at Zach, wondering how much Ruthie really knew. Did she know that Brian had shot at the patrol car? That Zach had chased him through the fields until he escaped by boat, but likely not before he was shot?

"The sheriff's department has been a big help. Thank you," Heather said. She knew they had hoped to limit the number of people who knew her location for security purposes, but she also realized it wasn't feasible.

"Not being from Quail Hollow, I couldn't do this on my own." Zach held out his hand to the young man leaning against the truck. "This gentleman is a deputy." The man tipped his head in acknowledgment.

"Another officer is going to arrange to drop off a truck on one of the nearby back roads for our use in an emergency, since mine is out of commission."

"Looks like you've covered everything," Heather said, dragging a hand through her hair, the exhaustion catching up with her. She hadn't slept well last night and today had been nothing but one stress-inducing event after another.

"My job is to keep you safe," Zach said.

"Well," she said, trying to sound more encouraged than she really felt, "hopefully this mess will be behind us soon and we can all go back to our regularly scheduled lives."

Ruthie grabbed a paper sack and opened it up. "I brought you some clothes."

"Thank you." Heather took the bag and set it in the back of the van. The fabric of the long dress felt heavy as she pulled it out.

"Do you really think this is necessary?" She ran her fingers down the ties of the bonnet.

"It's another layer of protection. I don't think Fox will be looking for an Amish woman."

Heather smoothed her hand down the pale blue fabric and a distant memory fluttered around the periphery of her mind. "I suppose not." She glanced around the open space of the barn. "Am I to get dressed in here?"

"We'll give you privacy." Zach tipped his head to the driver and they both stepped out of the barn.

"Would you like some help?" Ruthie asked. "There are pins to hold it closed."

"Pins?" Heather noticed the metal sparkle in the dull light.

"No buttons allowed."

Heather blinked slowly, unable to wrap her fuzzy brain around all the arbitrary rules. Rules her mother and father both had grown up following.

"Yes, I'd appreciate that."

Ruthie turned her back and Heather slipped off what her friend would call *Englisch* clothes and quickly slipped on the dress. "Okay, ready."

Ruthie spun around and her eyes widened. "Wow, you look… Wait…" She stepped closer and reached for Heather's hair, twisting it back into a low bun. With careful concentration, Ruthie reached into her apron and pulled out some bobby pins and secured her hair. "Almost ready." She stooped and reached into the bag and produced a bonnet. Ruthie secured it on Heather's head and stepped back. "There. You look right nice. Like regular Amish."

Heather touched the bonnet and was eager to see herself in the mirror. She hadn't had time to put makeup on this morning, so she imagined she did look like most other Amish women, even if she didn't feel like one.

Heather pulled up the hem of her dress and examined her purple sneakers. Ruthie laughed—the young woman had such an easygoing nature—and said, "You can always go barefoot. Or I'm sure I can find an old pair of boots."

Before Heather had a chance to comment, Zach hollered from outside the door. "You decent in there?"

Without saying anything, Heather walked to the opening where the truck was still parked, her heart racing in her chest. She felt a little bit like she was going to prom and about to show off her gown to her date, albeit the dress she was wearing was a lot plainer than the pink sparkly one she had worn another lifetime ago.

What Zach didn't say was telegraphed in his eyes. "I guess you're ready."

"Wait a minute," Heather said with feigned annoyance. "What about you? Aren't you supposed to be undercover?"

Zach made a sound she couldn't quite decipher.

Ruthie held up a finger and ran into the barn, then came back with a broad-brimmed felt hat. She handed it to Zach, who stuffed it on his head. "All right, then."

"We can find some of my *dat*'s clothes for you once we get inside."

"Ready?" he asked.

Heather couldn't read the expression in his shadowed eyes. A part of her felt like she was playing dress up, but nothing about this dangerous situation was pretend.

The truck that had provided Heather safe passage had pulled away and Zach escorted her across the farm, past the greenhouse and up the front steps of Ruthie's home. He continuously scanned the surroundings. Far too many places for someone to hide. But they had decided the less police presence here, the better. If Fox had somehow gotten off the creek, they didn't want to send out any red flares as to Heather's location.

Zach blinked slowly as flashes of memory assaulted him. The sound of the shots, the smell of the residue, his own jagged breathing in his ears…

There was no way he'd missed. *No way.* The first few shots he took were defensive shots from behind the safety of the tree. But the last shot, he had Fox in his sights.

As they climbed the front steps, Heather reached up and slipped her hand around the crook of his arm. "Are you sure this is a good idea? I don't want to put anyone else in danger," she whispered as Ruthie opened the door.

"This will all be over soon. I promise."

Heather dropped her hand and smoothed it over her dress.

"You look rather fetching," he said, keeping his voice low while trying to lighten the mood.

"Nice hat," she tossed back at him.

"I might see if we can add it to the U.S. Marshals uniform."

She turned to him and raised her eyebrows. She looked like she was about to say something else when his cell phone rang. Zach glanced at the screen and noticed it was a local call, probably the sheriff's department.

"I better take this. I'll be in shortly." He waited until Ruthie and Heather closed the door behind them. He stepped off the porch and hung in the shadows. "Marshal Walker."

"Hey, it's Gates. I have an update."

Zach held his breath waiting for the words like *body, dead, recovery, it's over*. Instead the local sheriff's deputy said, "We found a boat on the creek with some blood in it. But there's still no sign of Fox."

Zach swallowed hard. "What do you mean?" A thumping started behind his eyes and any hope that this situation was going to be resolved today ebbed out of him.

"The boat was found on the west side of Quail Hollow Creek. It wasn't anchored or tied down. We could speculate a lot from that."

Zach closed his eyes and pushed his hat up on his head and rubbed his forehead. "He might have fallen out of the boat."

"If that's the case, might take a few more days to find his body."

Zach turned around and glanced at the well-maintained house. A soft light glowed in the front window. He had to reassure himself that Heather was safe, regardless of the bad news.

Just a few more days.

But a niggling in the back of his head made him wonder if it really would be over in a few days. Fox was one tough egg.

"What are the chances Fox got out of the boat and is on the run? How much blood was in the boat?"

"The amount of blood itself didn't indicate a fatal injury, but a wounded prisoner won't make it long in the woods. We'll find him."

"And if he went into the creek?"

"Search teams are scheduled to drag a section of the creek in the morning. Hold tight."

"Will do." Zach ended the call and stood for a few more minutes outside. He drew in a deep breath, trying to calm his rioting emotions. The stillness on the farm was almost eerie.

Brian Fox was not going to get away. Law enforcement would either find him or his body tomorrow, in the light of day. Zach's job was to keep Heather safe in the meantime.

Chapter Six

"*Mem!*" Ruthie called as she led Heather into her home through a tidy sitting room and toward the back of the house. Every time Heather visited the Hershbergers' home, she was struck by how there wasn't a single framed photo in the room. Maybe she noted it because she regretted that she didn't have any photos of her mother, who grew up in the Amish way. The Amish were forbidden from having their photos taken.

"We're here. I have Heather Miller with me," Ruthie called cheerily, as if she had simply brought home a friend for dinner.

When they reached the kitchen, Mrs. Hershberger put the glass she had been washing into the drying rack and turned to face them. Her mouth opened as if she were about to offer them a greeting, when a look Heather couldn't quite define skated across the older woman's eyes. Her hands flew to her mouth in slow motion. Water rimmed her wide eyes.

"Oh, you look just like your *mem*, Sarah." Mrs. Hershberger walked over slowly to Heather and stopped in front of her. Heather half expected her to touch her face, but Ruthie's mother simply dropped her hands to her sides and studied her intently. "I saw the resemblance before, but now…" She clasped her hands and held them to her chest.

For a moment, any words were trapped in Heather's throat as the walls of the cozy kitchen grew close. She tipped her head and felt the tightness of her hair gathered at the nape of her neck. Finally she found some words. "My father used to tell me that I looked a lot like my mother, but I had never seen a photo of her." Her voice cracked. The fact that the Amish forbade their members from having their photo taken seemed like a harmless enough rule, but when you were a kid whose mom died when you were six, you couldn't help but be a bit resentful. Yet, unbeknownst to her, with each passing year she had apparently grown to resemble her mother.

"I saw the resemblance when you visited before." Mrs. Hershberger had started to repeat what she was saying earlier. "But now, without makeup and with the Amish clothes…" There was a quiet reverence to the older woman's tone.

"I hardly remember my mom, but I'm honored that you think I look like her. My father said she was a beauty."

Mrs. Hershberger dropped her hands to her sides and pink splotches colored her fair skin. "Oh, forgive me. That was rude. Please come in. Sit down." She pulled a chair out from the long pine table. "Can I get you something? Ruthie tells me you've run into a bit of trouble and need someplace to stay."

Heather's gaze drifted to Ruthie and she wondered how much she had confided in her mom. Mrs. Hershberger deserved the entire truth if she was opening her home up to her.

"Did Ruthie tell you what was going on, Mrs. Hershberger?"

The older woman froze, her well-worked fingers wrapped around the top slat of the back of the chair. "Please, call me Maryann. And yes, Ruthie told me you had an old boyfriend who might try to hurt you."

Heather made eye contact with Ruthie and smiled. Ruthie was both determined and confident, two qualities Heather imagined were not in overabundance in young Amish women—or in young women in general.

"It's more than that. He's actually my ex-husband, who escaped from prison after being sent there for killing his second wife."

Maryann gasped and walked around to the front of the chair and slowly sat down, as if the news had ripped the steel rod from her spine. She sat perched on the edge of the chair, seeming ready to bolt at a moment's notice. "Perhaps my daughter left out a few details."

"I didn't want to be a gossip," Ruthie said, joining them at the table and leaning eagerly forward as if afraid her mother was going to rescind the invitation.

Heather wondered if the woman was more horrified that she had been divorced or that her ex was an escaped convict. She hoped, despite the woman's strong religious convictions, that she wouldn't condemn her for putting her very life above the sanctity of marriage. Heather had long ago made peace with her decision and expected that God would forgive her.

However, during all her previous visits with the Hershbergers, Heather had omitted the darker side of her past. Had she not forgiven herself?

Heather ran the palms of her hands over the edge of the pine table. She imagined that not too long ago, it was surrounded by a big loving family who had now grown and moved on to create happy dinner tables of their own. The passage of time and her spouse's premature death had left Maryann alone with her youngest two daughters, Ruthie and Emma.

"I'd understand if you'd rather I stay someplace else. My ex-husband is both smart and ruthless."

Ruthie squared her shoulders, the light in her eyes suggesting she rarely had such excitement in her life. "Marshal Walker made sure no one followed Heather here. Precautions were taken. There's no reason to believe we're in danger. Besides, Heather needs someplace safe to stay."

Maryann's gaze drifted toward the front room. "And this law enforcement person—"

"He had to take a phone call. He'll be in in a minute," Ruthie interrupted her mother, obviously determined to convince her that they had to host their *Englisch* friends.

Maryann's lips grew pinched, then relaxed before she spoke again. "He plans to stay here, too?"

Heather caught Ruthie's eye, encouraging her to stay quiet so she could speak. "Yes, if that's okay with you. It'll be safer if he's here. For everyone."

Maryann smoothed the folds in her dress near her thighs. "I do suppose we have the room. But I'll need for both of you to respect our home. No phone calls. No guns."

"Mem," Ruthie groaned, sounding like a typical teenager. "He needs his gun."

Maryann hiked her chin, not about to back down. "He can keep it in the barn."

"Are you sure we're not an imposition? We can make other plans," Heather suggested, even though she wasn't sure what those other plans would be. Her preference was to stay in Quail Hollow, close to the final renovations of her bed-and-breakfast. But those were selfish plans.

"We have invited you into our home. You don't need to make other plans." The finality in Maryann's tone stopped Heather from questioning her host further.

"I'll check on Zach." Heather pushed away from the table. Just then Emma came running down the stairs. She greeted them shyly.

"Excuse me a minute," Heather said, not missing the look of surprise on Ruthie's fifteen-year-old sister's face. On the way to the front door, Heather caught sight of her sneakers poking out from the bottom of her dress.

Pausing at the front door, she listened to see if Zach was still talking on the phone. She didn't want to interrupt. She thought she heard him wrapping up the call. Reaching for the door handle, she said a silent prayer that he'd have good news for her.

Was it wrong to pray that Brian was dead?

Maybe. Perhaps she should pray that he was back in custody instead?

Drawing in a deep breath, she opened the door. Zach turned toward her. The deep lines of concern etched on his handsome face under the moonlight told her that her prayers would have to wait to be answered.

Zach slid his cell phone back into his jacket pocket, then took off his broad-brimmed hat and set it on a small table that sat between two rocking chairs on the front porch.

"That's not the face of a man with good news," Heather said, pulling the front door closed behind her with a quiet click.

He searched her face for a moment. "No, it's not. They still haven't located Fox."

The strings of Heather's white bonnet pooled around the hollow of her neck. Her hand fluttered around the tips of the strings. A part of him wondered if this ruse was being disrespectful to the Amish people of this community. Playing dress up to avoid detection.

"Is it wrong that I hoped he was dead?" Heather whispered.

"You have a right to be frightened." He ran a hand across his jaw. "I'm sorry I didn't catch him earlier, then neither one of us would be standing on this porch pretending we're Amish."

"Hmm…" There was a distant quality to her voice. "I thought being here in the country would be more peaceful. I guess I didn't bargain on Brian escaping from prison."

"None of us could have predicted that."

"I know." She drew in a deep breath. "Hey, listen," she said with a forced cheery tone. "Ruthie's mother is fine with us staying, but she asked that we don't use our phones in her house and she wants you to keep your gun in the barn."

Zach gave his head a quick shake. "Wait. What? I need to be able to protect you." He took a step back, then forward. "No, okay…" He ran the options over in his head. "It's probably better if I patrol the grounds tonight anyway. Yeah, that will work. I'll stay outside."

"You've got to be exhausted. You didn't sleep last night, either."

Zach blinked slowly but refused to admit how tired he was. Regardless of his exhaustion, he wouldn't be able to rest until Fox was no longer a threat.

When he didn't answer, Heather said, "I can keep you company."

He slowly shook his head. "I'd feel better if I knew you were safely inside. I'm going to see if Mrs. Hershberger will allow me to do a quick sweep of the house." He scratched his head. "Please tell me the Amish have locks."

"We have locks."

Both Heather and Zach spun around to find Mrs. Hershberger standing in the doorway. After telling Zach to call her Maryann, she went on to explain that not every Amish home had a lock, but Maryann had insisted her husband put locks on the doors and windows after her dear friend—Heather's mother—had been murdered.

Maryann turned to look Heather in the eye. "We all lost a little something the day your mother was killed. Some far more than others, of course. But many of us who called her friend forever lost a sense of safety."

Heather bowed her head but didn't say anything.

"I'm sorry for your loss," Maryann continued. "I'm not happy about the situation, but I'm grateful I can help my dear friend's daughter."

Until this very moment, Zach hadn't truly considered the amount of loss Heather had suffered over her short life. He had been too focused on his own.

Heather nodded, as if she couldn't spare any words.

"Locks are a good thing," Zach said, needing to focus on the task at hand. "I have my gun in its holster, but can I do a quick tour of your home, then I'll stay outside?"

"You're going to stay up all night watching the house?"

"That's my job." His gaze drifted to Heather. However, that wasn't entirely true. In just a short time, it was beginning to feel like far more than just a job. He would have thought he'd be able to keep it strictly professional, but something about this woman, even dressed in plain clothing, made him wonder... No, this *was* just a job. Even if he did enjoy Heather's company, he would never be able to see her without thinking of his sister. Who wanted to live life with those constant reminders?

Maryann clasped her hands. "Okay, you can come in the house with your gun." She pressed her hands together. "But, please, I don't want to see it. You can take one of the guest rooms. You need to protect Heather. Her mother and I were best friends."

"I appreciate that." Zach grabbed his hat from where he'd set it down. They all went inside the house and he personally saw to it that all the doors and windows were secured.

Long after the women retired upstairs, he stood in the dark sitting room staring out the window wondering if Fox was still stalking his way through Quail Hollow or if he lay dying deep in the woods. Or if his body had sunk to the bottom of the creek.

None of the ideas brought him peace. Nothing would bring him peace until he knew for sure that Fox could no longer hurt anyone.

One of the advantages of staying at a true Amish home was that Heather had been unable to watch TV and see what she assumed was the relentless, round-the-clock coverage of a convict on the run playing out over all the local news networks. However, her sisters had been inundated with the news and were wildly relieved when Heather reached out to them. She assured them she was safe, but couldn't share the details. They also had strict instructions to call the police if they noticed anything suspicious.

Over the course of the few days that she and Zach were at the Hershbergers' home, Zach had given Heather occasional news updates—editing out any parts that may have included her, per her request—but the only update she really wanted was the one that reported her ex-husband was back in custody.

Or dead.

Feeling a little stir-crazy as a light drizzle made the autumn day bleak, Heather got up from the breakfast table with plans to retreat to the solitude of the greenhouse to water the mums. Zach had excused himself a while ago to make phone calls on the front porch.

Heather cleared her dishes, then went out the back door. As she crossed the muddy driveway, she was again grateful Ruthie had found an old pair of boots for her.

She opened the glass door to the greenhouse and stepped inside. The temperature was cranked high, but it felt good on this damp, dreary day. She found she enjoyed working in the greenhouse. The Hershbergers sold plants and flowers to the public. On Sunday, a lot of non-Amish customers stopped by to purchase hay bales, mums and dried cornstalks for autumn decorations. Zach had insisted he and Heather stay inside. Out of sight. But once Monday, Tuesday and now Wednesday rolled around, the visitors dried up. Apparently the greenhouse was a weekend business patronized by tourists out for a country drive.

Zach had decided it was safe for Heather to stroll the property—not that Brian would be looking for his ex-wife dressed in traditional Amish clothing. She spent time in the greenhouse: watering the mums, deadheading the plants and general organizing. It afforded her the simple luxury of expending some of her nervous energy. Sometimes Ruthie or Emma came with her, keeping her thoughts occupied with things other than Brian Fox. She enjoyed listening to their chatter.

"There you are. I'm not going to want you to leave," Maryann said, stepping inside the greenhouse and picking up the garden gloves from the nearby shelf. Then her eyes widened. "I probably shouldn't have said that. I meant—"

Heather smiled. "No need to explain. Once I get the bed-and-breakfast up and running, I should make time for gardening. It's relaxing."

"Your mother used to say the same thing."

Heather met Maryann's gaze. "My mother liked to garden?" If Maryann wasn't such a kind, genuine soul, Heather might have been embarrassed by the raw desire to learn about her mother. Like a child eager to hear every last bit about the day-to-day life of Santa Claus.

"Oh, she loved to garden. She used to bring you and your sisters here on occasion, not that she had much free time while caring for her growing family and running a household. But she was the one who suggested we start a greenhouse."

Heather should have suspected considering her name and those of her sisters, Lily and Rose.

Maryann continued talking. "My husband had fallen

ill and farming was getting tough. This was something I could do with my daughters." Maryann adjusted the band of her glove. "My husband was sick for many years. Now it's just me and the two youngest girls."

The water from the hose was pooling at Heather's feet as she listened to the story, realizing her mother had probably stood exactly where she stood. Used the same hose. Felt the heat from the glass enclosure. She tried to still the moment, capture it, but curiosity got the best of her. "What do you know about my mother's death?"

The color drained from Maryann's face and Heather quickly added, "My father never talked about it and there's not a lot of information online."

"Online?" Maryann narrowed her eyes in confusion. Some of the younger Amish may have been familiar with their worldly neighbors' ways, but obviously Maryann had no exposure to computers or the lingo.

"I did a search on my computer. People can pull up old news articles. I learned that she was murdered and that she was found in the barn on my *mammy*'s farm." A flush of dread washed over her. She hadn't spoken out loud about her mother's murder since the day she was fifteen and had asked her dad about it. He'd shut her down in no uncertain terms. His grief had been so palpable that she hadn't dared ask him again. Now it was too late because he had passed away years ago.

Then a few years later, she met Brian and things spiraled out of control from there. Heather had been so fixated on protecting herself that she hadn't had time to reflect on the past. Only after Brian's incarceration did Heather feel that maybe she could reclaim some of her past. Figure out who she was. What she had lost all those years ago.

"The news articles were pretty vague." Heather studied Maryann's face, not wanting to rehash the tragic incident. "I imagine not many of the Amish wanted to talk to the newspapers or the police."

Maryann lifted her hand and shook her head. "I have tried to put it out of my memory." She pressed her lips together. "It was a long time ago. Maybe it's best if you forget."

"How can I forget something that shaped who I am? If my *mem* hadn't been murdered, I would have grown up in this Amish community. My entire life would have been different. Please, tell me what you remember."

Maryann peeled back the lid from a container of fertilizer and focused intently on scooping out the contents, then dumping the small beads into the pot of a mum, bursting with pretty purple buds.

Finally Maryann dropped the scoop back into the container and tore off her gardening gloves. She slumped back, resting a hip against the metal table. "The person who hurt your mother was an outsider. He was never caught." She looked up. "Don't ruin your future by searching the past. There are no answers. You must forgive him in your heart. He will be judged by God."

Maryann had grown somber and Heather regretted bringing up her mom's murder. If she couldn't have answers about her death, at least she wanted to know who her *mem* was in life. She decided to bring up the subject of her mother's life at another time.

A quiet knock sounded on the door. The two women turned to see Zach opening the glass door to the greenhouse. He wore black pants and a black shirt—most likely purchased from the men's department at some major retailer, certainly not Amish, but perhaps close enough from a distance if Brian was spying on them. He took off his broad-brimmed hat. "I didn't mean to interrupt."

"It's fine." Maryann tossed her gardening gloves aside and slipped out of the greenhouse past Zach. "I need to check on the girls. See that they're getting their chores done."

Heather watched Maryann leave, the fabric of her long dress swishing around her legs. She was sorry she had ruined the peaceful mood by her tactless questions about her mother's murder. Maryann had been her mother's dear friend.

Heather turned to Zach and noticed he was spinning the hat in his hands, a nervous gesture. Her heart plummeted. She sucked in a breath with eager anticipation. "Do you have news?"

Chapter Seven

"I don't have any news." Zach wished he did. He'd do anything to take away Heather's worry and see her smile. He blinked a few times, then stepped back, determined to maintain the wall of professionalism. He had a job to do. "Not concrete news, anyway," he clarified.

"What does that mean?" There was an edge to her voice as she turned away from him and shut off the hose in the greenhouse. She seemed to take her time rolling it up.

"Deputy Gates called me. They dragged the bottom of the creek and they haven't found Fox's body. The currents may have carried him out. Or maybe they didn't search the right spots. From the dock where he entered the boat to the point where we found the empty vessel was three-quarters of a mile."

"They may never find the body?" She crossed her arms and glared at him, as if somehow this was his fault.

"That's unlikely. But it might take a while. I'm sorry."

Heather bowed her head and ran a shaky hand across her hair, pushing back her bonnet. She took a moment to adjust her bonnet, then met his gaze. "What do I do now?" Her voice grew high-pitched. She waved her hand frantically up and down her Amish dress. The bonnet she had just adjusted. "Am I supposed to stay here? Hide forever?"

She spun around, paced a few steps, then turned back to him, shooting daggers at him with her steely gaze. She ripped off her bonnet and tossed it aside. It landed on the edge of a pot of mums in full bloom, dangled for a few seconds, then dropped to the floor of the greenhouse and settled into a puddle. He bent to pick it up, when she instructed him to leave it alone. With jerky movements, she yanked at the pins holding her hair in a neat bun at the base of her head. Her long brown hair cascaded over her shoulders in soft curls.

Combing her fingers frantically through her hair, she said, "I'm not going to spend another minute hiding." She drew in a ragged breath. "I wasted ten years already. Not to mention the years I had already wasted with Brian." She winced. "You said you shot him, right?" Her eyebrows rose as she waited for confirmation.

"Yes, I did."

"Then he's dead. I'm going to go back to living my life. Back to the bed-and-breakfast."

Doubt whispered across Zach's brain. His mind flashed back to the creek. To his erratic pulse pounding in his ears. Lifting his gun, aiming it at his target. He was a good shot. He *had* to have hit Fox.

Heather's life depended on it.

"Give it a few more days," Zach urged her. "They've extended the search north up the creek, cutting through the hills. If he lived long enough to get out near where the boat was found, he wouldn't have lived long. They'll find his body in the woods."

Her fingers edged with soil curled into a fist. "Then when his body doesn't turn up in the woods, you'll tell me to wait until they check north of there or west of here." Her face flushed red. "I have to believe he's dead. I'm done hiding."

Apparently sensing his apprehension, she stepped forward, looking like a woman straddling two worlds with her gorgeous long curls flowing down over her drab gray dress that only revealed the laces of her well-worn boots. She reached out and took his hat from his hands. A smile glinted in her eyes. "Now you don't have to pretend you're the Amish marshal."

Zach couldn't help but smile. "I thought I looked good in this hat."

She patted his chest. "You couldn't even commit to the entire ruse." She dropped her hand and adjusted the collar on his black golf shirt. "Now, *I* was committed."

He tipped his head and tried to read her. "It's not a good idea to go back to the bed-and-breakfast, you know."

"He's dead. I want to go back to my grandmother's house on Lapp Road and get the bed-and-breakfast ready for our first guests." Heather bit her lower lip and her eyes grew glazed for a moment, as if she were trying to figure something out. "I've lost five days. I'm expecting guests in just over one week. It's time I go back."

Zach ran a hand over his mouth. "I can't—"

"You can't what?" Anger sparked in her eyes. "I let a man dictate what I wore, when I slept, what I *ate*! I am not going to let you tell me what to do."

Zach held up his hands in surrender. "Can I at least

accompany you to the bed-and-breakfast? Stay a few more days. Until the body turns up."

"Your boss will let you stay longer?"

"He knows how important this case is to me." Besides, his boss owed him one for pulling him away from his vacation that he had planned to spend in his cabin surrounded by nothing but some dusty old books, a black-and-white TV and his feelings of guilt and self-recrimination.

Heather snagged the bonnet from the puddle on the floor and balled it up in her hand. "You're welcome to come to the bed-and-breakfast with me, but you know I'm going to put you to work."

"I wouldn't have it any other way."

A sense of pride filled Heather when Zach drove up to her grandmother's house. *Her* house now. They had used the unmarked vehicle the sheriff's department had left for their use until his truck was repaired. Ruthie had come along, insisting she needed to stay at the house to help with the preparations. Heather was happy for the company.

Looking at the house now was like seeing it for the first time. The workers had finished putting a fresh coat of gray paint on the shingled siding and the white trim gleamed anew.

For the briefest of moments she forget about all her troubles.

"Sloppy Sam did a great job," Ruthie said with a hint of pride she tried to suppress. The Amish were a humble people.

"Is there someplacc I could park? In the barn maybe?" Zach asked.

Heather shot him a sideways look, knowing it was unreasonable to think these precautions weren't still necessary. "Sure. The barn's fine." She herself had decided to park her little car behind the barn because she still hadn't mustered the courage to go inside the barn. Maybe she never would.

As the truck bobbled over the ruts in the dirt driveway, she gasped in excitement when she saw the completed back of the house. "The window has been installed. Here—" she patted the dashboard "—let me out." She tugged on the door handle and climbed out of the truck, unable to take her eyes off the completed addition. The siding. The painting. The window. All complete.

Excitement bubbled up inside Heather as Ruthie jumped out and followed her. Heather dug into the bag she had strapped across her body and pulled out the house key. She ran up the back steps and unlocked the door. She pushed it open and the smell of new wood mingled with that of fresh paint. The kitchen was untouched, per Heather's request, except for the updated appliances. She wanted to feel her grandmother's presence. The workers had even seamlessly extended the wood floor from the kitchen into the new eating area.

"This is better than I imagined," Heather said. Sloppy Sam had built a long picnic table that could seat plenty of guests.

"Sloppy Sam is a craftsman," Ruthie said.

As Heather's gaze moved to the freshly painted wall to the right of the window, she found herself drawn forward. She ran her hand over the flat surface where the man who had tormented her for years had stood. Where he had scratched his creepy message. But thankfully, the workers had seen to it that no trace was left.

"Things will get better from here, I just know it," Ruthie said, smiling.

Heather smiled in return. Maybe, just maybe, she could finally allow herself to have hope again for the future.

She heard Zach at the back door. She squared her shoulders and met him in the kitchen. He had their bags slung over his shoulder.

Ruthie approached him and took her bag. "Heather, would you mind if I went upstairs to unpack?"

"Of course not. Go on." Heather had converted the smallest room upstairs—one too small for paying guests—to a cozy room for Ruthie, who initially intended to stay over only on weekend nights when the bed-and-breakfast had guests. The rest of the week, Ruthie would live at home and help with the greenhouse. And Heather had no plans to host guests during the week.

Zach placed the other bags on the floor in the new addition. "Place looks great."

"It does." She bit her lower lip, trying to contain her excitement. The silence stretched on for a beat too long. Heather took a step backward. "Let me show you where you can stay. There's a small space downstairs on the other side of the kitchen. It only has a cot, but…" She hadn't really thought this through.

"It'll be fine. Really." A smile twitched the corners of his mouth. "I'll put my bag away and be right back. You can give me a list of things you need done." He held out his hand. "But from the looks of it, this place is ready for visitors."

His smile was contagious. "I can always come up with a list."

"I didn't doubt that."

Heather strolled into the kitchen and braced her arms on the oversize kitchen sink. How often had her *mammy* stood in this very same spot, mourning the death of her daughter and the loss of her grandchildren? Heather wanted desperately to change the course of the future. To find answers. To find happiness. And not to allow the ghost of Brian Fox to take that away from her.

"Okay, what's up first?"

She spun around and found Zach standing in the doorway with his arms crossed.

"Let me change, and then let's order a pizza for the three of us."

"Will they actually deliver way out here?"

Heather twisted her lips. "Oh, good point." She crossed the kitchen and opened the refrigerator, one of the few *Englisch* concessions to make running an "authentic" Amish bed-and-breakfast easier on her. Sure, she could have run a generator to all her kitchen appliances, but instead she had the contractor run electricity from the grid, definitely an Amish no-no, but her guests probably wouldn't think much of it. "I hadn't gone shopping yet, either. The few things Ruthie brought in the other day have rotted." For some reason, embarrassment heated her cheeks. Even after all these years, her response was instinctual. Brian would have yelled at her, called her an idiot, demanded his dinner. *Now!*

As her emotions welled and crested on a wave of panic, she reminded herself that the man standing a few feet away was not Brian. She swallowed back her emotions, closed the fridge door and turned to smile at him. "Any suggestions?"

"Absolutely. Let's go grocery shopping. I make a mean lasagna."

Zach laughed, apparently tickled by the surprise that must have registered in her eyes. "Don't you believe me?"

She held up her palms. "I have no reason not to. You've yet to disappoint me."

"I have no plans to."

Their eyes locked and lingered for a moment longer than was comfortable. Heather hadn't allowed herself to trust her feelings to another man after the havoc Brian wreaked on her life.

"Well—" Her voice cracked. "Give me ten minutes." She bent over and unlaced her muddy Amish boots and tossed them in the corner near the back door. Maybe she'd leave them there as part of the Amish decor. As she ran up the stairs of her new home, a sense of hope— real hope—for the future coursed through her.

Zach and Heather dropped Ruthie off to visit a friend while they went grocery shopping. It seemed Ruthie was excited to have a little freedom of her own. Her friend promised to hitch up her horse and bring Ruthie home sometime after dinner.

At the grocery store, Heather strolled ahead of Zach. She had a lightness he'd never seen in her before. Up to this point, all of their contact—from the first time he met her at Jill's trial—had always been during stressful times. Now he sensed she was finally allowing herself to believe she was safe. He just hoped she was.

Next to the stand of bananas near the entryway, she spun around. "I'm not much of a cook, but I'm not sure this little store carries everything you'll need."

Zach leaned over and grabbed a shopping basket. "I'm sure we'll find everything we need."

They strolled companionably through the grocery store, picking up lettuce, tomatoes, noodles, sauce, cheese. He hadn't realized how hungry he was until he had all the ingredients for dinner in the basket.

Once they had purchased the groceries and arrived back home, he unloaded them onto the counter.

"Tell me what I can do," Heather said. "I may not know how to cook, but I can follow directions."

"Is that why you hired Ruthie? To cook?"

"In part. But mostly, I knew I couldn't run the bed-and-breakfast all on my own." The look in her eyes suggested something more.

Heather looked away and rubbed the back of her neck. "Ruthie is going to stay here when I have guests. We've fixed up a cute little room for her upstairs. I'll pay her extra. I offered her room and board full-time, but I see now why she turned me down. Maryann and Emma still need her help at home."

"Yet the family needs the extra income."

Heather nodded her agreement.

Zach stopped breaking up the ground beef simmering in the pan on the stove and pointed toward the back door. "I'm going to make arrangements to have an alarm system installed."

Heather scratched her earlobe. "I can't afford that. I've spent everything I have on the remodel."

He watched her nervously tuck a strand of hair behind her ear while she pretended to be busy lining up the jar of sauce, ricotta cheese, and salt and pepper that he'd be needing shortly for the lasagna. His heart ached for her and he found himself drawn to her remarkable spirit.

"I'd like to install the alarm for you. A gift." He chopped up the ground beef with the edge of the spatula.

"Do you think I really need it?" Her soft tone sounded from just behind him.

He didn't turn around to answer. "I work in law enforcement. I've seen a lot of bad things in my career. You're out here in the middle of nowhere." He turned around, holding the spatula. A plop of ground beef hit the floor. They both squatted at the same time and bumped knees.

Heather laughed nervously and stood back up. "Here, let me get that." She tore a piece of paper towel from the roll, and from his crouched position he reached for the towel and she handed it to him. He wiped up the mess, straightened and tossed it in the garbage can.

Heather had gone pale as if a realization had washed over her. "You don't think Brian's dead, do you?"

He touched her arm. "I know I shot him. But it doesn't make any sense that they haven't found his body. However, even when we do have Fox back in custody or find out he's dead, it's not a smart idea for a young woman to live alone in a big house out in the country. You won't always have the benefit of houseguests." He pointed to the stairs. "We'll have a control panel installed in your bedroom."

She frowned at him as uncertainty flashed in her eyes.

"You're inviting strangers into your home. You need to take precautions."

A long-ago memory came to mind. His sister, Jill, had called him, panicked, frightened. She was afraid of her husband. By the time Jill met him at the door of her meticulously maintained home in the safe suburbs of

Buffalo, she had changed her mind. Told her big brother that it was all a misunderstanding. Brian stood next to his baby sister, a smile on his face, his arm draped over her shoulders.

His possession.

Zach's gut roiled at the memory.

Nothing he'd said had convinced his sister to open up to him. To tell him what was really going on. To leave Fox. That day, Jill stood in the doorway with a fake smile on her face.

If only he had…

He shook his head, trying to dispel the horrible memory.

Heather slipped in beside him and stirred the beef that was spattering on the stove.

"Oh, I'm sorry." He covered her soft hand with his, taking the spatula from her. "Some cook I turned out to be."

Standing close, she smiled up at him. "If you think it's important that I get an alarm system, we'll do it. But I insist on paying you back." She searched his face.

"I do think it's important."

Heather gave him a quick nod. "I don't want you to stay here out of some misplaced sense of obligation."

"What do you mean?"

"You're not responsible for your sister's death."

Zach stopped stirring the beef on the stove. How had she read his mind?

"Brian is—*was*—a very convincing man," Heather said, her voice low. "He was charming. He persuaded me to stay more than once. Your sister was a beautiful, smart woman—" her words made the back of his throat ache "—and she was no more at fault for what happened to her than you were. Trust me, I've had my own share of guilt about your sister. What could I have done to prevent it? But I remind myself constantly that Brian is the only responsible party." She reached out and cupped his cheek, brushing her thumb across his jaw. He stood frozen, not wanting to feel too much. "You don't need to stay. I'll be okay." A soft hitch caught in her throat, as if she wasn't sure she believed her own words.

Zach took her hand and kissed the inside of her palm. "Do you want me to leave?"

She lowered her gaze, then lifted it again to meet his. "No, I don't want you to leave."

The tension eased out of his shoulders.

She reclaimed her hand and fisted it to her chest. "Not until we have proof Brian's dead."

Chapter Eight

Heather enjoyed the meal she and Zach—well, mostly Zach—had prepared. It was her first dinner in her *mammy*'s remodeled home. And it felt wonderful.

The sun lowered in the sky as they chatted over a frozen cake from Pepperidge Farm—apparently Zach drew the line at baking. She stood up from the new table and turned on the kerosene lamps, which created a soft glow. She sat back down next to Zach, not eager for the evening to be over.

"When are your first guests scheduled to arrive?"

"Next weekend." She moved the crumbs of the cake around on her plate. "Barring any cancellations. My plan is to only book rooms for the weekend."

"Well, hopefully this other issue will be resolved."

Heather studied the palm of her hand. "I haven't watched any of the news coverage regarding the escape. I hope mention of an ongoing search for an escaped convict in Quail Hollow won't be bad for business."

Zach wiped his mouth with a napkin, then set it down, neatly running his fingers over the edge, creating a sharp fold.

"If I knew you better, I might think you were stalling," she said, trying to read his expression.

He drew in a deep breath. His dirty-blond hair looked darker in the heavy shadows. His eyes were hard to read. "The news mentioned that the search for Fox has focused on Quail Hollow because of you."

Heather's pulse whooshed in her ears as Zach's words seemed to be coming from miles away. "They mentioned me by name?" Of course they had. Hers was a juicy story. She swallowed hard. "Anything else?" She found herself holding her breath. "Did they mention my mother's murder?"

"Yes."

"How… Why?" But she knew why. Her mother's murder had been the only murder in the Amish community and now the next big story to hit the quiet town a generation later had a direct link: *her.* She groaned. "I wonder if this is going to ruin business." She snapped her gaze to him and laughed, rolling her eyes. "No, no, it'll be great for business. Like how people like to take tours of morbid things, like Lizzie Borden's house or…" She dragged her hand through her hair. "Not that my mother died here. But her body…" She let the words trail off, not wanting to talk about it. Her mother's body had been found in the barn out back. *Her* barn. Another part of her past that she'd eventually have to face.

Zach covered her hand with his. "A news truck was out in front of your house a few days ago, but Deputy Gates chased it away. I don't think they gave him much of a fight because you weren't here. There's only so much coverage we can give to an empty house."

"But now that I'm back?"

"If they come back, we'll deal with it then. The truck's in the barn, so that should buy us more time."

"I suppose you're right. Why borrow trouble?" Heather leaned her shoulder against his. He shifted and wrapped his arm around her shoulders. "You saw the news coverage. What are they saying?"

She settled into his embrace and tuned into his comforting stroke on her arm. "It's not important."

Her eyes slowly closed. "I suppose you're right. It's not going to change anything." She suddenly bolted upright. His arm fell away from her and she angled her head to study him. "Did they put a photo of me on the news?"

"Heather..."

She recognized a stall when she heard it. "Tell me. Did they?"

"They ran coverage from when you testified. So yes."

She stood, suddenly very exhausted. "You're right, I shouldn't have asked. I was really hoping to live in anonymity. I guess that was too much to ask." Gathering the dishes, she carried them into the kitchen and over to the sink, wishing she could crawl into bed and sleep. Forget about her troubles for a few hours.

"Look on the bright side," Zach said, bringing a few more dishes over. "At least the Amish don't watch TV."

She narrowed her gaze at him skeptically. "I have a feeling news like this will make its way around Quail Hollow, TV or not. Ruthie seems to know things from town before I do." She shrugged as she filled up half the sink with hot soapy water. "This is where I need to rely on my faith. Trust God that things will work out."

He gently touched the small of her back. "Trust God

and take precautions." She didn't miss the cynicism in his tone.

"I'll let the dishes soak and clean up in the morning. It's early yet, but I'm tired." Maybe relaxing with a book would settle her nerves. She leaned forward and brushed a kiss across his cheek. "Good night, Zach. Thank you for everything." She took a step back. "You should find anything you need in the guest bathroom. If that fails, just give me a holler."

He nodded. "Night, Heather."

A current of electricity ran between them. He was here doing a job and then he'd be gone. Did she dare trust her heart to him only to be hurt again? Like Brian had hurt her.

Zach was nothing like Brian.

But how did she really know? How did anyone?

When she first met Brian, she would have never pegged him for the man he turned out to be.

Dismissing her swirling thoughts, she spun around and ran up the stairs. She slipped into her bedroom and shut the door and turned the dead bolt. She'd sleep better with the lock in place even with Zach downstairs.

Heather flopped down on the chaise lounge, her mind still racing. She hadn't had affectionate feelings toward a man since... She traced the stitching on the arm of the chair and drew in a deep breath. She could still smell the subtle scent of his aftershave. Feel the solidness of his arm around her.

She grabbed the blanket draped over the back of the chair and pulled it over her. Maybe she was confusing her feelings of security and protection for something more.

Something she thought she'd never have again.

She forgot about the book she planned to read and started to doze. She snapped to attention at the sound of footsteps on the stairs. Groggy from sleep, she stumbled toward the door, yet managed to keep her bare feet silent on the cold hardwood floor. Her fingers faltered at the knob to the dead bolt.

Mouth growing dry, she opened the door a fraction, relieved to see Ruthie passing in the hallway. "Good night," she whispered.

"Good night." The shadow of Ruthie's hand lifted in a quick wave. "See you in the morning."

Closing her door, Heather turned the bolt, relieved to know she was no longer alone.

The slant of sun cut across the edge of her bed, startling Heather awake. She bolted up, then stretched across and grabbed her cell phone to check the time.

After eight!

Throwing back the covers, she got cleaned up and dressed for the day and ran downstairs, both refreshed and embarrassed. She never slept this late *and* she still had a list of things to do. A week had passed since Heather had returned to the bed-and-breakfast with Zach and Ruthie in tow. The house had been abuzz with activity: Sloppy Sam and his crew finishing odd projects, Ruthie making lists and Zach helping out wherever he could. Everything seemed to be coming together.

And still no sign of Brian.

When Heather reached the kitchen, she found coffee already made in the coffeemaker—another one of her *Englisch* cheats—but no sign of Zach.

Unable to resist, she poured herself a cup, then sipped it while staring out the window over the yard. In just over twenty-four hours her first guests would be arriving. That was when she saw movement by the barn. Squinting, she noticed that it was Zach. He had found a wheelbarrow and a pitchfork and was hard at work.

"What are you doing, U.S. Marshal Zachary Walker?" she muttered to the empty kitchen, reminding herself that he was here because of his job. But even at that, he worked harder than one of Sloppy Sam's crew members. Zach knew the ins and outs of home repair. However, the longer he stayed, the harder it was to remind herself that he was here on business. Thankfully, Ruthie's presence kept Heather's emotions in check.

All of them had a job to do. *Period.*

Carefully holding her coffee so it wouldn't slosh out of the mug, Heather slipped her feet into her black Wellies and stepped outside. The sun beat down on the gorgeous fall day. She drew in a deep breath and some of the stress of the recent events washed off her.

She stood on the back stoop, sipping her coffee, hoping to get Zach's attention. After a few moments, he set aside the pitchfork and grabbed the handles of the wheelbarrow and pushed it out into the sun and directly toward her.

He stopped and set the wheelbarrow down and smiled. "Sleep well?"

"I did."

He squinted up at her and lifted a hand to tent his eyes. "I thought I'd put some hay down here so the guests wouldn't have to slop through the mud."

Heather smiled. "Good idea."

"What are your plans for the barn? It looks like it could use some TLC."

Heather's gaze drifted to the barn and her pulse automatically spiked. She had never stepped foot in the barn, nor did she have immediate plans to.

"Is something wrong?" The tone of Zach's voice suggested he had to repeat the question. Had he?

"Um…" She scratched the crown of her head and set her mug down on the top rail of the small porch. "I guess I never thought about it much." *That's a lie.* The barn hunkered on the property like a beast ready to get up and strike.

"If I patched up the roof, it would prevent more rain damage. I'm sure tourists would love to go into a barn and explore, but in its current condition, it's a little dangerous."

"I'm out of funds for now," she said curtly, walking down to the wheelbarrow and grabbing a fistful of hay. She shook it out over the muddy path.

As Heather reached for more, Zach touched her wrist, stopping her mid motion. "Is there something you're not telling me?"

She sprinkled the hay over the mud, then brushed her palms together. She tucked her hands under her armpits as a sudden chill raced up her spine. "They found my mother's body in the barn."

Zach seemed to reel back. "Oh, I had no idea. I'm sorry. I shouldn't have pushed."

She shook her head. "No, it's okay. Part of the reason I came here was to face my past." Her tone was droll. "I had no idea I'd be facing so much of my past all at once."

"The offer still stands. I could patch the roof."

She scratched her neck. "Let me think about it."

"Okay." He turned and got to the business of spreading the hay.

Ruthie rounded the corner of the house and stopped.

"*Gut* morning," she sang good-naturedly. "I see you're finally up."

"Good morning." Heather smiled. "Yes, I was tired."

Ruthie brushed her hands together. "I planted some flowers by the mailbox out front. Sloppy Sam ran me home to pick some up from the greenhouse."

"Thank you. That's a nice touch."

"Did you still want to go to the grocery store this morning?" Ruthie asked.

Heather picked up her coffee mug from the rail and opened the back door, allowing Ruthie to go in first. "Yes. Let's finish our list first."

Before disappearing inside, she turned to Zach. "If you promise not to fall off the roof and break your neck, I think it would be great to patch the holes in the barn." She didn't need a liability on her property.

Heather could feel Ruthie's gaze on her. Most locals knew the story of her mom's murder even though it had happened before the young Amish woman's time. "I thought—"

"Perhaps someday I'd like to own horses. Maybe get a buggy. Do Amish tours." Heather smiled. "Lots of potential."

Zach covered his heart and gave her a solemn look. "Promise I won't fall through the roof."

"Please don't. That's the last thing I need." She shot him a pointed glare. "Be careful. I'm going inside. Ruthie and I need to make our grocery list."

"Do you need a ride?"

"No, my car is parked behind the barn. Hold on." She scooted into the house, grabbed the set of keys from the hook and returned, tossing them to Zach. He caught them in one hand. "Can you pull it around for us?"

A worry whispered across her brain. She prayed Brian hadn't taken his frustration out on her car as he had done on Zach's. She had gotten so spoiled this past week being driven around by Zach first in his loaned vehicle and now his repaired one, she hadn't given her car much thought. It wasn't much of a car, but at this point, she couldn't afford to replace it.

"Sure thing. I'll bring it around to the driveway."

Ruthie and Heather watched him jog to the backside of the barn. "Isn't he helpful?" Ruthie asked playfully.

"Yes, yes, he is."

Despite Heather's protest, Zach decided he should escort her and Ruthie to the grocery store. He was relieved to find her car had remained untouched. Maybe Fox hadn't noticed it parked behind the barn.

Once Ruthie and Heather were safely home and inside, creating a menu for the guests, Zach decided today would be a good day to inspect the damage to the barn. When his parents first got the cabin in the woods some ten years ago, Zach had done many of the repairs and updates. It had been a therapy of sorts.

He found a ladder in the yard and propped it against the side and climbed up and inspected the roof. With some plywood and shingles, he could make this thing as good as new. Well, at least it would be a start. The way it was now, rain would continue to damage the structure to the point of no return. *Maybe Heather would prefer that.*

Zach made a few mental notes, then climbed down the ladder. Far from the house so nobody would overhear, he decided to give Deputy Gates a call and ask him about Sarah Miller's murder. Gates seemed more than eager to discuss the case that had marred his father's tenure as sheriff.

"There had been a vagrant passing through town at the time of Mrs. Miller's disappearance. A middle-aged man who seemed to be homeless and acting strange. Might have had mental health issues. Anyway, he left town at the same time Sarah Miller went missing."

"Did anyone see Sarah with the man?"

"Not per se. But Sarah had been in town one of the days the man was begging for food outside the grocery store. Her children remembered that she gave him food. The Amish are kind that way."

"And you think maybe he became fixated on Sarah because of this?" Zach let out a long breath. Unstable people had become obsessed with their victims over far less.

"That was our best guess. But even with a sketch of the suspect widely distributed, no one identified the guy. Case grew cold." The deputy cleared his throat. "Now it's what, twenty-some years later? You're not thinking about digging into this case, are you?"

Zach turned and looked at the house. No one had come outside. "I guess the law enforcement side of me made me curious."

"Oh, plenty of people have been curious, but the case has gone unsolved. I'm afraid it'll always be that way. It was a dark page in the quiet town's history. My poor father, despite being retired, still brings up that case now and again."

"Sarah Miller's body was found in the barn behind the Lapp property?"

"Yeah..." Zach shifted his stance and hooked his thumb into his belt. "Hard to say if her body had been there all along or if the murderer had dumped it there just prior to her being found."

"Didn't the Millers use the barn?"

"Sure did. But Sarah's horse had gone missing, too. No reason to go into the stall without the horse."

"Did they ever find the horse?"

"Yes, about a week later. An Amish farmer from the next district over brought it around once word reached him about Sarah's disappearance."

Zach rubbed his jaw. "Thanks for the information."

Ending the call, Zach walked around to the front of the barn and entered it again, this time with a new awareness. It wasn't a large barn, so the fact that her body had remained missing for a few days meant that it had either been moved or hidden.

A little voice deep in his head scolded him for not just enjoying this fall day. And instead of appreciating the lull in the case against Fox and salvaging part of his vacation, he was mentally digging into a cold case.

Totally not his job.

But finding answers was important to Heather, so it had become important to him. He inspected the entire barn. Sun streamed in through the broken slats and dust particles floated in the air. A ladder was propped up against the loft. He hadn't remembered seeing the ladder there the night they searched the barn for Fox. Perhaps one of the workmen had brought it in more recently. He grabbed a rung and shook it. Seemed sturdy enough.

Carefully checking each ladder rung as he climbed, he reached the top and stepped into the loft. The strong scent of dried wood reached his nose. He crossed to the wall and slid open the loft door. He held on to the frame, realizing that though the drop to the grass below might not kill him, it wouldn't feel good.

And he had promised Heather he wouldn't break his neck.

From here, he had an unobstructed view across the yard to the upstairs bedrooms at the back of the house, including Heather's. Someone could sit here and watch.

A chill skittered down his spine. He pulled his cell phone out of his back pocket and turned on the flashlight. He shined it around the loft and stopped when he found a fast-food restaurant bag crumpled up. He picked it up and carried it over to the light by the opening. Unfolding the bag slowly, he smelled the not-too-old scent of French fries.

Strange.

He rooted around the bag and found a receipt. He pulled it out and stared at it, blinking rapidly. It was dated yesterday afternoon.

Chapter Nine

Deputy Gates left with the fast-food garbage and the assurances that it was probably just some local kids taking advantage of an abandoned barn. Sloppy Sam and his crew, once contacted, assured the deputy that they all brought lunches from home. Just to cover all their bases, the deputy promised to check if the restaurant had any video of the person making the purchase at the time stamped on the receipt.

Heather turned to Zach. "Do you think it's something more?"

Zach crossed his arms over his solid chest and sighed, which was far more telling than any words. "I thought it was important enough to call the sheriff's department."

Ruthie sat rocking in one of the chairs next to the wood-burning stove. "Kids go up into barn lofts all the time. Even Amish kids. It's a perfect place to party. No one can see you from the road."

"But it was just one bag. If it was a party, wouldn't there be discarded beer bottles? More garbage? Not just one fast-food bag."

Zach touched her wrist. "We have no reason to think it was Fox."

Heather lifted an eyebrow at the mention of her ex-husband's name. Of course she had been thinking it was Brian, but to hear Zach give voice to her suspicions made the fine hair on the back of her neck stand on edge. She cleared her throat. "Are we safe here?"

"I'll make sure you're safe. We have an alarm system now, too." The workers had installed it a few days ago. The modern technology may have detracted from the Amish vibe, but Heather had already felt safer at night when the alarm was activated.

Ruthie pushed to her feet. "Everything will be fine. And we can't let down our first guests tomorrow."

Heather nodded. "I suppose you're right. Oh, wait…" She hustled into the kitchen and came back with a slip of paper. "I almost forgot with all this craziness going on. I got a last-minute reservation. A young woman wanted a place to stay as a writing retreat. Something about a book deadline and she was looking for some quiet." She laughed nervously. "I hope I can provide the quiet she needs. Either that or fodder for her next story."

"Don't think like that. This is great. We have a full house," Ruthie said.

"Yes." Heather was afraid to allow the spark of hope flickering in her belly to burn bright.

"Let's continue with our plans as scheduled and not allow some garbage in the barn to throw us off course. Like Ruthie said, it was probably some kids." Zach gently brushed his hand down Heather's arm.

"I talked to my boss right after the incident here," Zach added. "He's going to put a call out and have a search party fan out from the barn. Can't hurt."

"But…" Heather stopped herself. She didn't want to sound like a petulant child whining that she thought Brian was supposed to be dead, not having fast food in her barn.

"It's a precaution. That's all. They're not going to allow anything to happen to you. *I'm* not going to allow anything to happen to you."

Ruthie gestured with her bonneted head toward the stairs. "Let's get the pink room ready. It has a nice chair and a desk. I'm sure our newest guest will love it. The afternoon light in the room is great, I mean if she's going to be in there writing a book." Ruthie drew up her shoulders and smiled brightly, as if work was a treat. "Isn't this exciting?"

Heather followed Ruthie upstairs. Her young employee's enthusiasm was contagious.

Zach couldn't sleep much, so he found himself patrolling the property, checking all the outbuildings, including the loft of the barn. The only thing that kept him company outside was the chill and the crickets.

There was absolutely no sign of anyone.

The stillness brought a certain peace to Zach, a man who was otherwise always on an assignment or surrounded by the buzz of his hometown. He enjoyed a certain energy from that, but stillness was good, too.

He made his way around the property once again, but this time he slowed by the barn and turned around and stared up at the house. The way the land rose to meet the barn, it gave a clear view of the house. Once again, he wondered if Brian had watched the house—watched Heather—while snacking on French fries and a burger.

Zach's phone dinged and he glanced down. A new

email had come in. Out of habit, he tapped through and opened it, surprised, or maybe not, that his boss was still awake at this hour and sending emails.

As he read, his stomach dropped. The sheriff's department hadn't found anything suspicious on the fast-food restaurant's video feed. The local high school basketball team and the requisite cheerleaders had gone in around that time for an after-school celebration. No sign of Fox. And since all indications were that Fox had perished, it was time for Zach to report back to the office. The U.S. Marshals office had other cases that now required his attention.

Frustration heated his cheeks. He was *not* going to leave Heather. Not yet. Something in his gut told him this case wasn't settled, the most obvious sign being that they hadn't found Fox's body. But it had been over a week. Where was it?

A little voice whispered in Zach's head. *Not going to leave here because you think her life is in danger or because you don't want to leave her?*

He honestly didn't know the answer. Perhaps a little of both. Less of the first, more of the second. At least that was what he wanted to believe. He wanted Heather to be able to live out her dream in peace.

It was after midnight. His boss was obviously up. Zach tapped the phone's screen and lifted it to his ear.

"Don't you ever sleep?" Kenner said by way of greeting.

"I could say the same thing." Zach ran a hand over his hair. He could use a trim. He liked to keep it military short.

"You got the email?"

"Yeah. What case do you need me back for?"

"A few. You know how it is. The caseload on your desk isn't getting any smaller."

"But—" he turned his back to the house, not that anyone was awake and in earshot "—I had vacation I didn't use when Fox escaped."

"I know." His tone suggested he wasn't going to give Zach any slack because of it. "But it's been a couple weeks. We need you back in the office."

"What if I told you I wasn't ready to come back? I need to stay to see this thing through."

"We both know Fox can't still be out in the woods."

"I'm not going to feel Heather is safe until I see his body."

"Heather, huh? I know how personal this case is," he said, his tone a mix of sympathy and understanding. "But perhaps you've made it even more personal."

Zach bit his tongue. Understanding he appreciated, sympathy not so much. The soft lilt of sympathy suggested that his boss thought he wasn't thinking clearly. That he had allowed his personal feelings to cloud his professional judgment.

"We both know this could drag on for weeks, months… It may never be resolved," his boss said.

Zach groaned. The thought of no closure twisted his gut. He needed to know Fox was dead. Then he could go back to his life knowing the man who had killed his sister wasn't roaming free.

"We've worked together for a long time. We've been friends for a long time," Kenner added. "Don't do this to yourself. Come back to the office. We'll get you busy on another case."

"Can I give you my answer tomorrow? I'm not sure I'm ready to come home."

A long, tension-filled pause extended across the line. Finally his boss spoke. "I'll give you till Monday morning. But I want your answer then."

"And if I don't come back?"

"I'm not going to lie. We need you here, and if you defy a direct order, it will affect your career."

"I'll take my chances." Zach pressed End and slid the phone back into his pocket.

A twig snapped behind him and he spun around as he reached for his gun.

Heather's hands came up and her wide eyes glistened in the moonlight. "It's me. It's me."

Zach's heart was up in his throat. "Haven't you ever heard you're not supposed to sneak up on a guy who has a gun?"

"I didn't want to interrupt your phone call." A hint of annoyance edged her tone. "Was that work?"

"Yeah." He started walking toward the house, not comfortable with having Heather out here in the open in the middle of the night. "Come on." He touched the small of her back.

Heather glanced up at him as they walked toward the house. "Yeah, it was work. But it's nothing for you to worry about."

"Please don't do that to me. I'm not a little delicate flower."

Shame heated his cheeks. "I'm sorry. My boss got info back on the video at the fast-food restaurant. Nothing indicates Fox purchased the food at the time on the receipt found in the loft."

"That's good, right?" She tilted her head, but he didn't want to meet her gaze. "Dead men don't get hungry, right?"

He couldn't help but smile. "No, they don't."

"Does this mean you're leaving?"

She must have overheard his conversation.

"I have to decide by Monday."

Heather held out her hands, indicating the house and the land surrounding them. "I think we have everything under control. I can't ask you to stay, even though the barn roof ain't gonna fix itself."

Zach laughed. "Yeah, maybe it is time to go home."

Heather ran the dust rag over the oak of the rockers, more for something to do than out of necessity. The house was ready. *More* than ready.

A mixture of excitement and a touch of disappointment ran through her. Today was opening day. The fruit of all their labor. Yet she couldn't shake the feelings of loss that had lingered with her as she drifted off to sleep and then again when she woke up.

Zach was leaving on Monday.

In the short time she had spent with Zach, she had grown to really like him, but now with him going back to Buffalo, they wouldn't be able to explore what might have been.

She flipped the rag around to find a clean spot and ran it over the windowsills. Maybe it was just as well. She didn't need the added complication of a man.

Footsteps sounded on the hardwood floor and Heather's heart leaped in her throat. She spun around to find Ruthie on the stairs. Heather tried to hide the disappointment she felt in her heart.

Ruthie must have witnessed it, because she made a dramatic show of pressing her hand to her heart. "I'm happy to see you, too, Miss Miller."

Heat fired in Heather's cheeks. "No, um...you surprised me. Good morning." She tucked the dust rag into her back pocket and smiled. "Ready for our first big day?"

"Yah." A hint of Pennsylvania Dutch slipped in. "We'll serve a light snack around seven this evening. Most of the guests will have eaten before they check in."

"Yes, that's the plan." Heather crossed the room and palmed the banister. "I appreciate all your help. I wouldn't be able to do this on my own."

A shuffling drew her attention to the kitchen. Zach stared at her with a funny expression on his face. She wondered if he had made a firm decision to leave on Monday.

Of course he had. He couldn't stay here forever.

"Anything specific you need me to do today?"

Heather clasped her hands together. "I think we're set."

Mr. and Mrs. Hopkins and Mr. and Mrs. Woodruff sat around the table and chitchatted, seeming like they were more interested in talking about who they knew in common in Buffalo than they were about talking to the real live Amish person walking in and out of the room serving shoofly pie and tea and coffee.

Heather suspected the guests had also discussed the search for the ex-convict who had made his way to Quail Hollow, but either out of consideration or maybe just by chance, she hadn't heard anything as of yet. She hoped it remained that way. She hated to be the focus of gossip.

Miss Fiona Lavocat, their last-minute guest, hadn't arrived yet. Heather pulled back the front curtain and a whisper of worry sent goose bumps across her skin. It seemed late for a single woman to be traveling alone.

Dropping the curtain back into place, Heather forced herself to relax her shoulders. She was probably project-ing her own feelings. That was what happened when you spent the majority of your adulthood hiding from an abusive ex-husband.

She smiled politely at her guests as she slipped past the dining area and into the kitchen. She turned on the tap and filled the sink with hot soapy water. Something about washing dishes by hand was therapeutic. Beyond her kitchen window, as she swished the inside of a tall glass with a sponge on a plastic stick, she saw Zach unloading some plywood from the back of his pickup truck. His vehicle provided the only light in the gath-ering dusk. She didn't want to read too much into the delivery. Was he going to be around long enough to fin-ish the job? He didn't strike her as the kind of guy who didn't finish what he started.

Maybe he was just picking up some supplies for Sloppy Sam.

A knocking sounded on the front door. Heather set the glass in the drying rack, wiped her hands on a dish-rag and hustled toward the door. She waved to Ruthie, who was collecting dishes from the table. "I'll get it." She'd much rather Ruthie entertain the guests.

Through the glass on the top half of the door, she noticed a young woman with long red hair falling over her shoulders. She seemed to be looking everywhere but through the window at Heather. She pulled open the door. "You must be Fiona."

The young woman adjusted her glasses and smiled. "I am. I had trouble finding the bed-and-breakfast." She hiked up the strap of her bag and bent her knees slightly to reach for the handle of her suitcase.

"Let me get that." Heather stepped onto the porch and reached for the bag.

"I've got it." Fiona lifted the bag into the house and set it down on the hardwood floor. She took in the room. "Wow, this is a real Amish house?"

Something about the way she said it made Heather bristle. She just hoped she was able to hide her reaction. Isn't this what she had wanted guests to think? Yet a little piece of her felt like she was trading on her family's past for profit.

Heather swallowed and forced a smile. "My *mammy* was Amish. This was her house." Her "go-to" had always been to say her grandmother was Amish, but what about her *mem*? What about her? However, truth be told, she had never been baptized—the Amish waited for adulthood—so although she had lived as the Amish until she turned six, she hadn't been fully brought into the faith.

She cleared her throat, wishing she could stop her rambling thoughts.

Fiona dropped her laptop bag by the door next to her suitcase and strolled around the room. "This is so cool." Then she stopped and turned around and made a strange I-should-have-thought-to-ask-this-before face. "I'm going to need to charge my laptop. Will that be a problem?"

"No, not at all. When I had the renovations done, I added a few modern conveniences. You'll find an outlet in your bedroom as well as one in the bathroom."

"Good, good." Fiona placed her hands on her hips.

"I should get a lot of work done here out in the middle of nowhere."

"How did you find us?"

"Your website. I googled B and Bs in Western New York. There were so many. There are a ton in Niagara Falls, but I wanted to find somewhere less…busy, I guess. Less temptation to go out and visit a wax museum or something." A grimace flashed across her face as if she had said something wrong. "Am I supposed to check in or something?"

Heather shook her head, feeling a little foolish. She figured she'd get into a rhythm soon enough. She slid up the cover on the rolltop desk, opened a notebook and entered Fiona's name. She had decided paper and pens would seem more quaint. However, she had the ability to run a credit card through her smartphone. Fiona reached into her bag and pulled out a roll of bills. "Is cash okay?" She shrugged, a sheepish expression on her face. "I don't have a credit card."

"Yes, cash is fine."

Laughter rose from the eating area. Even though the two couples had just met, it seemed they had really hit it off. Fiona glanced in that direction with mild disinterest. "Busy weekend."

Heather held up her hand. "You'll have your own bedroom. Ruthie picked out a nice room with a cozy chair and a desk. I'm sure it'll be very quiet. You can listen to the corn grow." Heather sometimes wished she could make herself stop talking.

"Sounds great." Fiona reached for her laptop case.

"Um, I do need ID. Do you have a driver's license? It's just a formality." Heather wasn't sure why she felt silly for asking this young woman for ID. She was running a business. It wasn't a paranoid thing to do.

Fiona seemed to flinch. "Oh, of course." She slid her fingers into a narrow compartment on her laptop case and pulled out a New York State driver's license. "I parked on the edge of the driveway behind the other cars. Is that okay?"

"Yes. That's fine."

As Heather jotted down Fiona's information so she could track the woman down if, say, she damaged her room, Fiona leaned in close and whispered, "I almost didn't book this bed-and-breakfast when I realized this was in the same town where they're looking for that escaped convict."

Heather froze, pen poised above the piece of paper. She slowly lifted her eyes to meet Fiona's. "Well, I'm glad you didn't cancel." Heather prayed that her expression didn't give away the emotions rioting inside her.

"Should I be worried?" The two women locked gazes a moment and Heather tried to decipher in that one look if Fiona knew of her personal ties to the missing convict.

"No, not at all." Heather noticed Zach enter the front door at that exact moment. "There's no need to worry. Law enforcement has combed this area, and if Brian Fox was in Quail Hollow, he's long gone by now."

A small frown tipped the corners of Fiona's mouth. The expression on her face shifted from mild curiosity to one of expectation as she stood clutching her bags.

"I'll show you to your room," Heather said, snapping the register closed and sliding the rolltop desk down.

"I'll show her to the room." Ruthie's voice startled Heather. The young Amish woman had entered the living room from the other direction just as quietly as Zach had, either that or Heather had just been a little jumpy.

"Thank you." Heather held out her palm to Ruthie. "This is Ruthie. Ruthie, this is our guest Miss Lavocat."

"Oh, please, it's Fiona."

"Okay, Fiona. Ruthie'll show you to your room."

Fiona lifted her shoulders, then let them drop. "Sounds good."

"I'll take your bag," Zach offered.

Ruthie slipped in and grabbed it. "No need. I've got it."

Heather sensed Zach watching her, but oddly it didn't unnerve her. She turned to him and smiled. "You've been working hard."

"I believe I've run out of daylight." He brushed his hands on the thighs of his jeans. "How do you contact your Amish contractor? Does he have a phone?"

"Yes." She feared the brightness of her smile wavered. Zach wanted to hand off the work. Did this mean he was leaving? "I have his number in my desk."

She took a step toward the desk and Zach said, "It can wait till tomorrow."

"Okay. I guess I should see if our guests need anything else."

Heather noticed that Ruthie had already cleared the table. Upon seeing her, the guests looked up expectantly. "You have a very nice home," Mrs. Woodruff said.

"Thank you. Can I get you anything else?"

They all said they were fine, so Heather excused herself and went upstairs, fully intending to come back down after her guests had settled in for the night and make sure the last few coffee mugs were cleared away and all the doors were locked. A niggling that she had forgotten something wouldn't leave her. Soon, she'd get into a routine, but she had to give herself some slack. This was, after all, her first night with guests in her bed-and-breakfast.

Zach had retreated to his room a few minutes earlier. From the upstairs landing, Heather could hear Ruthie talking to Fiona. She slipped into her room and wished she could have just crawled into bed and called it a night. Her eyes felt gritty and a headache threatened. She figured she better take something for it because she couldn't afford any downtime with guests in her home.

She opened her medicine cabinet and sucked in a gasp. Panic sliced through her as she reached in with a shaky hand and picked up a simple gold wedding band. With narrowing vision, she read the inscription:

Forever Mine.

Followed by the date of her wedding to Brian Fox.

The ring slipped out of her grasp and bounced around the bowl of the sink. She clamped her hand over it before it slipped down the drain. She scooped it up with her fingers and set it back on the shelf where she had found it and stared at it as the walls closed in on her.

Chapter Ten

Zach stood by the window and stared out over the farmland. He had enjoyed the hard labor today. It felt good to get out of his head for a bit. His boss was telling him he was needed at the office. But too much was left undone here.

They still hadn't found Fox's body.

A quiet knock sounded on his door and he frowned and turned around. He crossed the small room to the door and found a pale Heather standing in his doorway under the soft glow of the kitchen light. Behind her in the eating nook, the guests' good-humored conversation indicated they were oblivious to whatever had brought Heather to his door. She was shaking.

"What is it? Is everything okay?" He looked past her, half expecting Fox to be standing behind her. He blinked and the image disappeared.

Heather lifted a shaky hand and tucked a strand of hair behind her ear. "I have to show you something." Her voice trembled.

"Okay." He searched her eyes, but she seemed to be a million miles away.

As they walked past the guests, Heather smiled and said, "The upstairs faucet seems to be dripping in my bathroom."

Zach followed her upstairs and the door down the hall opened and Fiona peeked out, gripping her bathrobe closed at the collar. "Oh, I'm sorry. I heard voices and I wondered. I didn't mean to—"

"Everything's okay," Zach said. "Miss Miller has been having issues with the faucet."

"Okay. Well, good night, then." The young woman closed the door with a quiet click, leaving Heather and Zach in the hallway alone.

"Come on. Show me what has you so rattled," he said.

Zach followed Heather through her suite into her private bathroom. She stood with her arms crossed staring at the mirror, but not at her image reflected in it. "What is it?"

She pointed at the mirror. "Look in the medicine cabinet."

He pulled on one side of the mirror, then the other before he heard a quiet click and the latch released, revealing the medicine cabinet behind the mirror. A single bottle of pain reliever sat inside next to a simple gold wedding ring. He turned and looked at Heather. She had that glassy look again. He saw her visibly swallow. "The ring. Read the inscription," she whispered.

Zach stared at her for a minute longer before picking up the ring and turning it so he could read the inscription. Dread knotted his stomach as he realized the significance of it. "Your wedding ring?"

Her hand fluttered around the hollow of her throat.

"Yes." The word came out on a single breath. "He was here."

He cupped Heather's elbow and felt a slight tremble race through her. "When was the last time you went into the medicine cabinet?"

She blinked slowly, as if thinking. "I put the pain reliever in there when I moved in, but haven't opened the door since."

"When did you last see this ring?" He ushered her out of the bathroom and she sat on the edge of the chaise lounge while Zach paced the space in front of her.

"I left it behind when I ran away."

"You left it at the home you shared with Fox?"

She nodded and dragged a shaky hand across her hair. "I took it off and set it on the kitchen table. I wanted him to know I had left him. It was an act of defiance just before I took the biggest risk of my life." She lifted her watery gaze to him. "He was in my room. He's not dead."

Zach stopped pacing and crouched down in front of her and gathered her hands in his. "This doesn't mean that he's alive. He may have made his way up here the night he left the message on the back wall for you. He may have slipped upstairs, then escaped out the front door while we were by the back door. Any number of possibilities that don't include a return trip to your house."

Heather pressed her hands to her mouth. "How do we know for sure?"

He didn't.

"His body has to be recovered." It wasn't fair that Heather had to live with this doubt. Zach stood and gently brushed the back of his knuckles across her warm cheek. "I'm not going anywhere until then."

Heather nodded, but uncertainty flashed in the depths of her eyes. "Your boss…" They both knew that finding Fox's body wasn't a certainty. Zach couldn't stay here forever.

"My boss is going to have to understand."

"But…" Heather tried to argue.

"I need to make sure you're safe." He cleared his throat. "Now, about this ring. You were still married when you left Fox?"

"Yes. I had to leave him. If I didn't, he would have—" The word *killed* died on her lips. "I'm sorry."

"Don't be. How did you arrange a divorce?"

"I didn't for a long time. I had to stay hidden. But when Brian met Jill, he wanted a divorce and reached out to me through my sister. It was through her that I communicated with a lawyer and the divorce was finalized." She frowned. "I moved again after that. I couldn't risk him coming for me. No one disobeyed Brian and got away unscathed."

"No." No, they didn't. He had killed Jill the day after she called her big brother begging for a way out. He'd been out of town on a case. He'd told her to leave the house that night. To go to his apartment and lock herself in. Brian had found her. Slaughtered her on the back steps. Her favorite purple suitcase dumped on top of her lifeless body.

Heather untucked her legs and stood, sighing heavily. "I'm tired. I need to go to sleep."

"Of course." He smiled and backed out of the room, slipping out of the door that had been left ajar. He paused just outside the doorway thinking he heard footsteps somewhere on the second floor. All the rooms were occupied by guests and the hall was empty. It was now quiet downstairs.

Just to be safe, he double-checked the doors and windows throughout the house and then returned to his room on the first floor. With various guests in the house, it would be difficult to assure that all the doors and windows remained locked without scaring the guests. Nor could he set the alarm in case a guest wanted to go outside.

Why are you so worried? Dead men don't crawl through windows.

The ring had set off new concerns. Had Fox left it on his first visit? Or had he somehow returned?

Zach sat down on the edge of the cot. Until there was a body—definitive proof of Fox's death—Zach would remain vigilant even if it meant sleeping with one eye open.

With a bowl of fruit in her hands, Heather froze on the other side of the entry to the addition, where her guests had gathered. Fiona was holding court, her voice a hushed whisper.

"Brian Fox, the convict running loose in Western New York, had been married to Heather Miller."

"What?" one of the older gentleman said, either in disbelief or because he was hard of hearing.

"Yeah, she testified against Brian after he killed his second wife." Fiona relayed the information as if she was doling out juicy gossip on the middle school playground. Anger swirled in Heather's gut as this stranger violated her privacy. Why hadn't Fiona mentioned any of this to her last night when they chatted? Instead she acted as if she barely knew about "that escaped convict."

Heather had been so used to being tucked away, she'd never get comfortable with having the details of her life splayed out for all to see.

"You okay?"

Heather spun around and bumped into Ruthie with the edge of the bowl. "Can you put this on the table? I think they have everything they need for breakfast. I have to do something."

Ruthie took the bowl with a smile. Heather drew in a deep breath and opened the back door and stepped outside. The cool autumn air hit her fiery cheeks.

Her gaze drifted to the barn, where Zach was already setting up work for the day. She crossed the yard to him, her mood immediately lifting. He looked up from where he had a piece of wood balanced on a table.

"You really don't have to do all this." Heather tented a hand over her eyes and looked up at the barn.

"I enjoy it."

"I appreciate it." She stared at the small pile of sawdust on the hard-packed earth. "And thanks for being there last night. I don't know what I would have done. That ring really rattled me. You really think he left it the night he broke into my house?"

"I called in the information to my boss. He'll see that the proper authorities know of the development. But yes, I don't think Fox came back to the house. Even if he had survived, it would have been too risky."

"You don't know Brian like I do. He's not rational."

"Once we find him, you won't have to worry about him ever again." His gaze drifted to the back of the house, then to her. "My boss gave me another week."

"Because of the ring?"

"Yes."

A puddle of conflicting emotions pooled in her belly. She was relieved Zach was staying, but concerned that his reassurances regarding the ring were merely lip service. But what could he tell her that she hadn't already considered?

"I'm glad you're staying," she finally said. "I'd feel better if we had more answers."

"Me, too." He picked up a piece of wood and placed it flat on the workbench. "I figured you'd be occupied for a while with breakfast."

"Ruthie and I already set up the breakfast buffet. I had to get out for a bit." She crossed her arms and rocked back on her heels. "Fiona, our young writer, decided it would be fun to tell the other guests that I'm the infamous Brian Fox's ex-wife." Another wave of pinpricks washed over her. "As much as I hated hiding from Brian, I enjoyed the anonymity of it. I hate being the subject of gossip. It's so intrusive. And I can't imagine it'll be good for business."

Zach rested his palms on the plywood and squinted at the house. "Things will quiet down eventually." He drew in a deep breath. "You'll never be able to let it go completely, but the people around you will stop talking about it as they move on to the next drama."

"Mmm…" Heather feared things would never quiet down. That she'd never be able to face the past. *All of her past.*

She took a step toward the barn and her knees grew weak. "I haven't been in the barn since I learned that that's where they found my mother's body." A band of dread tightened around her chest and made her dizzy.

She touched the door frame, waiting, for what she wasn't sure. The scent of damp hay and aging wood reached her nose. A surreal feeling made the old wooden walls heave and sway.

Her father had said her mother had loved her horse and probably would have become a veterinarian if there were such a thing among the Amish. But generally the Amish only went to school through the eighth grade.

A person didn't need an education to live the Amish way.

Heather stepped into the barn and slowly walked toward the stalls where her mother's body had been found. She wasn't sure which one. One of the planks of wood along the back wall had rotted away due to dampness and age.

She turned when she felt Zach's hand on her shoulder. "I thought I'd feel something more knowing this was where my mother was found."

"I'm so sorry."

Heather turned away from the stalls. "The local sheriff was convinced it was a random person traveling through town. My father never wanted to talk about it, but he finally said that any leads never panned out. My dad said I had to forgive the man who killed my mother. That's the Amish way. My father had given up everything Amish, but he clung to that. Forgiveness. I think it's what allowed him to keep going." She dragged a hand through her hair. "I haven't been able to find forgiveness."

"You've had to deal with more tragedy in your, what—" He lifted his eyebrows.

"Thirty-two years." She smiled at his roundabout way of asking how old she was, not that it mattered.

"Yes, most people haven't had to go through what you've had to deal with in their entire lifetime."

"I'm not looking for sympathy. God has blessed me in more ways than I can count." She turned and stepped outside of the barn, letting the sun warm her goose-pimpled skin.

"How do you do that?"

Heather turned to look at Zach standing next to her. "How do I do what?"

"Have faith despite everything that has happened to you?"

Heather opened her mouth to say something, then thought better of it, considering his sister was dead.

"Tell me, what were you about to say?"

Heather met his gaze squarely. "I was going to say that I'm blessed to still be alive. To see the sunrise. To feel the cool air on my skin. But then I realized how trite that would sound to someone who had lost someone to murder. I imagine your sister also had faith."

"She did."

"Yet, despite her faith, evil found her. So I understand why your faith has been shaken."

A muscle worked in Zach's jaw. "At her funeral, the pastor said that God gave us free will. And it was free will that allowed the likes of Fox to kill my sister."

"And despite my mother's devotion to her faith, she, too, was murdered." The familiar guilt weighed heavy on her chest. It wasn't fair to push her faith. Zach had to find his own way through his grief and feelings of guilt. Much as she had struggled. Much as she *still* struggled.

But wasn't that part of faith?

Heather dried the last glass and placed it in the cabinet. The Woodruffs and the Hopkinses were on a buggy tour of Quail Hollow, while Fiona had settled into a rocking chair in the sitting room with her laptop.

"I'll start making apple pie for dessert. I think I have everything set in the kitchen for now," Ruthie said, giving Heather a pointed stare.

Heather recognized a dismissal when she heard it, but still she pressed. "What can I do to help?"

"You hired me to take care of the kitchen and meals. Let me do that. I have to earn my keep."

Heather dried her hands on a dishrag. She didn't want to offend Ruthie by suggesting she couldn't manage her job.

"I'll go…" To do what, she wasn't exactly sure, until she found herself in the sitting room watching Fiona type away on her laptop. The young woman's back was to her. An unexpected whisper of dread made the hairs on the back of her neck prickle to life. She wasn't sure why. Perhaps because the memory of Fiona eagerly sharing the Quail Hollow gossip unnerved her.

What is she really writing about?

Fiona stopped typing and clasped her hands, but didn't turn around. "I can't type when someone's watching me."

Heather cringed. She hadn't meant to appear to be snooping. "Sorry, I didn't mean to interrupt." She turned to walk away, then stopped and decided to approach Fiona. "Why didn't you tell me you knew I was Brian Fox's ex-wife?"

Something flickered in Fiona's eyes, then she had the good sense to glance down. "You heard me talking." It wasn't framed as a question.

"I did."

"I'm sorry. I should have been more discreet."

Anger simmered just below the surface. "You shouldn't have been gossiping." Heather took another step closer. "What are you working on?" she asked, an edge to her tone.

"I've got my first contract to write a romance." Fiona smiled, a hint of an apology in her eyes. She turned the screen so Heather could read it. The passage read very much like something from a sweet romance novel. Heather's cheeks grew warm at the unfair accusation that had crossed her mind.

Fiona's eyes opened wide as she sensed it, too. "You thought maybe I was writing about you." She gave Heather an exaggerated frown, her eyes magnified behind her thick lenses. "I would never do something like that. I mean, I used to write articles for newspapers, but I'd never do something like that on the sly. That would be unethical."

Heather drew in a deep breath. "I value my privacy."

Fiona pushed her glasses up on her nose. "Yes, I understand completely. I just came here to work on my novel. That's all. It was inconsiderate of me to be all gossipy at breakfast this morning. I guess I enjoyed the attention too much when the other guests started asking questions."

Heather shrugged. "Well, I guess the cat is already out of the bag. The guests may have questions. I'll have to come up with some answers."

Fiona shifted the laptop and frowned. "I wasn't thinking. I'm sorry." She tapped her chin with her fingers. "I thought you should know I read about your mother's murder when I was doing research on Quail Hollow after I found this bed-and-breakfast."

"Oh." Pinpricks blanketed Heather's scalp.

"If you're ever interested, *that* would make a fantastic true crime story. I'd be honored to write it. I'm sure it would be a bestseller. A murder in Amish country…" A faraway look descended into Fiona's eyes as the wheels of her mind turned.

Heather rubbed her arm as unease skittered across her flesh. "I like my privacy." She didn't care that her words came out clipped. They had already been through this.

"Of course. I'm sorry. I don't mean to be insensitive."

"Thank you. I appreciate that and I'd appreciate your continued discretion." Heather lifted her hand to the laptop, suddenly feeling very disconcerted. "I'll let you get back to work. On your romance."

Fiona's eyebrows flew up. "Do you read them?"

Heather smiled, still having a hard time figuring out this young woman. "Yes. I read across all genres. Haven't made much time for it lately, but now that the renovations are done, maybe I'll have more."

"You should also start one of those lending libraries for guests. The ones where they can take a book, leave a book. You could put shelves right in this room."

"That's a great idea." A few books would add charm to the mostly barren room. But Heather didn't want to overdecorate, which would be out of character for an Amish home.

Fiona leaned over and pulled a book from her bag resting against the rocker. "I'm almost finished with this one. I'll leave it here when I'm done. It can be your first lending library book."

"Sounds like a plan." Heather slid her fingers in the back pockets of her jeans. "Well, I better get a few things done before our guests return."

"If it's okay with you, I'll take my writing and my dinner up to my room later today." She lifted her laptop as if to prove a point. "I'm on deadline."

"Of course, I can bring something up."

"Oh no, I can come down and grab a plate. I just wanted you to know my plans so it wouldn't seem rude when I didn't join the other guests."

"This is your vacation. Do whatever makes you comfortable."

"Thank you." Fiona placed her fingers on the home row of the keyboard, but she didn't start typing. She turned to look at Heather. "I'm sorry if I caused you any pain by being gossipy. I'm not usually like that."

Heather tapped the door frame with her open palm. "Don't worry about it."

"Can I ask you something, though?" Fiona gave her a blank look.

"Okay." Heather didn't want to be rude, but she felt herself bracing for the question.

"Should I be worried that the escaped prisoner is going to come here? I mean, you hear stories all the time about innocent people getting caught up in domestic situations. Wrong place, wrong time sort of thing."

Heather had to focus on her breathing to control the anxiety that was welling up inside her. "We have reason to believe Brian Fox is dead."

Fiona's eyebrows shot up above the frame of her glasses and she had to catch her laptop before it slid off her lap.

"Really? What happened?" She clutched both sides of her laptop and a hint of apprehension flashed in her eyes.

"I can't really say, but law enforcement believes it's just a matter of time before they find his body."

"Oh." She lowered the lid of her laptop. "How does that make you feel? I mean, you were married to him."

Heather stared at this woman. Under normal circumstances, she wouldn't entertain such personal questions from a stranger, but this was a paying guest. What did she owe her? "The true Brian Fox is an evil person. He tricked me. And unfortunately, his own free will led him to wherever he is today."

"Dead?"

She prayed he was dead.

"Yes, he's most likely dead."

"Hmm." Fiona seemed to consider this information. "Well, it seems you've found yourself a great guy in Zach. I was chatting with him earlier."

Heather suddenly felt flushed and she wanted nothing more than to end this discussion. Her guest certainly knew how to interrogate someone. Maybe she had missed her calling as a reporter.

"Yes, he's very helpful doing projects around the house." Zach and she had agreed they wouldn't let any of the guests know he was in law enforcement. They didn't want to make them feel uncomfortable or worried.

Fiona adjusted the monitor on her laptop, then looked up at Heather. "That's great. Well, I shouldn't have pried. I talk too much sometimes."

Heather smiled tightly. "It's okay. But I'd rather not discuss the situation anymore, especially not in front of the other guests. Unless they have questions."

"Of course."

Heather turned to walk away. "Let either Ruthie or I know if you need anything."

"I will." Her fingers started flying across the keyboard before Heather reached the stairs.

Heather retreated upstairs and opened the medicine cabinet. It was empty save for the pain reliever. Zach had taken the ring for safekeeping.

A nervous energy she couldn't shake had her searching the entire room until she was satisfied that Brian hadn't left her any other unwanted gifts.

Chapter Eleven

A few days later, Zach toed his work boots off at the back door of the bed-and-breakfast and slipped inside. He drummed his fingers on his cell phone in his jacket pocket as he searched for Heather. He found her sitting at the rolltop desk making a few entries in the leather binder. The house had quieted down since the weekend guests had departed and he was grateful his boss had given him permission to stay in Quail Hollow for another week because it seemed like they were just about to get a break.

Heather ran her hand over the page and turned around; a smile lit her warm brown eyes. "The place is booking up. I might be able to make a go of this after all."

"I had no doubt you would." He leaned his shoulder against the door frame, hesitant to ruin the mood. But he had to tell her. He cleared his throat. "I received a phone call."

Heather slowly closed the book and turned to stare at him, taking in shallow breaths. "Tell me."

"A body's been found."

"A body? Brian's body?"

Zach held up his hand to caution her. "They believe it's him."

She threaded her fingers together and placed them in her lap, a show of restraint. Fox had done a number on her and now his delayed capture was tearing her up inside. Perhaps she didn't want to get her hopes up that this nightmare was officially over, however tragic the end result.

"I don't understand." She bit her lower lip. "Did something happen to the body? Why can't they identify it?"

Zach scrubbed a hand across his face, debating how many grisly details to share. But she deserved the truth. He crossed the room and sat down on the edge of a rocker. "Are you sure you want to hear the specifics?"

She stared at him with a steely expression. "I have to hear."

Zach nodded slightly, then said, "His face was destroyed. Deputy Gates mentioned that he had multiple wounds, including a gunshot to the face."

"If you hit him in the head, wouldn't they have found his body in the water when they searched it?"

"A working theory is that he survived the initial wounds, but then killed himself to hasten the end when he got desperate. He'd been on the run for a long time."

All the color seemed to drain from her face. "That doesn't sound like Brian. I think he'd chew off his arm before ending his life. How do they figure it's him?"

"Same general description—height, weight—and he had on his orange prison uniform under a jacket."

Heather slowly stood and put her hand down on the corner of the desk to steady herself. "Can I see the body?"

"I don't think that's a good idea. That's an image you'll never be able to get out of your head." Zach stood, watching her carefully.

"There are a lot of images I can't get out of my head. As warped as it sounds, knowing he can't hurt me again will give me great comfort." The tremble in her voice and the slight sway of her body weren't very convincing, but who was he to deny her this request?

"Where's Ruthie?" he asked, stalling. "Don't you two have work to do around here?"

"She's working in the greenhouse today." Heather crossed her arms and continued to press. "I need to see the body."

He stared at her a long moment before pulling his phone out of his pocket. "I'll call Deputy Gates."

"No, let's just show up. Harder to say no."

"I don't think this is a good idea," he repeated.

"Please."

"Okay. Grab your jacket."

Breathe in. Breathe out. Breathe in. Breathe out.

Heather tugged on her seat belt as Zach talked on the cell phone, getting directions from a dispatcher as to the location of the body. From what she could hear, personnel were still on location, bringing Brian's body out of the woods. Maybe Zach was right—maybe this was a bad idea.

But a stubbornness deep inside wouldn't let her admit her mistake. No, not a mistake. She was just afraid. She had to see for herself that Brian was dead, thus allowing her to live a life without fear. She couldn't bear to continue always wondering *what if*.

"You okay?" Zach asked when he ended the call and dropped the phone in the empty cup holder.

"I've been better."

"You don't have to do this."

"I know." She turned to face the window as trees, cornfields and the occasional house zipped by. She sat up straighter when she recognized where they were headed. "This is the direction of the Hershbergers' home. They didn't find him, did they?"

"No, the body was found by an elderly man walking his dog in the hills behind their house."

A new flush of dread washed over her. Had Brian been watching her when she had taken sanctuary there? She swallowed back her fear, praying she'd make it through the next moment. Then the next. One moment at a time.

They drove past the Hershbergers' home. There was no sign of anyone outside. About a half mile away, a dozen law enforcement vehicles, ranging from the local sheriff's department to New York State troopers, lined the shoulder of the road. Zach pulled in behind an ambulance. There'd be no need for that.

Heather reached for the door handle and Zach touched her knee. "Wait in the car?"

"I didn't come all this way to wait in the car." Besides, with her nerves, she was ready to jump out of her skin. She needed to get out and expend some of her nervous energy.

Zach met her around her side of the car and they approached the edge of the woods. A trooper stopped them from going any farther. "You'll have to wait here."

Heather let out a long breath, her stomach churning. A buzzing started deep in her head, much as it had when she was married to Brian and she feared him going off on her for no other reason than she used wheat bread instead of white. Or some equally frivolous reason that always kept her in a state of watchful anticipation.

"You don't look so good. We can wait in the car." Zach's voice sounded strange, as if he were standing far away and talking softly through a long tunnel.

"No. Just help me get through this… I have to do this."

Zach touched the small of her back and she fought every instinct to bury her face in his shoulder and let him protect her. Let him take all her fear and worry away. But she refused to be weak. A long time ago she had vowed to not rely on anyone but herself.

As she stood next to Zach, she stared up into the trees, a beautiful palette of oranges, reds and yellows, wondering how long Brian had been this close. *Was* he watching her when she was staying with Ruthie? The idea struck terror in her heart.

Breathe in. Breathe out.

Voices coming from the woods grew louder. Then flashes of orange caught her eye. Her adrenaline spiked. *Can I do this?*

Deputy Gates led the search team out of the woods. He was wearing an orange safety vest. He seemed to catch Zach's eye and made a direct line for them. "You shouldn't be here."

"I need to see the body," Heather rasped. The back of her throat ached.

The deputy slowly shook his head, looking to Zach for support. "Between the gunshot wound and animals, there's not a lot left. It's not a good idea."

Heather pressed the flat of her hand against her rioting belly and swallowed back her nausea.

"Can you give us more information about the hiker who found him?" Zach asked, shooting Heather a reassuring smile.

"An old-timer, George Campbell. Walks his dog everywhere. The dog stumbled across the remains. George called us in right away from his cell phone."

"Are you convinced it's him?" Zach asked.

The deputy ticked the items off on his fingers. "Peters Correctional Facility inmate uniform. Same height and build. And they're running the serial number on the gun they found with him." The officer's phone buzzed on his duty belt. "Hold up." He turned his back to them and took the call. His words swirled into a garbled mess, making her think of the old *Peanuts* cartoons when adults were speaking. She stared at the tree line, holding her breath, expecting men with a body bag to burst into the opening, wondering how she'd feel when they did. Relieved? Afraid? Sad?

The deputy turned back to them. "The serial number on the gun matches one of the guns stolen from a home near the correctional facility. The young woman who helped him escape is out on bail, but with strict instructions not to leave town."

Heather closed her eyes and nodded. "It seems everything's lining up."

"Yes. They'll run his dental records, which may take a few days, but I'm confident we have found Brian Fox."

"What do you think?" Heather asked Zach.

"I agree with the deputy. We've got him."

"I need to do this for my own peace of mind." Would refusing to see the body make her weak?

"Ma'am," the deputy said, "you wouldn't be able to identify anyone considering the condition of the body."

She felt Zach's gaze on her. Some of her conviction was draining out of her. "This is something I need to do." But really, she wasn't sure anymore.

"We'll run his dental records, which will make everything rock solid. Only a few more days and there'll be no doubt."

"What do you think?" Zach asked. "Please spare yourself the pain."

She looked up and met Zach's gaze, then slowly shifted her gaze to the men emerging from the woods. Rescuers carried a sled with a body bag. Her heart rate slowed in her chest as the world around her grew black. Only one image remained. The body bag.

Does it contain what's left of Brian?

The men stopped at the back of a black van. A man reached for the handle and opened the doors. They slid the body bag inside.

The body.

Heather's world swayed. She gently touched Zach's arm. "Let's go."

She didn't need to see the body. Brian was dead.

On the way home, Heather insisted they stop by the Hershbergers' farm to tell Ruthie and Maryann that her ex-husband no longer posed a threat to the quiet town of Quail Hollow.

They knocked on the front door, but no one answered.

"Let's try the greenhouse," Heather said.

They found them watering the mums. Emma was stacking empty pots in the back. Maryann saw them first. She turned off the hose and let her hands hang limply by her sides. Apparently their presence portended something really bad. "What is it?"

"Brian Fox is dead."

Ruthie's shoulders relaxed. "They finally found him. What a relief."

"Yes, that's why we wanted to let you know. They found him in the hills behind your home." Heather watched them closely.

"Oh, dear." Maryann glanced over toward her younger daughter, then back at them as she fidgeted with the folds of her long dress.

"No need to worry now," Zach said solemnly.

"Had you seen anyone out there lately?" Heather asked, still trying to wrap her brain around everything that had happened.

Maryann's eyes grew wide. "We were missing some eggs, but I assumed a critter had gotten into the hen-house. Do you think…?"

"There's really no way to know. But you're safe now." Zach touched the small of Heather's back, a gesture Heather found greatly reassuring.

Maryann stepped forward. "How are you? This hasn't been easy for you."

"No, it hasn't." She flattened her lips into a thin line, trying to tamp down her emotions. She had come here to reassure her dear friends, not to seek comfort from them. "I appreciate all your support through this. I don't know what I'd do without you. You've become like family."

Maryann smiled, her porcelain skin only a shade darker than her white bonnet. "Your mother would be so proud of how you handled yourself through all this." She clasped her hands. "You *are* part of this family."

A lump of emotion clogged Heather's throat. What she wouldn't do to have known her mother. Getting to know her mother's best friend was what she'd have to settle for. But she considered getting to know Maryann and her daughters to be a true blessing.

Ruthie smiled. "I love working for you, too. I have to tell you, though, I've been a nervous wreck since I first learned that man had escaped from prison. So glad he's not going to be a problem anymore."

"Now you can run the bed-and-breakfast without worrying," Maryann said. "You'll experience the Quail Hollow that we all know. It's usually so quiet and peaceful."

"I look forward to it," Heather said, suddenly feeling warm under the intensity of the sun through the glass of the greenhouse.

"Your mother always seemed so restless here, but I just know you won't feel that way. Not now."

An unease whispered across Heather's brain. *Restless?* Heather's father had assured her that her mother had been nothing but loving and doted on her children. Perhaps Maryann had misspoken. But now wasn't the time to get into that. Brian was finally gone.

Gone. Dead.

Guilt twisted in her heart. She shouldn't be happy that he was dead. What kind of person did that make her?

"Does that mean you're going home, Marshal Walker?" Ruthie's question snapped Heather out of her maudlin thoughts.

Heather shot her friend daggers but found herself holding her breath waiting for his answer. But what did she expect? Of course he'd be going home. Brian was no longer a threat. She was no longer in danger.

She glanced down at her fingernails, pretending not to care about his answer.

"Yes, my boss had given me a week extension to

stay in town, but now that the case is resolved, he'll be looking for me to get back to the office."

"When will you be leaving?" Heather wished she could take the question back. She hadn't meant to sound so needy.

He met her eyes and their gazes lingered. "I should probably head back in the morning."

The single word "oh" flew out of her mouth.

"Sounds like someone would like you to hang around."

"Ruthie!" both Maryann and Heather said in unison in similar scolding tones.

"What?" Ruthie's eyes grew wide, but she didn't look sorry in the least. Lowering her head to hide her grin, she deadheaded the nearest mum.

"Will we see you again, Zach?" Maryann asked in a motherly tone. "It was so nice to meet you."

"I own a cabin in the woods nearby. I'll make sure to stop by and say hello when I'm in town."

"That would be nice," Maryann said.

"I'm actually going there tonight," Zach said. "Make sure it's closed up before I head back home."

Heather drew back her shoulders and pointed at Ruthie. "Why don't you stay here tonight with your family? I'll pick you up tomorrow afternoon."

"Sounds good." Ruthie brushed the dirt off her hands. "Thank you."

Heather and Zach said their goodbyes, then walked out to climb into his truck. She buckled in and sighed, perhaps a little too loudly.

"I could wait until Sunday night to go back to Buffalo if you need help. My boss wasn't expecting me till

Monday. The roof on the barn is only partially finished, but Sloppy Sam said he'd get it done."

Heather shook her head, perhaps a little too adamantly. "Yes, the Amish work crew will do a great job. I can't keep you from your work."

"Can I take you for something to eat?" Zach asked as he pulled out onto the main road.

"Do you think we could pick up a pizza in town? I'm drained. I'd rather relax at home instead of sitting in a restaurant."

"Sounds good. If you don't mind, why don't you call ahead? We'll pick it up on the way home. We'll eat, then I'll go to my cabin for the night."

As Heather searched for her phone at the bottom of her purse, she had myriad emotions crowding her soul. She'd miss Zach. But it was time she faced her future as a confident young woman.

Without relying on a man.

Zach slid the pizza box on top of the stove. The smell of cheese and pepperoni reached his nose and made his stomach growl. He was hungrier than he had realized.

"Would you like some pop?" Heather asked as she stretched up into the cabinet and pulled out some paper plates. It was the most she had spoken since they had picked up the pizza. He had written it off as exhaustion from all the stress. "I have a few kinds here. Is a cola okay?"

"Sounds good."

She poured two glasses of cola and he plated two pieces of pizza. They settled in at the table next to one another enjoying the view through the new window overlooking the barn and the rest of the yard awash in the early-evening glow of the setting sun. With her food sitting untouched in front of her, she smiled. "This is just the view I imagined and this is the first time I've taken the time to enjoy it. Really enjoy it without the nagging dread that Brian was out there." She tilted her head and a light came into her eyes. "This is the first time that I've been allowed to enjoy it."

Zach's gaze drifted to the corner where they had found the graffiti the escaped convict had left. Zach had a hard time thinking of Fox as this beautiful woman's ex-husband. As his smart little sister's husband. The man had duped a lot of people, including the woman at the correctional facility who helped him escape. She was currently out on bail. But she wasn't his concern. The legal system would take care of her.

Making sure Fox couldn't hurt any more people had been his goal. After dinner, he planned to call Deputy Gates and find out where they had taken Fox's body. Even though he had talked Heather out of viewing his remains. *He* had to see them. *He* had to be convinced.

Zach took a bite of his pizza and the two of them sat in companionable silence as they ate.

"I've come a long way since the night you showed up at my back door." Heather's tone had a distant quality to it.

"You've always been a strong woman. From the first time I met you."

"If I had been braver, your sister would still be alive."

Zach put his piece of pizza down, realizing neither of them was going to eat until they had this discussion.

"You can't blame yourself. If you had stayed, you may have died. And you had no way of warning my sister. You didn't know. You have to move forward."

She traced the rim of her glass. "I'll never forget your father's face at the trial. He was destroyed."

A pang of guilt knotted his stomach. No one had empathized more with his father's pain than he had. As the big brother—in law enforcement, no less—he should have protected his sister.

"There's enough bad feelings to go around." He reached over and took her hand. "Let's move forward. It's over."

She turned to him and met his eyes. "It really is, isn't it?"

"Yeah. It is." He leaned closer and paused. A small smile played on her lips and she leaned closer to him. He brushed a gentle kiss across her lips. She tasted sweet from the cola.

He pulled back and looked into her eyes. A flicker of happiness danced in their depths, having replaced the fear and worry. She lifted her hand and cupped his cheek. "Thank you for being here."

Her fingers slid from his cheek and picked up her slice of pizza. "I guess we should finish up here. You probably have to pack for home."

He nodded and took another bite of his pizza, but he had suddenly lost his appetite.

Apparently his job here was done.

It was time to go home.

Chapter Twelve

Heather woke up early to the sound of rumbling thunder in the distance. She rolled over and snuggled into her covers, trying to put her finger on the emotion she was feeling. Hope? Renewal? Empty? Last night with Zach hadn't exactly gone as planned. She hadn't anticipated his kiss as they sat at the table enjoying pizza.

She threw back the covers and climbed out of bed. The kiss had sent tingles all the way to her toes, but she wasn't the type to have a fleeting romance. And based on her past experience, she probably wasn't the type to have any romance. She didn't trust her judgment when it came to men. She had been so, *so* wrong before.

But Zach was nothing like Brian.

Heather slipped into the bathroom and chuckled at her reflection in the mirror. Based on the every-which-way of her hair, she must have tossed and turned all night. With more than a little effort, she ran a comb through her long tresses. She had a quiet morning planned before all her guests arrived tomorrow afternoon. Five women were registered for a weekend getaway, but the weather didn't look like it was going to cooperate. Maybe with Ruthie's help she'd try a new soup for Saturday afternoon.

Twisting her hair up in a ponytail, she left her bedroom— leaving the door unlocked—and headed downstairs. The clock on the kitchen wall ticked away each second. The red light on the alarm pad indicated it was set. That was when she saw a piece of paper on the table. From Zach. Funny, she hadn't noticed it last night after he left.

She picked up the scrap of paper and realized it was his business card. She ran her thumb over the embossed letters of his name. Their relationship had been a professional one despite a little kiss.

That's all.

She frowned. Her heart disagreed. She should have felt more content. Safe, at least, after knowing her ex-husband was no longer out there. But instead she felt…lonely.

You won't feel lonely come tomorrow afternoon when the bed-and-breakfast is buzzing with guests. Enjoy this moment.

She grabbed a bowl of cereal and sat at the table overlooking the yard. The exact spot where she had sat with Zach twelve hours ago. The exact spot where he had kissed her. She touched her lips, remembering the warmth of his mouth on hers.

Why was she so quick to dismiss the notion of a relationship with him? He was a good man.

She was damaged goods.

Instead of obsessing, she focused on finishing her breakfast. She couldn't just wander around the house all morning, missing Zach, listening to the rain beat on the roof. She had to do something. She wasn't scheduled to pick up Ruthie until this afternoon.

Her gaze drifted to the barn. That was when she

knew what she had to do. Soon, the news coverage of Brian Fox would be a distant memory. Perhaps now was the time to focus on putting another tragedy behind her.

She put her bowl in the sink, then grabbed her rain jacket off the hook, stuffed her feet in her Wellies and headed outside. The cool autumn rain felt refreshing on her cheeks. She turned and locked the door behind her. Some things would die a slow death. However, she supposed locking doors and setting alarms were a smart way of life for any woman living alone.

She crossed the yard. Determination lead her toward the open barn door. She swallowed back her nausea. The dilapidated barn taunted her, as if it had taken on a life of its own.

"You can do this," she muttered to herself. The familiar tingling of a threatening panic attack bit at her fingertips. She glanced up. "*Mem*, stay with me. Help me do this so I can move forward."

Letting out a long breath through narrowed lips, she kept up her steady pace for fear she'd chicken out. The muddy path sucked the soles of her rain boots with every step. When she reached the open door, a chill slithered down her spine. With trembling fingers, it took her a few tries to catch the zipper on her raincoat and yank it up to her neck. Pulling her sleeves down over her hands, she slipped inside the barn. Her mouth went dry. She walked over to the horses' stalls. There were three of them.

Heather had no idea in which one her mother's body had been found. Tears stung her eyes as she peered into each one. She ran her hand along the half door, vowing to put the barn repairs at the top of her priority list. Her mother had loved horses.

Zach had already made a good start.

A horse or two would be a wonderful addition. She'd have to repair the fences, too, so they could safely roam the property. That was about the extent of what she knew about horses, but she figured Ruthie would be a wealth of information.

Heather swiped away at the tears and said a silent prayer for her mother. That she would rest in peace. And that Heather'd be able to live with not knowing what happened because sometimes there were no answers. She had to ask God for comfort and peace.

The sound of shuffling made Heather spin around. Icy dread coursed through her veins. She squinted into the heavy shadows as thunder rumbled overhead and a bolt of lightning made her jump.

Crossing her arms, she decided the noises she had heard were the settlings of a very old building during a storm. She turned to leave the barn when someone yanked a burlap bag over her head and threw her down onto the ground. Her elbow and hip slammed into the hard-packed dirt.

Her scream got lodged in her throat as she sucked in the gritty fabric of the burlap. Panic consumed all rational thought.

Before she had a chance to gain her bearings, someone jumped on top of her and tied her hands behind her back. As the person yanked Heather to her feet, Heather pleaded, "Stop. Why are you doing this?" Shadows moved quickly, masked by the heavy weave of the burlap.

The image of her mother, the one she had held in her six-year-old brain, floated to mind. Was she going to meet her Maker in the same place as her mother's body had been found?

Fear made it nearly impossible to think. Her pulse

whooshed in her ears, masking the subtle sounds swirling around her.

Heather was shoved a few feet and tossed to the ground again. She whimpered in pain but refused to give up. In a desperate attempt to escape, Heather bucked and kicked, but her attacker had the upper hand. Something hard came down across her head, the blinding pain making her nauseous and dizzy.

"Stop." The single word was slurred, sounding as if it hadn't come from her mouth. "Please."

The attacker used his advantage to tie her feet together. She struggled to see, but between the burlap and the heavy shadows and the throbbing pain in her skull, she couldn't make out more than shadows.

"Brian? Please." The words sounded hoarse as they rasped out of her throat.

Brian's dead. Isn't he?

A strange sound floated in the air. *Is that me sobbing?*

Her attacker dragged her as she bucked with her bound legs, unable to free herself. "Stop! Please!"

The attacker dropped her legs. Heather's attempt to scoot back was made more difficult by her bound hands and feet. Something slammed her in the head again.

She fell back. Her head slammed against the ground. Nausea welled up and her head throbbed as she struggled to maintain consciousness.

Please, dear Lord. Save me. Save me.

The sound of liquid splashing on the ground filled her ears and the smell of gasoline gagged her.

Oh no... Oh no...

Panic, and a concussion, no doubt, made her dizzy.

Her ears buzzed, but she heard the unmistakable sound of a match hissing to life.

* * *

Zach paced the small lobby of the sheriff's office waiting for Deputy Gates to return. Zach glanced at his watch. It was early, but the deputy had assured him he'd meet him here, even at this hour.

Impatience made him antsy. He knocked on the glass separating the common man from those who protected and served, an added security measure necessary in modern times. Quail Hollow wasn't immune to evil.

"Deputy Gates is on his way," the young woman said as she hung up the phone.

"Okay." Zach squared his shoulders, bracing himself for what he had asked Deputy Gates to meet him for. He had to see Fox's body. He couldn't leave any room for doubt.

Crossing his arms, he turned toward the window. A sheriff's patrol car pulled up and Deputy Gates climbed out. Zach yanked the door open and met his new friend outside.

"Morning," Zach said, biting back his frustration when he noticed the deputy reaching into the cruiser to pull out a tray of coffees.

"Morning," the deputy said. "Coffee?" He held out the tray.

Zach waved him off. "No." He opened the door to the office for the deputy, who seemed determined to keep walking, perhaps to get out of the rain. "Deputy, I was hoping to see Fox's body."

A buzzing sounded and the deputy opened the interior door to the secure offices. "Come on in."

Zach didn't want to go into the sheriff's headquarters. He wanted the deputy to escort him to the morgue. He could have gone himself, but he thought using local law enforcement would go over better. Besides, he had no official reason to see Brian's body. This was personal. Deputy Gates was his in. Less questions this way.

"Come back to my office." The deputy led him through a series of hallways to a cubicle in the center of a large office space, dropping off two coffees on his way. He slid the tray with one remaining coffee on his desk. "Sure you don't want one?"

Zach smiled tightly and finally accepted the coffee. "Thanks." He took a long sip, hoping the caffeine would fix his mood. "Now, about our phone call."

The deputy sat and rested his elbows on his knees. "That's why I brought you back here. News is going to hit soon enough, but we need to try to get a jump on him."

A ticking started in Zach's jaw. "What are you talking about?" The coffee suddenly felt sour in his gut.

"Fox's dentist expedited his X-rays."

"Yeah?"

"The body. It's not Fox's. The dental records don't match."

Zach slowly leaned back, the reality of the latest discovery washing over him.

"Who is it?"

"Too early to tell, but a young man went missing about twenty miles outside of Peters Correctional Facility. Law enforcement didn't connect the two until now. They're sending us the young man's dental records to see if it's him."

"Brian found someone roughly his height and build and faked his own suicide."

The deputy ran his hands up and down his thighs.

"He's smart enough to know we'd figure it out. Far as I can tell. He was trying to buy time."

Buy time.

The last two words bounced around Zach's head. *Buy time.* He slammed down his coffee, the contents of the cup sloshing over the edges.

"What's going on?"

"Send patrols to the Quail Hollow Bed & Breakfast on Lapp Road. I have to go. I have to get to Heather."

The tires on Zach's truck spit out gravel as he tore out of the sheriff's parking lot. He had to get to Heather. *Now!* He grabbed his cell phone and dialed Heather's phone number. Not a great idea while racing down a country road, but it couldn't be avoided.

He put the phone on speaker and the hollow echo of the ringing phone bounced around the interior of his vehicle.

"Come on, Heather. Answer, answer, *answer…*" He tapped the side of his steering wheel as anxiety charged through him.

Heather's voice sounded in his car speakers. "Hi, you've reached Quail Hollow Bed & Breakfast. Please leave your name and number and we'll get back to you. We look forward to your visit."

"Heather," Zach yelled, as if she might hear him despite the fact he was talking into her voice mail. "Call me as soon as you get this. The body was not Fox's. The dental records do not match. Lock the doors. Make sure the alarm is set. I'll be there in—" he glanced at the clock out of habit "—five minutes."

Zach ended the call and pressed the accelerator to the floor and the engine hummed. In the not-so-far distance behind him, he could hear sirens. He hoped they were racing to Lapp Road and not to pull him over for driving like a lunatic.

With a white-knuckled grip, he navigated the curve on Lapp Road. Up ahead, smoke filled the air in a thick black plume disappearing into the dark storm clouds. His heart plummeted.

"God, I know I haven't prayed since before Jill died, but if You have any mercy on a poor soul like me, please, spare Heather. *Please*."

His truck skidded on the wet pavement as he slowed at Heather's driveway. His truck bobbled over the ruts. He slammed the gear into Park and jumped out of the truck, leaving the door open and the engine running. He leaned into the bed of the truck and snapped a fire extinguisher off the brace holding it in place, grateful he had gotten his truck back from the collision shop.

He ran as fast as he could, feeling like he was approaching a forest fire with a squirt gun. But he needed something. God was guiding his actions. He just knew Heather was in the barn.

He yanked the pin out of the extinguisher and aimed it at the door and white foam coated the frame, but flames licked the dry wood farther in.

"Heather! Heather!" Zach screamed, then he hooked his arm over his nose and mouth and pushed into the smoky confines of the barn. Holding his breath, he went in farther until he kicked something soft.

Dropping to all fours, he breathed in a shallow breath and coughed, his lungs filling with the acrid smoke. He reached out and felt an arm. He felt around her shoulders, slid his hands under her armpits and dragged her out of the barn.

A wave of relief washed over him when he saw

Heather's chest rise and fall once he set her on the grass a good thirty feet from the barn. He tugged off the burlap bag from over her head and his heart dropped when he saw the blood around her hairline.

Out of the corner of his eye, he saw the deputy running across the lawn. Zach hollered to him, "Call an ambulance!"

"On the way." The deputy approached, hands fisted on his hips as he scanned the landscape. "Is Miss Miller okay?"

"Heather, it's Zach. You're going to be okay." He worked on the ropes that bound her hands and feet. When she started to cough, he helped her sit up.

"Water," Heather rasped.

Zach was vaguely aware of the deputy instructing someone to get her water. As he helped support her into a seated position, he scanned the landscape. Fox could be anywhere.

Zach pointed frantically at Deputy Gates. "Have your men search the fields. He can't be far."

"Who?" Heather coughed again.

"Fox."

Her eyes widened in her sooty face as rain plastered her hair to her scalp. She slowly closed her eyes and her body went limp. Carefully, Zach laid her down. A fear like he'd never known spiked through him. He couldn't lose Heather.

"Is that ambulance on the way?" he yelled.

The deputy spoke into his shoulder radio and then listened. "Two minutes out."

Zach slid his arms under Heather's armpits and knees and hoisted her up. Her head lolled against his chest. "Come on, honey. I've got you." He ran toward the driveway and heard the sound of approaching sirens, his footing unstable over the muddy terrain. "I've got you," he repeated over and over.

He reached the ambulance just as it stopped in front of the house. The paramedic jumped out and swung open the back doors. "What do you have here?"

"Smoke inhalation. Possible head injury."

Zach climbed into the back of the ambulance and laid an unconscious Heather on the stretcher. "I'm going with her. Can I close these doors? We have to get moving."

"Yeah, yeah," the paramedic said as she started working on her.

As Zach reached to close the back door, he realized with a sick feeling in the pit of his stomach that his truck was missing. It was possible someone had moved it, but he knew better. The search party wasn't going to find Fox in the fields because Fox had gotten away in Zach's truck.

Zach sat down on the bench next to Heather in the back of the ambulance. He pulled out his cell phone to notify the deputy of the new development. It helped to focus on details. Job-related tasks. Made him feel like he was accomplishing something when deep down he knew he was helpless when it came to what mattered most: Heather.

Zach ended the call and leaned forward, resting his elbows on his knees. He reached out and took Heather's limp hand in his and pressed her cold fingers to his lips.

Dear Lord, let her be okay.

Chapter Thirteen

The stink of the acrid smoke lingered in Heather's nose while a steady *thump-thump-thump* throbbed behind her eyes as she dreamed a million bizarre dreams of disjointed nonsense: swinging on a tire swing while pumping her legs toward the sky with a long dress flapping around her legs; serving guests at a long table that extended toward the horizon like one of those infinity pools; someone reaching for her through black smoke with strong arms.

Distant voices lulled her out of her strange dreams. It seemed to take a herculean effort to open her eyes. The voices grew louder and then grew distant again.

Finally prying her eyes open, she immediately regretted it as the long fluorescent lights in the ceiling were like a million pinpricks to her eyeballs.

"Ohh…"

A shadow crossed her face and a warm, gentle hand touched the back of hers. "I'm right here." It was Zach.

She tried again to open her eyes. This time, Zach's handsome face blocked the harsh lighting. He reached toward her and slid a piece of hair off her forehead. "Hey there. You had us worried."

"What…?" The memories of her attack assaulted her brain like a tsunami unexpectedly taking her legs out from under her.

"How long have I been here?" The intensity in Zach's gaze unnerved her.

"Twelve hours." He lowered himself into the chair next to her bed and a strange thought ran through her mind. Had Zach been by her side the whole time?

"Who attacked me?" She tried to lift her arm and she realized there were wires coming out of her hand. "What aren't you telling me?"

Zach took her hand in both of his. "Brian Fox is alive."

She tried to push up on her elbow and immediately regretted it when nausea rolled over her. "What?" She furrowed her brow. "Can you elevate the top of my bed? I need to sit up." This wasn't the kind of news a person took lying down.

Zach found the control and pressed the button and the top of the bed moved up as the motor hummed. Heather folded her hands on top of her stomach as she talked herself out of a panic attack. "What about the body pulled out of the woods?" Tears threatened, but she refused to give her ex-husband any more of her tears.

"Fox wanted us to think the body was his. Made it look like he committed suicide by shooting off his face. Then he had the added benefit of time. Bodies decompose. Animals…" Zach seemed to be measuring his words, but Heather didn't want to be coddled. She needed the truth.

"How did they figure it out?"

"When they finally got his dental records early this morning, law enforcement realized their mistake. I was on my way to tell you when I spotted the fire."

"You pulled me out of the fire?"

He nodded.

"Thank you." She blinked slowly. Thank God for putting him in her path.

"You didn't see him when he attacked you?"

"No." She ran a hand across her forehead. "Someone came up behind me and put a burlap bag over my head. He whacked me with something." She pressed her fingers delicately to her sore cheekbone. A small smile flickered at the corners of her mouth. "I can only imagine what I look like."

Zach tilted his head and stared intently at her, cupping her cheek gingerly with his hand. "I've never seen a more beautiful sight. I thought I lost you."

"You thought you lost me?" She hadn't meant to say the words out loud.

He ran his hand over his mouth. "I'm grateful I learned the truth and raced back to the bed-and-breakfast in time."

"Yeah, me, too." She leaned back on the pillow and groaned as the room spun around her. "The bed-and-breakfast. I have guests arriving tomorrow. Tomorrow, right?" She strained to orient herself. *What day is it?*

"Ruthie contacted them to cancel."

"I can—" The pain that shot through her head stole her breath away.

He gently placed his hand on her shoulder and helped her settle back in. "Even if you were physically able to run the bed-and-breakfast right now, the smell from the barn fire is heavy inside the house."

"Oh no." Heather blinked furiously, determined to keep the tears at bay.

Zach slid his hand down her arm and stopped at her hand. "Shh," he said, swiping his thumb back and forth across the palm of her hand. "Other than the barn, there's no damage to the house. Nothing that a little fresh air won't fix."

"Are you sure?"

"Yeah. Focus on getting better."

Heather raised her eyebrows. "Easy for you to say." She licked her top lip. It felt dry. Anticipating her needs, Zach reached over and poured some water from the pitcher into a plastic cup. The ice rattled as he held the straw to her lips. "Thanks."

Just then voices grew louder outside her door. Passing doctors or nurses. That was what she must have heard during her fitful sleep.

"Did the doctor say how long I had to stay here?"

"Okay, about that…"

"What?"

"I told a little white lie and said you were my fiancée. It was the only way I could get any answers. Even at that, I think she was afraid of breaking some sort of privacy laws, but she had mercy on me, I suppose."

"Okay, fine. How long?"

"Overnight."

"Oh." The thought of trying to get some sleep here with all the lights and sounds and… She supposed with a head injury, the doctor had to be careful. She tried to sound cheery. "I can go home tomorrow?"

"Not home. I assured the physician I'd take care of you."

She stared at him but didn't say anything.

"I'll take you to my cabin in the woods for a few days of rest and relaxation."

Heather sat in the passenger seat of Zach's borrowed truck with her eyes closed against the bright sunshine. Zach noticed she was finally able to open them when he turned up the long lane to his cabin. The mature trees created a canopy of darkness that seemed to provide some relief to her eyes.

"You doing okay? We're almost there."

"The doctor said the pain should gradually decrease each day. I'm looking forward to it." She let out an awkward laugh, obviously still in pain.

"Do you need me to get you anything? I can run out to the store."

"A comfortable place to rest and darkness."

"I can do that."

Zach parked the truck and ran around to her side to help her out. "I'll come back out for your bag." Ruthie had packed one for her.

Heather felt frail as he slid his arm around her back. He'd spent most of the previous night following up on leads on Fox. *Nothing.* His stolen truck hadn't even been spotted. Once he got Heather safely settled at the cabin, he'd return to the search. He couldn't sit this one out.

He reached around her and twisted the doorknob to the cabin. The door swung open with a screech and his father scrambled out of a chair, the newspaper on his lap fluttering to the floor. Zach suspected his father had been dozing.

Heather paused in the doorway and glanced up at Zach, curiosity glistening in her eyes.

"Heather Miller, this is my father, Charlie Walker."

Heather offered her hand. "Hello."

"Nice to see you, Miss Miller. We met briefly during the trial."

Heather's face grew somber. "Of course, Mr. Walker. I remember." Her hands fluttered around the hollow of her neck as her gaze dropped to the floor.

"So," his father said, perhaps a little too cheerfully, "I hear you took a knock to the head."

Heather groaned. "I suppose I'm lucky I have a hard head."

"Come on in." Zach encouraged her forward with a hand to the small of her back. "Do you want to sit for a bit or would you rather lie down?"

His father bent and picked up the newspaper that had slid to the floor. "Sit here. It's the most comfortable chair. I'll get you some water." Without waiting for an answer, his father crossed the room to the kitchen.

Zach helped Heather settle into the oversize chair. He slid a blanket his mother had crocheted off the back of the chair and spread it across her lap. She looked frail and the bruise under her eye had turned a purplish yellow.

His father reappeared with a glass of ice water and set it on the table next to her. "Here you go."

His father stood off to the side. "Are you hungry? I make a pretty mean grilled cheese."

Heather smiled. The first time Zach had seen her genuinely smile since finding her in the smoke-filled barn. "I'm not hungry now, but can I take a rain check?"

"Absolutely." He drew in a deep breath and let it out. "I'm going to take a quick walk around the exterior of the house. Give you some time to settle in."

"Thanks, Dad."

His dad put on his boots and coat and disappeared outside.

Zach sat down on the footstool in front of Heather and leaned forward, resting his forearms on his thighs and clasping his hands together.

Heather slumped back in the chair and groaned. "You're going out to look for Brian yourself, aren't you?"

"I have to. I can't—"

"Sit around babysitting me?" She must have recognized the bite to her tone and quickly added, "I'm sorry. That's not fair of me. It's just…" She adjusted the blanket on her lap. "I'm afraid."

Something told him she had rarely, if ever, admitted her fear. "My father is a retired marshal. He'll protect you."

Her gaze drifted to the door. "He's doing more than stretching his legs outside."

"Yeah, he's checking the property for any signs of Fox."

She drew in a deep breath and closed her eyes. "You have to find him. I can't live like this anymore."

Heather clamped her jaw trying to stop it from trembling. She wanted to be strong for Zach, but she was tired. Tired of hiding. Tired of hurting. Tired of wondering what was going to happen next.

So, so tired.

"I need to join the search party," Zach said.

"I get it." Heather tried to reassure him with a smile, but all she wanted to do was cry and take comfort in Zach's arms. But how was that fair when she was here and his sister was dead? At the hands of the man he needed to find.

Zach patted her knee. "Call me if you need anything." He frowned. "Cell reception out here is hit-and-miss. But there's a landline."

"And I'm here." Mr. Walker had come back in from outside, his nose red from the cold. He pulled back one side of his coat, revealing a gun. "I won't let anything happen to you on my watch."

Zach crossed the room to where his father stood. He clapped his father on the shoulder. "I don't anticipate any trouble, since this place isn't listed anywhere. Fox would have no way of tracking you here."

"But you found me." She hated the subtle tremble in her voice.

"We tracked you down through a real estate transaction. The land for this cabin was purchased by my grandmother. It would be impossible for Fox to make that connection." Zach snatched his coat from the arm of the couch. "I'll bring your bag in, then hit the road."

"Okay." Her mind raced, but she couldn't think of anything else to say. It wasn't fair of her to keep him any longer.

Mr. Walker sat on the couch and leaned over and opened a drawer on the coffee table. It was filled with old VHS tapes. "Feel like a movie?"

She didn't. But she didn't want to be rude.

"I might close my eyes, but I wouldn't mind the background noise." It might help distract her.

A minute later, Zach breezed back in. "I'll put your bag in the guest bedroom." He stopped on his way back through the cabin. "Last call. Need anything?"

She shook her head and immediately regretted it as pain ricocheted through her head.

"I'll check in. Keep you posted," he said, as much to her as to his father.

Heather heard the lock snap into place. Mr. Walker put a movie in and Heather found herself drifting off to sleep.

She wasn't sure how long she had been dozing when the smell of something on the stove pulled her out of her disjointed dreams. She opened her eyes and sat up and groaned at the pain. She tried to rub the crick out of her neck, but the pain persisted. She feared the only way she could get rid of this pain entirely was to obtain a time machine and go back to before Brian took a board to her head.

But why did he cover her head? Brian was the kind of guy who liked to see the fear in her eyes when he hurt her. She pulled herself upright and rested her elbow on the arm of the chair. Something uncertain niggled at the back of her brain.

"I thought you might have been more comfortable in the guest room, but I hated to wake you up." Mr. Walker stood at the stove in the kitchen and hollered over his shoulder.

"That's okay." She rolled her neck, relieved that the throbbing in her head had quieted to a dull roar.

Mr. Walker handed her a plate with a grilled cheese and some fresh fruit. She accepted it and scooted back on the chair. "Thank you."

He sat down on the couch with a plate of his own. He picked up the remote and turned down the volume on some Sandra Bullock movie. "Grilled cheese is my specialty."

Heather took a bite and her mouth watered. Around a mouthful of sandwich, she said, "This is the best grilled cheese that I've ever had. Ever. Ever." She took another bite, savoring the taste.

Mr. Walker smiled. The resemblance around his eyes to his son was uncanny. "I'm not sure it's that good."

"It is. And I hadn't realized how hungry I was."

"Well, I'm glad." He took a bite of his own sandwich and chewed thoughtfully. "After my wife died, I had to learn to cook. A person gets sick of takeout pretty quick." He stabbed a fresh strawberry with his fork and popped it in his mouth. "Zach tells me you opened a bed-and-breakfast here in Quail Hollow."

"I have. But it's off to a rough start." She cut her gaze to the handsome gentleman. "As I'm sure you're aware, the barn on the property just burned down."

"You'll have time to rebuild once that..." His jaw clenched. "Once Fox is back in custody."

Heather pulled apart her sandwich and stared at the long strand of cheese. "I know. I'm lucky to still be around to do these things." She cleared her throat. "I'm sorry about your daughter."

"You say that as if you somehow feel responsible for my daughter's death."

That same familiar guilt stole her breath. "I knew what Brian was capable of, yet I ran off and hid. I can't help but feel guilty."

Mr. Walker set his plate aside and rested his elbow on the arm of the couch. He stared off into the middle distance and took a deep breath, as if he were about to share a very painful story. Heather considered stopping him. She didn't want to cause the man any more pain, but something deep in her heart suggested he needed to talk. And she needed to hear this.

He ran a hand across his mouth. "For the longest time I blamed myself, too."

Heather's reflex was to tell him, "No, of course it's not your fault," but she knew how that worked. The guilty party never believed it anyway. She set her plate aside and held the blanket close to her chest.

"My wife died when Jill was only sixteen. I was always busy working. Away at a job. And when I was home, I was as strict and tough as when I was on the job. It was the only way I knew how to parent." Other than a quick sniff, Zach's father revealed no sign of emotion. "She met Fox when she was eighteen and they were married six months later." He swallowed hard. Jill's story sounded oddly like hers. Brian knew how to take advantage of vulnerable young women. "I think he was her ticket out of the house. She couldn't wait to get out from under my strict reign."

Heather opened her mouth to offer him some reassurance, as people often did with her. But he held up his hand. "My mind tells me I'm not to blame. That Fox was an evil man. But my heart hurts. If I had been able to provide my daughter with warmth at home, she wouldn't have been so eager to get out of the house. Or…" He turned and met Heather's gaze and something flickered in the depths of his eyes. "I can only imagine how different our lives would have been if my wife had lived. She and Jill were so close." He drew in a deep breath and let it out. "As you can see, there's enough blame to go around. Zach has his own burden of guilt, but he refuses to talk about it. Our goal has been to see that Fox pays. Control the things we can. Get him behind bars. *Again.*"

"I suppose that's a good strategy. Otherwise you can drive yourself crazy." Heather understood more than most what it was like to feel lost and hopeless. The need to control what little she could.

"Your testimony helped secure Fox's conviction. You did good. Please, never regret your role in this."

Heather nodded, a lump forming in her throat. "I really thought we'd be able to put things behind us once he went to prison."

Mr. Walker picked up his plate and moved the fruit around with his fork. "It'll be over soon. Fox can't run forever."

No, no, he can't.

Chapter Fourteen

The sun had dipped below the hills. The sky still held a hint of purple. The air had a bite to it. Even if Fox was able to stay on the run where temperatures could plummet well below zero once winter hit, he'd need help if he wanted to survive.

Help. That was what bugged Zach. Earlier, he had talked to his supervisor, who assured him the local authorities still had the woman who provided Fox with the tools to escape prison under tight surveillance as she awaited legal proceedings. They had positively identified the man who they initially thought was Fox through his dental records. He was a high school dropout who liked to spend his time at one of the taverns near the correctional facility. Apparently the dead man had simply been in the wrong place at the wrong time. Fox had either hitched a ride with the man or carjacked him. The ending had been the same: the dead man's car and body ended up in Quail Hollow.

Zach turned the heat on in the truck. He decided to call his boss again, who wholeheartedly supported his decision to remain in Quail Hollow. Yet no one had any updates. Then he called his father. Heather was sleeping and all was quiet at the cabin.

Thank You, Lord. The quick prayer had come naturally and Zach realized Heather had influenced him far more than he had ever imagined. It was easy to turn his back on his faith after Jill was murdered, but now as he turned to prayer, he recalled the comfort that faith could bring in times of crisis. His mother had taught him that, but he had forgotten. Heather had reminded him.

But he realized he couldn't keep Heather safely tucked away. That was why he had to get Fox once and for all. Growing desperate and frustrated, he decided he'd drive the roads of Quail Hollow one more time and see if he noticed anything out of the ordinary.

When he reached the Quail Hollow Bed & Breakfast, he decided to do a property check. All the doors and windows were locked. All appeared secure.

The smell of burned wood still hung in the air. If Zach didn't know better, he'd think someone had been sitting around a campfire. In the gathering darkness, the shell of the barn was a stark reminder of how much worse it could have been if he hadn't raced back here when he had.

He found himself pausing and saying a silent prayer of gratitude. God had truly put him in the right place at the right time to save Heather from certain death.

He strode back around to the driveway, hyperaware of his surroundings. He scanned the area with his flashlight. The light bounced off something metal across the street, partially blocked by the abandoned buggy.

Strange.

With his hand hovering over the grip of his gun, he turned off the flashlight and jogged across the street. When he reached the buggy, he flattened himself against it and moved under cover toward the vehicle that had caught his attention.

His pulse spiked.

His truck. The one that had been stolen.

Exactly where he had parked it the very first night he had arrived at the bed-and-breakfast when Fox escaped. Was this a message? That he had been watching all along?

He scanned his surroundings. No sign of movement. He slid the switch on his flashlight and lifted it to examine the interior of the cab. The beam of light lit on Brian Fox, head tilted back, eyes closed.

Adrenaline surged through his system.

Zach aimed his gun at the one man he hated most in the world. The man who had destroyed so many lives.

Tucking the flashlight under his arm, he yanked open the door and aimed his gun at Fox's head. The temptation to pull the trigger and kill the poor excuse for a human being blackened his heart. His hand trembled on the trigger and a voice whispered in his head, *That's not you. Don't kill him. Take him into custody. He'll be judged by someone far greater than you.*

Swallowing hard, Zach took a step closer and grabbed Fox's arm. A chill ran down his spine. Fox's head lolled over. His body was cool.

Zach checked Fox's pulse. Nothing.

He couldn't have been dead long.

But he *was* dead.

Definitely dead.

Zach holstered his gun and stood frozen for a minute, unsure of how to feel.

"It's all over," he muttered to himself. "It's really over."

He grabbed his phone and called Deputy Gates. "I found Brian Fox. He's dead."

"Where are you?"

"I'm across the street from Quail Hollow Bed & Breakfast."

"I don't understand. We've been patrolling that area."

"Fox was sitting in the driver's seat in my truck. The truck was partially hidden by an abandoned buggy."

"Couldn't have been there long. We've been thorough." He could hear a rustling. "The log says that a patrol was through there fifteen minutes ago."

Zach tapped the side of the truck with the palm of his hand. "Well, he's here now."

"I'll follow up on it. But are you sure it's Brian Fox?"

"Yes, it's definitely him. No gun blast to the face this time." He moved back in front of the open truck door. "I know I hit him when he was making his escape." He turned on his flashlight and saw blood staining his tan T-shirt. "So, either I hit him or someone else did. Either way, the road has ended for Mr. Fox."

Heather rolled over and slowly opened her eyes, surprised at how well she had slept. The bed was very comfortable, especially for a guest room. She pushed up on her elbow, testing to see how much pain she was in. The throbbing in her head had dulled and the bruise on her cheek was tender to the touch. But she'd survive.

She pushed back the hand-sewn quilt that someone— maybe Jill, maybe Jill's mother—had perhaps picked up at an Amish sale. The hardwood floor was cool on her bare feet, reminding her that winter was coming.

She pulled back the room-darkening curtains and stared outside. Clouds cast an eerie glow over the early morning. She reached over and picked up her cell phone on the bedside table—7:17 a.m.

Unease crawled up her spine as she imagined her enraged ex-husband skulking around the woods, determined to find her after learning that she had escaped the inferno, her certain death.

He had failed at controlling her, once again.

Crossing her arms over her oversize T-shirt, she turned away from the window. Curiosity had her moving toward her bedroom door. Surely Zach had returned sometime last night. Did he have news?

She paused at the mirror and smiled. She better take a few minutes to get presentable before she checked to see if her host was awake.

After she got dressed, she went to the kitchen. Zach and his father sat at the kitchen table drinking coffee. Mr. Walker looked up and smiled. He pushed away from the table and the back of his chair hit the door leading out to the backyard. "Good morning." He lifted his mug and took a sip, then set it down. "Okay, what kind of eggs would everyone like? I'll get the bacon on."

Heather narrowed her gaze. An entirely different mood settled, albeit subtly, into the cozy space, as if a weight had been lifted. Had something happened last night?

Zach stood and pulled out a chair for Heather. "Sit down. My father wouldn't allow us to help, even if we asked. What kind of eggs would you like?"

Heather lifted her hands, not wanting to be an imposition. "Whatever's easiest."

Mr. Walker grabbed the eggs from the fridge and spun around to face them. "Why don't I make a big batch of scrambled eggs?"

Heather's stomach grumbled. "Sounds good."

Zach grabbed a mug and the coffeepot. He set the mug in front of her and smiled. "Cream and sugar are right here."

"Thank you." She traced the handle of the plain ceramic mug, then met Zach's gaze. She almost hated to ask because she feared the answer, but she couldn't delay any longer. "Any word on the search?"

If she hadn't looked up from the sugar bowl, she might have missed the quick exchange between father and son. Her heart plummeted. "Do you have news?"

Zach let out a long breath. "Yes, I do." He seemed to be searching for the right words. Goose bumps blanketed her skin as she anticipated his update.

"Did Brian hurt someone else?" She swallowed around a knot of emotion.

Zach pressed his lips together, then reached across the table to cover her hand. His hand felt warm on hers. Comforting.

"What is it?" she whispered.

"Last night I was searching your property—"

"At the bed-and-breakfast?" She couldn't keep the tremble out of her voice.

"Yes. I found my stolen truck parked across the street with Fox at the wheel. He was dead."

Heather's hand flew to her chest as a flush of an emotion she couldn't quite pinpoint settled on her lungs, making it difficult to breathe. "Brian's dead?" She lifted her watery gaze to him. "Are you sure?"

Zach squeezed her hand. "Yes. I saw the body myself. There's no mistake this time."

She nodded slowly, as if in a fog. "It's over. It's really over."

"Yes. It's over. I wanted to tell you last night, but you were sleeping so peacefully I didn't want to wake you."

"How did he die?"

"Best guess? He succumbed to the wound when I shot him," Zach said. "I checked with the sheriff's department that he had been shot, apparently twice. An autopsy will confirm cause of death."

Heather pulled her hand out from under his and placed each of her hands on either side of her coffee mug, focusing on the warmth flowing off the ceramic. A tear trailed down her cheek.

Zach brushed the tear away. "I'm sorry you've had to go through all this."

Heather nodded again, trying to let the news settle in. "I can go back to the bed-and-breakfast. Get back to my life." She tilted her head toward him and winced at the pain. "I suppose you'll be getting back to Buffalo, too."

Zach smiled but didn't say anything. Heather didn't know what to make of it.

Heather felt a gentle hand on her shoulder. She glanced up into Mr. Walker's kind eyes. "Everything's going to be okay."

Heather's lips trembled. This man had lost his beautiful daughter and he was comforting her. She reached up and patted his hand. "Thank you for keeping me company last night. It meant a lot to me."

"It was my pleasure." He grabbed the pan of eggs from the stove and dished them out. He set three plates down on the table. "I can understand why my son talks so highly of you."

Zach cleared his throat. "We're not telling tales out of school, are we?"

Mr. Walker picked up a piece of bacon with his fingers. "I like to be helpful. My son here would be all work and no play…"

Zach laughed. "I'm a grown man. I think I can get my own dates."

Heather felt her face heat as she moved the eggs around her plate with the fork.

Zach took a sip of his coffee, then set it back down. "Can we just eat and enjoy the peace? We finally don't have anything to worry about."

Nothing to worry about.

Heather's mind flashed to the barn and her canceled reservations at the bed-and-breakfast. She had a lot to take care of—a lot to worry about—but God had seen to it that her biggest concern was no longer a threat.

She scooped up the eggs and couldn't believe how delicious they were. "These are fantastic. I'm not going to be in a hurry to go anywhere." Then realizing what she'd said, she quickly backtracked. "I mean…"

Both Walker men laughed. "We know what you mean," Zach said as he bit into a piece of bacon. "My father really knows how to cook."

Shortly after breakfast, Zach had plans to drive Heather home to the bed-and-breakfast. "You're welcome to stay at the cabin for a few more days to recover. My father loves cooking for you."

Heather tugged on her seat belt, seeming anxious. "As wonderful as that sounds, I need to get home. To start figuring out what I need to do to have the burned-out barn replaced. I need to reassure those who have future reservations that we'll be reopening for business soon. I can't afford to waste any more time. This is peak tourist season. Once winter arrives, business will slow down, maybe even come to a halt." She dragged a hand through her hair and sighed heavily, sounding weary. "And I can't put you and your father out any longer."

"Don't overdo it. Promise me? You've had a concussion." He wanted to say so much more, but now didn't seem like the right time. He didn't want to pressure her.

"I'll try." He knew it would be a struggle considering how determined she was to make a success of the bed-and-breakfast.

"I have to get back to Buffalo for work, but I could come back on the weekends and help you with projects."

Heather shifted in her seat but didn't say anything. For the first time in a long time, Zach felt an air of awkwardness stretch between them. Something that hadn't existed between them before. Perhaps he had said too much.

Zach cleared his throat, wanting to backtrack. "I figured you could use some help."

"I really could, but you have a life, a job, in Buffalo. I don't want to take advantage of your kindness. You've already done so much."

Zach knew a brush-off when he heard it, but he also realized Heather had been through an awful lot recently and it wasn't fair of him to expect her to make any other plans for the future other than getting her bed-and-breakfast up and running.

He slowed and turned into her driveway. His vehicle bobbled over the ruts created by the hardened mud. Sloppy Sam—Zach couldn't help but smile inside every time he thought of the workman's nickname—was installing a handmade sign on the front lawn: Quail Hollow Bed & Breakfast.

"Look at that," Heather said, an air of excitement in

her voice. "The sign looks beautiful." She climbed out of his vehicle and went over to chat with the Amish workman.

Zach parked and got out. He grabbed her overnight bag from the backseat and slung the strap over his shoulder. "Where do you want me to put this?"

"I'll take it." Heather held out her hand. "I don't want to hold you up."

"No, you need to take it easy. I'll carry your bag in and put it on the landing upstairs."

Heather smiled, a genuine smile. The weight of recent events seemed to have lifted and left a light in her eyes. "I won't argue. Upstairs would be great." She turned to Sam. "Thank you. The sign looks awesome." She traced the carved lettering with her index finger. "Just beautiful."

Sam tipped his broad-brimmed hat. *"Denki."*

Heather jogged and caught up with Zach. She slipped ahead of him and reached out to unlock the door to the house, when it swung open. She glanced back at him with a startled expression.

Was someone inside?

Zach was about to stop Heather's entry when Ruthie's voice rang out. "You're home!" Heather's shoulders relaxed at her friend's greeting.

"I am." Heather stepped aside to hold the door open, allowing Zach to pass.

"I'll run this upstairs." Zach patted her bag and jogged up the stairs. When he came back down, Heather was sitting at the table in the new addition while Ruthie put the kettle on.

"Stay for some tea, Marshal Walker?" There was something very hopeful, almost gleeful, in her tone.

"I should probably go."

"Don't run off. Not yet." Heather glanced at the seat next to hers. "Sit down a minute."

He sat down at the table, not eager to leave. "Our view isn't quite the same as it was a few days ago." In the bright sunshine, the loss of the barn was staggering. Heather seemed to stare at it for a long moment, as if reflecting on how she had almost lost her life in the raging fire.

Ruthie set out two cups of tea and a few cookies. "I'm going to run upstairs and do some cleaning." She paused in the doorway. "Thanks for keeping my *gut* friend safe."

Heather pushed the plate of cookies toward Zach and he waved them off and she laughed in response. "Yeah, I'm not exactly hungry, either. Not after that breakfast your father made us."

They sat in silence for a few minutes, sipping their tea. After a stretch, Zach stood up. "I guess I shouldn't prolong the inevitable." It seemed they were playing a game of who was going to say goodbye first.

Heather stood up, joining him. She placed her hand on his chest and leaned up on her tippy-toes and kissed his cheek. "I'll miss you."

Zach tilted his head back and smiled. "You know where to find me if you need a hand around here."

"Be careful what you offer."

"I wouldn't offer to help if I didn't mean it."

Zach cupped her soft cheek, then let his hand drop. He turned to leave before he changed his mind.

Chapter Fifteen

A few days had passed and Heather was feeling much better. The only outward sign of her injuries was a slight yellowish mark under her eye. Nothing a little makeup wouldn't cover up.

On her trip to the grocery store, the sun seemed brighter and the air smelled sweeter. She had said more than her share of prayers for Brian's soul, but now was her time to move on. Thank God that He had protected her and those she cared about.

Picking out the groceries for this weekend's guests had been a pure pleasure. The bed-and-breakfast had been aired out and was ready for guests. She could finally get on with her life without constantly looking over her shoulder.

As she wandered the aisles, her mind drifted to Zach. She missed him. He had called yesterday to check in on her, but the conversation had been brief. Perhaps neither one of them knew what to say after all they had been through.

His presence here had been part of his job.

That's all.

He owed her nothing more. Her feelings for him were born out of gratitude.

That's all.

Heather smiled at the cashier as she paid, then loaded the groceries into her car to head home. She thought of her mother as she drove. Apparently her mind wouldn't allow her to have a completely worry-free day. She supposed it was her nature. Her mother's murder had never been solved, but maybe it was time to put her mind at peace and focus on the fact that her mom wasn't suffering. She was in heaven. She wouldn't want her eldest daughter to waste any more of her life trying to uncover the evil of the past.

Even though Heather wasn't Amish, she needed to follow the Amish way in honor of her mother and forgive the murderer. Move on.

Brian was gone, that was the most important thing. That part of her past was over. She was safe.

Maybe it *was* time to let it all rest.

A car's horn honked behind her. She glanced into her rearview mirror and muttered, "Sorry," even though he couldn't hear her. She wasn't sure how long she had been sitting at the stop sign. She looked both ways and moved through the intersection.

The car behind her sped up and zipped around her. Heather cringed when she noticed a horse and buggy traveling on the shoulder in the opposite direction. The Amish woman frowned and pulled up on the reins when the car sped past.

It seemed the tranquility the Amish sought was forever being encroached upon by the *Englischers*. Heather wondered if she was respecting her grandmother's home by allowing outsiders in.

Her worries fell away when she arrived home and saw the beautiful sign Sloppy Sam had constructed on the front lawn: Quail Hollow Bed & Breakfast. She had to believe her *mammy* was happy to have family back in her home.

Her proud feelings were replaced by curiosity when she noticed a car parked in the driveway. She wasn't expecting guests. "Is that Fiona's car?" she muttered to herself. Had the writer shown up unannounced? Heather didn't think she was scheduled to stay. Maybe Ruthie had taken the reservation and forgot to mention it. Yet they didn't take reservations for a weekday.

Heather popped the trunk and grabbed a few of the grocery bags. She'd return for the rest in a few minutes.

When she climbed the steps to the porch, she heard loud voices coming from inside. She set the bags down on the porch and opened the door. Nerves tangled inside her stomach.

Fiona stood with her back to the door. Ruthie was begging Fiona to leave. From her vantage point, Heather couldn't see Fiona's face to get a better read on the situation.

"What's going on?" Heather asked, her mouth growing dry as her nerves buzzed.

Fiona spun around, her face radiating rage. Reflexively, Heather recoiled; her instincts told her to get away. The same instincts that had convinced her it had been time to leave her husband.

Confusion swirled in her brain.

"What's going on?" she repeated when no one answered her.

"Run," Ruthie yelled. The fear in her friend's voice struck terror in Heather's heart.

Fiona slowly pulled her hand out of her jacket pocket and pointed a gun at Heather's chest. "Run and either you or your Amish friend here dies."

Heather slowly lifted her hands in a surrender gesture. "No one needs to get hurt. Please, lower the gun."

What in the world was going on?

Fiona shook her head slowly. "No." Her clipped answer made Heather's stomach bottom out.

"I don't understand," Heather said as her vision tunneled onto Fiona's face. The determination in her eyes behind her thick glasses landed squarely on Heather.

"I tried to get her to leave, but she threatened me," Ruthie said apologetically. "She insisted on seeing you. I'm sorry. So sorry." Her voice trembled.

"It's okay, Ruthie. It's okay."

Fiona stepped closer to Heather and the smell of beer wafted off her breath. "What do you want, Fiona?"

"You."

The single word made her knees go weak. "I'm sorry. What?"

"You… I want you dead." Fiona flashed the gun as if it were no big deal.

"I don't understand. What have I ever done to you?" Despite insides of mush, Heather projected a commanding tone.

"Please, Fiona, don't hurt Heather," Ruthie said, on the verge of tears. "She's like a sister to me. Please."

Fiona's eyes darted around the room, as if she was trying to weigh her options. She grabbed Heather's arm and squeezed tightly. Heather didn't react. She had had a lot of experience in tamping down her reaction when Brian was raging. He'd fed off her fear and she'd refused to give him more fuel for his anger.

"Amish girl, sit down and shut up."

Ruthie lowered herself into a chair at the kitchen table and clasped her hands in front of her. All the color had drained from her face.

"It's okay," Heather reassured her. "Everything's going to be okay."

Ruthie bowed her bonneted head. A sob escaped her lips.

Heather's stomach twisted.

Fiona leaned in close to Heather and clenched her teeth. "I need a second to think."

Zach sat at his desk at the downtown Buffalo U.S. Marshals office. This was the part of the job he liked least: paperwork. And nothing created more paperwork than a dead escaped convict. He wouldn't be able to wrap up the case until Fox's autopsy was complete. He moved the mouse and the computer screen came to life. He had just entered his log-in and password when he heard a soft knock on the door.

He hit the enter key, then turned halfheartedly toward the door, expecting one of his colleagues, eager to hear about the big manhunt that had transfixed the state over the past few weeks. What he hadn't expected was his father, dressed casually in a golf shirt and jeans.

Zach removed his hand from the computer mouse and leaned back in his chair. "Hey, Dad."

"You look as excited about that paperwork as I used to feel." His father crossed his arms and gave him an easy smile.

"I don't suppose the paperwork is why any of us got into law enforcement."

"But it might be the reason we retire." His father

sat down in the chair on the other side of the desk and crossed his ankle over his knee.

"What brings you by?" Zach knew his father liked to catch up with his former colleagues now and again, but he usually gave his son a quick text letting him know he'd be in.

"I can't stop by and say hello to my son?"

Zach eyed his father skeptically. Theirs was a solid relationship, but not a touchy-feely one. "Sure you can. I'm glad you stopped by. I was hoping to take you out to dinner this week. Thank you for your help in Quail Hollow."

"No need to repay me with dinner. I was glad to help." His dad rubbed his hands up and down his thighs. "An old guy like me likes to feel useful now and again."

"Well, I appreciate it."

"Speaking of Quail Hollow, are you going to keep in touch with Heather Miller?" His father dropped his foot to the floor and leveled his gaze at his son.

Zach frowned and lifted his hand in a casual gesture, as if it were of no consequence.

"Life goes by too fast. You've been all about this job for a long time. You need to let someone in." His father tapped the edge of the desk with his fingers for emphasis.

"You know what the job's like."

"I do." His father sat back in his chair. "And I loved the job like you do. But what I wouldn't do to be able to go back and spend more time with your mother. I'd trade anything for it. Now I'm retired. And all alone."

Zach was about to tell his father that he had him, but he knew that wasn't what his father meant. His father had spent most of his adult life chasing criminals.

Then he lost his wife too soon. Then, tragically, he lost his daughter…

Zach cleared his throat. "Heather and I are clearly on two different paths."

"But perhaps God brought your paths together for a reason."

Out of the corner of his eye, he noticed his computer screen went blank. In the past, any mention of church, God or faith had made Zach bristle. But this time it hadn't. Heather's doing, most likely.

"Perhaps you're right." Zach raised his eyebrows. "Not really sure what I'm supposed to do about it. I don't want to crowd her. She's been through a lot. She needs time." Out of habit, he reached over and wiggled the mouse and the screen came to life.

"Well, I'll let you get to your paperwork." His father stood and paused in the doorway. "But don't give her too much time. She might meet herself a nice Amish guy."

"You don't have to do this," Heather said as she took a chance and backed away from Fiona in the small kitchen of the bed-and-breakfast, hoping—praying— she could find something to defend herself with.

Fiona wore a blank expression that unnerved Heather more than the fuming she was doing earlier. She seemed disconnected, catatonic. "You really don't get it, do you?" Her tone was flat.

Heather swallowed hard. "Get what?"

"It doesn't surprise me. He said you were a stupid woman."

Heather's heart plummeted and nausea roiled in her

gut as she took another step back and reached behind her to feel for the drawer where she kept the knives.

He...he...he...

Heather knew exactly who *he* was. She felt it in her bones. Brian Fox had manipulated another impressionable young woman.

Even in death, he was coming back to mess with her life.

The room grew close. Too close. A bead of sweat rolled down her back. She had to keep talking to distract Fiona. Distract herself from her rioting thoughts. "Who are you talking about?" Despite her best efforts, Heather's voice cracked. She needed Fiona to say it. To confirm what Heather already suspected.

Don't show your fear.

"He was obsessed with you. Even after everything I did for him, he still wanted you." Fiona's eyes narrowed into slits behind her glasses.

A buzzing hummed in Heather's ears and the ground shifted beneath her.

"*You* helped my ex-husband escape prison?" How could that be? Zach said they had already arrested someone and she was out on bail.

Fiona rolled her eyes, mocking her. "No, of course not. How would I do that? That other stupid woman who worked at the correctional facility helped him. He was just using her. Besides, she was stupid. She deserved to get caught."

Brian was charismatic. He knew how to charm women. Even in prison he had charmed multiple women into helping him. How had he reached Fiona?

Keep Fiona talking.

Heather's fingers brushed across a smooth drawer

handle. Inside were several serrated knives. Could she open it without drawing Fiona's attention?

Bigger question: Could she use a knife on another human being?

"How did you know Brian?" Heather scanned the room behind Fiona, calculating how difficult it would be to shove her out of the way and make her escape. But even if she could, Ruthie might not.

"I wrote him in prison because I wanted to write his story. *His* side of the story."

"Brian beat me. He killed his second wife. What more did you need to know?"

"That's *your* side of the story. He needed to be able to tell his."

A throbbing started behind Heather's eyes. "Brian's dead. Why are you doing this now?"

"You're the reason he's dead."

Heather's pulse whooshed in her ears.

"He said he'd be with me when he got out. But he was obsessed with you." Fiona turned her head and stared out the kitchen window toward the burned-out barn. A small smile played at the corners of her mouth.

Realization smothered Heather like a too-heavy itchy blanket on a hot summer's day. She struggled to catch her breath. This woman was completely irrational. "You tried to kill me in the barn. You were the one who slammed the bag over my head and started the fire."

"I didn't want you to see me. I wanted you to die thinking the man you tossed aside had killed you."

"But why?" Heather swallowed hard, trying to tamp down her panic.

"I thought he wouldn't be with me until you were out

of the picture. As long as you were alive, Brian would prefer you to me."

Heather tried to keep her breath even. "Brian's gone now. He can't be with anyone." She held her breath, watching Fiona's face flush red. Had she said too much? "What do you expect to gain now?"

"A little satisfaction."

"I don't understand." Heather's limbs trembled, fully realizing she was carrying on a discussion with someone who had discarded logic for some sort of warped revenge.

"He's dead because of you." This conversation was going in circles.

Pinpricks blanketed her scalp and she swallowed back her fear. "I didn't kill him."

Fiona turned and glared at Heather as if she had offended her. "Can you believe he got mad at me after he found out I tried to kill you in the barn fire? I thought he'd be happy that I had gone after the woman who put him in jail. But he told me I had no right. He told me he was still committed to you. That he had left you your wedding ring. Is that true?"

Ruthie gasped, but Heather kept her attention on the woman in front of her. "Yes," Heather said, afraid to lie. "He left it in the medicine cabinet. But I didn't want anything to do with Brian. I was done with him."

Fiona flinched, as if the words hurt, or perhaps confused her. "Brian was every bit as controlling as you said he was. But I thought if you were out of the way, we could be together." Her voice held a faraway quality. "But I was wrong."

"He's gone now. It's over. He can't hurt either one of us anymore. Don't you see that?"

"It won't be over until you're gone, too. Because of you, I couldn't have Brian. You destroyed everything. You need to pay."

"Fiona, think about what you're doing. You'll go to prison. You'll have let Brian destroy your life, too."

"It's already destroyed." Fiona lifted her hands to her temples, still holding the gun.

"Tell me how he died." Heather tried to distract her.

Fiona's lips began to tremble and she lowered her hands. "He was already nursing a bullet wound to the arm—the jerk was wearing a bulletproof vest when your boyfriend shot at him as he tried to get away on the boat."

Heather reached behind her and inched the drawer open a fraction as Fiona unraveled her story, seeming to revel in the details. Maybe she still planned to write this story.

Fiona continued, "But once I realized he had used me to get to you, I decided to put another bullet in him. End it for him. I waited until he was good and dead, then I left him in the truck across the street. It was all so neat. I had a perfect ending to my story. The bad guy gets his comeuppance." Fiona's finger twitched near the trigger, sending renewed unease twisting up Heather's spine. Fiona looked off into the distance, as if she was plotting something. "Heather Miller's ex-husband is found dead in her boyfriend's stolen truck. Readers love those kind of twists."

Fiona had gone over the edge. Heather had long ceased talking to a sane person, but she had to try if she hoped to get out of here alive with Ruthie. "No one would have ever known about your involvement. Coming here today couldn't be worth jeopardizing your freedom. Could it?" Heather held her breath, waiting for her answer.

"The story wasn't complete. Brian was supposed to be with me. I was going to write his *complete* story, which was supposed to end with me and him together. But he couldn't be with me because he was obsessed with you. He was always going to be obsessed with you. You ruined my happy ending." Her eyebrows rose in an awkward gesture, then her gaze lowered to her shaking hand holding the gun.

"It's not too late to walk away," Heather pleaded. "You can claim self-defense with Brian. And you haven't hurt me or Ruthie. You can walk away," she repeated, maintaining eye contact with her captor. The light from over the sink glinted off her glasses. "You can be the hero of your story."

Behind her, Heather eased the drawer open just a little bit more. She slid her fingers in and felt for the handle of a knife. Pinching it awkwardly with her fingers, she eased the knife out of the tray. It hit the edge of the drawer and clattered back down on top of the other silverware.

Fiona's eyes flared wide. She stepped back, kicked the drawer shut, lifted the gun and aimed it at Heather's heart. "Yes, I *am* going to write the ending. *My* way."

Chapter Sixteen

Heather held up her hands, trying to appease Fiona. Trying to make her forget she had just been caught trying to slide a knife out of the utensil drawer. "Please don't do this." She hated the squeak in her voice.

Ruthie cried quietly in the corner.

Heather would never be able to overpower a deranged woman with a gun, so her only chance was to talk her way out of this. Dread tightened like a band around her lungs. She hadn't been able to make any headway so far, but she had to keep trying.

"You're a writer. You want a great story? Why don't you write about my mother's murder?" Shame in the form of heat swept up Heather's cheeks. *Please forgive me, Lord, for using my mother's tragedy like this.*

Fiona lowered her gun a fraction, as if considering.

"I can give you my side of the story. How I grew up Amish and my father left the Amish community heartbroken after my mother was murdered."

"I told you that would make a great story. I'd probably become famous." Intrigue softened Fiona's tone.

"Yes, it's a story that needs to be told."

Fiona lifted an eyebrow, skepticism lining her eyes.

"Doesn't everyone like a good mystery?" Heather hated herself for using her mother like this.

"But, you told me you valued your privacy. You made me feel like a loser for being gossipy with your other houseguests." Fiona frowned, as if considering something. "I don't like being made to feel bad about myself. I would have just continued to spy from the barn without your criticism, but I couldn't get close enough."

"That was you?" Heather's hand flew to her mouth. *Of course.* The police had been checking the restaurant surveillance cameras for possible images of Brian. Fiona could have easily slipped in unnoticed between the cheerleaders who had been there at the same time.

"People have been underestimating me my entire life. I found a ladder behind the barn. Realized I could spy on you from the loft." Fiona hiked up her chin, obviously proud of herself. "About your mother's murder…"

Trying her best to sound calm despite having a gun aimed at her, Heather said, "I've had time to think about it since we first talked. My mother's story needs to be told. Maybe your book will lead the police to her killer."

Something flitted in the depths of Fiona's eyes. "Exactly. That's why I started writing true crime. The victim's story needs to be told."

"You were never writing a romance?" Heather wasn't sure why she even asked, perhaps just to keep Fiona talking.

Her captor shrugged. "I dabble. But true crime is my passion."

"But why did you want to tell Brian's story and not Jill's? He wasn't the victim."

Fiona froze and her nostrils flared. "Sometimes the story the media portrays isn't the truth."

"My mother and Heather's mother were best friends when Mrs. Miller disappeared," Ruthie said in a soft, frightened voice from her chair in the corner.

Heather's heart stopped, uncertain what Fiona would do with that information. Heather never had any intention of sharing her mother's story—not with Fiona, anyway—she was just trying to talk her way out of this situation. Buy some time.

Fiona turned slowly to look at Ruthie. "Is that so?"

Ruthie's eyes grew wide. She nodded.

Fiona spun around and grabbed Heather's pony-tail and pushed her toward the front door. She pressed the gun into her spine. "Get up," she yelled at Ruthie. "We're leaving." Ruthie jumped up and knocked over the chair.

Heather's scalp ached as Fiona shoved her outside, down the stairs and toward her car. Ruthie followed behind.

"Where are we going?" Heather asked.

"We have to get out of here. I know. I watched this place for a long time. Workers might be here soon." Fiona's gaze darted around. Her grip tightened on Heather's ponytail. "Besides—" her tone grew curious "—I want to meet Ruthie's mom now."

Fiona reached into her pocket and pulled out the keys and opened the trunk.

A weight pressed down on Heather's chest and she could already feel the suffocating heat and closeness of the trunk. "Please, please, *please*, don't do this." She made eye contact ever so briefly with a terrified Ruthie.

"Get in the trunk or I'll kill you and your very helpful friend." Fiona shrugged, as if taunting her. "Ruthie gets to ride up front and give me directions to her mom's house."

Ruthie looked like she was about to pass out.

Realizing she had no option, Heather lifted a shaky leg and stepped into the trunk. Just as she was debating how she could gracefully climb into the space to become Fiona's hostage, her kidnapper planted both hands on Heather's back and shoved her in. She landed heavily on a partially sunken spare tire, some half-empty water bottles and a pair of tennis shoes.

Before she had a chance to make one last plea, Fiona slammed the trunk shut, leaving her to suck in stale carpet fumes.

Heather could hear muffled voices as Fiona undoubtedly threatened Ruthie at gunpoint to comply. Car doors slammed. The engine started. Desperation and exhaust fumes made Heather dizzy, yet she pushed with all her might on the trunk lid. It didn't budge. Heather didn't know a lot about cars, but she suspected this old beater was manufactured before safety experts put releases inside the trunk.

Panic made it difficult to think. *Breathe. In through the nose, hold for three, out through the mouth.*

Dear Lord, help me. Help me and Ruthie.

The cell phone sitting on the corner of Zach's desk vibrated. He considered letting it go to voice mail as he tried to catch up on a mountain of work, but something made him pick it up.

"Marshal Walker?" came the breathless voice over the phone line. "This is Sloppy Sam."

Zach pushed back in his chair and it bounced off the

wall as he stood. Dread coursed through him. "What's wrong?"

"Are you still in Quail Hollow?"

"No, I'm back at my office in Buffalo. What's going on?"

"I showed up at the bed-and-breakfast to tie up a few loose ends and the back door was open and a kitchen chair was knocked over. Miss Miller's trunk was open with groceries inside. Seemed like someone left in a hurry. I wanted to make sure Miss Miller was okay. I thought if you were still in town, maybe she was with you."

"No, she's not." Heart beating wildly in his chest, he swallowed hard. "I need you to hang up and call the sheriff immediately. Tell him what you just told me."

"*Yah*, I will." Sloppy Sam ended the call.

Zach stared at his phone as panic crashed into him. He drew in a deep breath, knowing he had to keep calm. He dialed Heather's number and waited. Her cheerful voice sounded on the voice mail. He waited and left a message. "I need to make sure you're okay. Call me as soon as you get this message. Thanks."

Zach pushed back his chair and snagged his jacket from the coatrack in the corner of his office. Shoving his arms into his jacket, he ran to the elevator. He found himself praying for Heather's safety.

He had to get to Quail Hollow. Make sure she was okay.

When he got down to the parking lot and into his brand-new truck, he called Deputy Gates to make sure Sam had called it in. At least now Zach knew someone local was looking into it.

"Call me if you get any leads. I'm leaving from Buffalo for Quail Hollow now. I should be there in an hour."

"We'll find out what's going on," the deputy reassured him.

As Zach tore out of the parking lot, he couldn't imagine what had happened. He had thought the danger had passed once Fox was found dead.

He slowed at a red light, then pounded on the steering wheel. "Come on. Come on. Come on." He glanced both ways, and once it was clear, he blew through the light.

Fiona hadn't driven far when the car bobbled over an uneven road, making every contact point between Heather's body and the trunk of the car ache.

The car came to a stop. Heather strained to listen over her heavy breathing. She knew the trunk wasn't airtight, but the darkness and the stale smell did nothing to alleviate her fears.

The engine cut off. A door slammed. Footsteps.

Please open the trunk. Please open the trunk. Please open the truck.

Anxiety made her heart race.

The footsteps grew more distant and Heather nearly cried when she was abandoned in the trunk with something sharp digging into her side.

Help me, dear Lord. Help me.

Heather wasn't sure how much time had passed when she heard voices. One was Fiona's. Her pulse spiked when she recognized the other: Maryann's.

Where was Ruthie?

"We don't have many plants left. Our peak season is in the spring. All the mums are picked over," Maryann said.

"That's okay." Fiona's voice grew closer. "I had something else in mind."

"Oh…" Maryann sounded confused, but not frightened.

Please leave her out of this. Please, please…

The sound of metal scraping—a key inserted into the trunk lock—didn't provide the sweet relief she had hoped for. Instead she feared for what Fiona would do to Maryann once she saw Heather in the trunk. She'd be a witness who needed to be eliminated.

The crack of light grew larger. The first thing Heather saw was Maryann's horrified face. The Amish woman covered her mouth with her hands. "Heather…"

Ruthie stood nearby. Terror making her mute.

"Ah, yes, sweet Heather. Not exactly what you were expecting." Fiona was talking to Maryann, but she had a gun trained on Heather.

"Oh, my. What's going on?" Maryann backed up and hit her heel on the door of the greenhouse. She turned to her daughter. "Ruthie, what's going on?"

"I'm sorry, *Mem*" was all she could say.

Heather blinked against the bright light after being held in the darkness of the trunk. Fiona had pulled the car around to the back of the greenhouse, where it would be hidden from those searching for it from the street. *If* anyone was searching for it.

Ruthie stood clasping her hands with silent tears falling down her cheeks.

"Leave Maryann out of this," Heather said, fully realizing she wasn't in a position to make demands.

Immediately Heather figured she had said the wrong thing. Fiona would do exactly the opposite of what Heather wanted her to do.

"I need Maryann for my story. You know, the one you promised me about your mother."

Maryann's brow furrowed as she struggled to comprehend the situation.

"Get out." Fiona pointed the gun at Heather. "And you two," she said to Maryann and Ruthie, "don't go anywhere."

Heather braced her hands on the edge of the trunk and dragged herself out. The ground beneath her swayed. Her feet tingled from the awkward position she had been forced to take in the trunk. She blinked, trying to orient herself. Despite the overcast day, going from the black of the trunk to the light of day felt like tiny pinpricks in her eyes.

"Quit *rutsching*," Fiona said when Heather tried to squirm out of reach. "Did I say that right? Quit squirming, right? I figure if I can sprinkle some Pennsylvania Dutch throughout the book it will make it more authentic. I hear Amish books are big sellers. I had done a little research before coming to Quail Hollow, but I never realized it would come in handy so soon."

"I can help you with that," Heather said in a desperate attempt to appeal to this crazed young woman. "I spoke Pennsylvania Dutch for the first six years of my life. You don't need them."

Fiona gave her a strange look. "Get inside. All of you." Maryann started walking toward the front of the house when Fiona yelled, "No, the back door."

Maryann led the way, then Ruthie, Heather, followed by a gun-toting Fiona.

Fiona made them sit down at the kitchen table. "If anyone thinks they're going to be a hero, I'll shoot

Maryann first." She frowned, a feigned sympathetic gesture that came off as garish. "You all can't get away."

Fiona reached into the bag strapped over her shoulder and pulled out a yellow legal pad. "I prefer to work on my laptop, but I know electricity can be scarce out here." Her words held an air of disgust.

Fiona threw the legal pad on the table. "I wish I had more time to prepare for this interview, but I'm good at working on the fly." She sounded almost gleeful. "Answer the questions honestly." She lifted her eyebrows. "And don't worry. You can help one another if you don't know the answers."

"You can't expect us to answer questions under duress." Heather pushed back from the table. "Why don't you put the gun away and we can chat calmly?"

Fiona aimed the gun at Heather. "You're trying to trick me."

Heather squared her shoulders. She was tired of dealing with bullies. "You can't expect us to answer questions while you're pointing a gun at us." She stood and kept moving so that Fiona had to turn away from Maryann and Ruthie. Fiona's rage grew as she tracked a defiant Heather into the front room. Heather had counted on it. She glanced over Fiona's shoulder at her dear Amish friends. She gave them a subtle nod and mouthed the word *run*.

In her attempt to flee, Maryann knocked Heather's chair over and it bounced off the floor.

Fiona spun around. Heather grabbed a glass pitcher off a shelf and brought it down over Fiona's head. The woman crumpled to the floor and her gun clattered across the hardwood.

Blood pulsing in her ears, Heather stepped over

Fiona to grab the gun. At the same time she yelled to Maryann and Ruthie, "Run! Get out!" When Ruthie paused, Heather yelled, "Go, *now*! Call for help."

The Amish woman she had grown to love like a mother moved toward the door, her long skirt fluttering around her legs. Ruthie followed. Heather bent for the gun when Fiona dived at her legs, taking her down. Heather landed on her shoulder with an *oomph*. Twisting, she stretched for the gun while Fiona clawed at her legs.

The tips of Heather's fingers brushed against the cool metal.

A scream tore from Fiona's throat as Heather stretched with everything she had to gain control of the gun. If she didn't get the gun, Fiona would kill her for sure.

Chapter Seventeen

The closer Zach got to Quail Hollow Bed & Breakfast, the more fried his nerves became. Deputy Gates had promised he'd call once Heather was located. The silence of his cell phone was unnerving.

He just passed the location where the body had been pulled from the woods behind the Hershbergers' place. The trees dotting the hillside were in peak fall colors. Evil had touched even this beautiful place.

Dear Lord, please help me get to Heather in time.

He didn't know what had happened to Heather, but every ounce of his being knew it was bad.

An image of his sweet sister came to mind.

Let me be there for Heather. Please. I can't let her down, too.

The cell phone on the seat next to him rang, startling him. He had waited the entire drive for it to ring, and now that it had, he was afraid to answer. He had dealt with hundreds of life-and-death situations in his job and now he was truly afraid. Afraid that he may have lost Heather forever.

Drawing in a fortifying breath, he pressed the accept

button. "Marshal Walker," he said into the air with his phone set on hands-free.

"It's Deputy Gates…" A determined voice filled the cab of the truck. He bolted upright and his seat belt snapped against his chest.

"You found Heather."

"A call came in from the Hershbergers' residence, Maryann and Ruthie are hiding in the barn. Someone is holding Miss Miller at gunpoint in the main house," he said in clipped tones. "We're headed there now."

Zach slammed on the brakes. "I'm a minute away."

"Wait for backup," the deputy said. "We're en route."

"Okay." Zach ended the call and pressed the accelerator and did a quick U-turn and headed back toward the Hershbergers' farm. He wasn't going to wait for anyone. Not if it meant saving Heather's life.

Zach pulled over about a hundred feet from the handmade wooden sign by the road that read Greenhouse. Apparently the Amish were on the nose in their advertising. The cornfields from the neighboring property would hide the truck. Provide him with the element of surprise.

Zach climbed out and closed the door with a quiet click. He pulled his gun out of its holster and ran toward the driveway, his heart in his throat. When he reached the end of the cornfields, he paused and peered up toward the house.

According to the deputy, Heather was being held captive in the main house. He scanned the windows and didn't notice any movement. He broke away from his hiding place and sprinted toward the house. He took cover by the side of the building, catching his breath.

He listened. He could hear rustling from inside, then a crash. Shouting.

Time was running out to save Heather. Crouching, so as not to be seen from the windows, he moved toward the porch and silently climbed the steps and prayed for backup.

When Heather couldn't reach the gun, she twisted her body around, despite Fiona clawing at her legs. Heather freed her legs and kicked Fiona as hard as she could. Her shoe made solid contact and a horrifying crack came from Fiona's jaw as she fell backward and let out a whoosh of air. Heather scrambled and reached for a table to pull herself up.

"I'm going to kill you," Fiona screamed.

The front door burst open and Zach stepped in, training his gun on Fiona. "Stop."

Relief washed over Heather. *Zach,* she breathed.

Before Fiona had a chance to get her legs under her, Zach strode across the room. He shoved his gun back into its holster and quickly put handcuffs on Fiona. "Stay put."

Zach turned and reached for Heather's hand, pulling her toward him. He cupped her cheek with his hand and smoothed his thumb across her skin, leaving a trail of warmth. "Are you hurt?"

Heather shook her head against his hand. "How did you know I was here?"

"Let's just say your friends were worried about you." He tipped his head.

Heather narrowed her gaze, confusion making her thinking fuzzy. "Thank God." She raised her eyebrows. "Oh, my. I have to make sure Maryann and Ruthie are okay."

Zach brushed a soft kiss across her forehead and she smiled up at him. "They are. They called the sheriff's department. Deputy Gates is on his way. He can take care of Fiona."

"I'm not going anywhere." Fiona tried to get her feet under her, but she couldn't seem to with her hands hand-cuffed behind her back.

Zach grabbed Fiona's arm and yanked her to her feet.

Heather shook her head. "She had befriended Brian. She wanted to write his story." She turned and glared at Fiona.

Heather took a big step back when Fiona puckered her lips as if to spit on her.

Heather blinked slowly, trying to tamp down her growing anger. She was done being the victim. She spun around and walked out onto the porch. She'd fill Zach in with all the details soon. But right now, she needed to find her friends. The cool air felt refreshing on her warm cheeks. Out of the corner of her eye, she saw movement.

She turned and saw Maryann and Ruthie running toward her, their long dresses flapping around their legs.

Heather ran down the stairs and pulled Ruthie into an embrace. Then she quickly let her Amish friend go. "Thank you for calling the sheriff."

"I've never been more grateful we had a phone in the barn for business purposes." Maryann reached out and squeezed Heather's hand.

A commotion drew their attention to the front porch. Zach led Fiona out in handcuffs to the newly arrived sheriff's deputy.

"Are you okay, Maryann?" Heather asked.

"*Yah.* I'm fine."

"I'm sorry you got wrapped up in this."

"I've had enough excitement around here to last me a lifetime, that's for sure." Maryann shook her bonneted head. "Everything's okay now."

Zach joined them after Fiona was secured in the back

of the patrol car. "Is everyone okay? Does anyone need medical attention?"

"Neh," Maryann said. "I'm fine."

"Is she going to jail?" Ruthie asked.

"Yes. Then she'll await trial," Zach said.

"But she won't get out to hurt us?" Ruthie asked.

"No, she won't."

"I need to go inside. Sit down." Maryann walked toward the steps.

Ruthie turned to follow her in and Heather called out to her, "I'll be in in a minute to help you clean up." She didn't think there was too much damage, but some furniture and items had been upended when she and Fiona had struggled. And the glass from the pitcher would need to be swept up.

Heather felt slightly awkward as she and Zach stood in silence watching the patrol car pull away. Deputy Gates said Heather could come in later to file a report.

"Ruthie and Maryann have become like family to you."

Heather rubbed her upper arms for warmth. "They have. I'm so grateful they're okay." She stared at the empty road. "If only Brian could have put his charms to work for something positive." Heather sniffed and drew her shoulders up.

"You're going to have to relay the entire story of what happened here to the sheriff's department," Zach said, placing his hand on the small of her back.

"I'd be happy to never hear Brian Fox's name again."

"Me, too. He's caused a lot of havoc in our lives."

Heather lifted her hand toward the house. "Well, I better go help them clean up." With her heart beating in her throat, she took a few steps toward the house, then turned to call Zach's name when he said hers at the same time.

"You go first," Zach said, smiling.

Heather cleared her throat and she grew light-headed. "Okay, I'm just going to say this because about thirty minutes ago I thought I had bought the farm. Well, I had bought the farm, but…you know what I mean."

Zach nodded, a light glowing in his eyes. He seemed to be enjoying this. "Go on…" he encouraged her.

"Anyway… I should know that life and a future are not guaranteed for anyone. And—" she lifted a shoulder, feeling so far out of her element she wanted to run into the cornfields and hide "—is this thing between us going to lead anywhere?"

Heather was standing in front of him pouring her heart out. All of a sudden, her face flushed red and she threw up her hands. "Just… I don't know. Forget it. I need to go help them clean up." She spun around.

Zach reached out and touched her arm. "Heather. Wait."

She stopped with her back to him and paused a minute before turning around. When she did, she had tears in her eyes. Without saying anything, he stepped toward her and pulled her into an embrace. He ran his hand over her head, feeling her silky smooth hair and breathing in the fresh scent of her cucumber shampoo.

"I've faced a lot of bad guys in my career. Been put in a ton of hairy situations. But I have never been more frightened than when I found out you were in danger today." He pulled away slightly and cupped her face in his hands and pressed his lips against hers. After a long moment, he pulled away. "I don't know what I would have done if I had lost you."

Heather smiled and a tear trailed down her cheek.

"I should have never let you out of my sight," Zach said.

She swallowed hard. "You have your job in Buffalo. I have the bed-and-breakfast here in Quail Hollow."

"Those are jobs. You're more important to me than a job."

A small line creased her forehead, indecision flashing in her eyes. "But I've worked so hard on the bed-and-breakfast. I wanted to honor my family."

A small pool of dread gathered in his stomach. Didn't she feel the same way? He dropped his hands and stepped away. He needed her to understand exactly how he felt, then he'd walk away if that was what she really wanted.

He met her gaze. "I think I'm falling in love with you, Heather."

She reached out and took his hand in hers. "You're such a sweet man. But I can't give up everything here for you. I know you're nothing like Brian, but I need to be independent. Not cave to the wishes of a boyfriend."

Zach tried to process everything that she was saying to him while not showing the disappointment on his face. "I wouldn't ask you to leave Quail Hollow. We can work something out. Buffalo's not that far. I could commute. Or find a new job. They need law enforcement here, too."

It was Heather's turn to touch his cheek. "I care for you a lot, Zach. But my heart needs to heal. I've been through so much that I don't trust myself."

"I understand. And I'll wait for you."

Epilogue

A year later...

Heather handed Ruthie the last dish. Her Amish friend dried it and put it away in the cabinet. The Quail Hollow Bed & Breakfast was booked solid this weekend. The fall foliage was at its peak, the sun was shining and a big event was happening in their very backyard. The tourists who'd happened to book this weekend were in for a very big treat.

"I don't know why I'm so nervous," Heather said, drying her hand on a dish towel.

"No need. The members of the Amish community are experts at barn raising."

Heather touched her hair, trying to remember if she had even combed it this morning. "Do you think we have enough food?"

"Of course. And don't forget many of the wives will be coming with picnic baskets, too."

Heather let out a long breath. Through the kitchen window, she noticed her neighbors starting to arrive and strolling over to the foundation that had been set last week in preparation for the walls and roof. "I suppose we should get out there."

Ruthie smiled and held out her hand as if to say, *After you*.

Heather stepped outside in her jeans and T-shirt, surprisingly not needing a sweater in October.

Ruthie came up beside her. "Um, you realize you can't help rebuild the barn, right? The men do the work."

A row of buggies were lined up along the property. The men had unhitched the horses and let them graze in the fenced-off area. Heather couldn't wait to have her own horse there.

"Oh, I know. I'm afraid of heights anyway."

"Do you think they'll let *me* help?" Zach strode through the gathering crowd of Amish workmen on the lawn and stuffed a broad-brimmed hat on his head. "Like my hat? Sloppy Sam let me borrow it."

Heather couldn't help but smile. "You made it!" She and Zach had been carrying on a long-distance relationship for the past year with Zach coming to visit Quail Hollow when he could. And Heather visiting Buffalo during the quiet season. They had also spent some time together during the subsequent trials. The woman who had helped Brian escape from prison was serving a minimum of seven years in prison. Fiona had received a much harsher sentence for killing Brian and kidnapping Heather, Maryann and Ruthie. Fiona would never likely see the light of day again. Heather was satisfied that the impressionable young woman wouldn't be bothering her anymore, but she couldn't help but feel sad that Brian Fox had destroyed yet another life.

"I wouldn't miss this barn raising for the world," Zach said. "The Amish could teach us a thing or two about getting things done." He took a few steps and studied the construction zone. "I see they already laid the foundation." He turned around and smiled at Heather, a smile that melted her heart. "A strong foundation is key."

Heather crossed her arms as a warm tingle raced down her spine. "A strong foundation *is* very important."

"Hey, I thought you wanted to help," Sloppy Sam hollered as he pulled a ladder from the back of his wagon.

Zach tipped his hat. "Duty calls."

Heather smiled and watched Zach jog over to offer a hand.

Ruthie leaned over and whispered into Heather's ear. "He looks very handsome."

"You're never going to stop, are you?"

Ruthie playfully tugged on the strings of her bonnet. "*Neh.* Everyone needs their happily-ever-after."

Zach put in a full day's work unlike any he had ever had. Despite being active and physically fit, every single muscle in his body ached. All the Amish neighbors had left for the day, with a handful promising to return tomorrow for some finishing touches.

Zach stepped back and admired the structure that had gone up quickly by the well-timed work of the Amish. He considered himself blessed to have experienced such teamwork. Such community. It was heartwarming.

Running the back of his hand across his forehead, he let out a long breath. The sky behind the barn—a barn that hadn't existed just twelve hours ago—was gorgeous, a mix of deep purple, orange and red.

"It's beautiful, isn't it?"

Zach turned around to find Heather walking across the lawn, dressed in jeans, a T-shirt and a light jacket. Her long brown hair was twirled into a loose bun. "Yes, beautiful." But he wasn't referring to the barn or the sky behind it.

A light twinkled in her eyes and she tipped her head shyly. "I can't believe how quickly it went up. I love it."

"The community has really embraced you."

Heather pressed her hands to her chest. "I'm blessed." A hint of nostalgia tinged her tone. "I feel like the new barn is like a rebirth. No longer a reminder of the tragedy that was, but rather hope for the future." She dragged a finger across her lower lip. "I think I've made peace with my mother's death, despite the unanswered questions. I've found forgiveness and I know the man who took her from us will be judged in the end."

She drew in a deep breath and smiled despite watery eyes. "Come spring, I'll house my own horse in the barn. I'd love to ride."

"Sounds like a great plan." Watching her intently, Zach took off his hat and tossed it on the grass. "I also have plans for the spring."

"Oh?"

Zach had a hard time reading her expression. Dread? Excitement? Anticipation?

He slid his fingers into his back pocket and eased out a diamond ring. He must have touched it a million times during the workday, assuring himself it was still there. Assuring himself that Heather also felt the same way about him.

Her gaze dropped to the ring pinched between his fingers. Her eyes flared bright. He dropped to one knee. "Miss Heather Miller, will you marry me?"

* * *

The ground under Heather's feet shifted as Zach's words took a minute to hit their intended mark.

Will you marry me?

Zach watched her, anticipation etched on his handsome features.

"But your job in Buffalo…" She turned around and flung her hand awkwardly toward the bed-and-breakfast, completely refinished, as if to say, *And my work.*

The new barn… Her plans for a horse.

Her mind swirled…

"We can work around that. A job is a job. But I can't live my life without you. That I know for sure. I've missed you over this past year. I don't want to do long distance anymore."

Hope, excitement and love blossomed in her heart.

Heather leaned over and cupped his cheeks in her hands, drawing him to his feet and pulling him into an embrace. She loved the feel of his solid chest, his firm grip, his warm lips on hers.

He pulled back and looked at her, a question in his kind eyes. "You never answered me."

"Yes, *yes*, I'll marry you." Butterflies flitted in her stomach and she could feel the joy radiating from her soul.

He stepped back and took her hand and slid the ring on her finger.

"I love you, Heather."

"I love you, too."

Zach lifted her hand to his lips and kissed her fingers.

"So, you finally did it."

Heather spun around at the sound of Ruthie's voice.

"You knew?" Heather asked.

"It was simply a matter of time. I think everyone knew you two were destined for each other, except you."

Heather took a step back and Zach hugged her from behind. She tilted her head back to rest on his solid chest. He ran his knuckles gently up and down her arm.

"I'm thrilled for you guys. But does this mean I'm out of a job? I heard Marshal Walker's a great cook," Ruthie joked.

"He *is* a great cook, but you've got official bed-and-breakfast duty."

"Sounds perfect," Zach said.

Heather looked up at Zach and he kissed her on the nose. "It *is* perfect," Heather said.

"The kitchen's all cleaned up. Sloppy Sam's going to give me a ride home." Ruthie took a step backward.

"Oh, really?" Heather said playfully.

"Knock it off," Ruthie said. "I think we've had enough lovey-dovey stuff for a while."

"You never know," Heather said. "You never know."

Ruthie waved her hand in dismissal. Heather thought she heard her giggling as she strolled away and hopped up into Sam's wagon.

Zach threaded his fingers with hers. "I should probably call my father and share the good news. He was convinced you'd find yourself a nice Amish guy if I didn't make my move soon."

Heather leaned over and grabbed the broad-brimmed hat from the grass and stuffed it on Zach's head. She leaned up on her tippy-toes and planted a kiss on his lips. "As much as I love you, you'd never pass for Amish."

* * * * *

Save $1.00

on the purchase of any
Love Inspired®,
Love Inspired® Suspense or
Love Inspired® Historical book.

Available wherever books are sold,
including most bookstores, supermarkets,
drugstores and discount stores.

Save $1.00

on the purchase of any Love Inspired®, Love Inspired® Suspense or Love Inspired® Historical book.

Coupon valid until June 30, 2018. Redeemable at participating retail outlets in the U.S. and Canada only. Limit one coupon per customer.

Love Inspired®

Inspirational Romance to Warm Your Heart and Soul

Join our social communities to connect with other readers who share your love!

Sign up for the Love Inspired newsletter at **www.LoveInspired.com** to be the first to find out about upcoming titles, special promotions and exclusive content.

CONNECT WITH US AT:

Harlequin.com/Community

 Facebook.com/LoveInspiredBooks

 Twitter.com/LoveInspiredBks

LISOCIAL2017